Lily K

The Soulless

Written by Lily K

Copyright © 2021 Lily K

ISBN-13: 979-8-7547-0240-0

Character Sheets and Illustrations in the Collector's Edition by Dani
Adam Octavian
Cover and Portrait Art by Lily K

Edited by Katie Volker

DEDICATION

I dedicate this book to my amazing editor Katie Volker, who helped me through this huge journey with her infinite knowledge, care and kindness. To Dani Adam Octavian, who agreed to do the illustrations without a second thought and helped me to get better at digital art too. To Jeffrey Pierce, for all his advice and time he gave to this book. To Jonna Robertsen for taking the time to help with the poems and join the beta reader team. And therefore, I dedicate this book to all my amazing beta readers: Armineh, Kevin, Jasper, Nadine, Liv, Yasmin, Jeffrey, Katie, Dani and Jonna.

Lily K

Lily K

CONTENTS

The Soulless

Lily K

Acknowledgements

This book has been through a lot, to say the least.

I originally wrote it in 2015 and it actually ended up reaching a few publishers and one of them was very much interested. The only mistake was that I wrote it in my mother language so I needed to translate it and my English was not on that level just yet. Let's just say that it ended up being a failure due to multiple reasons and it got me so upset that I didn't go back to it.

Then 2021 rolled in. A new publisher appeared and wanted to get the whole manuscript as they loved my synopsis and the first chapter, I sent out back in 2015.

Panic.

Instantly.

I knew that if I was going to translate the whole thing then I will need the best editor I can get. So, I wrote to one of the greatest people out there, my podcast co-host (To All the Films We Judged Before – check us out on YouTube and Anchor) and my dear friend **Katie Volker** and I asked her if she would be my editor. To be fair, if she would have said no, I probably wouldn't have done it at all. I just... I don't see how it would have looked like, but Katie...

She is amazing.

I would like to say a huge thank you to my friend for all her patience with me when I used very strange sentence structures or made up words that didn't even exist. For our endless Zoom calls on Mondays where we edited together. For her determination to see it through and for the amazing flavours she added to 'The Soulless'. It just simply wouldn't be the same without you Katie. My dears, please buy this book, I NEED to pay this woman because she deserves every single penny.

Watch out for my illustrator who designed the 2 scene illustrations and all the character sheets: **Dani Adam Octavian**. They offered their help without a single question; I was completely new to digital art and I just knew that I needed someone professional. Dani was the first one I reached out to and the rest is history. Dani, you are the best of the best, thank you for understanding my impatient ass and guiding me through the hard times.

I would also like to shout out **Jonna Robertsen** who I asked to look through the poems as she is an unbelievably great poet and I highly recommend checking her out on Socials (and hopefully soon getting her poetry book as well!!). I sent over the poems and riddles and she was done within two days. Thank you so much my dear friend that you took the time not only for this, but for other things as well.

Because, before I could thank anyone here's the second part of the story. You might be asking:

"If a publisher reached out, why are you publishing through Amazon?"

Well. They ghosted us. We don't know if they were scammers or data fishers, but they completely disappeared before the deadline arrived. I had to take precautions, so I changed all my passwords, strengthened the whole signing in procedure and simply hoped that they didn't steal any of my info or bank account details. While they gave us false hope, they actually failed on whatever they were planning to do. The book was ready, the artworks too and the beta readers (you'll be able to read what they had to say a bit further down) wrote their reviews as well, so I just had to figure out which way to go. The rest is history...

Let me continue then.

A big thank you to **Jeffrey Pierce** who took time to read my book while writing his third one in the Reckoning series.
https://www.thereckoningseries.com/

He also gave Katie and I valuable advice and I can safely say that he is one of the smartest and nicest human beings on Earth.

Thank you for all my amazing Beta Readers:

Armineh Davis

Jasper James Thieme

Nadine Martin

Yasmin Gibson

Kevin Clawson

Olivia Diaz

Jeffrey Pierce

Jonna Robertsen

Katie Volker

Dani Adam Octavian

And alas... thank **YOU** my dear reader for deciding to pick up my book and give it a go. You are awesome and your support means the world. Book Two is already in the works and trust me... it will be a wild ride.

I

The Prophecy

CHAPTER 1
YANDANA

"SAM"

The City of Dreams.

Right. More like The City of Snobs. When I arrived in Yandana I was - of course - amazed by its glory. This was, after all, the symbol of the New World. After the Great War, the Elves and Fairies decided to unite their already strong Kingdoms, and it all started with the marriage of the Elven King, Oberon, and the Fairy's Queen, Beatrice. The building of their Capitol - right in the middle of The Broken Ground - was their declaration of victory above every other Nation.

Yandana - which literally means Glory in Elvish - was the perfect mixture of the two tribes' architectural wonders. The immaculate structures of the Elven stone buildings surrounded the cobblestone streets, while the magical Fairy trees towered above all of them. Each of them gave home to at least twenty houses that were structured from the branches of the tree. They were all around Yandana, planted in a perfectly symmetrical shape around the different parts of the city. If you were to look from above, you would see them forming a circle distinct from the winding pattern of the city streets.

It was possible to see the city from miles away thanks to the palace in the middle of the Capitol, which was even taller than any of the Fairy trees. The enormous towers were built using the noble white stone of the Dwarves. They completely destroyed one of the abandoned Dwarven cities in order to get their hands on the stones that were carefully carved by the once great tribe. The King and Queen's decision meant that their name became equal to destruction. They didn't respect anything or anyone other than their own. Some believed -

1

including me - that by building the palace's tower so high they were also telling everyone that they were always looking down on them.

The roof of these towers were made from pure gold. It was actually quite blinding to look at them when the Sun was high in the sky. But their way of showing superiority didn't end with the roofs; the main building of the palace was surrounded by the statues of their heroes, and - naturally - the King and Queen themselves. To me, it was the ugliest thing that I've ever seen in my life.

The only part of Yandana that was bearable to be in was the Noble Gardens. I'd spent many days there just wandering around the blooming bushes, the great big trees and the colourful flowers. It was so different from the city itself that it served as a breath of fresh air when walking around the streets that screamed "WE'RE BETTER THAN YOU". It simply became too much.

I have lived in Yandana for sixteen very long years. Of course, it wasn't the brightest idea to live in a city where they would kill me for simply existing, but when you're escaping a terrible fate anything else is better.

My name is Samantha Tanan and I'm a Halfling. My mother, who was an Elf, fell in love with my monster of a father, who was a Human. Their love had been forbidden ever since the Great War. The only races that are allowed to mix are the Elves and Fairies, and the only reason for that is that the children who come out of those marriages are considered perfect creations. I know how it sounds, but the mix of Elven nobility and Fairy beauty was undeniably different from what people were used to seeing on the streets and therefore they enjoyed a life of respect, no questions asked.

However, the same could not be said about me. I wouldn't call myself ugly, but I am definitely nothing special to look at: I am short and my face is dull, surrounded by long red hair which hasn't been cut for sixteen years and my only means to hide the one thing that could give away my heritage. Thanks to my long hair, the people of Yandana aren't able to see my half-grown pointy ears. They're nowhere near as long as they would be if I were fully Elven. They're the only thing I inherited from my mother; not her beauty or her tall figure, just the ears. I've only heard stories about her as she wasn't even there to raise me. My father tried that for fifteen miserable years. I lived with him in Irkaban in nothing but fear and agony. When I left it was the happiest day of my life. He made sure I hate who I am even more than I already did.

Yandana wasn't always bad to me. In the beginning I had a job. I worked for the biggest inn on the west side right up until the point the Innkeeper tried to have his way with me and, when he was unsuccessful, he called the Guards on me and told them I was a thief. So I left the west side of Yandana behind and moved to the North End where the Nobility lived. Not one of them would hire me for even the simplest work, so I ended up on the streets, just trying to survive day to day until I finally became what the innkeeper said I was: a thief.

I've been chased for stealing food or clothes or… gold. So far, I've been lucky and mostly smart enough to not be caught by any of these morons who call themselves the King's Guard. If they were ever to catch up with me it would mean my immediate death.

My days were pretty much the same: trying to survive.

My "home" was the flat roofs of the Elven Houses. I've found them to be much safer than staying on the cobblestone streets, or somewhere in a dark alleyway. I was out of sight from the Guards, but also out of reach of a horrible band of homeless folks who had been causing trouble all over Yandana. I hated being associated with them. I only stole things if I really needed to and I wouldn't have hurt anyone even if my life depended on it. These people, who consisted of mostly disgraced Elven boys and a few Human soldiers who escaped from the dungeons, didn't value anyone's life. They were feared by many and no matter what the King's Guards did they always managed to escape. I'd only come face to face with them once. It was a narrow escape, but my natural agility meant I could climb to safety. That unfortunate meeting led to my life on the rooftops. They didn't come out during the day, but they were out in full force at night. I often heard them roaming the streets, yelling and laughing, or fighting with the Guards, when they were able to catch up with them.

On the day my life changed forever, my morning started off the usual way. There was no sign of trouble; everything seemed calm. I climbed down from the roof I slept on the night before - I had stayed there a few times - and into the alleyway next to the house before walking out on the busy main street. People were making their way towards the marketplace that was at the east end of the road. It was a special day for the city because vendors from other kingdoms arrived with their best cargo to sell their wares. Yandana ran on trade, so the city's vendors were hard at work making sure they were ready for the day's rush. But it was special for me too, because it meant that my only friend in the world would be visiting the Capitol.

Polly was the sweetest woman I'd ever known. I travelled to Yandana with her and her husband Charles when I fled Irkaban sixteen years ago. We became friends during the long journey and she promised me when we parted ways that we would meet again. So we did. Every sixty days, they came back to sell their goods at the market. Polly was an extremely talented tailor which served her perfectly as Elven and Fairy Nobilities loved her creations. They were always sold out by the day's end and returned to Irkaban with an empty carriage. Charles passed away a few years back and this wonderful, kind woman almost died from the grief. She didn't return to Yandana for a long time after, but eventually she returned. Her joy might have diminished, but her pure heart wasn't. She always treated me like family, so I always pretended that I had a good life. I hated myself for it, but I knew that it would have broken her heart if she knew about my situation. Whenever she came, I braided my hair - while making sure that it still covered my ears - stole a new dress to put on instead of my raggy shirt and trousers and washed myself clean from the dirt.

People still pushed me to the side no matter what I was wearing, but I didn't care too much about them. I don't think any Elf or Fairy ever looked at me unless it was in pure disgust, or I bumped into them accidently. Being invisible to them meant that I didn't have to worry all the time.

The market was already packed with people as I arrived. The biggest square in Yandana - named Emerald - gave home to it. Vendors set their tables up in mostly straight lines providing an easy flow for the people. The thing that always struck me first were the different smells lingering in the air, the delicious richness that came from the foods right at the entrance, but as you made your way more into the centre, the aromas coming from flowers, the fine leather works, all mixed together in a overload of the senses. The noise was also shocking at first, practically unbearable to those who were not used to the big crowds, but it was something that quickly faded from the minds of the people as they made their way through rows of delights.

I had to fight my way through many people before I finally spotted Polly's stand. She had the most beautiful tent behind her table where the ladies and gentlemen could try on her wares in peace. The dresses she tailored were so unique compared to what people were used to that I wasn't even surprised that there was already a crowd of young girls surrounding her. I squeezed through which resulted in a lot of huffs and puffs on their end, but I didn't care. Polly was showing a long purple dress that had these light green motifs sewn into its low neckline and sleeves, when she spotted me out of the corner of her eye. Her smile became even brighter.

"Dear ladies, I'll be back shortly. My daughter Mary will assist you," she announced to the crowd, stepping away from the table and coming straight over to me. She gave me the biggest, warmest hug, planting a big kiss on the top of my head. She was two heads taller than me so it wasn't really a challenge for her to do so. Even though she was in her later years, she was absolutely gorgeous to look at. Long ice white hair; hazel brown eyes; strong, defined cheekbones. She always smelt like roses.

"Sam, I am so happy to finally see you!" She exclaimed. "Come, we have much to talk about." She began to lead me away from the crowds.

After a short walk, we sat down on a bench under one of the Fairy trees. Its leaves were a light brown colour. All the different trees had varying coloured leaves depending on the Fairy families who occupied them. Their obsession with connecting everything to colour always baffled me. I mostly wore black which, in their books, literally meant that I was a moody outsider. These brown leaves signalled that the tree was home to middle-class families. Bright green was a sign of Nobles, yellow belonged to the Royalties and a washed out greyish colour was representative of peasants. There was only one tree in the city with that colour. If they married Elves, they would colour the houses in the correct colour.

"How have you been?" Polly asked as she held my hand.

"Great! Yes. We had a busy week in the inn, but you know me, I love it when that happens." I was lying through my teeth. I really didn't want to upset her in any way. "How about you?"

A strange sadness appeared on her face. She squeezed my hand a bit harder. "Sam," she started, trying to bring a smile back onto her face, "after talking with Mary and her husband..." She swallowed hard and moved around on the bench uncomfortably. "We decided I won't be coming to Yandana anymore."

"What? But why? Are you ill?"

"No, no," it was as if she could feel my worry, and her smile became a little brighter because of it. "But I am getting old, Sam. I will still be making dresses in the comfort of my home, but Mary will be travelling with it to the market." She paused for a moment, looking out at the people milling about. "It's time for me to rest a little."

"I see," I replied, my voice coming out a little smaller than I had meant it to.

"But please, if you ever come back to Irkaban, make sure that you'll visit me. My door will always be open for you."

"Of course, Polly." I never wanted to step foot in that town again. There were too many bad memories in that place.

We talked for a little while longer before we decided to head back to the market. I felt incredibly sad knowing that I wouldn't be seeing my friend anymore. She was the only one who had shown me any real kindness.

An idea was slowly forming in my head. I wanted to do something for Polly before our inevitable goodbye. She never failed to bring me gifts, or to give me food - which often proved to be life saving - so I made a decision as soon as I left her by her stand. I needed to get her a gift.

Stealing something during the market meant a greater risk of getting caught. Fortunately, I had my own tactics to avoid the Guard's watchful eyes. It didn't always work, mind you, but I prided myself on being one of the best thieves in Yandana.

I walked around all the rows to see what the different vendors were offering. Flowers would have been too general, while clothing was literally useless to give to Polly, so I decided to find her some jewellery that would be fitting for her appearance. Near the end of the last row, I spotted the most beautiful necklace I'd ever seen in my life. It was silver and the pendant was a Unicorn. I knew instantly that it was the perfect one. I decided to come back for it closer to sunset, when people would have started to head back to their homes.

I left the market behind and made my way towards the Noble Gardens further up north. The streets of Yandana were inconsistent to say the least, where some were wide enough for two carriages to easily get by, others were so narrow that a maximum of two people could squeeze through them. It didn't mean much to the Fairies as they tended to fly around the city, only walking if their partner was an Elf. I squeezed through one of the narrow streets but when I came out the other end I immediately regretted my decision choosing the shortcut.

The King's Guard were out in full force, at least thirty or forty of them. They all wore the King's bright white armour with the Fairy Queen's long iridescent robe. Their helmets were the shape of an Eagle head. I always found their outfits ridiculous and pretentious. They were holding back the crowd on both sides of the street which only meant one thing: The Royal Carriage was heading towards the palace.

My fear of being discovered rose as the Guards and the many Elves surrounded me. As the people were backing down towards the side, a woman pushed me so hard that I fell to the ground right into a puddle. The dirty water covered me, ruining my dress. The woman didn't even look to see what she did and nor did any of the other Elves. The Royal Drums sounded and the crowd burst out in cheers. I took a deep breath, stood up and took off the dress, still dripping. I was glad that I decided to keep my old clothes under it. I used the dress's clean side to wipe down my face before throwing it on the ground. I hated Elves so much. I hated their pretentious nature, their holier-than-thou attitude to anyone who isn't them. Through my sixteen years in this city I had yet to meet one who showed even the smallest of kindness.

I turned around just in time to see the Royal Carriage. One of the princesses was sitting on it, waving to the people with a bright white smile on her face. I had to admit that the beauty of Elven and Fairy halflings made me stare in awe every time. The princess had light brown skin, flawless, almost glowing. Her flightless, small wings were golden yellow and were in perfect contrast to her chestnut brown curly hair. A gorgeous dark blue dress was tightly wrapped around her body. She had a round face, slightly angular purple eyes and big, full lips. Her half-grown pointy ears had long silver earrings dangling down from them. The whole crowd was in awe of her. I quickly looked down when her gaze turned to my direction and didn't dare to look up again until I heard the Guards yell "all clear!"

The crowd flooded back onto the street as the Guards followed the carriage in two straight lines. I let out a sigh of relief and continued on my way, finally reaching the gates of the Noble Gardens.

The smell of flowers was a breath of fresh air. I wandered my way down a path that was made from small pebbles. Young couples were walking through the Garden, some of them in love, others out of duty to their families. Arranged marriage was not uncommon, and you could easily tell which couple was which.

I went off the path and made my way through the trees to my favourite spot. It was the only willow tree in the garden with silver leaves. When I sat under it I always felt at peace, like the world just faded away. Everything was quiet. I sat down next to the trunk, putting my back against it, and I took out my small book from my back pocket. It was my only possession. The Little Book of Tales. The only good thing my father ever did for me was giving me the ability to read. My only good memories with him were our lessons, the only times we'd laughed together.

The Little Book of Tales contained three stories: Ser Desmond and the Dragon, The Red Tree, and The Tale of Three Cities. I had read through them at least a hundred times. I knew them by heart, but getting my hands on a new book was impossible. Books were only available in the Royal Palace for royalty and some of the Nobles. King Oberon was of the belief that too much knowledge would start another War. He was a strange man. I honestly think he was crazy. The Great War messed up his head. He was the one who gave the order to execute King Herald and his family; he was the one who forbade mixing between races other than Elves and Fairies, and according to some stories he killed more people during the battles than any of his soldiers.

I held onto my little book like my life depended on it. As I sat there, the cold breeze brushed by my face, getting under my clothes, bringing with it the smell of flowers. I looked up at the branches of the willow tree. A squirrel was eating his nut, stuffing it into its little face. For a second I felt like I was up there too, feeling the roughness of the branch under my feet. It felt so real. I shook my head and opened the book.

Ser Desmond and the Dragon told the story of a Human knight who travelled through the Kingdoms to find his bride. He searched for her everywhere but no matter who he met - whether it were Dwarves, Fairies, Elves, Handors, or even his own kind - no girl was good enough.

One day, as he was making his way up on a hill, a large grey Dragon appeared. The knight immediately pulled out his sword, ready to fight, but the legendary creature began to speak. To his surprise, it told him that she was actually a cursed princess that only a knight like himself could save from being imprisoned in the form of a Dragon forever. Ser Desmond didn't believe the creature at first, but he listened, still on guard, and as their conversation went on for three days and nights, he fell in love with the Dragon. He put away his sword in the morning of the fourth day. Ser Desmond declared his love for her, waiting excitedly for the curse to be broken, but instead the smart Dragon grabbed him and swallowed him whole. That's how a long journey to find the perfect bride led to the demise of a desperate Knight.

Every time I read through the story it made me chuckle. I'd never understood love or why some people needed it so much. I saw it happening all around me - the Noble Gardens was always a perfect place for people to show the world that they found their other halves.

I was deep into my thoughts when the sound of footsteps brought me back to myself. I sprung to my feet and looked around, ready to run if it was necessary. Two young men appeared holding each other's hands. When they noticed me they stopped in their tracks. They looked at each other then back at me, a bit confused by my presence. I smiled at them, took a quick bow and left. I didn't want to get into any unnecessary conversations.

I walked around the Gardens to enjoy the quiet a bit longer. I only started to make my way back towards the market when the air started to grow colder. I knew I'd made the right decision when Emerald Square came into view. Many of the Elves were still there, but most had already left.

As I got closer to the row where I saw the vendor I felt my nerves getting to me. I was on edge. All I could think about was Polly and all the good she'd done for me. I needed to get that necklace for her before she left Yandana behind forever.

I scanned the area: no Guards were nearby, which was a good sign. The way to the building I had chosen as my escape route was clear, but I would only need it in case someone caught me in the act. I watched the people around the jeweler, looking for a mark. A Bulky Man was standing on the opposite side, looking at some leather bags. He was my man. I decided to use my best ruse: The Blind Girl.

One last deep breath. I was doing this for Polly. I headed straight for the man and bumped as hard as I could into him. Reflexively he turned around, pushing me right into the jeweler's stand. People around us yelled out in surprise as I cried out as loud as I could, knocking as much of the jewelry to the ground as I could.

"Is this how people treat the blind?" I yelled, indignant. It was my best performance yet. The jeweler ran out from behind his table, panicking.

"I am so sorry, ma'am!" Exclaimed the Bulky Man. As they helped me to my feet, I slid the necklace into my back pocket.

"Are you alright?" The jeweler asked and I had a hard time keeping my focus on my performance because his breath was so bad.

"I am still in one piece. Did I knock over anything?" I allowed as much innocence to drip into my voice as I could.

"It was entirely my fault, I will pay for the damages," the Bulky Man replied, and I had to keep a straight face, but his reaction surprised me. They let me go, I smiled as widely as I could.

"Thank you, dear ser." I bowed my head a little, and started walking away, holding my hands out for the act. I knew they were still watching me.

I was nearly out of sight, when out of the corner of my eye I saw a hand reaching for mine. Before I could think, instinct took over and I dodged out of the way causing the Guard to almost fall on his face. The necklace slipped out of my back pocket and clattered to the ground. I heard the jeweler yell out, but couldn't quite make out what he said. The Guard looked down at the necklace, then up at me.

"Hey-" he started, but before he could say anything else, I moved, snatching the necklace from the ground and began to move.

The Guard was smart, and stood in the way of my planned escape route, forcing me to turn around and bolt the other direction, one thought on my mind as I did so:

I am so tired of running away.

I soon heard orders being screamed behind me, people yelling as I quickly ran past them. I reached the other end of the market and, by sliding through one of the stands, I was able to avoid a second Guard as he appeared right in front of me. I ran out onto the main street, but my relief didn't last long as they suddenly became very crowded.

As I was making my way through the wide streets of Nobletown, I couldn't help but notice that more and more people appeared from the houses. They were all wearing the most beautiful dresses called Ilyon, the official dresswear of the Elves and the Fairies in a time of celebration. It almost stopped me in my tracks as I started thinking about what was going on, but as one of the Guards yelled out behind me I started to run again.

The streets started to become way too crowded to move through and I felt the awful look the Elves gave me, a dirty homeless girl, fleeing for her life. The Fairies flying above us were laughing and singing, not paying any attention to what was going on down below. In my haste, I ran straight into a bunch of the young Elven women who started calling me nasty names and would not let me through. I started to panic when I suddenly felt a strong grip on my arm. The Elves stopped talking and stared at whoever grabbed my arm. It wasn't a fearful gaze; it was more in awe. I tried to wrench my arm free, but the stranger's grip was too strong and I felt them dragging me into a nearby alleyway. When I finally turned to look at his face, my jaw hit the floor. Even in the dark of the alley, I knew who he was.

Killian Fin, a soldier and the only Human to be given a noble name by the King and Queen. They called him 'Malion Arur', which roughly translated to 'Bravest of Men'. Giving a Human an Elven name was unheard of; it was a huge honour, and not one taken lightly.

CHAPTER 2
THE LONELY HOUSE

Killian Fin dragged me further away from the crowd, never once looking down to face me. All I could see was his back, his long jet-black hair and his armour the colour of the Sun, with his symbol - the Owl - burnt into his shoulder pad. I never understood why he'd chosen it.

Eventually, we arrived at the gates of the Noble Garden and he finally stopped. He finally turned towards me and I felt a sudden burn in my chest. He had the beauty of any of the Elves and Fairies combined. He didn't look like a Human at all. His eyes were black as night, he had a perfectly crafted face and shaped lips. He looked directly in my blue eyes and I suddenly felt embarrassed. It felt like he was looking straight into my soul.

"Are you hurt?" he asked. I was so baffled by the question that I forgot how to form words. "Sam, are you hurt?"

"How do you know my name?" I asked, my voice small.

"That doesn't matter right now. The guards are looking everywhere for you."

"Do you think I don't know that?" I paused. "Wait, you're not gonna hand me to them?"

"No, why would I?" He looked up suddenly, and I was relieved that I didn't have to look into his eyes any longer. "Do you know The Lonely House?"

"Behind the North Gates? Of course, everyone's heard of it."

"Great. Head there, I'll come for you as soon as I can, but I am afraid that right now we have to part ways."

"What are you talking about? Why are you helping me?"

"Sam-" He cut himself off, taking a deep breath before looking me dead in the eye once more. I couldn't help but hold my breath. "Just trust me," he continued, desperation in every word. "Please."

I nodded. None of it made sense, but I didn't have any other options. If Killian Fin said he was here to help me, then maybe luck had finally shifted in my favour. He turned on his heel and was gone in an instant. It took me a moment to gather myself, but before long I began running to the Noble Gardens.

I quietly made my way through the huge trees and bushes that surrounded the Noble Gardens. The sound of footsteps made me stop, and I shrank down to hide myself in the growth. A piece of parchment paper, battered and torn, carried here on the wind, caught my eye. Picking it up, I realised it was a flier for the Noble Ball at the palace. Now I understood why the streets were so crowded with Noble Fairies and Elves: they were thronging to the palace to find their future partners. It always seemed a very old-fashioned way of finding someone who you can grow old with, if you ask me. The sound of footsteps passed. I stuffed the parchment into my pocket and picked up my pace.

It didn't take me long to arrive at the North Gate after that, and to my relief there were no crowds, just two Guards standing there. I took a deep breath and started walking towards them hoping that they wouldn't ask any unnecessary questions. As I approached, one of them immediately held up their hand.

"Where are you off to at this time of day?" The Guard on the left asked. It was starting to get dark.

"I'm looking for my uncle," I replied. "He was supposed to arrive home around lunch time, but he never did. He was out hunting so I thought it was better if I went and checked on the old fella." The lie slipped easily off my tongue.

The right one chimed in. "Why haven't you alerted the guards?"

I smiled. "No need, I know my uncle. He probably drank too much and stood for too long in the scorching sun." They both chuckled.

"We all know the type," the left Guard continued. "Off you go then. But if you aren't back by High Moon, you're both going to be locked out of the Capitol for tonight."

"Duly noted, ser. Good day to you."

I quickly moved on and picked up my pace again when they were far behind. Finally, as I walked up to the small hill, I saw it: The Lonely House.

It wasn't wise to have a house outside of the Capitol. The Leongrass, a mercenary group, were famous for attacking villages and farms - robbing them, raping the women and abducting their children. One lonely house did not stand a chance against them.

But this house was different from the others. Everyone knew about it in Yandana, because it was the stuff of nightmares. Parents told horrific stories about it to their kids to make sure that none of them even thought about going near it. I'd heard many stories involving angry spirits and all kinds of monsters living there. As I came up on it, my trembles became more regular. I didn't usually fear anything, but I wasn't a fool: this house gave me the creeps.

I was getting closer when I spotted a light in the window. I froze. Was someone living in there?

With the fading sunlight I was starting to get cold and I didn't have my cloak, so I started moving again, slowly. My steps became more and more cautious as I got closer to the front door. Instinct was holding me back from knocking, but I couldn't stay out here. Suddenly, the door blew open and I jumped back several feet. An old man stepped over the threshold. He looked as if he was at least 90 years-old, with long white hair, beard, and possibly most surprising: a Druid's robe.

I couldn't believe what I was seeing. A Druid? Just outside of Yandana? He waved at me. I looked around, but there was nowhere else to go. If I was going to get murdered, it might as well be by a ghost.

"Welcome, my child." He said, his voice a bit shaky, almost rusty, but it felt kind.

"Ser." I bowed my head to him as I approached. Ghost or not, Druids held a level of respect unlike anyone else. But he laughed.

"No need for formalities around me, Sam." He knew my name too? The look on my face must have given me away because he grabbed my hand, comforting me. "I will give you all the answers you seek. Come into the warm."

I followed him inside and found the interior wasn't anything like I expected. It was quite nice actually. Everything was carved from wood except the fireplace, in which the Druid's magic-created blue flames were blazing. On the left side of the room were two doors leading into what I could only guess were a washroom and a bedroom. On the right hand side was a large window - the one I saw the light coming from - looking straight out at Yandana. A peculiar smell hit my nose - it was a mixture of the wood and herbs, many which were hanging down from the ceiling. I sat down right beside the fireplace on a very wonky chair and started to warm myself. The old Druid soon arrived with a cup of hot tea.

"Thank you, ..?" I said, unsure what to call him.

"Felnard, my dear. The name is Felnard." He smiled at me again, and for whatever reason it felt like home.

"Thank you, Felnard. I hadn't had tea in ages." I drank it quickly, the tea warming me from the inside as the fire warmed my skin.

"Would you like another?" He asked.

"No, thank you."

"You are a very polite halfling, I must say." Fear passed through me, forcing me to my feet ready to run, but the old Druid raised his hands. "Worry not Sam, I'm not here to persecute you. I told you, all I have are answers for you."

"How do you know so much about me?" I asked, not knowing if I was really interested in the answer. I wanted to leave as quickly as possible, my mind kept yelling at me to run.

"I've been watching you the past year or so, my dear. In fact, I've been looking for you for a very long time now." He stood up and walked to a shelf next to the door. He grabbed a big heavy book and walked back over to me. There was something about him that I couldn't quite put my finger on.

I pressed on, "I've never seen you in Yandana."

"Oh no, no." He seemed very amused by me. "Let me rephrase myself. My friend was following you. I believe that he was the one who directed you to me today."

"Killian Fin is your friend?" He chuckled again.

"Indeed."

"And why were you two looking for me? To hand me over to the King?"

"Oh, my dear sweet child, no!" He sounded genuinely surprised that I would even ask. "All the things that I will reveal to you today may come as a shock-"

"Trust me, we are way past that point where I am shocked," I said, unable to really believe my ears.

"-but you need to hear them." He looked at me, pointedly. "You're special, Sam."

I put the teacup down. "You must have made a mistake here," I replied, a little incredulous. "Trust me, there's nothing special here."

"Oh, but that's where you are wrong." He smiled mysteriously. It didn't help put me at ease. He opened the big book in his lap and without any further question started reading:

Long ago, before the Sevens and the appearance of the different tribes, there lived two sisters: Radona and Elemris. They were the darkness and the light, the evil and the good, the Moon and the Sun. They lived in harmony with each other and began creating the world as they imagined it.

However, Radona's greed was too big, and soon she stepped onto a very different path.

In secret, Radona started creating blood-thirsty demons, the stuff of nightmares and pure horror, but she wasn't careful enough. Her creations escaped from their prison and began attacking the peaceful world of their own creation. The tribes were suffering and Elemris' anger was bigger than her love for her own sister. She was able to stop the abominations by imprisoning Radona and banishing her into Darkness with all her horrible creations.

However, Radona was smart and, before her sister marched up against her, she created a prophecy that would free her again, bringing eternal darkness to all the land. Elemris found the Prophecy and, after reading it through, her heart broke. She handed it to her most trusted creations, the Noble Grabodans, to protect it from the hands of The Soulless, the only one with the power to free Radona.

Finally, before the beautiful Elemris laid down to her forever rest, she made sure that The Soulless' job would be even harder:

Only one shall be able to destroy the Prophecy so it will never reach the hands of the Soulless: A halfling, whose heart is pure, whose soul shines bright like the Sun, and whose mind is open to wonders.

I shall give the Destroyer the power of Magic.

Felnard closed the book and looked at me eagerly. "So?"

"Very... nice tale." I didn't understand, so I just smiled. "I've never heard it before."

"It's about you!" He exclaimed, and before I could stop myself I burst out laughing.

The softness disappeared from the corner of his eyes, his expression changing in an instant.

I quickly continued. "There's one big problem with your theory, ser," I was pretty sure that he was a lunatic, but I tried to keep my tone even, "I am a woman and you, as a Druid, should know that women don't have magic. It is only the privilege of men. Everybody knows this. So, I am sorry, but I really can't be your halfling, super... destroyer... or whatever that book said." The words sounded ridiculous even as they came out of my mouth. He considered me for a moment, before extending his hand to mine.

"Give me your hand, child," he said it like an order, but I still hesitated. "Don't be afraid." His smile returned as he said it. Slowly, I extended my hand. He took it forcefully, firmly, and before I could stop him he cut my palm.

It all happened way too fast. I fell hard, backward onto the wooden floor as I pulled my now bleeding hand away from him. I watched as the blue flames in the fireplace suddenly turned dark red and rose up to the ceiling, shifting and changing, before taking the shape of a dragon. It hung there for a moment - magnificent, terrifying - before burning out, the fire returning to its normal blue state.

"What the…" I said, breathless. Did I do that? Felnard was laughing then. He stood up and offered me his hand. I ignored it and stood on my own, stepping further away from him, cradling my bleeding palm.

We stood there, staring at each other in tense silence, before the sound of the door opening made me turn. Killian stepped in, dishevelled and a bit out of breath, eyeing us both with an intense curiosity.

"We were right!" Felnard yelled, and I watched as a huge, beautiful smile spread across Killian's face, eyes bright with hope as he looked at me, and then back to Felnard. He strode past me, over to the Druid, and I sat back down in my chair.

I didn't hear what they were talking about as I got lost in my thoughts. I couldn't believe what happened. Women can't have magic. They don't have magic. Easy as that. Sagar - the first recorded man with magic - only gave it to other men, everybody knew that. So what happened? How was I able to-

The feeling of a hand on mine pulled me out of my spiral. Killian was trying to open my palm, and I let him. Felnard raised his right hand and with a woosh the wound was gone.

I looked up at them. I could feel tears threatening to spill, but I held on. It took me a moment to realise Killian was still holding my hand.

"I know this is a lot, my child," Felnard said. I'm not a child, I thought back. I'm a thirty-year-old woman. But I held it in. "We've been looking everywhere for you," he continued, "there aren't many halflings left who aren't the descendants of Fairies and Elves. When Killian spotted you a little over a year ago, you were our last hope."

"But… How did you know that I had magic? I didn't even know about it." I looked at Killian, who finally let go of my hand.

"It was the third time I spotted you. You were attacked by a group of young boys in an alley, do you remember?"

It took me a moment. "The… Harlington brothers," I said, recalling the memory. "Yes, they liked to come after me whenever they could."

"But not after that day, am I right?" I didn't answer. He was right. I haven't even seen them for months now. He continued. "I was ready to step in when one of them pushed you on the ground. You yelled out and, I don't think you even noticed, but a huge wind knocked all four of them off their feet. I couldn't believe my eyes. I think you were so scared that you didn't even look up for a good minute and by the time you did-"

"They were gone," I finished.

"I knew right then and there that it was you who we were looking for."

I sighed, my head still spinning from all the information. "No, this can't be possible. I'm pretty sure I'm a girl, have been my whole life, so unless there's been some kind of mistake -" They both laughed.

"You are very much a woman, my child," Felnard said. He dismissed the moment with a wave of his hand. "This was a lot to take in. Why won't you lay down and rest? I have a bed ready for you."

I tried to respond but my mouth refused to form the words. I looked at them again. Either they were crazy or I was, either way my head was throbbing and I couldn't concentrate any longer. "Alright."

I later woke up to the sound of murmured talk outside. I looked around in the small house and found that Felnard and Killian weren't here. I stood next to the window, looking out at the landscape of Yandana. It seemed so far away from here.

After a moment, I went back to the bedroom where, on the small nightstand, I noticed a bunch of new clothes. They were clean, the smell of roses coming off them in a comforting wave. I couldn't quite believe they were there for me, but as I unfolded them it became pretty clear they were my size. I didn't understand it. No one other than Polly had ever done something like this for me.

Then it hit me: Polly. I didn't say goodbye to her.

I reached into my back pocket, the cold silver of the necklace touched my hand. My only friend in the world left Yandana thinking that I didn't find it important to say goodbye to her.

I pushed the thought from my mind - it was too painful to even look at right now. I grabbed the top dress on the pile and left the house. I saw Killian and Felnard a little way away from the front door, discussing something in hushed tones. I didn't want to talk to them, I simply wasn't ready to get back into the conversation about who they think I was supposed to be, so I headed straight to the back of the house - making sure they weren't watching for me - and then down towards the nearby forest.

As I went deeper in the fresh air helped to clear my head. I was nothing more than a homeless girl and a thief who fled from her home when she was just a teenager. And then two lunatics walk in my life and tell me that I'm the answer to some centuries old prophecy. But the fire. The Dragon. Was that an illusion from Felnard? But then what about the story Killian told? Felnard wasn't there for that.

I broke the treeline and found a crystal-clear lake. The water was expansive before me, reaching beyond my sight, and almost supernaturally still. The quiet bird song in the distant trees was helping to calm my nerves. I walked down to the water's edge, in awe of it all. I slipped off a shoe and touched my toe to the surface. It rippled out, but seemed okay. I took a moment to take off all my dirty clothes and waded slowly into the cold water. The chill of the water brought me back to myself even more.

As my long hair got wet I felt its heavy weight. I hadn't touched it in years, the red waves pouring down past my knees, darkening as they hit the lake. I looked down at my own reflection. I studied myself, searching for the look of a saviour. But all I saw was a nobody.

I pushed my hair behind my disappointing ears and, for the first time in forever, I let myself cry. It was too much to take in all at once. All my sadness and loneliness broke out in heaving sobs and I didn't stop them.

The loud snap of a branch made me turn, my guard back up as quickly as it came down, but it needn't have. I couldn't believe my eyes.

A herd of stags walked out to the edge of the lake. The biggest one, the leader of the pack, came straight over and stood in front of me. I was overcome with the strangest feeling, like I somehow knew this animal. I held out my hand, staying as still as I could so as not to frighten him. Slowly he stepped forward, pushing his nose into my palm, his eyes closed. He trusted me. I felt it. I stood up and hugged the neck of the stag. The relief I felt when this royal animal allowed me to do so. I only let him go when I heard footsteps. I looked at him and said without words: It's time to go. Within seconds the herd was gone.

I didn't know how to explain what it was that just happened, but as the footsteps came closer, I ducked down into the water so only my head was visible. Killian appeared from the forest. He had taken off his armour. He had black shirt and trousers on so his sleek figure was showing more visibly. He stopped as soon as he noticed me and turned to his side.

"Are you alright?" He asked, clearly trying to give me some semblance of privacy.

"Yes. I just needed to freshen up."

"Understandable." He nodded and I saw as he quickly glanced at me again.

"Can you... turn away?"

He turned his back to me, and I quickly got out of the water and put on the purple-coloured dress. Despite my outfit from the day before, it still felt weird as I rarely wore skirts. I slid into my shoes and walked towards him. He turned around.

"I've... never introduced myself," he said, almost sheepishly.

"You didn't have to," I replied. "I know who you are. Everyone does."

"I would still like to. My name is Killian Fin, my lady. It's a pleasure to meet you." He bowed in front of me and I couldn't help but smile.

"Sam Tanan. The pleasure is all mine, my lord." I bowed too. He held out his arm and I took it. Together we started heading back through the woods.

"I am sorry if we scared you yesterday. Our nerves got the better of us."

"How long have you been helping Felnard?" I asked.

"Five years now, ever since he left Lendala to look for the Halfling. But sometimes it feels like it's been even longer than that." He sighed as I looked at him, and for a second it felt like he was carrying the weight of the world on his shoulders.

"And how did it all start?"

He stopped abruptly, took a deep breath and I noticed that he was careful not to look at me as he replied. "It's a long story," he said. "For a later time." The curtness of the response meant that I just nodded in response. We started moving again and suddenly I could not believe that I was holding onto the Killian Fin, Hero of all.

"Felnard's nephew arrived," he continued. "He'll be coming with us on the journey." It was my turn to stop.

"What journey?" I let go of his arm. He looked taken aback by my question.

"To destroy the prophecy as it is your destiny to do so." That strange feeling took over me again. I simply could not help myself. First it was just a giggle then it grew into uncontrollable laughter. "Did I say something funny?" He was looking at me as if I'd grown a second head.

"Oh, you most certainly did." Disappointment appeared on his face but I didn't care. What were they thinking? They reveal this to me and I will run straight into danger's arms? "I'm no one! Just a thief who doesn't have any-" I stopped myself, because I was desperately holding onto the hope that Polly was still my friend, "-family, whose name is unknown to others and-"

"You're wrong." He cut me off and caught my gaze. I once again felt like he was looking straight into my soul. A shiver ran through me as he stepped closer. His appearance, his every move, demanded respect, but I saw something else too: he was scared. "I know that this is too much at once, but we can not change our destiny, Sam. I know you-"

"You don't," I snapped at him. "You don't know me. Just because you've been following me around for a year does not mean that you know a bloody thing about me." I could feel the tears fighting to the surface again, but I held them back, pushing forward. "Look, I am sorry. It's just... I can't go from being a nobody to the saviour of the Broken Ground in a day."

"We are the victims of our own circumstances," he said quietly. He looked down, staring at the ground. "Please, just…" I suddenly felt sorry for him. He had an enormous sadness in his deep black eyes. I don't know what came over me, but before I could think about it-

"I think the animals understand me and I understand them," I blurted out. He looked surprised. "Is that… part of my magic?" He smiled.

"I think Felnard can answer that question better than me." He held out his hand again for me to take. I looked at it for a second before taking it once again, and we walked the rest of the way back to the house in silence.

When we arrived back Felnard was outside and, to my surprise, he was petting a donkey while giggling like a child. The scene was more than a little confusing, but I decided not to say anything.

A very slim man appeared from the house. His skin was dark and I immediately knew that he was a Druid too. A huge scar was running through his left eye, leaving his iris white and milky. The scar seemed like it came from an animal and not a weapon, but what really gave him away was he shared Felnard's inquisitive expression. He had a curiosity in his eyes unlike anyone I'd ever seen in Yandana. He watched us as we made our way towards them and a nervous smile appeared on his face.

"Vendal," Killian called out to the man, "this is Sam Tanan. Sam, Felnard's nephew Vendal Heron." I held out my hand.

"Nice to meet you," I said.

"You're the Halfling?" He asked, ignoring my greeting. I put my hand back down. He looked just as confused as I felt ever since last night. Felnard joined us at that moment.

"I am," I said, trying to maintain some dignity in the situation.

"This is a woman, uncle." He was staring at Felnard as he said this, and I couldn't help but feel like a show pony. Felnard took a deep breath.

"I'm aware."

"Women. Can't. Have. Magic," he said, punctuating every word to make sure he was very clear.

"That's what I said!" They all turned to look at me, then turned back to each other.

"She does have magic, Ven. I saw it with my own eyes," Killian said, and Felnard nodded so hurriedly that I was afraid his head would fall off. Vendal looked at me again, but this time, he was scanning me from head to toe. I could tell he didn't believe his friend or his uncle. I'd never felt more uncomfortable in my whole life.

"Alright. Prove it then." He folded his arms, waiting to be blown away by my powers. I first looked at Killian, who smiled at me with great confidence, and then to Felnard, who seemed a bit more sceptical but still reassuring.

"I don't know... how?" I said slowly. I saw a smirk appear on Vendal's face and I felt a sudden flush of anger burn through me. While I agreed with his scepticism, I didn't appreciate being looked down on. Embarrassment turned to spite as I considered the facts: I could not deny what happened the night before or with the stag in the lake. Then the idea came. I turned towards the forest. I had no idea what I was doing, but I took in a deep breath and concentrated.

"What are we waiting for?" Vendal whispered, loud enough so I could hear, but his uncle shushed him. After what felt like an excruciatingly long time, finally the stag stepped out of the woods. The noble animal stopped right in front of me and once again, without any fear, he let me touch his nose. I turned towards the three men and they all had the same amazement in their eyes.

"Well, shit," said Vendal, and for the first time in 24 hours I felt a sliver of vindication.

"You are even more special than I first thought," Felnard whispered as he moved next to me and touched the neck of the stag. It didn't run away. I felt Killian's eyes on me but I did not turn to look at him.

"It seems you're a Paradion as well," Felnard continued. The word threw me off so much that I suddenly lost my connection to the stag and the animal quickly turned and ran back to its herd in the forest.

"A what?" I asked.

"You were born under the Red Moon, am I right?" Felnard asked with confidence.

"I… don't know. My father never talked about it."

"Uncle, that's impossible," Vendal chimed in.

"You saw what she did and you are still in doubt." Felnard shook his head disapprovingly. Vendal sighed.

"It's just… Come on! Up until this point the tale of Radona and Elemris was nothing more than a legend. And now you're telling me that really is all true? That she is the Destroyer? And the Soulless is probably on the rise out there somewhere?"

"You've seen the signs, Vendal." Felnard's voice was no longer calm and kind. It had an edge I wasn't expecting. The young Druid deflated completely, his eyes kept bolting between me and his uncle. Killian didn't say a word and neither did I. Before Felnard could say anything else, Vendal turned and walked back into the house. Felnard let out a huge sigh of desperation.

"I am sorry, my child. My nephew is usually far more composed than this." He shook his head, attempting to regain some of his composure. "Anyway, you have no time to waste." He looked at Killian. "You have the gold I gave you, my friend?" Killian nodded. "Good. Go to the Noble Stables and get three of their best horses. Your journey will be long and, I'm afraid, quite dangerous. Get weapons for yourself and the girl. Sam," he turned towards me, and handed me a heavy pouch which I guessed was full of gold. "Get some supplies and clothing as it-"

"I don't want to do this, Felnard." The Druid looked at me with utter disbelief.

"Do you want to go back to the streets? Do you want to live in fear that one day, someone will discover that you are a Halfling born from a love that was unforbidden? Do you want to be alone forever?" I turned away. His words cut too deep.

"I'm terrified."

"You would be a fool if you weren't." The old man smiled comfortingly and suddenly closed me in a hug. "You won't ever be alone again," he whispered, so only I was able to hear it. I held him back for a moment, before he let go of me and headed back to the house. I turned to Killian who handed me the reins of the donkey.

"You'll need Martha." I smiled and nodded and we left the Lonely House behind.

Killian left me to go to the stables, leaving me at the North Gate with

Martha. Walking through the streets of Yandana felt strange after all that happened in little over a day. Everything was quiet. Barely anyone walked the streets and there wasn't a single Fairy flying overhead. I gave thanks to The Big Silhoue for it. With every step I was considering running away. The pouch probably had enough gold in it for me to start a whole new life somewhere else. But what Felnard said kept creeping up on me. Ever since I had left my abusive father behind in Irkaban, I'd been alone. I had no friends, no family, no one to turn to when I needed to. It was just me and my shadow. I knew every street in Yandana and every secret it held, but it was nowhere near to what I considered being home. Did I even know what home meant? Being around these strange men who thought I was some kind of saviour felt weird and scary, but at the same time it felt like I mattered. I was someone. They knew my name, they wanted to help, and truthfully it just felt good to talk to someone. I sighed and didn't even notice I'd stopped until Martha nudged my back with her nose. Did I really understand animals? It certainly seemed like it, but I couldn't comprehend how it was possible.

I turned to the left to make my way to the market, but I stopped dead in my tracks. The King's Guard, four of them, were blocking my way. They were deep in conversation, but I recognised one of them. It was the same Guard who was chasing me yesterday after I stole the necklace. I wondered if he would recognise me considering that I was no longer dirty and my clothes resembled the ones Noble Elves wore on an easy day. I started walking towards them, keeping close to Martha.

"I am telling you; it was Malion Arur," said the Guard who was chasing me yesterday and his comrades started laughing. "I'm not joking. He came out of nowhere, grabbed that thief and ran away with her."

"Well then, he was probably doing you a favour, Alten," said another trying to swallow his laughs. "I bet he took her straight to the king."

"No! He was saving her!" The Guard named Alten blurted out and they all laughed at him again. "Fine," he continued. "How do you explain that the Malion Arur never arrived at the Ball then?" They all stopped laughing as I was getting uncomfortably close to them. I held my breath, but they continued to pay me no mind at all.

"Come on, Alten," a brown hair guard said, his braids peeking out from his helmet. "Killian Fin would never choose a homeless girl over the honour of being the first Human to have the hand of an Elf."

When I reached them, they parted and let me walk through without even looking at me. I couldn't believe my ears. Was it true? Did they offer a Human the hand of an Elven maid?

"Where was he then?" Alten asked, and I suddenly felt eyes boring into my back. I quickened my pace.

"I don't know. I don't know the guy."

I didn't hear the rest of their conversation as I finally made it out of earshot and arrived at Emerald Square. The market was quiet which made my supply run easier. I couldn't believe what the guards were saying about Killian. I knew he held a lot of respect, but the fact the Elven King and Fairy Queen would even think of allowing him to choose a bride from their own kind was insanity. They were breaking their own rules. It was a bigger honour than receiving an Elven name and Killian had left it all behind to help a crazy old Druid and me? Why would he do that?

I bought the food as Felnard ordered me to do so, grabbed warm blankets, cloaks for all three of us and a new shirt and trousers for myself. When I left the last stand behind, Martha's bags fully loaded up, the thought of leaving - once again - crossed my mind. But that conversation I overheard made me realize that I couldn't do it. Killian, and probably Vendal too, had sacrificed things in order to help me. If I were to run away, I would be no more than a coward.

I looked back at the market. Elves and Fairies slowly started to appear from their houses and the sight of them felt strangely unfamiliar. I did not belong to Yandana. From the Elves' absurd buildings that all displayed their so-called Nobility, to Fairy huts up in the big trees all around the city. This world was not my world, and they hated me here. I was no more than an unwanted fly in their eyes.

I started to make my way back to Felnard's house, but as I was going through the main street, I saw the same four guards emerging from the left. They were still deep in conversation, not really looking at their surroundings. The guard named Alten seemed to be looking for something and it didn't take me long to realise it was me he was looking for. I slowed down to make sure I didn't draw attention to myself. The other three were laughing really loudly and I heard Killian's name being brought up again. I passed a bunch of Elven ladies who were also talking about my saviour from the day before. It seemed like everyone was talking about him and how disrespectful he was for not showing up on the ball to choose a bride for himself. I saw some crying over their lost opportunity, while others claimed that they wouldn't let a Human touch them. I was starting to feel uncomfortable when I noticed that the four guards were no longer in front of me. I quickly picked up my pace again and a huge wave of relief came over me as I saw the North Gates. However, my relief was short-lived as their voices shot up behind me.

"Have you seen the new recruits?" Asked one of them, I couldn't tell which and I didn't dare to look back at them.

"Oh my… they look like a small breeze could blow them away," laughed another.

"Alten, are you okay?" That question cut through my nerves in an instant. I knew Alten was looking at me, I could feel his gaze on my back.

"Yeah…" he said slowly, and then suddenly: "Miss!"

I didn't stop until I felt his hand on my shoulder. I almost jumped out of my skin.

"Miss, you dropped this."

I looked down to see he was holding an apple out to me. I forced myself to smile and took it from him, but he quickly grabbed my hand before I could pull it away.

"Have we met before?" He asked, studying me.

"Oh no, kind ser," I answered quickly. "My father sent me to buy supplies for our journey back home."

"Where's your father?"

"He's waiting for me at the edge of the forest. I should really get back to him, ser, he must be worried for me by now."

To my relief he let go of my hand, but was still looking at me. I bowed quickly and then started to walk away, hoping that he wouldn't stop me again.

By the time I stepped out of the North Gate I finally managed to catch my breath. Martha was nudging me with her nose so I gave her the apple Alten just handed me. I looked back: no one there. I let out a huge sigh and felt my heart slow down.

Eventually, I made it back to Felnard's. Tying Martha up outside, I headed into the house. There was no sign of Felnard or Vendal anywhere. Did something happen to them?

I stepped back out and heard their voices in the distance. They were coming back from the forest, Vendal carrying two buckets while having a heated discussion with his uncle. As they spotted me, I watched as their discussion ceased immediately. When they closed the distance between us Felnard patted my shoulder and went straight into the house. Vendal put down the two buckets and turned to me, oddly fidgety.

"I apologise for the way I was behaving earlier," he said, a little reluctantly. He wasn't even looking at me properly.

"Don't worry about it," I replied. "It is just as unbelievable to me as it is to you." I tried to give him a reassuring smile, but he just nodded and left.

"He'll come around." I turned towards the voice. Killian stood with three incredibly beautiful horses. One of them was jet-black with a white patch on its nose, while the other two had mixed brown and white colours. I walked up to them and was instantly drawn to the black horse. "That's Agarta," he continued. "Figured you'd like her."

"She is gorgeous."

"Yes, she is." I felt his gaze on me but I didn't care. "Did you have any trouble?"

I had been contemplating for a while if I should ask him about what I heard, but decided against it. We didn't know each other and I didn't want to offend him.

"No," I lied.

"Great."

The moment stood a little awkwardly, and I wondered if there was as much he wasn't telling me as I was unwilling to ask.

We went back to the house leaving the supplies outside with Martha. Vendal was packing his things together and was back in his Druid robes. Felnard sat next to the fire, staring straight into it. The moment felt paused, like if I just stayed silent maybe nothing would happen ever again. The temptation died with the thought of Alten, his gaze trying to place me. There was no hiding from any of it. I swallowed.

"So," I started, surprising myself with how loud my voice was as it broke the silence. "What's the plan?"

Felnard turned to me so suddenly I had to take a step back. His face lit up with joy.

"My child, I am so proud of you," he said and I saw a strange twitch run through Vendal's face. "Vendal has everything with him. You all will start in the Druid capitol, Lendala. We have an old friend there named Rowland, he'll be able to help put the pieces of the puzzle together a bit better."

"We don't know enough about the Grabodans," Vendal cut in. "There are some gaps in the story that we need to sort out. We believe that Rowland will be able to point us in the right direction."

"I thought Grabodans were extinct," I said.

"They are, but you're not looking for them, you're looking for the place where they may have kept Radona's prophecy. There are some who claim that the Prophecy is no longer in their temple."

Felnard stood up and he looked older than ever. He held both my hands in his.

"This is an enormous quest my dear, it won't be easy. You will have many battles you have to fight, but you won't be alone. Please. Trust my nephew and my dear friend." He looked to the two men as they made their way outside. He then suddenly lowered his voice.

"You need to open your heart more, Samantha." I hadn't heard my full name in a very long time.

"I don't-"

"You'll understand," he said, cutting off whatever protest had begun to come out of my mouth. "I know you will."

He gave my hands another pat and led me outside. Killian and Vendal had finished packing up the horses and Martha, so all that was left was… me. I got on the back of Agarta and looked one last time towards Yandana. The place where I lived for so long, but maybe 'living' wasn't the right word.

We said our goodbyes to Felnard and rode off into the unknown.

CHAPTER 3
THE RUINS OF THE OLD KINGDOM

It was pure torture. For the first two days none of us said anything, we just rode through the valley, barely looking around and only listening to nature. I felt way too awkward to actually open my mouth and say anything and I had the sneaking suspicion that Killian and Vendal felt the same way. What really didn't make any sense was the fact that they didn't even talk to each other even though I thought they were supposed to be friends. We were sitting around the fire for two continuous nights without a word. I was considering leaving them and heading straight back to the Guards so they can torture me instead. It would have been better than two completely silent men.

On the third day I couldn't take it anymore. I decided to start asking them about their lives.

"So…" I started and it startled my two companions so much that Vendal yelled and Killian put his hand on his sword. "Woah!" I put my hands up, defensively. "Do I frighten you that much?" They both started laughing and so did I.

"I guess we are all on edge," Killian said, smiling

"Alright, let's change that. How did you two meet?"

"I saved his ass," said Vendal immediately.

"Now, wait, it wasn't that simple."

"Come on. It's okay, we've all gotten into trouble because of some nice maiden." The Druid winked at Killian who flushed slightly. I didn't know if I wanted to hear the story.

"Fine, fine. He saved me."

"Our friend over there," Vendal nodded towards Killian, who couldn't help but smile as Vendal started to talk, "came to Lendala because of an invitation from the Head of the Druids. It was a formality since he received an Elven name."

"Oh Lord." Killian moved behind me so he didn't have to see my reactions.

"And in Lendala," continued Vendal, "the only women around are the wives and daughters of Druids and let me tell you something Sam, they are gorgeous."

A flush of embarrassment ran through me so instead of looking at Vendal, I fixed my gaze between Agarta's ears, hoping that the redness on my face wouldn't become too obvious.

"So one night, Killian and his Guard buddies are out in the local inn, having some drinks and celebrating. A few drinks in, Killian and this woman are all over each other, and the woman leads him outside right when the Head of the Druids arrives."

"I will give you five gold if you shut up now, Ven," Killian said behind me, deadly serious. Vendal just flashed a grin.

"The Head of the Druids turns to the woman: 'My dear Elena, what are you doing with this man?'" Vendal had to hold back his laughter. "'Answer me, my dear wife!' He demands and that's when I stepped in, grabbed Killian and said-"

"Come on old friend, how many times do I have to tell you that this woman isn't your mother?" They said it together in perfect harmony and burst out laughing. I laughed along, but my heart wasn't really in it. I can't quite put my fingers on what was holding me back.

"And that's how we met," said Killian as he pulled up beside me once more.

"It's a good story," I replied as honestly as I was able to.

"What about you Sam?" Vendal asked. "Any friends or lovers?"

"No," I tried to force a smile. "None of the above."

The young Druid seemed surprised. "Really?"

"Yeah. It's hard to make friends while living on the streets." Another lie, but I couldn't talk about Polly. A sudden tension appeared between us all. "Sorry, didn't mean to bring down the mood."

"No, you're all good," Vendal reassured me without hesitation. I took a glance at Killian, who suddenly seemed incredibly sad. "Well, now you have us."

"What do you mean?"

"Trust me, we have such a long road ahead of us that we will either love each other by the end or hate each other," he said gleefully.

The conversation kept going. They told me stories of incredible escapes, unfortunate encounters with women and funny stories about Felnard. Vendal didn't say it, but I could tell that he was worried for his uncle. He talked about him with such care in his voice that it left an aching in my chest.

We stopped next to a lake at midday and started eating. Vendal talked a lot. Now I'd gotten him talking, he wouldn't stop. He seemed to be enjoying the sound of his own voice while Killian went a bit quiet. There was something strange about him. One minute he seemed like the kindest, most caring soul, the next he wouldn't even look me in the eye. I didn't know what was going on with him, but I had a feeling that it had something to do with why he started helping Felnard in his quest. He spent a lot of time taking care of his weapons, but I noticed really early on that he did not wear his signature armour at all. It felt like he was hiding.

Vendal, on the other hand, seemed to be opening up more and more. He was a very funny man. He laughed a lot and loved his stories. That's why it didn't even surprise me when he suddenly stood up, threw down his robes and went straight into the lake without a word of warning. I would have been happier without seeing him completely naked, but I didn't say a word as I quickly turned away.

After we all had our well-deserved rest, we got back on our horses and continued our journey.

The landscape was incredibly beautiful. We were in the last days of spring so the trees and bushes had started to lose their flowers and put on their beautiful green leaves. In Yandana, because of the Fairies, all the trees kept their flowers. It never changed. There were flowers everywhere in the Capitol. It was a nice change to see how nature turned into different shades of green.

For the next three days, we had fun telling stories and creating theories on what might lie ahead of us. However, the next morning I felt an uneasy feeling creeping in. Killian's whole demeanour had changed. He went completely quiet and there was a peculiar look resting on his face. Vendal seemed to shift into a much darker mood too. He was jumpy and a bit all over the place. Was it possible that both of them had a rough night's sleep? It would have been odd I guess, but not unimaginable.

I was taking care of the horses and lovely Martha before we set off to continue our journey when Vendal appeared next to me. He just stood there awkwardly for a short few seconds and stared at me. It gave me the most uncomfortable feeling. I stared back.

"We..." he started and trailed off. He turned to look behind him. Killian was gathering the blankets a bit further away from us. When he turned back to me, he lowered his voice so I had to step a bit closer to hear him. "We are entering the Ruins of the Old Kingdom today." He paused and I was sure that he was waiting for a reaction that I wasn't able to give him. He sighed. "The Kingdom that once belonged to the Humans."

The realisation hit me. I peeked at Killian who seemed oblivious to what we were talking about.

"Oh..." It was all I could mutter.

"Killian will act all tough and what not, but..." I could see he was searching for the right word while I was keeping my eyes on our companion. Finally he said: "He is ashamed, Sam."

"Ashamed?"

"Of what the Humans once did. If it weren't for them, The Great War would never have happened and we would still be united." A new emotion appeared on the Druid's face that took me a moment to place. He was sad.

"Killian can't be blaming himself for that, right? It happened ages ago, we were all born on the Broken Grounds, we didn't even know what the Sevens were like."

"Yes, Sam, but he is still a Human, you know. He carries around the sins of his ancestors and I know that he does everything he can to distance himself from that history."

"I see."

I'd never thought about it that way. For all I'd heard about Killian and the things that he did, it just seemed like that he was Noble by nature, that he just simply always wanted to do the right thing. I'd never considered the guilt. He started walking towards us.

"Are we ready to go?" He asked as he put the blankets on Martha's back.

"Yeah mate," Vendal smiled at him. "Let's go."

We all mounted our horses and set off. I started to dread the moment when we would lay our eyes on the ruins of the Old Kingdom. I kept looking at Killian who seemed completely zoned out. He didn't say a word and wouldn't look at us at all. Vendal seemed just as troubled as him. The sun was starting to go down when we laid our eyes on the ruins. The first thing that appeared was the silhouette of a tower. As we were getting closer the holes and burn marks on its stone structure became visible. It was a miracle that it was still standing at all. A sort of deep sadness took over all of us. There were piles of rotten and burnt wood all over the grounds and a few stone structures that must have been the base of some glorious buildings in the past. I didn't know much about how Humans built their cities back in those days, but I was sure that it was nothing like the buildings in Irkaban. The new Human world screamed defeat to whoever stepped into it. There was nothing glorious there.

As we were getting closer to some of the ruins, it was easy to see how hard Killian was trying to hold himself together. I felt for him. I wanted to comfort him, but I wasn't sure I could. Just as I was getting my courage together to do so, Vendal was already by his side and he did something that only true friends would do, he patted Killian's back and handed him something that I couldn't quite see. The soldier looked up at him and a smile appeared on his face. Vendal didn't say anything, but he kept close to his friend to make sure that he wasn't alone with his thoughts. I kept behind them to give them the space they needed.

A whooshing sound came out of nowhere and it was followed by a pain I have not felt before. I grabbed my shoulder tightly and I must have yelled out, because I faintly heard the yells of Killian and Vendal somewhere in the distance. I reached to feel what was causing the pain when Agarta suddenly cried out and dropped me from her back. As I hit the ground, I heard a snap and the pain exploded in my right shoulder. There were voices all around and as I managed to finally look up: there were men coming from all directions towards us.

Killian appeared near me; he was running towards the charging men with his sword in his hand ready to strike down. Vendal was on my other side, his eyes rolled back to their sockets as he was making his connection with the elements all around us. I saw heavy stones flying through the air towards our attackers, smashing into many of them. Strong lianas broke out of the ground grabbing many of the unknown soldiers and dropping them mercilessly from high above.

Then, without any warning, it was all over. A tall man grabbed Vendal from behind holding a big knife to his throat, which in itself shouldn't have stopped the Druid, but he saw what I didn't. Someone yanked me up from the ground by grabbing my long hair and I yelled out in pain. I heard Killian scream out my name before dropping his sword and surrendering to the men around him. A big, very muscly man appeared, riding on the back of a griffon and my stomach dropped. It was Cutter Callaghan and his band of mischieves, the Leongrass.

Cutter dismounted from the back of his griffon. He was enormous and even though I knew he was Human, he looked more like a Giant. He wasn't wearing a shirt so his battle scars were all visible. The largest one started on top of his left shoulder and cut through his whole chest down to his waist. His long blonde hair was greasy and disgusting as was his face. He had rotten yellow teeth and similar coloured eyes. His beard was braided and was bouncing off of his chest. He stopped right in front of me and his smell made me want to throw up.

"Who shot the girl?" he yelled. The guy who was holding Killian dropped him right next to me. I caught his eye.

"It was me, boss," said a voice behind us, and then all I saw was a quick movement. Cutter grabbed his knife from his side and threw it. We only heard a big thud as his man hit the ground.

"Bunch of idiots, they can't even aim." He muttered to himself before his gaze turned to me. Cold shivers ran through my whole body. "Hey there, pretty."

"Leave her alone." There was such anger in Killian's voice that it scared me a bit. He looked furiously up at Cutter who started laughing.

"Oh look boys! We captured the bravest man in the world! It's Killian Fin himself." His men started to laugh as they heard the name, but they fell silent again when Cutter raised one of his huge hands. "Bring her to me," he said and the soldier behind me grabbed my braided hair, revealing my ears as I was pulled to my feet. Vendal and Killian yelled out in anger.

"Well, what have we here?" Cutter grabbed the pointed top of my ear and yanked it forward. I grit my teeth, trying not to show any weakness. "This is a Halfling, boys." His spit hit my face as he spoke and I felt my stomach turn.

"Let us go, you monster." I said it without even thinking and Cutter's face suddenly turned red with anger.

"Monster, eh?" He nodded at the man who was still holding me by my braided hair.

I heard the sound of the blade cutting through the air and suddenly there was nothing holding me up anymore. I fell hard on my knees and my hand automatically shot up to my hair. My head felt light. I turned to see the man behind me holding the other end of my plait, the hair on my head suddenly barely grazing my shoulders.

I felt a dam break inside me as the strange feeling I felt at the lake rose up in my chest and, before anyone could react, the huge griffon grabbed Cutter by his shoulder and I felt the animal's strength shoot through my own veins. He threw him away like he was no more than a ragdoll. Then he turned his beautiful eagle head to the soldiers who ran towards him and dispatched them without a problem. The griffon's huge claws cut through their stomachs and throats like knives through the butter. The pain in my shoulder grew stronger and my strange connection to the animal started to fade. The world slowly turned black around me.

It was just a dream. No more than a wild dream. But then if it was just a dream, why was my shoulder hurting? I sat up and immediately felt a pair of hands close in on my face. It was a gentle touch which prompted me to open my eyes. Killian's face was full of worry as he was looking at me with his piercing black eyes. He said something, or more like asked something, but I couldn't make it out. My hand was searching for my hair and then it hit me: it wasn't a dream. I stood up so quickly that I instantly felt dizzy and would have fallen right back if Killian didn't have his arms around me. He closed me in a hug and his hand was gently stroking my hair. Sound started to come back to me and I had to realise that I was sobbing while Killian kept repeating in a soft voice.

"I'm sorry. I am so sorry, Sam."

I was seeking refuge in his arms but as he muttered those words I slowly let go of him. As his face came to view I saw guilt written all over it. I reached up without even thinking about it and stroked his cheek.

"It wasn't your fault," I croaked out, and as I tried to raise my other hand the pain made me take a step back. I folded up the sleeve of my shirt and a strange black marking, almost like a vein, led up from my wrist to the middle of my lower arm.

"It's the price we pay when our magic comes from a place of anger and hate." I quickly turned as I heard Vendal's voice behind me. He was putting down a load of wood he had been collecting for the fire. He looked incredibly tired.

"You know... even after what you did with that stag, I didn't believe that you had magic," he admitted, regretfully. "But what you did yesterday..." Yesterday? A day passed by since the attack? "I will never doubt you again, but I need to start training you."

"What?" I asked, puzzled. Vendal walked past us to the fire. It was really cold and the stars started to appear above us. We were no longer near the ruins of The Old Kingdom, instead we were somewhere deep in the Pinetree woods.

"Druid magic is difficult to master and if we use it for evil, we have to pay for it. It was something Sagar made clear before giving magic to men hoping to avoid the use of magic for anything sinister." Vendal snapped his finger and the fire was lit. We all sat down around it and I noticed that Killian was keeping very close to me.

"That line that appeared on your hand after taking over control of the griffon is called The Mark of Sagar. If you use too much dark magic that line will start spreading, and if it reaches your heart, it will kill you." Vendal was being very direct, serious, holding intense eye contact with me.

"I... didn't even know what I was doing. When that man cut-" I stopped myself. I felt that strange feeling rise up in my chest again and I had to push it down with everything. I knew it was just hair, but that hair kept me safe from the eyes of others. I felt naked without it, and my ears...

"I know," said Vendal quietly. "But... you are the Destroyer, I now have no doubt about it."

"Ven-" I started, but he raised his hand to silence me.

"I will teach you how to use your magic starting tomorrow. Killian," he nodded towards his friend, "will teach you how to use a sword. We need to prepare you, Sam."

I looked down on my boots. Fear creeped in my bones. I opened my mouth to protest, but then I felt Killian's hand close on top of mine and I let out a sigh instead.

"Alright."

"Good," said Vendal. Then, suddenly remorseful, he said: "I'm sorry that we weren't able to protect you. We shouldn't have left you behind."

"No." I said it with a bit more heat than I intended. I finally looked up, darting my eyes between the two of them, the both of them looking back at me. I suddenly realised I was on my feet. "I will not allow this. You did nothing wrong. Do you hear me? This wasn't your fault."

They nodded, slowly. I couldn't quite tell if they were hearing me or were a little afraid. Either worked. I sat back down. "I don't want to hear about it again."

"Duly noted," said Vendal, smiling. A breeze of relief took over me.

"What happened to Cutter?" I asked, eager to move on.

"Well," Killian slipped his hand out of mine, continuing, "after you fainted the griffon slowly started to calm down, but was still defensive after the attack from the soldier. We carried you away, but unfortunately I did see Cutter escaping as I looked back to make sure they weren't following us."

I didn't say anything. I couldn't. The way the griffon threw him away I was sure he was dead, but I guess he was even stronger than he looked. The next thought hit me like a brick.

"Where are the horses? And Martha?"

"Don't worry," Vendal smiled, clearly amused at my worry. "They're fine, see?" He nodded and I saw all our animals were there. A little skittish, but unharmed. I let out a sigh of relief but at the same time I felt myself getting a bit light headed.

"You still need rest," Killian said, his voice soothing.

"Yes... yes, I believe I do."

I got up and walked back to my blanket, Killian spotting me to make sure I was okay. Before I laid down he looked at me.

"I like your hair like this." He said it quietly, just for me. I couldn't help but smile.

Sleep came easy, but so did the nightmares.

I was in complete darkness, but still I felt someone looking at me. And then a voice came, barely audible behind me.

"So, you are the Halfling..."

The voice sent shivers down my spine. I couldn't tell if it was a man or a woman talking and I couldn't see anyone. I felt a sudden push from behind and I fell to the cold ground.

"You're not much to look at, to be honest."

The voice came from the left, a bit louder than before. I looked around as I slowly stood up and I suddenly felt a familiar hold around me. It was Killian, but his face dripped with disgust as he looked at me.

"Don't touch me you filthy Halfling!" he yelled, pushing me away from him and drew his sword. I braced myself, arms flying in front of my face, but before he could attack me he disappeared into thin air. A tall figure was standing in his place.

"Look at you," the figure said, disdain in every syllable. "Are you really the one my sister sent to destroy my Champion? Hah... pathetic."

She stepped into the small circle of light and took my breath away.

Radona. It was Radona.

She was gorgeous, the palest thing I'd ever seen in my life. She had a slim figure but it wasn't covered by a dress, instead a thick black smoke shifted with her, covering her, and her long dark hair was moving around her like hundreds of snakes. And her face. Her face was picture perfect. Beautiful, round eyes that were the colour of blood; full, delightful lips; harsh cheekbones and jawline. Her presence was undeniable.

But she was pure evil. I could feel her darkness radiating off of her, the kind that made you want to curry favour. It was overwhelming, and dangerous.

"You are a nobody." She said it slowly, like she was making sure I understood every word. She closed the gap in a few strides. "You won't stand a chance against my champion."

She looked at my hand, the one that had the Mark of Sagar.

"Interesting," she said, eyebrow arched in intrigue.

And then she screamed in my face and disappeared.

I put my hands on my ears but soon there was nothing but darkness around me. All that was ringing in my ears and lingering in front of my eyes were the words and face of Killian.

Don't touch me you filthy Halfling.

I woke up bathed in my own sweat. I could hardly breathe, it felt like someone sucked all the air out of my lungs. Vendal was next to me in a blink of an eye. He put his hand on my forehead and his voice echoed in my head:

"CALM DOWN."

Instantly, I could hear all the noises of the forest around me and my vision was clear enough that I could see the Druid kneeling in front of me.

"Are you alright?" Vendal asked.

"Yeah. Yeah, just a bad dream," I said, taking deep breaths. I could still see Radona in my head. "Sorry. I didn't mean to scare you."

"Don't you worry about that." Vendal smiled.

It was still dark. Killian was sleeping peacefully close to the fire. We sat down quietly a bit further away from him. "I was just looking at our map and the instructions my uncle gave us. We should be reaching a small-town tomorrow by the name of Allion. I think we should stop there to recharge and to fill up our supplies. Maybe we could spend a good night sleeping on an actual bed."

"That sure would be nice," I smiled, and then I had a thought. "But..." As soon as my hand was close to my ear he spoke.

"You're all good. Other than the Elves and Fairies, no one cares about your kind of Halfling. Humans and Druids don't give a damn about who they run into. Allion is somewhat of a collecting place of misfits." He smiled mischievously. "We will most likely run into disgraced Elves, drunken Druids, loads of mercenaries and who knows what else. It also has one of the biggest marketplaces in the whole of the Broken Ground."

"I feel like you've been to Allion before." I tried to let the irony sink into my voice.

"Oh, trust me... I have." He winked at me. It made me more uncomfortable than I'd like to admit. I tried not to let it show. He continued: "We're going to find everything we need there. Lendala should be another four days' journey from there so I don't think a little extra rest will work against us in the long run." He yawned loudly.

"Off you go." I gestured towards his blanket. "I will keep watch."

"Are you sure?"

"Yes, I am wide awake and have no desire to go back to sleep."

"Alright. If you insist."

And with that he was gone.

My eyes rested on the peacefully sleeping Killian. There was something strange pulling me towards him ever since he saved me from the Guards in Yandana. It wasn't the same type of connection I felt with the animals or anything else. It felt very different, and it was growing stronger as the days were passing by. I felt like I knew him, even though that was impossible. But the way he talked to me and looked at me made me feel like he might be feeling the same way as I did. A smile appeared on his face and I knew that he was having much sweeter dreams than I had.

Why was he there? Why did he appear in my nightmare? And why did Radona seem... surprised when she saw the Mark of Sagar?

I knew little about Sagar, well, just the general things really. The Druids believed that Sagar was the very first of their kind, and it was he who decided to share his gift with the Chosen Ones.

The tale said that the news of Sagar's incredible powers spread through the Realms like wildfire. So the Kings and Queens of the Sevens decided to invite the strange man into the Palace of Peace that lay on the shore of the Enormous Sea. Sagar accepted the invitation and was soon standing in front of Queen Margot and King Tidios of the Human Kingdom; Queen Alberta and King Marius of the Dwarven Kingdom; Queen Seleca and King Myron of the Giant Kingdom; Queen Olion and her bride Arya from the Fairy Kingdom; the widow King Shan from the Elven Kingdom; General Kirkby, the representative of the Grabodans; and the Emperor of the Handor Empire, Landlow Mortem.

Sagar showed the Royals many of the things he was capable of, but not the full extent of his powers. He knew that if he were to show them his full potential the hunger for power could easily take the minds of good people away.

The reaction he got was quite unexpected, even for him. The Giants feared his power and outright refused to give him any access to their Kingdom. They didn't care about the pleas of the others, they stood up and left the Palace of Peace. The Dwarven King and Queen were in awe, but when Sagar offered them the gift of magic they politely declined. King Marius believed in equality and he knew that if only some of their people were able to do the same things as Sagar, it would only lead to dissension between the clans. They did, however, offer their undying respect for Sagar and whoever may become his children. They left the Palace with peace in their hearts.

Queen Olion and her bride were hungry for the power that magic could have given to them, but Sagar didn't offer them his gifts. He said that as long as they were controlled by their own greed, they did not deserve it. The Fairies were deeply offended by his words and left the Palace without another word.

It was Queen Margot and King Tidios who showed the deepest respect for Sagar, and thus they received his gift. But the Queen's Soul could not take it in. She began to age rapidly in front of their eyes. Sagar was baffled by what happened and withdrew his gift from the woman, returning her to normal. Apologetic, he instead gifted the Queen with fertility, ensuring that the lineage of King Tidios would continue.

Sagar knew, in that moment, that he could not give away his magic to women. Something was holding it back.

Elven King Shan also showed deep respect to Sagar, and so he gifted it to his people too, but Emperor Landlow Mortem refused Sagar's gift. He knew his people and he decided that they did not deserve it. His real reason, however, was much simpler: he was afraid that whoever would receive the gift would try to take his empire from him. Instead, he promised Sagar safe passage to the Empire.

General Kirkby was the only one who had questions. He wanted to know how the Human got his powers. Sagar shared his story with him, but once he offered his gift the Grabodan instead offered him to live among them. That surprised the man, but after careful consideration he declined as he had much to do with his soon to be born children: the order of the Druids.

Those who received the gift all left behind their Kingdoms, creating a new and powerful nation of the Druids without any Kings or Queens to rule over them. They served only one man, and that man was Sagar.

CHAPTER 4
ALLION

Vendal didn't teach me anything the next day, he was too busy gushing over his memories of Allion. He told us elaborate stories of mischief and regrettable nights. Killian was in a much better mood than before and was laughing at everything his friend was saying. I, on the other hand, could not stop myself from checking on the Mark of Sagar every few minutes.

It scared me. I didn't want to use dark magic, in fact, I didn't even know I was using it. What if it happens again? How do you control your emotions enough to avoid something like that happening? Are there Druids walking around in Lendala wearing the Mark? I'd never heard about it before, nor had I seen anyone with it but then again, Druids were usually wearing long sleeved robes. I couldn't see anything on Vendal's arm, that was certain. Considering the stories he had, I was surprised that he never lost his head and used "dark magic".

I had so many questions, but I didn't want to disturb his good mood. After what went down by the ruins, we sure needed it.

"Maybe that pretty Elf is still working in the inn, Killian, I am sure she would be happy to see you again."

That snapped me out of my own head. I looked at the two of them in front of me. Killian smiled.

"Do you still remember her?" Vendal asked.

"How could I forget?" He replied, and that made Vendal burst out in laughter. The way they were talking about their adventures with women started to get under my skin. It seemed like they had forgotten I was one of these "women" they were so cavalier about.

"Hey." I heard Killian say, but it took me a moment to realise that he was calling out to me. I looked up at him, attention alert. "Are you good, Sam?"

"Yes!" I answered, burying my irritation. He nodded at me and turned back to face the road.

I shifted a little in my saddle and felt a sharp pain shoot through my shoulder. I winced audibly and grabbed at it instinctively. I tried to pass it off, but the sound made Killian and Vendal turn, suddenly stopping their horses. I brought Agarta to a stop as well.

Killian dismounted and came over to me.

"Come on," he said, holding his hands up towards me.

"I'm fine."

"No, you're not. We shouldn't have let you ride your own horse; that wound is still fresh. You'll ride with me."

He said it with a voice that told me it's better if I didn't argue. I waved him off helping me down from Agarta, leading to a far less graceful dismount than I had hoped. Killian tried to hide his smirk, so I shot him a look. It didn't help.

I had to let him help me up onto his horse - my arm wasn't in good enough shape to lift myself - but I scowled the whole time to make my point. Vendal grabbed the reins of Agarta and Martha and knotted it on his horse's saddle. Killian got up behind me and his arms were quickly around me as he grabbed the reins.

"Are you comfortable?" I could hear an element of amusement in his voice, which I elected to ignore.

"Yes," I lied again because the truth was that I'd never felt more uncomfortable in my whole life. I could feel Killian's warm breath on the back of my neck and his every movement. I felt Vendal staring at me and as I paid a quick glance at him, I saw a strange expression on his face. He was smirking.

"When are we gonna get there?" I asked quickly. This was all getting old very quickly.

"Shortly," answered the Druid and even in his voice I could tell he was letting a thought go.

"Good." I nodded, not knowing what else to say. We started moving again.

"Were you born in Irkaban, Sam?" Killian asked. It came so out of nowhere that I had to giggle. I felt him frown. "Did I ask something funny?"

"No, sorry, sorry." I said, pulling myself together. "No, I wasn't. My parents met not far from Yandana, in a small Elven village Peldona."

"Oh, the village of Sins," said Vendal, but I paid him no mind.

"And, according to my dad, that's where they stayed while they were waiting for me to arrive."

"What happened to your parents?" Vendal asked, more seriously this time.

"My Mom left after I was born. I don't know her name or how she looked. Dad took me back to Irkaban to raise me on his own, which turned into so much abuse that after fifteen years of suffering I stood up and left and did not stop until I reached Yandana." I said it as nonchalantly as I could, but years like that leave a mark.

It was quiet for a moment before Vendal spoke.

"For the blessed Sagar's sake, life was not kind to you Sam."

"Vendal!" Killian's voice completely changed in tone. It wasn't kind or nice, it was full of anger. The Druid looked apologetically at his friend and then me.

"Sorry, Sam, that was rude."

"No, no. It's the truth." I smiled. "It's okay, honestly. I had the life I had so far, but it's in the past. I am happy to be in better company, finally."

Vendal nodded, looking grateful for my immediate forgiveness, but as he looked at Killian, whose face I couldn't see, his smile disappeared and he didn't speak another word, nor did we.

Allion was so different from Yandana. It was a small town, but we heard the noises even before we laid eyes on it. It was full of life. Vendal's face lit up as soon as we entered and people were flooding the streets in big crowds. The houses around us were all different shapes and sizes and even different colours. I didn't know where to look first as there were so many things to see. People were laughing and singing all around us. Elves, Fairies, Druids and Humans were all over the place, all of them making their way towards a wide-open space that I could only guess was the market Vendal mentioned.

If the houses were colourful on the way in, the burst of colours that welcomed us to the marketplace were unbelievable. Up until that point I didn't even know there were so many colours existing in the world. We passed person after person and I saw things that I never thought were possible. Elves were kissing humans. Not just for the fun of it, but because they were in love. A whole family passed us with an Elf father, Human mother and Halfling children. I couldn't help but turn after them and met Killian's smiling face. He was looking at me in amazement. I felt my cheeks blush and I quickly turned back. He let go of the rein with one of his hands and he reassuringly squeezed mine.

By the time we arrived at the inn, Vendal was full of joy. The inn's name was 'The Peeking Owl' and it made me think of Killian's royal symbol. Was there a connection there? I filed that thought away for later.

We all got down off the horses, grabbed our supplies and went in. There was barely anyone in the cosy inn's lounge area where a big, rounded woman was serving lunch for the wayfarers. The whole interior was made from pine and the smell was intoxicating. There were at least twenty small, round tables placed all around with beautifully crafted chairs. The fireplace was made out of black stone, the kind that was only found up on the Smoky Mountain. As the waitress came out from behind the bar, I clocked a painting on the wall behind her: a small brown owl peeking out from behind a barrel.

"Bertha!" Vendal called out to the woman, who turned to look at us. Her face broke out into the biggest grin I'd ever seen.

"I can't believe my own two eyes. Is that you Venny?" She said, putting down the food she'd been carrying to give us her full attention. I had to swallow my laughter.

"It sure is, and I brought Killian too." Vendal smacked Killian on the back.

Her eyes widened and I was sure she even blushed at the sight of him. Her already enormous grin somehow got bigger. I noted Vendal didn't bother to introduce me as well.

"Come on boys, just come on now," she said, ushering them over as she rushed behind the wooden counter. We approached as she bent behind it, producing two keys and placing them down when she finally noticed me.

"Oh!" She exclaimed, as if I had just appeared from thin air.

"Oh my, sorry Bertha," Vendal said. "This is Sam. She's travelling with us."

"I see... Well, I'm sorry, but I only have two rooms free." She seemed a little rocked by my presence.

"That's fine," Vendal waved, dismissing the problem. "Myself and Killian will share."

"Great," Killian sighed, "I guess I'll sleep on the floor again?"

"You guessed right." Vendal said, winking. He continued:

"Tell me Bertha, do you still have that Elven employee? You know, the wild one?"

"You mean Lilian? No, I had to kick her out. She was making men go wild with jealousy over her. Two of them even got into a fight and broke my favourite chair." She seemed legitimately broken up over the chair.

"Sad," said Vendal, shaking his head. I could feel Killian rolling his eyes next to me and I couldn't blame him. Vendal picked up the keys, thanked Bertha, and we all headed upstairs. Ven gave me one of the keys and we parted ways to our rooms.

It was really a simple room. A rusty - and dusty - old bed, the smallest window I've ever seen, and a single chair under it. I was relieved to see that there was hot water already right next to the door as I entered.

After closing the door, I immediately took off my dirty, bloody clothes. I washed myself the best I could, including my new hair - a process that took far less time than I was used to - and felt like a completely new person when I finished. However, to my great disappointment, the only other clothing I found in my bag was a green dress. I was sure that Felnard put it in there as I remembered seeing it previously in his house. What is it with these men and their insistence on putting me in dresses? I wondered to myself. I sighed, resigned, and put it on. It was this or the rags I was shot in, and I didn't think that would go down so well in town.

When I looked at myself in the mirror, I started. I looked different. My skin seemed healthier and my short hair looked better than I expected. I pushed it behind my ear and smiled, thinking about the Halfling children I'd seen on our way in. In this town, I didn't have to hide my heritage in fear of getting captured by the King's Guard. The concept was foreign, but not unwelcome.

I stood there for a long time before someone knocked on my door.

I opened it and there stood Vendal, now wearing his red robes that looked really good on him. Together, we headed back down to the lounge where Killian was waiting for us, having a conversation with Bertha who looked up at him longingly.

As we walked towards him, I suddenly felt eyes following me. I stopped and looked around. In a dark corner at the back of the lounge I could see someone was sitting in a chair, hiding in the shadows. I couldn't tell if it was a man or woman, but the person was definitely looking at me. I reached for my hair, but Vendal caught it, pulling me on toward Killian and away from the prying eyes. Killian finished his conversation and turned to join us. It took Bertha a moment to turn back to her duties after he left.

"Alright," Killian said. "Supply run."

"We need extra clothes," I said, unable to stop myself from looking back at the stranger before turning back. "Food, most definitely food as well."

"Great. Can you two take care of it?" Vendal asked, hopefully.

"Actually," Killian said, "I want to take care of something while we're here." Jealousy turned my stomach, but I tried to push it away.

"Oh…" Vendal's energy completely dissipated.

"It's okay Vendal," I said quickly, seeing the disappointment on the Druid's face as he realised that he had to join me for the supply run. "I can do it alone."

"Are you sure?" They asked simultaneously, which made me giggle.

"Yeah. Pretty confident."

"Great!" Vendal yelled, and he was gone. Killian looked troubled.

"Are you sure that you're gonna be okay?" He asked, all concern.

"Course, go on and take care of whatever business you have." I smiled and left quickly.

I didn't wait for him to answer. Instead, I headed straight for Martha and left with her back to the marketplace. I passed one of the kissing couples again and saw another family with Halfling kids. There was something so odd about seeing Halflings simply existing in the world. Years of having to hide made me realise I never even considered life could be anything else. It made me happy to see that not everyone of us had to go through the same fate, and that parents can actually be pretty great as well, but it made me sad too.

A larger group of young women were walking in front of me. They didn't have clothes as beautiful as the Elven ladies had in Yandana, but they were still very pretty. They were laughing at something and turned to every single man that walked past them. I only just realised that they were the so-called Joy Girls when one of them moved away from the group and walked towards an older Elf who was holding out a pouch. The older Elf took the woman by the hand, leading her into his home. I saw him pull her in and kiss her, pulling off her clothes as the door closed.

Yandana did not have any Joy Girls. It wasn't prohibited, but also they didn't need them. Every year they held a celebration to pay their respects to the

Goddess of Love, Nihue. I hated the city around that day and usually spent the whole time outside of the walls. Nobles usually held the celebration in their houses while the lower-class citizens held it in one of the three big inns, and the peasants… in the street. They all came together and held an orgy to pay their respects to the Goddess. I'd always found this to be the most disgusting thing imaginable. What went down between two lovers shouldn't happen in front of others. I only witnessed one of these celebrations, when I worked for the inn the first year I arrived in Yandana. Some of the images were burnt into my mind forever.

As I stepped into the marketplace, I heard music. I could hear a girl singing somewhere nearby and it sounded beautiful. I took my time looking around to see what everyone had to offer and found the strangest things. One stand had little boxes on it but the vendor, a small bulky man, wouldn't tell me what was in them. I had to buy one to find out, which didn't seem like a fair deal so I left it behind. On another there were dozens of beautiful flowers in a variety of colours, but there was one that seemed to be translucent which stood out to me.

"You like it?" The lady behind the stall asked.

"I've never seen anything like it."

"It's called a Mood Flower. They are very rare; they never die and they show the exact mood of the person who's wearing them by changing their colours." She picked up the flower, and I watched as the petals shifted from that translucent shimmer into a deep, verdant green. It was stunning. I reached out to stroke the petals, which twitched under my fingers.

"That's why they cost 3 gold," she said, smiling. I pulled my hand back. It was way more expensive than I expected. I could feel condescension radiating off her and was starting to feel uncomfortable. I managed to muster a polite smile.

"Thank you."

I left the stand behind and continued my journey through the market. I quickly found clothes for all three of us and I bought enough so we could swap them more regularly. I got a carrot for Martha - who seemed very happy with the treat - and by the time I reached the end of the first row, the bags on Martha's sides were full of supplies again. I didn't want to leave though, so I walked through the second and third row, looking through everything thoroughly.

When I reached the end of the fourth row my heart almost stopped. Not far from the marketplace, I could see the stables, and in the stables… was a Unicorn.

I squeezed my eyes shut and opened them a few times, disbelieving. It still seemed to be there. Quickly, Martha and I walked over to where it stood.

The Unicorn was there, no question, real as any one of us on the streets. The kids around it were in awe of its beauty and I saw out of the corner of my eye that a woman was weeping. I just couldn't believe it. Unicorns were very rare. So rare in fact, that many people never got to see them and those who did were considered to be lucky for the rest of their lives.

As I was looking at the animal, I felt a weird vibration in my body. It took me a moment, but it was clearly there. A connection. The Unicorn was looking straight at me and I could suddenly feel everything it was feeling. Warmth spread through my shoulder and I knew that my wound had healed. I didn't even have to check it. I whispered thank you, and the connection was just as quickly gone as it came. The animal turned its back to the people and walked to the far side of the stable.

I couldn't help but smile. Martha and I turned around and started walking back to the inn. We were only halfway through one of the rows when I heard a voice:

"There you are."

I turned but no one was talking to me. I noticed a younger girl running towards a man and jumping into his arms. Young love.

Then I turned back and jumped out of my skin. Killian, now standing in front of me, started laughing.

"Didn't you hear me before?" He grinned.

"It sounded like it was coming from behind me," I said, grabbing my chest and taking long deep breaths.

"We have to ask Ven to check your hearing."

"Very funny."

I noticed that he wasn't wearing the same clothes as before. What he had on was much nicer looking, looked like noble clothing.

"I am funny," he said as we started walking together. "Did you get everything?"

"Hopefully," I nodded. "Were you successful in… you know… whatever you needed to do?"

"Yes." He sounded sad all of a sudden.

"You alright?"

"Yeah. I visited the widow of one of my comrades."

I felt embarrassed. I was so sure that he was going to visit one of his maiden lovers and I couldn't have been any more wrong about him.

"He died acting on my orders. He left behind the love of his life and his children and I received an Elven name…" He sighed.

"I'm sorry Killian, I didn't know."

He smiled a little weakly. "It's okay. She's fine, and the children are fine too. That's all that matters." He paused for a moment, looking out over the market. I found myself struck by how much seemed to be going on with him just under the surface.

Pulling himself back to reality, he continued.

"I always send half of my payment to her and whenever I can I visit them.

She is an excellent seamstress, as you can tell." He twirled, confidently showing off his new clothing.

"You look very good."

"Thank you, my lady." He bowed and I couldn't help but giggle when we heard a distinct voice.

"This tramp? She isn't a lady, my good lord."

A woman stepped in front of us. She barely had any clothing on, her brown hair was in elaborate curls and ugly grin sat on her face. She looked at me in disgust.

"A handsome man like you deserves someone beautiful..." She stepped closer to Killian. "Like me."

As she was trying to touch the man's chest Killian grabbed her wrist. "Oh, I see you like it rough, big boy?" She moaned seductively.

"The only ugly woman I see here," Killian said between his teeth, almost hissing, "is you."

He pushed her out of the way without another word and we started walking again. She watched us walk away, trying to hold her bravado after the interaction before turning to find someone else to pick up.

"Don't pay any mind to her," Killian said to me. "These women are nasty. They would do anything for a few gold, including selling their bodies."

I didn't say anything. Suddenly, he grabbed my arm, making me stop in my steps, eyes intense as he looked at me.

"You don't believe her, right?"

"It's not important Killian. Let's just head back to the inn." I said, avoiding his gaze. I shook off his warm hand and started walking again.

As we stepped in, the overwhelming warmth welcomed us. The fire was crackling in the fireplace and there were a few more people in as the night was setting in. We took the supplies upstairs and made our way back down to have dinner. To our huge surprise, Vendal was sitting at a table talking to a woman. She was an Elf, but the pointy end of one of her ears had been cut off. She had a square face, narrow green eyes, a tiny nose and full lips. Her cheekbones were strong and she had a slim neck. She was wearing a black silk dress and she was picture perfect. Vendal was listening to her so intently that he was startled when Killian put his hands on his shoulder.

"Vendal, my dear friend, can you introduce us to this breathtakingly beautiful lady?" He extended his hand to hers in greeting.

I left. It wasn't intentional, I just turned around and headed straight for Bertha at the bar. I leaned up on the counter, took a deep breath. I buried my face into my hands for a quick second to find my composure. I could feel Bertha studying me but she didn't say anything. She was busy cutting up the bread for the stew.

I turned my head towards the window and watched the people passing by. I needed to get out of my own head. I had this same feeling take over me once before. He was an Elven boy and my heart always beat faster when I saw him on the streets, but I was always invisible to him. My father's words rang in my head: Love isn't for everyone. I just had to learn that lesson again.

"Are you gonna eat here, sweetpea?" Bertha asked. I just nodded. She put down the stew and the fresh bread in front of me and left to give out the food to everyone else. I wasn't hungry.

"What are you doing?" Vendal's voice cropped up behind me. I didn't turn around.

"Eating," I replied, though I clearly wasn't.

"Is something wrong, Sam? I wanted to introduce you to Neyra-"

"No," I cut him off, then forced a smile. "I'm all good, I just don't feel like talking. I'm sorry. Have fun though."

I left him by the counter and before I headed back upstairs, I took a quick glance at Killian who was clearly having fun talking to the Elven girl.

I closed the door of my room behind me and felt that throbbing feeling rising up in my chest. I tried to push it down, but I couldn't control it. The wind broke in the window and the pain erupted in my hand. I grabbed it as I fell to my knees. It burnt, fire coursing through my veins. I couldn't keep my eyes open without seeing stars. It took a few minutes, but the pain slowly disappeared. I rolled up my sleeve and Mark of Sagar was up in my elbow bend.

I started crying. Days of ongoing frustration built up in me, and with the tears some of that baggage came bursting out. I didn't want to tell my companions how scared I was or how I still thought that me being the Destroyer was impossible. I didn't say a word to either of them about Radona appearing in my nightmare and how even as she looked at me, she found it funny that out of everyone I was the one who was supposed to defeat her Champion.

I was alone. More than ever before. I was nothing more to these men than a job that they needed to complete. They didn't know me and I didn't know them. Laying on the cold floor of my room I once again wished to be back in Yandana, no matter how much I hated it there.

The cold breeze finally prompted me to get up. One of the pieces of broken glass from the shattered window was sticking out of my left calf. I grabbed my old shirt and tore it up into small pieces. I sat down on the bed and put my left leg up. I took a deep breath and pulled out the glass, fast. It didn't hurt as much as I thought it would. I tied the pieces of the fabric around the wound as tightly as possible and then just lay back down on the bed. I didn't have any idea what to do with the window but the guilt I was feeling for damaging the inn, creating problems for Bertha started growing on me.

I don't really know how long I was laying there motionless, but the sound of Vendal and Killian's voices coming up the stairs made me snap out of it.

"Did she say anything?" Killian asked.

"She said that she didn't feel like talking," Vendal replied.

"That's strange." Killian paused and there was silence for a few seconds. "Do you feel that?"

"Yeah…"

Vendal sounded a little uneasy and I knew that they must have felt the cold air that was slipping under my door. I turned my back to the door. I heard the knock just as I was expecting it but I didn't answer. Knock again. No answer. The door opened with a click.

"Blessed Sagar," I heard Vendal sigh. He must have done something, because the cold suddenly disappeared. "What happened?"

"I don't know. Sam…" I felt Killian's gentle touch on my shoulder, but I kept my eyes shut. "She's sleeping and… oh no…"

He must have noticed the bandage on my leg. I felt him shake me again.

"Sam."

"I'm fine," I said, knowing that they wouldn't leave until I responded.

"What happened here? Did you use magic again?" Vendal asked. His concern surprised me. I sat up, pulling my dress down over my bandaged leg.

"Yes," I said and this time it was the truth.

"But why?"

"I don't know, but I am fine, so if you could please…" I gestured toward the door.

"Sam," Killian said suddenly. His voice had that same edge to it like before. He was angry. "What's going on with you?"

"Nothing."

"Samantha." His voice suddenly became soft again, that was it. I felt my eyes tear up. The two men looked at each other and I heard a third voice inside my own head:

You need to open your heart more, Samantha.

Something clicked, I finally understood what Felnard meant. I couldn't hold all of it - the expectation, the fear, the inadequacy - by myself. So I started talking. I said more than ever before. I told them how I felt, how I was doubting myself and I told them everything about Radona in my nightmare. They listened and never once tried to stop me as I was telling them everything that was tainting my soul. When I finally finished it was like a big rock fell from my chest.

They were quiet for a moment after I stopped. They'd both taken seats - Vendal on a chair, Killian at the foot of my bed. Vendal broke the silence.

"Sam…" There was such an overwhelming kindness in his voice that it brought out more tears from my eyes. He looked at me, incredibly serious. "You're not just a job."

"You never were." Killian looked up at Vendal. I saw Killian give him an almost imperceptible nod, which Vendal echoed. It said go ahead. Vendal stood up.

"When Felnard first told me the tale of Radona and Elemris, the Prophecy of the Soulless and the Destroyer, I thought that my uncle was mad. The way he believed in it scared me to my core." He started pacing back and forth in the small room. "So, I did the dumbest thing possible and left him behind. That's when my road intertwined with Killian, when I saved him from death penalty after he laid his hands on the Head of the Druids' wife. He was so grateful that he told me I could stay the night in the guest room that Rowland gave him before I started my journey. But... something happened that night that we haven't told you about."

"What?" I looked at Killian who took a deep breath.

"We dreamt."

"Okay?"

"About you, Sam. Both of us, on the exact same night, without ever seeing you before."

I wasn't sure what I was expecting, but it wasn't that.

"We saw you just as vividly as we can see you now, and we weren't the only ones. Felnard dreamt of you, and that's when our lives became inseparable. We started searching for you, and the dreams became more and more regular as we got closer to where you were. It took us years to find you, but we had to."

"Because you saw me in your dreams?"

"It wasn't just that," Killian interjected. "We saw ourselves with you."

"In my dream, you were lost and I was guiding you out of the dark," Vendal said.

"In Felnard's dream," Killian continued, "you were falling and he was trying to catch you while riding a griffon. But you were just falling infinitely."

"And in yours?"

Killian took a deep breath.

"In mine..." he hesitated, but Vendal nodded encouragingly. "We were running towards each other but whenever our hands would finally touch... a woman appeared, snatching you into the darkness and I was just standing there unable to do anything to save you from her."

I pulled my knees to my chest, processing everything they just told me. Finally, I asked:

"Why didn't you tell me all of this?"

"How would you have reacted if three complete strangers would have started to talk about how they saw you in their dreams?" laughed Vendal.

"You weren't exactly normal when you did turn up," I said, but he was right, I probably would have run away as quickly as possible. Vendal shrugged, conceding the point.

"Why were you so hostile when we first met?" I asked him.

"Because I couldn't believe it." I furrowed my brow. "Sam, we were searching for you for more than five years. Imagine seeing someone in your dreams for five years, every single night and then all of a sudden, they are standing in front of you."

"I see," I said, even though I really didn't.

"We want to help you with every inch of our body and soul, Sam. It..." Killian stopped himself. "You are not just another job for us. You mean way more than that."

"That all being said, Radona appearing in your dream is reason to worry."

Vendal sat down in the chair, and I noted that the window behind him had been repaired, if it had never been broken. A dark look came across Vendal's face as he said:

"The Soulless might be on the rise."

I touched the Mark on my arm. "She appeared right after the Mark of Sagar..."

"It is the sign of dark magic. She must have felt it even in her prison." Vendal was deep in thought, just staring at the floor.

"I'm sorry Sam, if we made you feel like you couldn't talk to us," said Killian a bit more quietly. I looked at him. He was fidgeting with his fingers, his composure tense. He looked at me and there was that strange emotion on his face again that I saw once before.

"It's more than that. I was just..." I took a deep breath. "Nobody's ever wanted me to share my thoughts before."

"Sam-"

"Agh!" Vendal suddenly yelled. "I can't even think about this tonight, it makes my headache worse. Let's just... let's continue this talk tomorrow, please."

Killian looked at me, and I realised he was waiting for my approval to drop the subject. I smiled a little, and gave a small nod.

"Alright." Killian said, and stood up from the bed.

The men started to shuffle out of the room when Vendal suddenly burst back to life.

"Oh! Before I forget!" Vendal turned to me and he kneeled down so suddenly that even Killian seemed puzzled by it.

"I like you Vendal," I gave him a quizzical eyebrow, "but I don't think I am ready for marriage."

"Silly girl," he laughed. He gestured. "Give me your leg."

I did as he asked. He took off the bandages, put his hand on my leg and closed his eyes. A sudden warmth ran through my leg, similar in kind to when the Unicorn healed me, and when the Druid took his hand away a small, faded scar was on my leg.

Vendal looked bashful. "Felnard can do it without even leaving the tiniest of scars. I don't know why it doesn't work for me." He stood up, groaning like an old man. "Sleep well Sam. See you in the morning."

"Thank you for... listening." I smiled at them and then they were both gone.

That night, I dreamt about a woman. I couldn't see her face. No matter how I tried to get around her, I was only able to see the back of her head. She was singing a song that I'd never heard before whilst washing her clothes in the river. Then, a sudden noise startled her and a young man appeared from the woods on the other side of the water.

The man was tall and skinny. He had something in his hands I couldn't make out. When he saw the woman, he stopped in his tracks. How could he not hear her as he was approaching? The woman stood up and did some strange movements with her hands and a sudden smile appeared on the man's face.

I woke up to the sound of heavy footsteps. The sun was shining through the window giving light to the dark corner of the room. I got up very grumpily, my legs still half asleep. I stood next to the wall for a few seconds and gathered my strength. I braided my hair faster than I had ever done before. When I saw myself in the mirror again, I felt good. My ears were out for everyone to see and for the first time in forever it didn't bother me at all. I changed into the dark blue dress I bought on the market - it surprised me at the moment, but something about it stood out to me, and for the first time I felt good wearing it - and slowly made my way down.

There were barely any souls in the lounge. Bertha was preparing breakfast behind the bar and welcomed me with her biggest smile. I sat down right next to the fireplace with the cup of tea she handed me and slowly started drinking. I was so deep in my own thoughts that I didn't even notice the arrival of my companions. They both sat down in front of me and I took a quick glance at them. They were smiling but I paid no mind to them. I wanted to take another sip from my cup when the realisation hit me. I looked up at them again, or more specifically up at Killian and I almost started to cry. He had cut down his long hair so it was a little under his ears, just like mine. Vendal didn't have long hair so he was just smiling.

"What did you do?" I asked, swallowing down my tears. Killian laughed.

"It was time for a change, I guess." He winked at me and I could no longer hold back my emotions. I leaned over the table and closed him in a tight hug. No one has ever done something so nice for me before. I let him go when I heard Vendal's soft chuckle and blood rushed to my cheeks immediately.

I quickly pulled myself together. "It... looks good on you."

"Thank you." He smiled.

"Gentlemen." We turned, collectively.

The Elf from last night was standing behind Killian and Vendal. She was smiling.

"My lady," she looked at me and bowed a little. "My name is Neyra Lin, it's a pleasure to meet you."

"Sam Tanan, pleasure to meet you too." I lied through my teeth but forced a smile on my face in the process. She sat down right next to me.

"I brought what you asked for," she said, and I realised I was missing some information.

"Excellent," Vendal said, apparently very pleased with whatever that meant.

Neyra continued. "Leanne is still alive. She married the Druid, Herald, and they live in Lendala."

"What's going on?" I asked.

"Oh, sorry Sam, we forgot to tell you yesterday," Vendal said. "Neyra will be joining us to help on the journey."

I suddenly felt sick to my stomach.

"Oh?" I said, as innocently as possible.

"I used to work for the King-" Neyra started and out of pure instinct I went to grab my hair, but I, once again, had to realise that I couldn't. Neyra smiled.

"Don't worry, the main part is the used to. I hate the Elves."

"But you are…"

"I am an Elf too, yes, but I wish I could be literally anything else." She pointed at her ear and I understood the implication. She cut her own ear off. Blase, she waved it off. "It's a long story. What's more important now is that after my chat with Vendal and Killian yesterday I realised that I could be of assistance on your quest."

My eyes darted toward the two men. We'd never discussed if we were allowed to talk about our journey and where it was leading us, but since they so casually told everything to a complete stranger, I figured we were free to talk about it all.

She continued. "I worked in the Elven archives and they have information about, well, everything."

"And who is this Leanne?"

"She is a historian," Vendal answered. "We think we have the best chance to find out what happened to the Grabodans and the Prophecy if we talk to her. My uncle used to be in touch with her a lot, but one day she just didn't respond so we didn't know what became of her."

He didn't look at me as he explained this. Instead, he kept his eyes on the beautiful Neyra. It was quite clear that he fancied her more than a little. I shared a quick knowing look with Killian and somehow my chest felt lighter.

"Alright," I said, putting my tea down on the table. "Welcome on board Neyra."

CHAPTER 5
THE LOSS OF A NOBLE CREATURE

We decided to stay in Allion another day after we had our breakfast. For me that meant seeing the Unicorn again. I couldn't stop thinking about it. Vendal decided to get some herbs from the market and, to his great delight, Neyra offered to go with him. I couldn't help but smile seeing the Druid's ear to ear grin. After all his talk about winning over ladies, his shy behaviour towards the Elf felt a bit strange. He was saying nice things to her, being genuinely complimentary, effusive, but still I was expecting him to take her to his room on the first night and that never happened. Killian decided to visit his friend's widow again, knowing how much the children adored him.

After we all parted ways, before I made my way to the Unicorn's stable, I wanted to properly discover the colourful town. Other than Irkaban and Yandana, I'd never seen any other settlement. The streets were already packed, the sound of chatter filling the air as people were making their way towards the market. It was hard moving against the flow, but I managed.

I noticed how narrow the buildings were. They looked very odd but I guess they had their own practical use. The way colour was used for them was something I couldn't get over; the main colours I saw were yellow, pink and purple, but there were a few blue and red houses too. I wanted to stop someone and ask what all the colours meant, but it was hard to tell who was local and who were just wayfaring strangers passing through the town like we were. As I walked through many dirt streets, I saw more and more Halfling families. One family had eight kids running around them and I could hardly believe my eyes. They were happy. No doubt about it, just pure joy on their faces.

I had to keep forcing the thought of my own father out of my head.

I came to a stop as I reached the edge of the town. A few wooden houses were standing there with farmers doing their job, working hard. Satisfied I'd seen everything, I turned back around and, being my clumsy self, I bumped into someone. I looked up and was surprised to see Neyra standing there.

"Hi!" She said, cheerfully.

"Neyra? Where is Vendal?" I looked around, searching for my Druid friend, but he was nowhere to be seen.

"Oh, I left him in the market. He started talking about herbs and I'm gonna be honest with you…" She leaned closer and said in a hushed voice, "it was boring."

"Well, I am not surprised." I forced a smile on my face. I didn't know how to feel about the girl. "How did you find me so quick?"

"Quick? I've been looking for you for ages now."

"What? I only just…" I looked up. The Sun was already high in the sky. "Oh."

"I'm not blaming you; there's many things to see in Allion."

We started walking back together, wandering side by side in silence. I couldn't tell if the situation was awkward or I was. I cleared my throat and broke the silence.

"Have you been here before?" I asked.

"Just once," she replied. "Elves have an archive in every major city. Don't know why though. It was official business, but I did get out to look around a bit. If I could choose a place to live, this would be it."

"Why can't you?"

"Why can't I… what?"

"Choose a place to live?"

"Oh." A troubled look flashed across her face. "I mean, I guess I could. It's more that… I don't really want to." We turned into an alley and a disgusting smell stopped us in our tracks. "Oh my!" Neyra exclaimed.

"What is that?"

The door to a tiny house flew open and thick green smoke spilled out and filled the street. An old woman came crashing out, yelling horrible words, followed by a man who appeared behind her coughing like crazy.

"You idiot! I've had enough of your stupid experiments!" The old woman yelled and left the man behind while trying to catch her own breath. She walked past us and disappeared in the crowd in the other street.

"Are you okay?" I heard Neyra ask as she approached the coughing man. He just nodded, unable to stop his coughing. Neyra grabbed him under the arm and helped him walk away from the smell and the smoke so they were no longer around us. The man sat down on the stairs to one of the houses and was finally able to take some deep breaths.

"Thank you…" He said after a moment. "Sorry about my mother." He gestured towards the street that we left behind.

"If you don't mind me asking, what were you experimenting on?" Neyra crouched down in front of him so they were eye to eye.

"Herbs," he answered simply and I had to choke down a laugh.

"We have a friend who would be delighted to talk to you," Neyra smiled as I desperately tried to keep myself together.

"I see…" The man eyed me carefully before shaking his head. "Well, anyone who's interested in my job can find me in my house." he stood up, looking toward where we came from. "The smoke should be gone by now. Thank you for your help ladies." he quickly bowed and left us behind.

"Well… that's a reminder that we should keep our eyes on Vendal when he starts doing his potions," Neyra said, beaming.

"Definitely," I replied, finally breaking into laughter.

We made our way back to the market while talking about silly things. Neyra had many stories about what's been going on in the King's Palace. She quickly clarified that despite popular belief and rumours, Halfling's born from forbidden relationships were not given the death penalty. They had a far more terrible faith for them: They were sold as slaves to the nobles, working for their houses, or stayed in the King's Palace to do all the work there. They wouldn't get any recognition for their work and were lucky if they got food every day. Neyra felt ashamed even though she had nothing to do with the King's horrible actions. She explained that once she saw how royalty and the nobles were treating the Halfling prisoners, she left. Cut off the pointed end of one of her ears, which was the royal sign of outcast Elves, and left Yandana behind.

I was lost in my thoughts when she nudged me with her shoulder.

"You are deep in your thoughts again, Sam." She said in a kind manner.

"Sorry, I do that a lot. I just… after hearing all this, I feel really bad, because I-"

"Judged me?" I nodded and Neyra laughed. "Don't worry, I didn't take it personally. I saw how you looked at him."

I stopped. Looked at who? The Elf turned to me as she noticed that I wasn't by her side anymore. She walked back to me, putting her arm around my shoulder and pushed me to start walking with her again. "Don't worry, I won't say a word."

"I don't really know what you are talking about."

"Oh, dear. I knew Killian before. He spent many hours in the palace and you should have seen the maidens staring after him with big hopeful eyes. He is a very handsome man, despite coming from the Humans. I am not surprised he caught your eyes too."

"I don't look at him like that." I said quickly, not daring to look at the Elf to my side.

"If you say so." She said, but she didn't believe me at all, I could tell. "He looks at you the same way."

"What?" I stopped again, but Neyra kept walking.

"I have an eye for these things, you know." She said, chuckling. I darted after her.

"Then you must have noticed how Vendal was looking at you," I slung in response, desperately trying to veer the conversation away from me.

"Of course I have!" She exclaimed and looked at me. "He's a man. He'll know what to do if he wants me and given how he was staring at me, stripping me in his head… I give him…" She looked up at the sky, feigning then back at me. "Five days before he makes a move."

"Are you that certain?"

"I am. Do you want to bet on it?"

While we were talking, we reached the market and the chances of bumping into Vendal had doubled, but before I could think it through-

"Sure." I said.

"Alright. What shall we bet on?"

"I thought you had that figured out too."

"I've never made a bet in my life." She replied and we both burst out laughing.

I don't know what happened exactly, or how she did it, but talking to Neyra felt like talking to someone who I'd known for a long time. She was the friend I'd never had and after a bad start on my end, we quickly found our common ground. At that moment, it felt like life could not get any better.

We made our way through the market rows laughing and sharing stories, unable to decide what we should put up for our bet. When we made our way through the last row, we bumped into Vendal, whose bag was so full with different herbs that he couldn't even clasp it shut. When he saw us, he got all excited and he started explaining what he got and how he would make potions out of them, so we didn't have to worry about anything on our journey. He joined us when I told them about the Unicorn and claimed that he will definitely need luck. Silent, mutual understanding between myself and Neyra meant we didn't share our meeting with the potion man.

The Unicorn was there, still. More beautiful than I remembered from the previous day. Neyra and Vendal were both in awe. We sat down on the logs that were placed around the stable and just watched the animal in complete silence. I felt calm while I was there. All the negative thoughts left my mind and instead, for the first time, I was focusing on the future. Seeing the world throughout our journey, getting to places I'd never been before, but most importantly strengthening the bonds with my newly found friends. I felt a wave of joy wash through me and I just smiled.

It was the familiar voice of chaos breaking out behind me that woke me up from my daydreaming and brought dread in its stead. People were screaming in fear and running in every direction. I heard the sounds of arrows cutting through the air and watched as one of the women who had been sitting with us crashed down at my feet, mangled and bloody, an arrow sticking out of the centre of her chest. Neyra yanked me down as another arrow flew by, inches from my head. We ducked down behind the logs for cover and I finally got a look at the assailants:

Leongrass.

We sprung to our feet and made a break for it. Vendal and I knew all too well that they were looking for us, although they couldn't have been certain that they would find us in Allion. Their appearance meant that Cutter was alive. I had to push that thought away as we zigzagged through the streets, avoiding the mercenaries causing havoc in the thoroughfare.

After a long detour we arrived back at the inn. Vendal ran to Bertha, asking her if Killian had returned. Neyra made her way up to her room to gather her belongings and I was on my way too when I heard the innkeeper say that our fourth companion hadn't come back. I stopped Vendal at the door.

"I know where he is." I said confidently, remembering where we met up the previous day.

"Sam, you-"

"Vendal, trust me. Let's meet at the other end of the town, where the farmhouses are. Neyra will know where to go." It wasn't a request. The Druid nodded and I was out of the inn.

I ran as fast as I was able, all while avoiding all the panicking people who were trying to find their way back to the safety of their homes, although I wasn't confident that walls could protect anyone from the men of Leongrass. I saw children crying on the sides of the street but I couldn't stop; I had to find Killian.

I was running past a small alleyway when I spotted him. He was running in the other direction. I turned around and bolted into the small alley. I yelled after him, but my voice got lost in the screams of the townsfolk. He took a left turn and I followed quickly behind. Finally I spotted him at the other end of the street talking to a blonde-haired woman. A crowd of people were blocking me and then my stomach turned. Killian handed a pouch to the woman who immediately jumped into his neck and kissed him. I had to close my eyes to try and refocus myself on the situation, when the sudden shock of death screams brought me back. A group of Leongrass men tore through, their swords making quick work of anyone who got in their way. I backed into the doorway of a house to shield myself from the swathes of people, before turning back and screaming Killian's name again. I had to back into the doorway once more as another wave of people trampled by. By the time I looked back he was looking straight at me, but the blonde woman was no longer there. I managed to push my way through the last two men and ran to him. I grabbed his hand without a word and pulled him towards a now-empty street. I wasn't sure which way to go so I was only concentrating on avoiding the crowds. I spotted a dog and my heart flipped. When I whistled the dog immediately ran to us.

"Lead us out of here," I said. The animal started running and we followed him.

It felt like an age, but I finally spotted the wooden houses and I knew that we reached the edge of the town. The sight that beheld us, though, forced us to stop.

A smaller group of the Leongrass men were rampaging through the crop while young maidens were fleeing to the forest and back into the town. Killian began to draw his sword but I stopped him. If we started killing Cutter's men, he would know that who he'd been searching for was right under his nose. No one would dare to fight these men in a town like Allion, not unless they were fools.

The dog grabbed my skirt and started pulling me away, so we followed him in silence, Killian resheating his blade. As we took a sharp turn we bumped straight into Neyra and Vendal with all our mounts behind them. They signalled us to stay quiet. We heard the screams of people not far from us. A door opened a bit further down the street, and a man stepped out. Neyra and I stared at each other in bemusement. It was the potion man we helped before. He waved us over frantically. Vendal led the horses and Martha into a narrow alley that was next to the man's house. We could only hope that no one would find them there with all our supplies on their backs. We ran into the house and as the door closed behind us we finally took a deep breath.

"They are looking for us," Vendal said. "Neyra and I overheard them talking. Cutter is here as well." A lump formed in my throat. I still couldn't forget the way he looked at me that day.

"He also wants the unicorn," said Neyra and I looked straight at her. I didn't even think, I just went for the door. But before I could open it Killian pulled me back.

"You can't risk your life for an animal. Your life is far more important." I looked him dead in the eye and hoped that he could read all the pain and anger that was consuming me. To his credit, he just stared back, holding my gaze with equal ferocity.

"Don't mean to interrupt," the man who saved us said, interrupting. "But your friend is right, young lady. You should-"

"Malvin?" Vendal's voice rose. "Is that you?"

"Vendal? Oh blessed Sagar, it is you!" They hugged each other and while everyone was distracted by their reunion, I snuck out.

The dog was still there, waiting for me. We sneaked through many small hidden alleys, carefully avoiding all the commotion that was happening on the bigger streets. We got to a tall wooden fence that was closing off a bunch of houses from the main street that led to the market. The dog, without even thinking, slipped through a hole under the fences, one that I could clearly not fit through. I put my ear against the wooden structure and just listened. I heard a few footsteps, but nothing else. I gathered my strength and jumped up to grab the top of the fence and pulled myself up. I didn't jump down straight away, getting a lay of the land first, but other than one old man making his way into his house and a few dead people lying on the streets no one was around. I jumped down as quietly as I could and rushed to where the dog was waiting for me in the opening of another very tight alley. I had to turn to my side to squeeze through between the two houses while my companion had a much easier job. When we emerged, we were just a few steps away from the stable.

All at once, I stopped breathing.

Cutter was standing in front of the Unicorn; the noble animal was snorting nervously and was stamping his hoof. Behind Cutter stood the griffon and at least twelve of his men.

"Bring me its horn," he ordered his man and I was ready to jump when someone's hand closed around my mouth and waist.

"We can't expose ourselves, Sam," Killian whispered in my ear as he held me tight.

The two men jumped into the stable and grabbed the reins of the Unicorn. The animal's neighs were panicked, like cries for help, and I felt my eyes fill up with tears. Killian was taking heavy deep breaths behind me as we were hiding from view. He started to pull me backwards but I desperately tried to free myself from his grip, thrashing uselessly. I saw a third man jump in with a huge sword in his hand while the other two were holding the Unicorn in place.

"I am so sorry, Sam." Killian pulled me back one final time, lifting my legs off the ground. I kicked the air, still trying to get a purchase on something. We heard the Unicorn one last time, then everything went quiet. My fight died. He put me down.

Dark clouds started to form in the sky, quickly covering the Sun and the day turned into night. The wind roared through, and we struggled to stay on our feet. We faintly heard Cutter scream to his men and a few seconds later the huge griffon with its leader on its back rose above the town and disappeared. It started raining mercilessly. Killian finally let go of me and I ran straight towards the stables. I heard him scream after me but I didn't care. I was soaking wet within seconds. Cutter and his men were all gone, all that was left behind them was destruction.

And there it was.

The Unicorn was laying on the ground, motionless, its horn gone and its neck tainted with blood. I fell on my knees next to the animal and pulled its heavy head on to my lap. I wept like a child, the immense sadness taking over my body and soul. Lightning struck in large arcs across the sky, colouring the dark clouds. I felt a hand on my shoulder. The unicorn's body turned into silver dust without warning and the wind carried it all away. I was shaking from all the crying and the cold that had taken over the spring's warmth. Nature was crying for its child.

I slowly stood up, shrugging Killian's attempts at comfort off of me. I didn't want to see him and I didn't want to talk to him. I turned around and ran away before Killian could say anything else, the dog following me closely. I didn't stop at the house where our other two companions were and I didn't stop at the edge of the town either. Instead, I continued straight into the woods. Deeper and deeper we went, my feet simply following the order to take me away. As the trees got larger, the ground became more and more uneven. Roots spilling out onto the forest floor. In my carelessness, I caught my toe on one and fell sprawled out onto the ground. I didn't get up. Just kept crying. The dog laid down next to me and we stayed like that for who knows how long while the rain kept falling.

The woman was sitting on a log, waiting. I couldn't see her face, but soon the skinny tall man appeared again on the other side of the river. He was glowing with happiness. He put a blanket down and sat. The woman started doing those funny signs with her hands again and to my surprise the man responded the same way. I watched as they communicated like this, back and forth, the content of their conversation a mystery to me. I didn't understand why they wouldn't just simply cross the river to talk. It didn't seem that deep and it wasn't fast flowing either. I got closer to the woman to try and see her face, but her long black hair kept blocking it from me. I reached out to touch her shoulder-

Someone was yelling my name. I opened my eyes but quickly closed them again. When I opened them once more, I could see the Sun was shining through the leaves and I could barely see anything for a few seconds. I slowly got up and quickly realised that the dog was no longer curled up next to me. I looked around for him, but he was gone.

"Sam!" I heard the voice again and I knew that it was Neyra.

"I'm here!" I yelled back and heard the sound of running. Before I could say another word, the Elf closed me in a tight hug and she was followed by Killian and Vendal and all our animals.

"I'm sorry for what happened to the Unicorn, Sam," she said quietly, pulling back. "Killian told us."

"Yeah, me too." I patted her back and felt another shiver run through me. Vendal grabbed his cloak from the back of Martha and gave it to me.

"You couldn't have stopped them, Sam," he said in a failed attempt to soothe.

"You don't know that." My anger started to rise up again.

"I did what I had to to protect you," Killian cut in, his voice low and even. As I looked at him and his confident demeanour, I felt my rage take over.

"*Protect me?* I could have easily taken over control of that griffon and-"

"NO!" Killian yelled, completely out of character. The severity of it almost shook me back, but my rage continued.

"What do you mean *no*? Why did you have to stop me? A unicorn is DEAD, because we didn't do anything, because we were cowards!"

"If you had marched in there Cutter would have hung you up and bled you like a pig, and then I... we-" Killian was fuming, but there was something else there too, underneath, but I didn't care.

"What? Come on! Tell me!"

"No." He said it simply - a man who could tell if he opened his mouth again, he wouldn't like what came out. He turned his back to me and that was all that was needed for me to flip.

I screamed, the anger tearing at my throat, and suddenly a huge wall of fire rose from the ground, stopping Killian from leaving and scaring all the animals away. My arm burnt up from the pain and I started crying again, but more from frustration than sadness.

Vendal rushed forward, waving his hand in a particular way and the fire wall disappeared.

"Oh, for fuck's sake, Sam!" Vendal cried out as he saw that the Mark of Sagar was getting closer to my shoulder. "What did I tell you?"

"Nothing, because you've taught me fuck all you dick!" I snapped at him. Vendal recoiled like I'd slapped him, and all the anger I had been using sapped away from me in an instant. "Vendal, I'm sorry, I didn't-"

"No," he said, steeling himself. "You're right. But you need to make more of an effort to control your emotions, okay? I know it's hard and I know that right now this hurts. I may not know how it feels to connect to animals on such a deep level, but we are worried about you." I looked up at him and to my surprise he was tearing up.

"I'm sorry." I said. He came over and put an arm around me.

"It's okay."

By the time we gathered all the animals it was dark, but we decided to start our journey nonetheless. We made our way through the forest in dead silence. Vendal was leading us up front, then came Neyra, myself and Killian closed the straight line that we were riding in. I was still furious because I couldn't get what I saw on the street out of my mind. Was Neyra right before? Did I really have feelings for Killian? Did it matter at all if I did? I was freezing, no matter how much I held onto Vendal's cloak, the shivers wouldn't stop. I had changed into dry clothes but it didn't seem to make a difference. Agarta must have felt how I was wiggling in my saddle because she stopped abruptly and that made it even worse. I begged her to move but she wouldn't. I felt something warm being laid on my back. Killian was giving me his cloak. He didn't say a word, pushing ahead to ride next to Vendal. Neyra glanced back at me and winked.

As the Sun started to rise and light was making its way through the thick canopies again, the warmth came as well. I took a deep breath and started to feel better. The forest slowly started to come to life all around us. Birds were singing their morning songs and we could hear the shuffling of other animals too on the forest floor. To everyone's surprise, Vendal started humming in sync with the birds. His humming then changed to whistling and it was a melody that I'd heard before somewhere:

Over the mountain

The Soulless

Under the clouds
A druid was singing
With utmost delight
Ay-la-la-la-la Ay-la-la-la
His song was bright
As the Sun's scorching light
Ay-la-la-la-la Ay-la-la-la
He sang about women
Who brought joy to men
And men who disheartened
Every woman!
Ay-la-la-la-la Ay-la-la-la

We all started laughing once our Druid friend stopped singing. We were getting near the edge of the forest when I heard the voice.

Sam, it whispered. I pulled Agarta to a halt and listened. The others stopped as well after Neyra noticed that I wasn't following them anymore. Vendal opened his mouth to speak but I shushed him, pointing to my ear, indicating to them to listen.

And we did.

Sam.

There it was again! Much clearer. I looked around, searching for the source when a bright light appeared not too far from us. The others turned to look as well, but we all had to cover our eyes as the light grew bigger.

Sam.

I slowly put down my hand and opened my eyes. I let out a small yelp.

There... was the Unicorn. Healed, standing in all its glory.

"I can't believe this." I heard Neyra say.

"How is this possible?" Killian gasped.

"I think our Sam has greater power than we originally thought," Vendal finished, smiling at me in wonder. They all looked at me, I could feel their gaze on me. I got out of my saddle and walked to the Unicorn.

"How?" I asked.

Your tears. They came from your heart. There's nothing purer than that.

"So, I-"

You saved me. Yes. And I will pay my dues to you now. The creature tilted its head forward and as its horn touched my forehead I fell to my knees from the sudden power. I heard the others yell in panic but I raised my hand to stop them.

My seal will protect you from any dark magic, Paradion.

The Unicorn's whole body started to shine and again blinded us all for a second. When it faded, the Unicorn was gone.

"Sam!" The others ran to me. Vendal gasped.

"I can't believe it," he said. I opened my eyes and took Neyra's outstretched hand. "You have the seal of a Unicorn."

"It said… that it will protect me from dark magic," I mumbled, still a bit dazed from the experience. Vendal grabbed my hand and pushed up my sleeve. The Mark of Sagar was completely gone.

"What the-?"

"This is very powerful magic. The only other living being that ever had the Seal of a Unicorn was Sagar because…" He hesitated, suddenly a little sheepish.

"With this," he continued, "there's nothing stopping someone from using their magic for evil things."

I kept my tone clear; "I would never do that."

"I know, but now starting your training and learning to control your emotions has become more important than before."

I nodded. I looked at our other two companions and rested my eyes on Killian.

"I'm sorry," I said and he finally looked at me with his mesmerising dark black eyes.

"Me too."

"I don't mean to break up this nice moment, but I am hungry, I am tired and I need to wash myself desperately. Can we please go?" Neyra begged.

"We sure can," agreed Vendal "About the whole 'wash myself' thing…"

"Not a chance, Druid."

CHAPTER 6
THE MOOD FLOWER

"Just try it again. Please."

Vendal was begging me through his teeth as I was sitting there unable to produce anything magic related. We'd been at it for hours without any progress. I tried everything he said to light the fire.

"But I can't do it!" I said it more angrily than I'd intended to. Killian and Neyra, who were practicing sword fighting in the distance, stopped what they were doing and looked at us. We were sitting next to the river where we set our camp up the previous night.

"Sam…"

"No. No," I stood up. "I don't know what Felnard was thinking, but he was apparently wrong about me, alright?"

"Sure," Killian said, as he walked up to us with Neyra at his heels. "Just give up."

"*Excuse me?*" His audacity was beyond everything else. I hated that smug smile on his face.

"Just give up. That works out for you all the time, doesn't it? As soon as there's any sign of trouble or emotions involved, your answer is to run away and act like you are the only one who can have problems-"

I screamed at him and as I stormed the remaining distance between us to try and slap him. A deafening *crack* broke through the air as a huge bolt of lightning struck the tree behind him. Killian clapped his hand over his mouth with an unbelievable amount of sarcasm.

"Oh my days, I didn't expect this."

"Did you want this?" I turned to Vendal, fuming.

"Not really, but it's something at least," he replied, still shocked by what happened.

"Good." I turned back to Killian and slapped him as hard as I could. The sound of it was almost as loud as the lightning. "You idiot, I almost killed you!"

"But it worked, didn't it?" He was holding his cheek with a smirk on his face. Anger crackled up inside me once more, but I brushed it off. I sat back down in front of Vendal.

"Let's continue, please."

The Druid explained to me that magic doesn't require magic words like the Dwarves used to believe. In reality, you were either born with magic, or you could fight however hard you want for it but you wouldn't be able to ever learn it. The only thing he could teach me was how to reach the magic that was inside me without using my anger as a source for it. Everyone who has magic uses a different technique to bring it out, but the most common method was learning to understand everything that was surrounding us. He told me to empty my head out completely and just listen. So, I closed my eyes and took a deep breath.

I heard Neyra and Killian practicing. Iron clanging against iron. I heard the breaths that Vendal was taking, deep and purposeful. I heard my own thoughts going around everything that happened with us but I said to *stop it* myself, everything went quiet for a second.

I heard movement. Slimy skin was digging its way through earth, and a little bit above that, hundreds of little feet were running around, working on a structure. The scenery changed around me. It wasn't the earth anymore, it was water flowing around me, carrying sticks and leaves above its surface and giving life to many creatures under itself.

A strange force pulled me out of the water; a new sound hit my ear. A bear was walking through the forest, and I realised I could see everything around it with its eyes: the trees, the grass, the ground under its huge paws… and then I suddenly came back to where I was sitting.

"Well?" asked Vendal curiously.

"This is amazing. Everything is a-"

Neyra's laughter completely pulled me out of the moment. I looked towards them and the Elf was holding onto Killian's arm while they were both laughing.

"Hey," Vendal said, pulling my attention back to him. "They don't matter right now."

"Do you mind if we… stopped for today? I'm tired." He nodded.

I got up and walked to my bag. I grabbed new clothes from it and moved far away from my friends toward a nearby river. Two days had passed since everything that happened with the Unicorn and I had been exhausted ever since. Vendal was training me all the time; he kept all his focus on me no matter how hard I tried to push him into Neyra's arms. He wouldn't budge.

I was dirty and felt disgusting so getting into the cold river was a true blessing. I dived under but as soon as I came back up, I felt cold again even though the Sun was shining brighter than ever before. I didn't get out of the water; I embraced the cold. I spent some time swimming around the same spot when I heard footsteps approaching.

I quickly swam behind the reed to hide, but it was just Killian. He was soaked in sweat from the sword fighting practice he'd been at for hours. He stretched his arms and stopped a few feet away from where I was. I stayed hidden, curious, waiting to see what he'd do, but when he got out of his shirt, I quickly coughed loudly to warn him that I was there too. The sudden sound definitely startled him and he looked into my direction. His chest was covered in old scars.

"Who's there?" he asked.

"Just me," I answered, still hiding behind the reed.

"Sam?"

"Of course, can't you recognise my voice?"

"Are you hiding from me?" He asked, amusement hiding under his words. I kept peeking at him. His whole figure was very toned and it made me feel even more awkward than I usually was around him.

"Yes, because I am naked and this river is crystal clear." I explained, a bit frustrated.

"Oh, you're just shy then." He was playing with me; I knew he was.

"And what if I am?"

"Nothing, nothing at all. But I am getting in this river too whether you like it or not." "Can you at least wait for me to get dressed and leave?"

"Nope."

Then he pulled down his trousers so quickly that I barely had time to turn away. I heard him wading into the water. "This is really cold."

"It is." I answered and peeked back over my shoulder at where he was.

"I saw that!" He yelled and I felt the blood rush into my face. He laughed. A good, hearty laugh; unembarrassed and real, joyful. It suited him.

"You're in a good mood," I noted.

"Yeah, I've missed all this fighting even if it's just practice," he replied. I heard him swim around somewhere behind me. "Sorry I made you mad before."

"It's okay."

"Hey, what are you guys doing?" Vendal's voice came from the treeline.

"Are they here?" Neyra asked, not far behind.

"Looks like."

"Ven, you could at least warn me so I can turn away," Neyra said playfully, I didn't have to look to know that the Druid was already out of his robes.

"Where would be the fun in that?" Vendal laughed loudly and came straight into the water. "Ugh, this is really cold."

"Where's Sam?" I heard Neyra ask and I just raised my hand. "Found you. Don't stare, boys!" she yelled, and a second later she was swimming towards me. "Hey there, shy little girl."

"Hi." I was trying to hide my lady parts with my hands.

"You don't have to hide from me," she said, grabbing my arms and pulling them away.

"Neyra!" I exclaimed in horror.

"What's going on?" Vendal asked suspiciously.

"Neyra, let me go!"

"Come on, ain't nothing wrong with showing some flesh." She giggled but I couldn't stand the thought that the men who were approaching us could see me without any clothes.

"Neyra-" I said through my teeth but she didn't budge. "Fine," I said confidently, because I felt what none of them could. The two men yelled as Agarta galloped into the river. I stood up and hid my body behind hers. We walked to the shore and I grabbed all my clothes and quickly put them on, then sat up on Agarta's back.

"Coward!" Neyra yelled after me.

By the time they came back to the camp my hair was already dry. I was packing our things back to Martha and on the horses back when I heard their loud laughter behind me. I didn't pay much mind to them, but my Elven friend was quickly next to me, her hair soaking wet, still dripping. She started to help without saying a single word; only a peculiar smile on her face. I didn't say anything either.

Not long after we were on our way again. If Vendal was right, we only had another two days left to travel. If Lendala was anything like Allion I knew that I would love it. To my relief, Neyra was keeping Vendal away from me as we were riding through the lands. She kept talking to him, laughing at his jokes and throughout all of it I observed everything she was doing.

Showing affection came naturally to Elves and Fairies. One of their most well-known attributes was their hunger for love and fornication. There were many tales that involved these big heroic acts performed purely out of love when it came to their culture. One of them was the tale of Dalian and Moneai:

Dalian The Knight was the greatest hero of Elves who always did what was right. He fought in wars, saved young maidens and children from the grip of death, and worked on rebuilding cities and towns. He enjoyed the love of everyone around him, but no matter how many people surrounded him, he felt alone. He'd been offered many young virgins to marry but he said no to every single one of them. As years passed, his sorrow grew greater and greater. He still did what he had to, but he came less successful in his quests. Maidens and children were dying, wars were lost, and cities collapsed. Dalian's name quickly became one with a curse.

One faithful day, an old man came to Dalian's castle begging for his help. The knight kept saying no to the elder, who sat in front of his gate for five continuous days without any food or water. Dalian's good spirit rose above his self-pity and sorrow, and eventually he gave the man everything he needed to make sure he wasn't dying.

He also promised him that he would do what the old man was asking from him. And so, he did.

He travelled through treacherous lands until he reached the Scorched Fields where the most feared monster - a huge snake - was keeping the old man's daughter as his prisoner. The snake was waiting for Dalian.

'How did you know that I would come for the maiden?' the knight asked.

'I know about everything,' the snake hissed.

'Then you must know that I will kill you today.'

'Why would you do that?'

'To save the lady, of course,' the knight said, a bit puzzled by the question.

'The only way to save a lady is through killing?'

'No, but you are keeping her prisoner and for that you must pay.'

'I do not keep anyone here as a prisoner.'

'Stop playing games with me snake! Your fate is inevitable!' yelled the knight fearlessly and charged towards the snake. But the animal did not move, just kept staring at the man. Dalian raised his sword above his head but right before he would have struck down, he stopped in front of it. His sword was still up high but his eyes locked with the snake's. They stared at each other as the Sun rose above them. He watched as the snake slowly turned into a beautiful Elven woman. Dalian dropped his sword and fell on his knees, begging for his life.

'Stand up, my dear knight,' the woman said. 'Why did you come to search for me?'

'Because your father kept begging me for days to save your life.'

'But you didn't want to come at first, right?' she asked

'No and for that, please forgive me. I didn't trust myself that I would be able to save you. I was afraid that I would fail.' Dalian started crying, but the beautiful Elf caressed his face with her soft hand, filling the knight's empty soul with warmth and light.

'All that matters is that you are here; it doesn't matter why you decided to come.'

The beautiful maiden locked her hands with Dalian's and let him lead her out of the Scorched Fields that became full of life and greenery with every step they took together. When they arrived back at the knight's castle, the old man broke down in tears upon seeing his beloved daughter again. Before he could offer any reward to Dalian, the knight refused to accept anything. The young maiden, whose name was revealed to be Moneai, left with her father.

For days and days Dalian was happy, but soon his joy started to fade as he could not stop thinking about Moneai. His thoughts kept lingering on to her and an emptiness rose in his chest. He wouldn't fall back to his old ways so he made a decision. He got on the back of his fastest horse and rode to the house of the old man where Moneai was waiting for him. Dalian ran to her, but he hesitated for a second.

'I missed you.' He said and a beautiful smile appeared on the maiden's face.

'And I missed you too.'

They did not need to say anything else. Dalian asked the old man for his daughter's hand, to which he said yes.

Dalian took his beautiful bride back to his castle and soon all his glory was restored. He was blooming with love and promised himself to never love another again. But he couldn't keep the promise.

When his first daughter was born, he realised that there was still room in his heart.

We set up camp under a big willow tree. Neyra and Vendal were inseparable by the time the night came. They ended up leaving Killian and I behind to collect wood for the campfire. After we got all the blankets out, made sure that the horses and Martha were all provided for, we both sat down at the same exact time.

"If they won't come back soon, we're gonna freeze," I said, starting to feel the cold set in. I didn't even have to say anything else to have a cloak around me a second later. "Thank you." I smiled, blushing. "You're a real gentleman."

"I try to be," he replied. He went to say something else, but stopped himself. It was a thing he always did when he felt nervous.

"You can talk to me, you know," I said, trying to encourage him to finally open up.

"What you saw back in Allion," he started, and the image came rushing back to my mind. I forced myself to keep a straight face. "She was just overwhelmed, I think. It didn't mean anything." He looked at me with his eyes full of anticipation. I wasn't sure how to respond and definitely didn't understand why he felt the need to try to explain it all to me.

I looked away. "Was she the widow?"

"Uh, yes," he said, oddly rattled. "Gabrielle."

"She's lucky to have you. Not many would do what you are doing for her and her family." I was really hoping that our other two companions were making their way back to us as I started to feel more on edge with every passing second.

"I guess not." He took a deep breath, before saying: "I had a bride once."

"What?" I looked up at him.

"Yeah, before I joined the army. She was awful to me. Always mocking me for everything I did. no matter how hard I tried it wasn't enough for her. When the Elven army accepted me - a Human - among their ranks, her behaviour changed. She was kind and caring, kept bragging about me to her friends and

I, being the foolish young man I was, believed her sudden affection towards me." He laughed, incredulously, and brushed back his short hair. "When I received my first payment, I spent everything on her. When I received my second payment, I started to build her dream house. I kept giving and she kept taking and then, when I arrived home after losing all my comrades to battle and receiving an Elven name in return... I found her in our bed with another man."

My heart skipped a beat. Killian's eyes were filling up with tears and he quickly wiped them away.

"Killian-"

"That wasn't the worst part," he continued, and I heard a bitterness that wasn't there before. "The worst part was realising that I never even loved her. I knew exactly how horrible she was but I kept trying to feel something, at least."

He swiped his face again, desperately trying to get rid of his tears. My heart broke for him. In that moment, I saw more than the soldier or the handsome bachelor: I saw a boy, one searching for love like the rest of us. I shuffled closer and wrapped my arm around his shoulder. He didn't look at me. I felt him shivering.

"Hang on, here..." I took off the cloak he gave me and put it around him. He pulled it tighter about himself as a form of acknowledgement.

Since there was no sign of Vendal and Neyra I closed my eyes. I was searching for the fire in the landscape around me. I couldn't feel any among the many voices in the surrounding nature. I took a deep breath, held out my palms and blew on them. A small fire rose up in my hand but didn't burn me.

"Oh blessed Sagar!" I yelled out in excitement. I looked at Killian who was just as amazed as I was. "I did it!"

"You definitely did," he said looking at me and I could still see tears glittering in his eyes. I smiled softly at him.

"You will find love, Killian. I am sure of it."

I wasn't sure what made me do it but I leaned closer to him and planted a kiss on his cheek.

"BLESSED SAGAR!" Vendal's voice tore through the wood. I jumped, moving away from Killian. "You did it!" he said excitedly as he was running towards us. He quickly dropped the wood in front of us, arranging it, and I placed the fire on it. As Neyra approached I saw an all-knowing smile on her face.

"Where have you been?" I asked, like a mother watching her children come home late.

"Oh... we... well..." Vendal started mumbling but Neyra just stepped in front of me and to my biggest surprise handed me a flower. It was the transparent flower I saw in Allion's market.

"You won our bet," she winked at me and then proceeded to sit down next to Vendal.

"I guess we have new lovebirds among us," Killian said, smirking, and I was in awe of how quickly he was able to switch back to his immoveable demeanour.

"How did you know?" I asked Neyra but she just shrugged.

"I have a good eye for these things."

"Wait, what did you girls bet on?" Vendal asked after realizing what the Elf said to me.

"Nothing that concerns you," Neyra replied, planting a kiss on his cheek. She gave me a knowing look as she pulled back, and I couldn't help but smirk.

"Okay..." he said, a little bemused.

"Now, come on. Put the flower in your hair Sam, I want to see how you are feeling." Neyra said excitedly and I couldn't help but notice her taking a quick glance at Killian. I put the Mood Flower in my hair and waited.

"Oh. Yellow, huh?" Vendal said.

"What does yellow mean?" I asked.

"That you're happy," Neyra answered in a disappointed tone. She was clearly hoping for a different colour.

"I am." I smiled.

Early the next morning, I woke up to Vendal shaking my shoulders. I couldn't believe him. He was dead set on continuing practice and I knew I couldn't escape him. Killian and Neyra had already gone to train.

The Druid was merciless. I couldn't do anything he asked me for. He kept bugging me to reach deeper down and even though I was able to concentrate and hear everything again, I wasn't able to summon magic. So, instead, he forced me to meditate more and then to try over and over again. But no fire, no water, nothing came to me no matter how hard I tried to reach out for them. Vendal kept staring at me and then without any warning he hit my leg with a stick. I yelled out in pain, he hit me again on my arm. I swore at him, but then he hit me a third time on my other leg. There it was. The willow tree came to life and its long branches wrapped around Vendal and raised him from the ground. I quickly took control over my anger and the branches let go of the Druid, who fell on the ground with a thud. He looked up at me and smiled.

"Interesting."

That was all he said. Then he made me meditate again. When I opened my eyes again, Killian and Neyra arrived back from their practice. Vendal called them over and looked at me expectantly. I sighed. I knew that nothing would happen but I closed my eyes anyway, ready for them to be disappointed again.

And then, suddenly, there it was.

I grabbed a connection to the first thing I could reach and a strong blow of wind made every fallen leaf dance around us in a circle. I heard Neyra's excited giggle as I opened my eyes. When I saw Vendal's smug smile I lost the connection.

"Very interesting."

He walked away without saying anything else. Killian shrugged and we all started packing up our things. I didn't understand the Druid sometimes.

To all of our surprise we reached Lendala before nightfall. The Druids' capitol was half the size of Yandana. Its buildings were grey and, to be honest, very boring. There weren't many people on the streets as we entered, but just like Allion, the city had all sorts of people within. The streets were wide and easy to navigate, which was a nice change after our previous experience. In the middle of it all stood the Druids' Academy that was cut off from the rest of the city with enormous walls and a wide river that was protecting it from any unwanted visitors. It was created entirely by the Druids. The only way in was through the bridge and the large golden gate which was protected by guards.

Vendal led us to a huge inn that was twice the size of any I'd seen before, and for a good reason as it turned out. It was entirely packed with people. Wayfarers searching for Druids' healing, or vendors who were bringing in everything that the Druids might need, and even guests of the Head of the Druids himself.

A small man greeted us, introducing himself as Tobias. He had big ears and a small head. He looked quite comical but was incredibly kind. He had three rooms available, but we quickly realised that we could only afford two. Neyra and Vendal wanted to be together so that left me with having to share the room with Killian. I felt a bit uncomfortable, but accepted it. We took all our belongings up and as I set foot in the beautiful room I sighed with relief: there were two separate beds in there and a closed off room in the back where the hot water was set up for bathing. We put down everything and went back downstairs to eat dinner.

"Alright, here's the plan," Vendal said through mouthfuls of food. "Me and Neyra will go to the Academy to start researching tomorrow, and to talk with Rowland who - hopefully - will be able to help, but just to be sure you two will head to Leanne's house."

"Actually," Killian said, "I will go and look for work."

"What?" We all asked in unison.

"We're running out of gold and who knows how long we'll need to stay here," he explained.

"Good thinking," Vendal agreed. "Sam, will you be fine on your own?"

"You know I will be." I waved him off and noticed that Neyra was looking at me intensely. "What?"

"The flower," she said, anxiously.

"What about it?" I asked again.

"Wow, you are pissed!" yelled Vendal and I quickly took out the flower from my hair just to see the angry orange colour disappear from it.

"I am not," I said and slid the flower into my pocket. "Must be something wrong with it."

"Why are you pissed?" Killian asked.

"I am not... pissed." I said as calmly as possible.

"That flower never lies." said Vendal and I shot him the deadliest look. "I'll shut up now."

We finished our dinner and parted ways by our rooms. Vendal and Neyra seemed extremely excited to get rid of us. We waved them goodnight and went into our room without bothering to say a word to each other. Killian had become awfully quiet ever since he told me about his bride. He kept avoiding me and only said something when he really needed to. I went into the separate room to freshen up and get the road's dirt washed away from my body. When I finished Killian was already in his bed, his back turned to me. I walked as quietly as possible over to my own bed. I sat down and took out my comb from my bag, combing through my tangled hair before laying down. I almost screamed when I noticed that Killian had turned around and looked at me.

"Sorry," he said softly.

"I thought you were already asleep." I quickly grabbed the blanket and pulled it up as I realised that I was in my nightgown.

"If you want me to, I can go with you to Leanne's house tomorrow." I looked at him.

"What about the work? I mean, if we really are running out of money what you suggested makes perfect sense. I was actually thinking about asking the innkeeper here if I can stand in to work down the price of the room instead of paying for it."

"You were?"

"Yeah, I don't think that I would be of much help to Vendal and Neyra in the research."

"I can look for something after we talked with Leanne," he said. I nodded.

"If you insist."

"I do insist." His confident smile appeared on his face. "You know, you should learn a bit of close combat in case you can't work your magic."

"Ouch," I grabbed my heart mockingly. "That hurt." We started laughing.

"Sorry, I didn't mean it like that," he said.

"No, you can't save yourself in this situation. You said what you said."

"Well... I will make it up to you, I promise."

"You better. But I'm not gonna lie, I was thinking about asking you to teach me some tricks too."

"Tricks?" he raised one of his eyebrows in question.

"Come on, you know what I mean. I do know a few things, I had to learn them while living on the streets-" I stopped myself as I thought about Yandana. "It feels like that's a lifetime ago."

"The first time I saw you -" He had turned to look at me properly now, propping himself up on his arm. "- you were sitting by the fountain in the Queen's Square. I wanted to go and talk to you at that moment, but Felnard made it clear that we couldn't until the time was right. You went back to that fountain every day at the same time. Why did you do that?" He was studying me, searching my face for answers. There was something dangerous in the question - like he was trying to pry secrets out of me. I decided to relent.

"That's where the cart that I travelled on to Yandana dropped me off sixteen years ago. I went back because I kept hoping for... something. I don't even know what. Maybe another cart to take me away." I forced a smile on my face. "Eventually you came and my life became better since then." He smiled back, but I could see in his eyes that he felt sorry for me. "Let's sleep, we'll have a long day tomorrow. Good night, Killian."

"Good night, Sam."

I blew out the candle and fell into restless sleep.

CHAPTER 7
PARADION

The man was sitting on his side of the river, hopelessly waiting for the woman. He stood up and walked around from time to time then sat right back down on the ground. He threw rocks in the river for a while, picked out the grass from the ground, but eventually he stood up again. He looked across the river where I was standing even though he clearly was not able to see me. Then he turned around and left. A few seconds later, the woman ran right through me, I gave out a horrified yelp and struggled to find my footing again. I ran after the woman who was heading straight for the river. To my surprise, and hers, I caught her hand. She looked back at me and for the first time since I started dreaming about her, I saw her face. I was looking at Radona. But it wasn't really her. Yes, she looked exactly like her, but this woman's face was full of warmth and kindness. I was so shocked that I didn't notice her hand slipping through mine as she was no longer able to see me, I cried out after her and-

I woke to someone shaking me, hard. I was trying to fight whoever was holding onto my arms to no end. Finally, I opened my eyes and was able to stop, recognising who was holding me. My breathing was rapid; I was gasping for air. Killian, all calm and concern, helped me sit up and then sat down next to me, taking me into his arms. He was caressing my shoulder while my breathing returned to normal; nice and slow. I was gripping hard into his other arm with both my hands, rocking back and forth and Killian was moving with me until he slowly stopped me from doing that too. I don't know how long we were sitting like that on my bed, all I knew is that my eyelids were getting heavy and I soon fell asleep again.

Later, when I opened my eyes, I didn't know where I was. I felt a steady movement under my head. I was holding onto someone's arm and that's when

I remembered what happened the previous night. I tried not to panic. I lifted my head from Killian's chest and as I sat up, he soon followed suit. He gently touched my back.

"Are you okay?" he asked in a quiet whisper. I nodded.

"What happened?"

"I woke up to your screaming in the middle of the night. I shook you awake, but you were in such a panic that you grabbed hold of me. I didn't want to leave you alone. I'm sorry, I know it was inappropriate of me to-"

"No." I finally looked at him, cutting him off. "Thank you. I would have been up all night if you-" I swallowed my nervousness down. "Thank you," I said again. He smiled.

"No problem."

Suddenly our door opened and Neyra let out a big, purposefully dramatic, gasp.

"You two?" she asked in a high pitch voice but we both answered at the same time, basically screaming.

"NO!"

"Nothing wrong if you-"

"Neyra!" I said in a raised voice.

"Right. Breakfast is ready downstairs and we should talk through a few things before we part ways." Killian was already on his feet getting dressed, and I followed suit. "See you downstairs!" She called out after us as she left.

When we arrived downstairs the lovebirds were already there. Neyra must have told Vendal what she thought she'd seen because the druid was watching us with a huge grin plastered on his face. Killian must have given him a look, because he darted his eyes down to his plate and didn't say a word.

After breakfast, Neyra told us where we'll be able to find Leanne the historian. Vendal handed us a piece of parchment with all the questions we needed to ask her, then we all left the inn, but the streets were no longer empty like when we arrived; they were packed with people. Young Druids in yellow robes were making their way towards the Academy with a Master who was leading them ahead. The Master had black robes. Vendal had explained the difference between each of the coloured robes to us, but since he was always wearing different coloured ones, after a while I forgot how he said the assignment worked. I did, however, remember that black was the colour of the oldest and wisest Master Druids. I watched him as Vendal and Neyra followed the younglings while Killian and I went the other way.

As we walked, I saw Druids in blue, green, red, purple and white all around us. Some of them were deep in conversation with each other while they were making their way to wherever they needed to be. Others were talking to themselves, which was a bit disturbing to witness to be honest. The younger druids however were true to their age. They were running to the Academy, yelling jokes to one another, calling each other nasty names and acting like real children do. I knew that there were many Druids, but it was still strange to see just how many of them were actually on the streets. Naturally, there were vendors making their way towards either the Lendala market or the Academy - the beautiful wives, daughters and sisters of these magicians - but it almost felt like there were more Druids than anyone else.

Soon, I noticed that people were staring at me, but then I realised the reality of the situation: People were staring at Killian.

While we were in Allion not many people paid any mind to the Hero of All, but Lendala was different. Here, Killian enjoyed the same respect as he did in the Elven and Fairy Kingdom. People were starting to greet him as we walked towards our destination; young girls were acting all nervous and flirtatious as he passed, and the older women were straight up undressing him with their eyes, but he didn't pay any mind to them. When it became too much and a few decided to walk up to us just so they could talk to him, he grabbed hold of my hand signalling to everybody that he wasn't alone.

We left the bigger crowd behind, arriving on the street that Neyra was telling us about and kept on the lookout for a bright green-coloured door, which we discovered at the very end of the zig-zag street. Killian knocked on the door, but when it opened, I saw that all the blood rushed out of his face. The woman who was standing in front of us was gorgeous. She had long black hair, round face and huge green eyes. She was wearing a very revealing dress and she was in the same shock as Killian himself.

"What are you doing here?" she asked, not even noticing me.

"Well-" started Killian but I cut him off.

"We're here for some information."

She looked at me for the first time - barely more than a glance, but it was at least an acknowledgement of my existence - then was quickly out of the door, pulling it closed behind her and pushing her finger to Killian's chest, forcing him to back into the wall of the house opposite.

"If my father finds you here again, he's gonna murder you, *Killian Fin*. Don't you remember how angry he was? He swore to Sagar himself that he will take your life!" She yelled in such anger that I was afraid that her head was going to blow right then and there. Killian didn't dare to move.

"How could you be such a fool?" She asked, and the next moment grabbed the man and kissed him passionately.

My stomach turned, I felt sick and dizzy. An immense sadness rose up in me and I had to force it back down before my powers had a chance to manifest themselves.

"What kind of information do you need?" Her voice felt like it came out of nowhere. She was facing me while elegantly swiping her lips.

"They told us you are a historian who could help us." I said, strictly looking at her. She laughed out loud.

"Oh, that's not me. That's my mother. She isn't here. She'll be back in three days and-" I turned my back to her and left. I heard her yell something like: 'You're welcome, bitch!', but I didn't care how rude I was being.

Instead, I got back on the crowded street and got lost in the sea of people. I was winding my way back to the inn, but stopped when I found myself in a big open square. Young girls were dancing and singing close to a fountain in the middle of the square. A group of Druids were practicing on the other side. Each of the students were sat staring at a medium sized rock on the ground. Some of them concentrated with their eyes closed, while others were staring at their rocks like nothing else existed in the world. Their Master just smiled as he watched them exert some kind of will over the stones. Only one of the students was able to lift the rock off the ground, but he got so excited that it immediately fell back and hit his foot. The Master laughed, patting the successful student on the back and encouraging the rest to try again.

I walked to the fountain and sat down on the edge of it, turning to watch the town move around me. Cats started to appear from every direction and were making their way right toward me. I felt the stone ground under their soft paws. There was gasping all around me as a few dogs came rushing in too, and then the birds appeared up high. I only realised what was truly happening when an old Druid in black stepped in front of me. He came as close as he was able to next to the animals. The girls stopped singing and dancing and were just staring at me. I looked up at the Druid and the amazement on his face.

"You are a Paradion," he said, eyes wide.

"Good for me," I answered, still not understanding fully what the title meant and not entirely in the mood to be anything to anyone. The Druid hushed away a few cats and slowly sat down next to me. His face was heavily wrinkled but his eyes bore knowledge beyond time.

"What's your name, child?"

"I'm-"

"Sam!" Vendal and Neyra appeared from the crowd, seeming just as confused as I was. Vendal immediately bowed a deep, respectful bow when he saw who was sitting next to me on the fountain.

"Master Rowland."

"Vendal!"

Happiness shone through the old man. I helped him stand and we walked to my friends. I lost all connection to the animals so they quickly fled from the square.

"You know this young lady?" Rowland continued.

"Of course, she is with me. Her name is Samantha Tanan." The old Druid looked at me with bright eyes.

"And this is Neyra Lin." Vendal gestured to Neyra and the Elf bowed gracefully in front of the Master.

"Delighted to meet you, ladies. And what do I owe the pleasure of meeting all of you at once?"

"We actually arrived here hoping to talk to you, Master Rowland, and ask for your help."

"Certainly! Shall we go back to the Academy?"

Vendal and Neyra nodded with enthusiasm. I deposited Master Rowland from my arm onto Vendal's and took a step back.

"I will-" I said, clearing my throat a little. "I will go back to the inn."

"No, absolutely not my child. You're coming with us." Rowland gave me the kind of look that made me feel as if he was piercing deep into my soul to see what he might find there. "It's not every day that a Paradion enters into Lendala. Come." He gestured to the students.

"Children, we are heading back to the academy."

"Yes, Master!" They replied in unison. This was not the type of man you said no to, and so we all followed him.

The Academy was more beautiful than anything I'd ever seen. An intricate stone building full of arcades and towers one higher than the other. The front of the building housed a sprawling courtyard full of visitors and a few of the older students running around in it.

We made our way into the Great Hall where Master Rowland sent the children off to find another of their teachers. As we were making our way up the stairs, I noticed that the walls were covered with names. I stopped part way up the stairs to admire how intricately each name was carved into the stone. I got such an intense feeling of pride from all of them. Vendal explained that they were the names of all the students that have ever stepped foot in the Academy, even if they never finished their studies.

Many people who arrived in Lendala after they discovered that they were born with magic left the Academy before completing their studies to spend their time discovering the world instead of learning what they might be capable of. Others, who did finish their studies, went out to cut through the Enormous Sea in search of the mysterious Other World, the existence of which many were quite confident in. These wanderers have never returned to the Broken Ground. Many more went off to join the service of royals, stayed behind to teach the next generation, or started their own research on undiscovered fields.

We went up three sets of stairs before we finally arrived at Rowland's office. Two guards were standing in front of the imposing iron doors. When they saw the Head of Druids, they both saluted him and, with great effort, opened the doors for us.

If the building and the Great Hall were both breathtaking, they were nothing next to Rowland's room.

The skeleton of a dragon was hanging down from the ceiling. On both sides of the door, huge shelves full of books rose high to the very top of the ceiling. In the middle stood Rowland's huge desk, full of papers and a big stack of books. A black cat was sleeping on the Druid's chair. Behind the desk was a windowed door, leading out to the balcony from which the whole west side of

Lendala was clearly visible. Rowland nudged the cat from his chair and sat down, gesturing to us to do the same. Three other chairs appeared out of nowhere to accommodate us.

"How's your uncle, dear boy?" he asked curiously.

"Oh, Felnard is fine. Keeping his eye on Yandana, like you asked him to."

"Excellent."

Like he asked him to? It struck me how little I knew of the intricacies of my companions' lives.

"So, am I right when I say that my old friend believes that this young lady here is the Destroyer?"

My jaw dropped just like Neyra's, but Vendal's face did not move. He just nodded.

"I figured," Rowland smiled.

"We are searching for the Prophecy." I cut in, but Rowland didn't respond. He seemed to be both processing the information and completely unsurprised by any of it. We sat in silence for what felt like a decade, before finally he asked me:

"Do you know what a Paradion is?"

"Felnard mentioned something about the Blood Moon, but that's all."

"Red Moon, but indeed."

Rowland stood up and went to his bookshelf. He didn't even have to search, just grabbed the book he was looking for immediately, a gesture only performed by one extraordinarily comfortable in a space. I couldn't help but note how the room seemed like an extension of him, rather than a place he simply existed in. He sat back down and opened it.

"Paradions are so rare that we only know about four of them. There are many things that have to align for their birth. First, the Red Moon that only appears every hundred years. Second, those born under the Red Moon must be Halflings. And third... They can only be women."

He smiled and turned the pages until he arrived at a painted picture. He turned the book towards us and I instantly recognised the two women.

"Radona and Elemris," I said and, if it was possible, he got even more excited. "They were... Halflings? How is that possible? I thought they were the first of their kind."

"That's exactly the point my child. They didn't belong to only one race; they were a mixture of them. Illustrations are often wrong when it comes to them. They had wings, like fairies. Barely any illustration shows them like that. They were tall and thin like the Elves," he pointed at Neyra. "They had scales on their legs like the Handors. And they could change size into that of the Giants or Dwarves."

"I didn't know that," Vendal mumbled to himself.

"They were the first Paradions. And then," he turned a few more pages and a beautiful Handor girl was looking back at us. "Amelaya. Her tale is the saddest of all."

"I've never heard of her," I admitted.

"Then allow me to share with you the tale of the Black Roses."

In this tale, a Druid saved a little boy from a pack of bloodthirsty wolves. The boy, after having survived the ordeal, agreed to serve his saviour in whatever way he could. However, after a few years, the Druid realised that the boy had a head for magic and decided to make him into his apprentice.

As years passed by the boy grew stronger and stronger, an even more powerful Druid than his own Master. On his deathbed, the boy made a promise to the old man: he promised that he would only use his magic for good. Once he left Lendala behind, he decided to see the world and learn about the people who lived all across the Sevens.

After visiting the Dwarves, Giants, and Humans, he made his way to the Handor Empire - a land of which he only heard tales of. They greeted him with kindness and the Emperor provided the young man access to all their knowledge and history.

He felt strange at first; it didn't feel like the Handors belonged to the Sevens. Their views on life were more civilised than what the man had seen before. They did have strict rules, but it worked for them flawlessly. And their people looked different from everyone else. They were a bit taller than the Elves, but could not be mentioned on the same page with the Giants. Instead of skin, their whole body was covered in iridescent scales. Humanoid, yes, but incredibly strange. They had long tails which ended in a big sharp sting. The men didn't have any hair or anything that looked remotely like hair, but the women had long tentacles that lived their own life like snakes on their heads.

It took a long time for the young Druid to adjust to their lifestyle, but he became quite fond of them over time. Even he could not have predicted that something even bigger than all knowledge was waiting for him in the Handor Empire:

Love.

He caught sight of the beautiful young woman outside the walls of the city and immediately ran after her. He reached her in the forest and was surprised to see that she was Human, not a Handor. It was love at first sight. Her name was Amelaya. For reasons she would not reveal to the man, they could only meet under the dark of night, outside the city. The young Druid, infatuated by her in the moment, didn't argue.

For night after night, they'd met under the starry sky, but soon it wasn't enough for the man. He wanted to marry the beautiful girl. He started begging her to at least point him to her father's direction, but she kept saying no. One fateful night, Amelaya could no longer bear her lover's pleading and revealed to him her true self.

The Soulless

Amelaya was Handor, and the daughter of the Emperor. She transformed out of her Human form right in front of the man.

The Druid was scared. All his life he had learned that women could not do magic but there it was right in front of his eyes: a woman doing magic. He was confused and angry so he started cursing Amelaya. He screamed horrible things at her, but the most awful one that left his mouth was one word: 'Monster'.

Amelaya begged him to forgive him, cried after her one true love who so cruelly turned his back against her once she revealed her secret to him. The young Druid, in his infinite anger, put a curse on the Handor Empire. A monsterous rose bush appeared in the middle of the capitol. The man's curse was death itself.

'When the last black rose blooms, that will be the end of the Empire itself.'

The Druid, in his shame and horror, killed himself right in front of Amelaya, whose heart broke into a million pieces. She had brought an inevitable fate to her own people simply because she loved a man who couldn't accept her for who she really was.

Amelaya turned into an Eagle and flew far away from her people, unwilling and unable to stay and watch them turn into dust.

Some say that she is still alive, that she roams the skies above the Dark Forest where the Handors hid after turning into savages. Others think that Amelaya left the Sevens and disappeared somewhere in the Enormous Sea. Truly, though, we will likely never know.

We all sat in silence for a while after Rowland finished the tale. Neyra was near tears. Vendal kept fidgeting with his fingers in order to distract himself. I was just staring at Rowland as a question grew loud in my mind.

"Are you meaning to tell me that Amelaya, a Paradion, was able to shapeshift into anything she wanted?"

My companions both looked at me, their eyes huge in recognition. Rowland started to chuckle.

"And so were Radona and Elemris and therefore, so are you." I started laughing. "I know it is a lot to take in my child, but your ability goes way beyond just connecting with animals. Why do you think that Druids are able to connect to every single element, all that surrounds us, but we are unable to hear and understand animals or other people for that matter?"

I stopped laughing. I always wondered why Vendal was never able to connect to animals the same way that I was. "It's something to think about, no?" He smiled seeing our confused faces. "However, when it comes to the Prophecy and the Grabodans, I can't help you."

"What?" We asked all at once.

"We do have the library at your service but I'm afraid I've never really got into their histories so I probably know as much as you do. However," he slammed the book shut and threw it on top of the very unstable stack. It teetered dangerously for a moment, before settling. Rowland seemed entirely unbothered.

"Leanne, the historian could help."

"Oh right," Neyra started, "what ha-"

"She isn't here. She'll be back in three days," I answered quickly, signalling to Neyra with my eyes not to ask any other questions from me. She understood.

"Right. Well." Rowland stood up and started leading us toward the door. "My children, I will tell the Guards that you all have my permission to use the library, so come by whenever you desire. I'm afraid I now have to get back to my duties."

We left the Academy behind a bit disappointed. Vendal was buzzing about the fact that I might be able to shapeshift which I still found to be a ridiculous children's tale and nothing more. Neyra was deep in her thoughts not talking to us at all.

When we arrived back at the inn, the innkeeper pushed a chewed-up piece of paper into my hand. It said that Killian took on a hunting job that would come with a high payment of gold and he probably wouldn't be back for a while. We agreed that Neyra and Vendal would start searching for answers in the Academy library and I'd stay behind just to avoid unwanted attention. Ven was sure that Rowland had already talked about the Paradion who arrived in Lendala.

After giving ourselves a bit of time to rest, my two friends left and I made my offer of work to the innkeeper. He accepted only because the young girl who was supposed to help him didn't show up.

And so the days started to go by a routine. I got up before anyone else, went downstairs, had a quick breakfast (usually just bread and eggs) and started helping with the preparations. Vendal and Neyra came down as other wayfarers ate their food and left for the Academy. The innkeeper, Tobias, put all the cleaning work in my hands, so I swept the floors, changed the hot water barrels in every room, cleaned all the windows, then got back down to help serve the lunch. My companions would only return after night had already fallen, eat a little, share what they'd found with me - which was usually nothing that we didn't know already - and then they went upstairs. I cleaned all the tables, put up the chairs and closed the inn door taking a look outside before heading upstairs. After four days I excused myself for the day and headed back to Leanne's home. I was hoping that the beautiful girl would not be the one who opens the door.

As I was making my way through the streets, I noticed that a few Druids were staring at me and would start whispering once I walked by them. I picked up a quicker pace and actually felt relieved when the bright green door came to view. I stopped in front of it, took a very deep breath and knocked. I didn't have to wait for too long. The door swung open and there she was: the woman from before. I rolled my eyes, but forced a smile on my face.

"Can I help you?" I could tell she didn't recognise me at all which made the exchange a lot easier.

"Hi. I'm Sam. I am looking for Leanne."

She looked me up and down then nodded.

"MOM!" she yelled. After a few short moments, a small plump woman appeared. She had a warm smile sitting on her face, green eyes glittering and white hair up in a big bun. "She's here for you," her daughter said, gesturing to me dismissively.

"Thanks darling. Aren't you going to help out Tobias?" I had to hold back a gasp.

"I was just about to leave."

She walked past me, giving me a little push with her shoulder. I didn't pay any mind to her, my attention focused on Leanne.

"And you are?"

"Sam Tanan, I was sent by Felnard."

That wasn't the truth, but I hoped that if she heard the Druid's name that it would give me a greater chance to talk to her. Her face lost all the warmth it held and I was afraid that she might faint. "Leanne?"

"I haven't heard that name in a very, very long time."

She was considering sending me away - I could tell from the way she kept glancing at me - but then she stepped back from the doorway and let me in.

The walls of the house were full of pictures of historical figures, drawn on brown pieces of parchment closed into beautiful wooden frames. She led me through the living room, down a very tight aisle straight into a big, dark room. It had bookshelves all around and two separate tables under the window. In the far-left corner, a painting - still in progress - was standing. It portrayed a strange human-like creature. Its body was humanoid, but the head was that of an eagle and feathers were covering every inch.

"Are you here to ask about the Grabodans?"

"Yes. Yes, I am," I nodded but couldn't take my eyes off the painting.

"You are looking at one of them." She pointed at the painting, coming to stand beside me. "Their general, Crixus, who was believed to be the last of their kind."

She then moved past me and over to the painting, covering it with a cloth. She gestured toward two armchairs and we both sat down. "Would you like a cup of tea?"

"Sure, thank you." She snapped her fingers and I watched as a Dwarf ran into the room. A woman. I'd only seen Dwarves in books but I was confident that one just stood next to me.

"Two teas, Dolores, quickly."

"Yes, my lady." She bowed her head and left just as fast as she arrived. I knew I was gaping at her as she left, so I thought it better to just ask.

"Was she a-"

"A Dwarf? Yes, darling. She's paying off her debt to my husband," she said in a chatty manner. I didn't dare to ask what kind of debt she was talking about because I was already uncomfortable being in her presence. "So, I guess Felnard still hasn't given up on his search?"

"No," I replied, trying to appear bashful. I had to tread carefully; I didn't trust Leanne at all. "I am helping him with his research."

"I see. Well, he never bothered to ask me about the Grabodan history; he always had a funny way of looking at women who were smarter than him." She said with her nose pointed high in the air. Dolores came back and put down two beautiful ceramic cups on the table in between us.

"Thank you," I said, and she looked surprised.

"Anything else, my lady?" she asked, turning to Leanne.

"No, you may leave. Get back to your other duties." The dwarf left the room. "Where were we? Ah, yes! The Grabodans. What would you like to know darling?"

"I would like to know what happened to the last Grabodan and the Prophecy he was guarding."

"Well," she took a sip from her tea. "As I said, as far as we know, the last Grabodan was Crixus. They all used to live up on the highest peak of Irkaban and they were definitely guarding something there for a long time. However, when the Great War broke out, the Grabodans decided to stand with the Elves and go to their aid. Only one of them stayed behind - Crixus, who didn't believe that the War was more important than their duty." She let out a huge sigh. "His people never returned."

"I didn't know that."

"Of course you didn't," she snapped but almost instantly put on a delighted smile. "That's why you are here, darling. After the Great War, many have climbed the Grabodan Mountain and other than one, no one else returned. The girl, Enel, her name was I believe, only got away to deliver a message from Crixus. The Grabodan felt that his life was coming to an end. He left the Mountain behind, but to where he was going and what he was taking with him would only be revealed to the one true heart."

"One true heart?" I asked and Leanne nodded.

"Many have tried to get into their temple but it is said to be protected by magic that can only be broken by this... person." She gestured vaguely as she finished her tea.

"So, the answer to where his resting place is, is up on the mountain still?"

"Indeed, darling!" She beamed, but in a sarcastic way I didn't care for. "I don't think that one true heart would be Felnard's... he is a bastard." She said spitefully. I just nodded and stood up.

"Thank you for all your help, Leanne."

"My pleasure." She didn't stand up. "I trust that you can see yourself out."

"Yes. Have a lovely day."

She didn't acknowledge me further, so I turned and left as quickly as I was able. Before I stepped out, I looked back at the Dwarf who was watering the plants near the room I was in. She looked at me, gave a small smile and turned back to her work.

All the way back to the inn I couldn't stop thinking about everything I'd learned from Leanne. I went back to work helping Tobias, but my thoughts were so all over the place that I kept bumping into everything. When Vendal and Neyra arrived, I told them everything Leanne told me. The Druid's best guess was that the One True Heart meant the Destroyer. They were relieved by the new knowledge as they were still unable to find anything new in the library.

After they finished eating Vendal went upstairs, but Neyra stayed down to help with the packing away - much to Tobias' delight. He called it an early night after serving the last guest in the lounge. We worked in silence until the old man who was reading next to one of the windows decided to head upstairs. I started putting up the chairs when Neyra turned to me.

"So... no news from Killian, huh?"

A shiver ran through my whole body. I had thought a lot about our fourth companion. I shook my head.

"What happened? He was so eager to help you with Leanne, but when w-"

"Nothing." I said way too quickly and the Elf was on my case immediately.

"Did you bump into one of his lady friends again?"

"I don't know what she was to him. She freaked out on him for showing up and said that her father will kill him if he sees him and then she kissed him! I had nothing to do there so I left. That's all that happened."

"I see."

She didn't say anything else. Her sudden silence made me turn to her. She was all-in when it came to stories like this, but now it seemed like she didn't care.

"What?" I asked impatiently.

"I mean, you clearly got jealous." She answered like it was the most obvious thing in the world. I shook my head.

"No."

"Sure."

"Neyra."

"I believe you."

"No, you don't." I turned away from her and grabbed another chair.

"Why do you care if I believe you or not?"

"Because you're my friend and... I don't know."

"If I were to believe you, that would mean that you can convince yourself that you have no feelings for our handsome knight."

I stopped. She was right. She came to me and grabbed my shoulders.

"Look at me." I did as she said. "It's okay. I know that being in love is scary sometimes, especially if we feel like our feelings are not returned."

"You don't understand, Neyra." But she was watching me intently, a glint of something in her eye.

"*You've* never been with a man." She punctuated the sentence by pointing at me. I gave myself away instantly; I could tell when Neyra beamed at me. "Remember, I know everything. I figured it out that day by the river. You've never been with a man; you're not happy with yourself, and therefore you find any and all possible excuses as to why it makes complete sense that you're alone."

I looked at her, mildly dumbfounded.

"I hate you sometimes," I murmured, and then paused, holding onto the legs of one of the chairs I had just put up on the table. "But... you're also not entirely right."

She seemed surprised. I sat down on one of the chairs still down.

"I left Irkaban because... one night my father came home more drunk than he had ever been before. Instead of hitting me, like he might usually... he tried to force himself on me."

I let what I said hang in the air for a moment. I wasn't looking at Neyra, but I could feel her eyes on me.

"He realised what he was doing pretty quick, and as soon as I was out of his grip I left."

Neyra sat down next to me in silence. Her eyes were flickering back and forth, staring into nothing, processing. I continued.

"And then in Yandana, a few years later, an innkeeper tried to do the same. I fought him and managed to knock him out. That's when I ended up on the street. I didn't trust anyone - not men, not women. I let dirt sit on my face. I could have stolen clothes, but chose to stay in the raggy ones just to be safe from any potential hurt. And I became invisible to people."

I cleared my throat, and smiled meekly. I turned, then, to face Neyra properly. She was still gripping the side of the chair as she had when she sat down. The sound of my shuffling caused her head to snap up and look at me.

"I know when I am invisible, Neyra. I liked an Elven boy once. Used to be the highlight of my day when he appeared on the street with his friends. I stole nice clothes, brushed my hair and even cleaned all the dirt from my face in the hope he might notice me. He never did."

"Sam-" Neyra said, reaching out for my hand, but I pulled away.

"It's okay. Love isn't for everyone. That's what my dad always said to me and no matter how much of a monster he was… he was right in this one thing."

I stood up. Neyra didn't say anything else, but while we were cleaning the place, I kept feeling her stare at me.

I'd never told anyone about all that happened to me; I knew that my story would only make people sad. But I trusted Neyra. I trusted her not to judge me or give me pity when I didn't need any. When she was done sweeping the floor, she excused herself and went upstairs to get some well-deserved sleep. I stayed for a bit longer. I sat next to the fire that still had a bit of life left, giving a hollow light to the room. When there were only the embers left, I stood up and headed for the main door. I opened it and I looked out as I always did.

There was no one out there.

.

II
The
Journey
Ahead

CHAPTER 8
THE BOOK OF SAGAR

"VENDAL"

I hated mornings.

Not always, mind you, but lately they had become harder and harder to manage. Sure, I had the most beautiful woman in my arms, but after staring at her for a good few minutes the reality of heading back to the Library hit me like a ton of bricks. While I was studying at the Academy, I spent most of my time there and was honestly hoping that I wouldn't have to do it again once I was out. Oh, how life has a funny way of working.

Sam was already downstairs. I admired her devotion to the job; if it wasn't for her, we couldn't have stayed in the inn. Four days had passed since she talked with Leanne, but Killian was nowhere to be seen. I'd found the mercenary who recruited him for the hunting and he just said that the orders were clear:

They shall only come back when they have the beast.

As to what beast he was talking about, we had no idea. So we waited, and decided to get back to our research in hopes of finding some useful information regarding our quest.

I was surprised to see that Neyra and Sam still weren't making any effort to talk to each other for more than a few words. No matter which one of them I asked they didn't tell me anything, so I just embraced the awkwardness. Never understood women and, up until meeting Killian, I hadn't even had any experience with them.

Druids had some funny rules, and one of them was not being able to touch another person until after leaving the Academy. The Masters believed that it would only mean distraction from the hard work that needed to be put into the studies. Many, in my honest opinion, left the Academy because they had had enough of seeing the women of Lendala day after day without being able to touch them without some serious consequences. The Head of Druids wasn't a fool - he knew that simply saying no to a bunch of randy boys wouldn't do the trick, so he bewitched the main gate. Whenever someone who hadn't kept his oath stepped through it, the gate would stop them from moving ahead. They could only go back the way they came and were never allowed to step foot in the Academy again.

I bumped into Killian on my first day of being a fully recognised Druid. He was so drunk, I remember being so disappointed when I first saw him. He wasn't how I imagined the famous Malion Arur to be - flirting with every girl who came his way, being all over one woman after the other, yelling from the top of his lungs - but somehow, I was able to sense his sadness. It didn't show on his face or in his behaviour, but it was there, surrounding him like a dark cloud. I saved him from certain death and on that same day our lives became connected forever.

I still didn't understand why he'd lied to Sam about his dream. I knew well enough that he was the only one of us who'd dreamed about the girl in a positive way. Felnard and I had had horrible nightmares, but in his dreams, he often saw her as his lover, his bride or his saviour. He'd been acting very strange around Sam from the beginning. He was the one who wanted to find her the most, yet his behaviour changed instantly around her. I tried to ask him many times what happened, but he never answered me honestly.

During our first year searching for the Destroyer, we had many adventures enjoying the company of women. He taught me a lot about them and - not to brag or anything - but I soon became more successful with the ladies than he was. They would often choose me instead of the always brooding knight. Our second and third year we got into a lot of trouble while searching through Irkaban and the Human villages; they weren't too keen on seeing Killian. They often called him a traitor for choosing the Elves instead of his own people. I knew it hurt him in ways he would never have admitted to anyone. Felnard had to save his skin more than once from fights when things got way too heated and he couldn't keep his mouth shut any longer. Even he couldn't defeat a dozen angry men.

By the fourth year we were desperate. We'd almost given up all hope of ever finding the "Destroyer" my uncle kept talking about, but at the same time our dreams and nightmares were becoming more regular and intense. We knew exactly who we were looking for but it felt like the world didn't want to give her to us. Finding her in Yandana was not at all what we expected, knowing her heritage and how the people there treated her kind.

I kept my eyes on Sam too. Saved her without her knowledge more than once when the Guards almost caught her. Many times, I followed her in the

Noble Gardens to her favourite willow tree; it felt like it was the only place she was able to find some peace. As I was watching her, I couldn't help but feel bad for her. Not because of her life, but because the time was coming when we would ask her to give it up for everyone who had looked through her before. I was afraid *for* her. It would have been too much to ask from anyone. I had many fights with Felnard and Killian because of what we were about to do, but it was to no end. I knew I was right about how it was too much to ask, and they were also right about not having any other choice. Felnard started to see the signs that pointed towards *The Soulless*. He was on the rise, my uncle was certain of it, and if one thing was consistent in my life it was my faith in his word. He was never wrong.

Neyra shook my arm and I realised that I wasn't paying any attention to the book in front of me yet again. She was just as tired as I was - well, not because of the ongoing search, but because of all the hungry Druid eyes that had followed her in the Academy. A group of younglings even approached her one day to ask the silliest questions. She'd been answering the first few of them but quickly got tired of the puppy-eyed boys. She threatened to tell their Master what they'd been asking of her and they scattered.

"Are you okay, my love?" She asked me, her voice was soft and loving.

"Yes, sorry, I just got lost in my thoughts." I took her hand and planted a kiss on it. "Did you find anything?"

"You know the answer to that question." She sighed and I saw her glance up.

The Library was located in the Northern Tower. It spread up through thirty dizzying floors. A grand spiral staircase was placed in the middle of the hall with suspension bridges connecting it to every floor. The Library had been entirely built by the Dwarves, who wanted to show their utmost respect to the Druids. Once they were finished, Sagar asked them to carve their names into the door that led there.

"Well, we could do something else?" I smiled mischievously. Neyra bit her lower lip which never failed to make me like her even more. I leaned closer to her. "There's usually nobody on the 30th floor."

Neyra looked around. We were on the 14th floor and there were only two other people in there with us. She relented.

"Fine. But you have to be quiet, I don't want one of those perverted boys catching us!"

"I have to be quiet? You're the one who moans like a-" She put her hand on my mouth, shushing me. So I licked it.

"Ew!" She exclaimed. I laughed, full of mirth. She scowled at me as I continued to grin at her.

"Fine. I guess you're not getting any of *this* today." She gestured to her body, turning away from me and pretending to go back to her book. I just kept watching her, knowing she could feel my stare as she couldn't help but glance up at me every few seconds or so. Eventually I stood up and moved behind her, slipping my arms over her shoulders and caressing her skin lightly. She shuddered a little under my touch.

"I know you want it too," I whispered into her ear.

She tensed for a moment, trying to resist, before she sighed and nodded. I grabbed her hand and we left all the books behind at the table. We checked every floor as we made our way upstairs, but I was right. The most abandoned was the last one.

The bookshelves were not as tightly placed as on the other floors, some of them didn't have anything on them. The reading tables were placed under the big window that provided a view to the yard and the forest that surrounded Lendala.

Neyra pulled me behind one of the bookshelves, out of view of the staircase. She was a true Elf when it came to making love. She was wild and passionate, a real control freak, but I didn't mind it. She was kissing me with such hunger that it put to shame every other woman that I'd ever dealt with before. One of her hands was on my neck while she grabbed hold of my belt with the other one. I started kissing her neck which I knew would make her shiver through her whole body and I loved that. My hands were already on the lace that was holding her dress on her gorgeous body when we heard the footsteps. I'd never been more disappointed in my life. I quickly buckled back up my belt and walked out first from our hiding place. My jaw hit the floor.

"Master Rowland!" I ran to his aid; he was the oldest Druid after all. "What are you doing up here?"

"I have a book to return, my son," he said. I was surprised. He had his own private library in his office, why would he ever need to use the public one? "How's the research going?"

"Not great." Neyra appeared and I saw the old man's big smile as he saw her.

"You know," he said, pointing toward her ear as he sat down by one of the tables. "I could fix that for you."

"No need, Master. It's a good reminder." She answered as politely as she was able to. She absolutely hated talking about her ears.

"I understand," Rowland mumbled. He put the book on the table and my eyes widened.

"Master, this doesn't belong to the public library," I stated, curiously.

"Does it not? Strange." He looked at the cover, squinting at it, playing the fool. He shrugged.

"Well, it's a heavy book, so would you be so kind as to take it down to my office once you are… ready." He winked at me as he stood from the table.

I didn't even know what to say; I was trying to form words but nothing came out. I ran my fingers over the cover, feeling the leather which bound the pages together.

He was by the staircase when I finally found my thoughts again.

"And one more thing," he said, turning back to us. "I know what young love is, but try not to celebrate it here." A peculiar smile ran across his face and he disappeared as quickly as he appeared.

"This is unbelievable, Neyra." I said, quietly.

Neyra gave me a puzzled look. I tapped the cover.

"This is the *Book of Sagar*. Only the Head of the Druids is allowed to read this. That's a total of, like, six or seven people in *history* who have ever opened it. Ish. I don't remember how many of them were there." My words came out so rapidly I realised I hadn't breathed properly. I sucked in a huge breath.

"Isn't he gonna get into trouble?" She asked with a worried look.

"Only if anyone sees us with it," I grinned. I was so excited that I couldn't stay on my feet any more. I sat down and Neyra joined me. She grabbed a quill and ink and a piece of parchment from the stack that was placed on the table. She knew just as much as I did that, we needed to write down everything that might have been of importance.

The book looked untouched. The red leather binding shone as brightly as if it had been brand new. A complex, winding tree was burnt into the cover with one word under it: *Sagar*.

Once upon a time, when the World was still new, a young Human child lived a happy life in a small village. He was always considered special, as he had shown at a young age that, in addition to learning quickly, he looked at the world much more maturely than the other children his age. His mother enthusiastically taught him everything she knew about their world. She told him about all the people who lived all over the land - about Grabodans, Elves, Dwarves, Fairies, Handors, Giants and Humans. The young man was fascinated by the tales, so when he turned seventeen, he set off to discover the land of the Sevens for himself.

He visited every Kingdom; enjoyed the massive feasts of the Dwarves and their famous hospitality; learned all about the beauties of the body from the Elves; sincerely loved a beautiful Fairy girl; laughed with the Giants, and admired the strange and dazzling dances of the Handors. The Grabodans were the only ones who turned him away.

He left the Rocky Mountains of Irkaban, the home of the Grabadon's tribe, in desperation. Tired, tormented, he reached the pass, which led through the high rock walls. By then, it was raining and the wind was raging. After some thought, the boy decided to wait for the storm to pass, and only then continue on his journey. After some searching, he found a cave where he retreated from the weather. Inside, he found that the cave stretched back into a long, dark tunnel, leading deeper under the cliff. It didn't take long for his curious nature to get the better of him, so he set off to see what the cave was hiding.

He travelled along; the only light provided by his torch. He was amazed when he noticed something clear in the distance after one turn. As he got closer, he realized that he had not reached an exit, but that a fire was burning inside the cave.

He stopped. He couldn't bring himself to move on. For the first time in his life, he was frightened by the unknown. But his desire for knowledge prevailed and as soon as he reached the fire, he was terribly shocked.

There, sat alone in the dark cave, lit only by the fire in front of him, was a man.

His long red hair covered the entire ground, snaking out to points like the roots of a tree. His face, clean, spotless like a baby's. Lips thin, eyes a deep shade of ebony. The man offered him a seat and the boy accepted. Quickly, the young boy asked question after question about who he was, what he was doing in the cave, and why he was wearing such weird clothes. The man just giggled.

"How old are you?" Asked the boy.

"Does it matter?" The man asked back, tilting his head to the side in curiosity.

The boy was baffled by the question. "Of course, everything matters."

"Everything and nothing, age and timelessness. Everything has a match. The darkness has the light and the evil has the good. They are part of the great cycle in which we live."

"Everyone knows that." The boy was becoming inpatient.

"You think so? Because your thirst for knowledge is unquenchable, others may still live in darkness, yet they will not be less. Our world will be imperfectly perfect because we don't know everything there is to know." The man laughed and the boy felt a warmness run through his body.

"What is the meaning of life without knowledge? It's like trying to quench your thirst without water."

"What is the meaning of love? What is the meaning of hatred? What is the point of the question?" It annoyed the boy that he did not understand the strange man's words.

"At least tell me what your name is."

"Sagar."

"My name is Sagar, too." The boy stood up, the man moving with him. "Impossible." Whispered the boy. They closed their mouths. They jumped, danced, laughed. They held out their hands to each other, and when their fingers touched Sagar felt a full, infinite force running through his body. He felt everything around him. He could feel the worms digging deep in the earth, the birds flying down and around the mountains, the slow breathing of the trees, the peace of the world.

He left the cave as a wise man, which closed forever after his departure.

"Wait, so the Grabodans were not part of the Sevens?" Asked Neyra, a bit confused.

"Yes, they were. It was the Druids who weren't part of the Sevens. By the time they came into existence the Sevens were already established. Since the Druids were a mixture of different races, they didn't earn a separate place among the others."

"I see. You learn something new every day. Although, this story didn't make too much sense to me."

"He found... himself in that cave. His real self, the one that had all the knowledge he desired."

"You didn't understand it either, did you." She asked, but it was more of a statement.

"No. Not really. No."

We both started laughing. The book was filled with history. From how it all started; the gifting ceremony - which literally everyone knew on the Broken Ground - how he built Lendala; his adventures to the different nations. It was more like a journal than anything else.

Our excitement started to vanish when we found the entry he wrote about the Grabodans. As it turned out, he eventually took General Kirkby's offer, and - only ten years before the Great War broke out - left behind Lendala and moved to Irkaban to live with them.

The Grabodans were very different from all the other nations. They kept their culture to themselves for a good reason.

Their architecture was way more advanced than I'd ever thought was possible. All of their buildings looked like upside-down nests built completely from marble stones. They stood out from the greyish rocky landscape. They guided me up a staircase they had carved out of the mountain itself to the highest peak, where they had built their temple.

It was the most beautiful building I'd ever laid eyes on.

It was a circular structure, with just one great hall. Intricately designed pillars were holding up its dome, giving off a golden glow. On top of the dome sat a huge statue of an eagle with open wings spread wide out to each side. It was guarded by more of their soldiers than any other part of the city down below.

A sign was painted on its facade which I didn't recognize at all. It was an open eye, with a straight line that bisected it vertically down the middle. The line ended in a semicircle at the bottom. I asked them what it meant and they said it was the sign of the two creators of the World - Radona and Elemris. I found myself questioning my own knowledge as I'd never even heard their names before.

I read through the story of Radona and Elemris for Neyra as she didn't know much about them. I saw fear spread over her face when the role of the Destroyer was revealed.

"This is madness," she whispered, looking bluntly at the table. "Is this really what we're asking Sam to do?"

I hesitated. She had the same question as I had ever since we found Sam. "I know it's a lot."

"A lot? Ven, this isn't just 'a lot'!" She stood up from the table, suddenly restless with the weight of it all. "I can't believe this. You shared with me many things, but you somehow failed to mention this part."

"I told you she was destined to save our world, Neyra. Trust me, I don't like this either, but… Felnard and Killian are right. She is the only one who has a chance to succeed."

I touched the scar on my face. It was a grim reminder of what happened when I didn't trust my uncle.

"I just-" She turned back and angrily slammed her hands on the table. "Sam went through a lot, Vendal. What she told me of her life... It's haunted me every day since then." She took a shaky breath. "It makes me wonder if the bastards who hurt Sam deserve to be saved by her."

I couldn't hide my surprise. Neyra was so different from anyone I knew. She'd been through a lot of her own hard shit, things that even made her deny her own heritage.

"You don't mean that," I said.

"You know, I am not so sure. You haven't seen how Halflings like her are treated in Yandana. It was-"

"It was only a matter of time before she would have ended up in the King's dungeons, my dear." I cut her off. She gave me a dirty look.

"Elves don't deserve to be saved."

"Does that include you, then? What about me and Killian? The people of Allion? The Druids, the Humans or-"

"Enough, Ven." She said in a much quieter voice than I expected.

"Not everyone is as bad as the people who hurt Sam. Not every Elf is the same as the King or other Nobles. You're different from them and I bet there are many more like you."

I put my hand on hers and I took it as a good sign that she didn't pull it away. She finally looked at me.

"I know." She was near tears. I stood up from the desk and pulled her into a hug. We stood there for a long moment before she spoke again.

"She needs us," she whispered in my chest.

"We'll be here for her, always."

After she calmed down a little, she excused herself and headed downstairs for some fresh air. I stayed behind with the book. I knew that we had to use the gift we got from Rowland for everything it was worth.

I found myself rendered speechless after hearing about such a dark legend. If it was all true... it meant that we were all in grave danger.

And there was only one thing that proved the legend to be true.

The Prophecy stood on an altar in the middle of the temple hall. It was protected by four heavily armed Gabodans in black armour. The Prophecy itself was a scrolled-up piece of silver paper, a dark glow gently pulsing around it. Everyone could touch it, but no one was able to open it. The seal that was used was protected by dark magic. It really was only meant for either The Soulless or Elemris' Champion, The Destroyer. I felt the burden become heavier on my shoulders with every piece of knowledge I gathered.

General Kirkby eventually asked for my help. I agreed.

That same day, I put a spell around the temple that prevented anyone other than the Guardians and myself from entering, but it wasn't enough. So, in order to assure that only the Destroyer could get her hands on the Prophecy, I set up a

I turned the page, but it was blank. I couldn't believe it. I turned the rest of the pages and they were all blank too. Panic struck. I hid the book under my robes and set off straight to Rowland. I ran down the stairs, almost falling a couple of times, bumped into a few younglings, then, once I was out of the library, I bumped into Neyra. I grabbed her hand without a word and dragged her with me. When we arrived at the office the Guards let us through just as Rowland promised they would.

He was sitting on his balcony with his black cat in his lap. I took out the book from under my robes and asked a bit rudely:

"What happened to the pages?"

Neyra looked at me baffled by my outburst.

Rowland just smiled, unshaken by our sudden appearance. "Ah, the mysteries of Sagar."

"What?" Neyra asked, confused. She took the book and once she realised what I was talking about, anger distorted her face too.

"My boy, the Head of Druids before me, the one before him and the one before him, all tried to figure it out without success. I did too. The answer is: we don't know." He shrugged like it was nothing. "My theory is simply that Sagar never finished it."

"That's impossible!" I exclaimed.

"Why?" He asked, that smile playfully on his lips again.

I was taken aback by his question. He was right.

"Now, if I am correct here, you now know more than when you started the journey. That is something, no?"

He looked up at both of us. I was tired. I put down the book on the table next to him, turned on my heel and left without saying a word. I was fed up with how ignorant everyone seemed around us.

Neyra caught up with me in the yard. The grass, thanks to the Druids, was greener than anywhere else. The bushes were neatly cut back and surrounded the statue of Sagar in the middle. I sat down on the bench that was in front of it, looking at the man who started it all. Neyra sat down next to me. She wrapped her hand around my shoulder and kissed my cheek.

"I read the last part," she whispered in my ear. "I have a theory."

"I'm listening." I looked at her; her excitement was palpable.

"When I worked at the archives, I also had access to the library. There was a book in there with three tales."

"The Little Book of Tales."

She nodded, her eyes glittering. She turned towards me completely, putting her legs up on the bench too.

"The last tale in it, The Red Tree, remember what the Druid had to do in order to get inside its trunk?"

I didn't remember; I hadn't read the book since I was a little boy.

"He had to get through three tests!" She started playfully poking my shoulder. "I think that Sagar might have done the same in order to ensure that only the Destroyer could get in the temple."

"I mean, you might be right, but I guess it'll be something that we'll only find out for sure once we are there."

I saw I disappointed her by not being as excited as she expected me to be. I smiled.

"Rowland is right too, though. We now know more than we did before, which is a win."

"You are not an easy man to please." She said, pretending to be angry with me. I kissed her neck and she started giggling. "Stop it!"

"I am very easy to please when you are involved. I'll just eat you up!"

"Ew, you idiot!" She gently pushed me away, smiling shyly. Then she sighed. "What would you do without me?"

"I would have to deal with the longing looks the other two give each other completely alone. It would be miserable."

We both started laughing while a group of young Druids walked by us. They looked at us suspiciously but we didn't pay them any mind. Neyra stood up, stretched her arms and took a deep breath.

"We could watch the sunset today."

"Or…" I stood up too, hugging her from behind. "We could do something different."

"Ven, not everything is about sex."

"I know. Fine, let's watch the sunset." I agreed, a bit hesitant. "I know a good spot."

We walked around the city, met with some of my old friends from the

Academy, saw a group of the younglings getting chased by an older lady, young druids looking longingly at women as they passed by. Neyra found them hilarious; she was convinced that even their spit was dripping on their clothes. She didn't believe me when I told her that I successfully got through my studies keeping my oath. I took it as a compliment, it meant that I knew what I was doing.

I led her straight out of Lendala, into the forest and finally to Enyla Lake. There were a few couples, three or four families were already there, sitting on the grass. Children were running around, playing together. The sky was already painted with the red stripes of the setting sun. We sat down a bit further away from the others. Neyra laid her head on my shoulder.

"How many girls did you bring here?" She asked after a little while.

"None."

"Ven, you can't lie to me." She looked up at me with her beautiful green eyes. I shrugged.

"No one was special enough." I smiled, planting a gentle kiss on her perfect lips.

"You're a real charmer, Vendal Kin."

CHAPTER 9
THE HUNT

"KILLIAN"

Mercenaries.
Criminals.
Deserters.
I didn't belong at all. I chose my darkest clothes for the journey and made sure to always have my hood up so none of them could recognise me. I only signed up because we desperately needed the gold they paid.

And I couldn't be around her any longer.

The urge to hold her in my arms had grown stronger in me; I wanted to keep her safe from any harm, but at the same time I was the one who kept hurting her, even if she did everything to try and hide her emotions from me. Sam was so different from the women I had known before. From… Thana, my once bride. But I wasn't sure what was pulling me towards her. Was it the years of dreaming about her without knowing who she was as a real person, or was it *her*?

It was our seventh night out. I was sitting next to the campfire while the other men slept in the tents. I liked taking the first watch because it meant that I was able to take my hood down and, of course, I didn't have to listen to the other nine idiots talking. It was quiet and peaceful, although after a while the big guy, Ed, started snoring.

I dropped another piece of wood on the fire when I heard some coughing. I was reaching for my hood when a rough voice spoke.

"No need for that, kid."

It was Allen, the mercenary. He was a very tall, slim guy. His long face was weirdly asymmetrical, with crooked teeth, a long nose, narrow blue eyes and long nasty looking blonde hair. He was younger than me and yet he kept calling me 'kid'. He sat down beside me.

"I know who you are."

My whole body tensed up and I slid my right hand to the hilt of my sword.

"Don't worry. I won't say a word to anyone, Killian." Even his smile was crooked.

"And I should trust you? You're a mercenary."

"And you're a Human who chose Elves and Fairies over his own kind," he replied in a calm manner.

"You don't know shit about why I did what I did." I let go of my sword, but turned my head away from him. I didn't wish to have a conversation with him, let alone this one.

"It was because of a woman, right?" He asked, his face unreadable.

"No, it wasn't. And it's not your business anyway."

He raised his hands in defence. "I ain't trying to come off as rude, kid. Just always had a curious nature, that's all."

I was pretty good when it came to reading people, but as I looked at Allen, I couldn't decide what to think of him. He seemed harmless, but at the same time there was something off about him.

"What are you doing here?" I asked him, trying to get a better feel of who I was dealing with.

"I need the money. Like all of us do, I suppose. My wife's at home, pregnant."

"First child?"

"Third!" He laughed, but it sounded like a snort. "Hope it's a boy, finally. These girls are jumping on my nerves."

"I bet," I nodded. Allen just stared ahead into the fire.

"Hope we'll catch that bastard Gutagi tomorrow. When I left home, we barely had any food."

I felt a bit bad. It didn't feel like an act, but I still didn't believe him fully.

"I'm sure we will. Ed says we are near its nest." I tried to smile at him comfortingly. Allen nodded.

"Yeah. Are you going back to someone, kid?"

"My friends, and-"

I stopped myself. What had gotten into me? I usually composed myself much better, especially around people I didn't know.

"Now you must be thinking about that special someone." His half smile was back, looking at me through his eyebrows.

"She is just a friend too." I said, cursing my current inability to shut up.

"Nah, listen to me now; don't waste your time. If you like that woman, you just tell her. Ladies don't like to wait around for us to gather our courage, yanno?"

There was the way he talked that set alarms off in my brain. His accent kept changing. I knew I was already way deeper into conversation with him than I wanted to be, but there was definitely something there. My ears didn't lie to me.

"When I first saw my woman, I immediately walked up to her and started trying to say the sweetest things."

"You might be right," I replied, trying to keep suspicion out of my voice.

"Of course I am!" He laughed again, but it was different than before. I could feel it, *something* was wrong. I smiled, attempting to disarm.

"Will you take the second watch?"

"Sure thing, kid. Off you go to sleep."

I left him by the campfire. I walked over to my tent but I didn't go in. Instead, I snuck around the back of the camp and sat down under the tree that was near it. I was in complete darkness, but thanks to the fire I was able to see if someone was making its way toward my tent.

But the camp stayed quiet. Allen didn't even move from his place. Maybe I was paranoid? My eyelids started to feel heavy and soon I fell asleep.

It was the same vast darkness I'd always seen in my dreams.

I started walking, the only sound was my own footsteps. Suddenly, a light appeared in front of me. It grew brighter and brighter until eventually it filled everything around me.

I was in a wooden house. The interior was clean, everything was neatly placed, and the smell of fresh pie filled the air. I walked towards the front door and opened it.

As I stepped out, I realised it was Felnard's house.

It was his, but it felt so different. I looked around, but Yandana was nowhere to be seen. Was it really Felnard's house? I started walking around the outside of it when I saw her.

Sam.

I hadn't had any dreams of her ever since we'd found her in Yandana. She was just standing there, hanging up the laundry while humming a familiar song. I took a deep breath and walked to her. She looked different, her face was clear of all the trouble that was always sitting on it - the worry, sadness, loneliness she carried. Here, she was glowing with joy, a beautiful smile spread across her face. Her perfect ocean blue eyes were full of life and love. A white dress tightly wrapped around her body, its long train flowing in the wind.

I stopped right in front of her. She held out her hands towards me and I let her touch my face.

"Why are you sad?" She whispered softly, caressing my face.

"I'm not. I'm happy to see you," I replied, even though I felt the uncertainty in my

voice. Truthfully, I didn't know what I was feeling at all.

"Then why do you keep hurting me?" She asked, and her eyes suddenly filled with sadness and pain. I tried to pull away, but she came closer.

"Look at me, see what you did to me!" She was screaming now, pointing at herself. A black dot appeared on her chest and rapidly started spreading on the dress, soon completely covering it.

"Sam!" I screamed, trying to wake myself up at the same time. She leaned right next to my ear.

"You need to be there for her, otherwise she'll lose."

It wasn't Sam's voice anymore.

The woman let me go and I stumbled back, getting a good look at her. Her skin was dark as night, a silvery glow surrounding her. Beautiful golden brown curly hair floated around her. Her dress looked like it was created from the purest white flowers. And her face... her face was mesmerizing. Bright white eyes, golden eyebrows and lips, framed in a round face.

"Who are you?" I asked, my voice coming out a lot smaller than I wanted.

"Protect her!" And as she smiled, I felt like my heart was going to burst out from my chest as it filled with pure happiness. I nodded. "Now, wake up!"

As I opened my eyes, I saw Allen standing over me. He was smiling at me, but it wasn't friendly. There was barely any light around us as dark rain clouds had taken over the sky.

"Wakey-wakey kid! It's time to go. The weather is not in our favour today." I immediately reached for my hood but I saw that everyone was already glancing at me.

"Great." I growled, more to myself. I stood up but Allen didn't move.

"You were dreaming about the girl, am I right?" He asked, winking at me. I didn't understand his implication, until I saw his gaze wander down.

"Fuck." I turned away from him as quickly as I could. "Would you mind?" I said in a raised voice, very embarrassed.

"It's okay bud, it happens to the best of us. Sam must be a very gorgeous girl."

I felt my blood froze in my veins. Did I say her name out loud while I was sleeping? I turned to watch Allen walk away back to the camp, still watching me, that stupid smile still cut through his face.

After we decamped, we followed Ed - our tracker - even deeper into the woods.

It was unusually quiet all around us. There was no bird call, no insects chirping - nothing. An uneasy feeling soon took over. It felt like we were being watched as we moved as silently as possible through the trees.

The Gutagi - the beast we were after - was a species created through dark magic by a crazy Druid - the first and, so far, only Druid to have died from the Mark of Sagar. Vendal had given me a whole lecture about it while he was telling me the history of his people. When the mercenary told me what they were after I was honestly surprised that they would even dare to go out. Gutagis were very difficult to kill due to that same dark magic that had created them. They built enormous nests in the darkest parts of the forest to protect themselves and their nestlings. They hunted animals like deer, stags and - in extreme cases - even bears.

No one knew what the Druid was trying to do when he created them, as they were untamable even for him.

Suddenly, Ed raised his hand forcing us to a stop. Nothing changed around us as far as I was concerned, but he clearly noticed something that we hadn't. Allen already had his throwing blades ready, which were laughable to say the least. Our only chance to weaken the bird was the rogue Druid that had come with us, Lesal. He was a scrawny man - the robe that he was wearing practically swallowed him whole.

The Gutagi appeared without warning. It was almost five feet tall. Its wings seemed to have dwindled, but it was moving towards us in a breeze thanks to his two enormous, muscular legs, which ended in huge claws. The bird-like creature's spine arched gracefully, making it easier for it to move incredibly fast. Its feathers were reddish in colour, growing out of dense, rock-hard black scales. Its neck was long, head unbreakable, and its beak as strong as iron. It darted straight for Lesal. It seemed as if the beast knew that he was the Druid among us.

"Protect Lesal!" Ed yelled. We formed a circle around him, weapons drawn. "Don't shoot it until the Druid says so!" He continued quickly to our archer, who was at the ready. As we solidified our position, I saw the Druid begin moving his hands to form the somatic part of something he was casting.

The Gutagi reached us before the Druid was able to say a word. It struck down with its beak, easily picking up the frightened archer and throwing him right against the trunk of a huge beech. I felt the crack of his body impacting the tree in my own.

"It's done!" Lesal yelled just before the bird attacked once again, this time taking out a man who deserted the Human army, breaking his neck.

I launched forward as soon as the Druid gave the signal. I raised my sword but as I brought it down on the creature, it easily dodged out of my way, turning its full attention to the Druid. But Ed saw what was coming. He successfully wounded the animal on its side with his greatsword, right below the wing. The Gutagi howled in pain. It pushed itself from the ground and as the legs made an impact on Ed's chest, we heard his bones breaking into a million pieces.

By the time I was on my feet again the Gutagi had taken out two more people who had tried to stop it from reaching the Druid. It had forgotten about me, or might have thought that I was also already dead, so I snuck up on it and plunged my sword in its back in one swift move. The animal cried out again, but this time it was deafening. I dropped to my knees, clamping my hands over my ears to protect them from the sound. I saw Allen and Lesal do the same just in time. The other two members of our party who were still standing weren't fast enough and we watched in horror as their heads literally exploded from the sound. The cry finally died as the Gutagi fell to the ground. Lesal's ears were bleeding - it seemed he didn't cover them properly - and he was sobbing. Allen looked dizzy as he struggled to keep on his feet. I got up slowly. I took a few steps towards the creature. I pulled my sword out from its back and with one strike cut off its head as Ed had told us to do.

"That was... too close," Allen noted. Lesal's cry grew louder and he yelled out in a distorted voice:

"I can't heal myself."

"We need to get help for him." I put away my sword but I felt a sharp pain almost immediately in my hand as a *whooshing* sound cut through the air.

"Not so fast."

Allen was holding his throwing blades up and one of them was already in my arm, near my shoulder. I looked up at him and found he seemed... different. He had recovered from the death cry and I saw he was a lot more muscular.

He was no longer a Human, but an Elf.

"I know you," I whispered in recognition.

"Well, I am honoured. *The* Malion Arur knows me," he laughed, dropping the whole act, accents and all. The Druid stood up and walked next to him. I quickly realised what happened. It was a famous disguise trick; Lesal must have created an illusion.

"You're one of the King's Guard."

"I am. Alten Bar. Pleasure to meet you finally, Killian Fin." He bowed, deep. Lesal looked nervous and still in pain. "The King and Queen were very disappointed in your failure to show up to the Royal Ball. They wanted to give you the hand of one of their beautiful daughters, you know?" He started slowly circling around me.

"Well, please send my apologies, but I can't be forced into a marriage I don't want."

"Well, that's where you are wrong." He smiled, smug. "They gave you an Elven name, the only Human... They welcomed you in, so now it is your duty to marry one of their daughters."

"Then I am giving back my name. Do you want me to write it down?" He spat at me, his face distorted with anger.

"You ungrateful little shit."

"Master-" Alten threw the blade without a second thought and Lesal collapsed immediately to the ground, the sound of his blood gurgling in his throat audible. Alten kept his gaze on me as Lesal eventually expired.

"I saw you with her, you know? With that homeless girl. I am guessing that she must be your dear Sam." I pulled out my sword and almost instantly another blade was in my arm. I yelled out in pain but held the sword right to his throat.

"Don't take her name in your mouth!" He raised his hands, that smug smile still sitting on his face. I wanted to kill him; every inch of my body was ready to strike him down.

"You have two choices here, *Malion Arur*. You will either come back with me willingly or I will have to force you to return."

That was all I needed. I struck down on him, cutting deep into his right shoulder before he could dodge away. But he was fast; he threw another triangle blade right into my side.

"You fool!" He yelled, angry. He wasn't as well composed as before. He pulled out his long sword and raised his weapon in the air, but I took my chance, getting on my knee and striking the blade right into his stomach. His eyes bulged out from their sockets, mouth half open. His sword clattered to the forest floor in a heap and fell to his knees. I stood up, pulling the sword out of his stomach.

"You talk too much, Elf," I said, bitterly, and cut off his head.

I stumbled back a bit as the adrenaline slowly left my body and pain radiated through my hand and side. I looked down at the blades and one by one pulled them out. They were all marked with King Oberon's royal sigil: a bear head. I tore off the bottom of my shirt and wrapped the pieces around my wounds.

I searched through Alten's pockets and found the parchment I was looking for:

Alten Bar

You are now in service to our King, Oberon and Queen, Beatrice.
You can use whatever non-lethal force in order to fulfil your mission:
Bringing back Killian Fin, bearer of the Elven name: Malion Arur, the Bravest of Men, to Yandana.

No harm shall come to him.

May Silhoue follow
you on your journey,
General Len Hiu

"Well, you already failed to follow one of your orders." I slid the parchment into my back pocket.

I grabbed the head of the Gutagi, which was much heavier than I expected, wrapped it into my cloak and put it over my shoulder. I started walking, but I couldn't leave. I looked back at the dead, my companions for the past eight days. I sighed in exhaustion but put the prey down.

It took me a long time to dig enough holes for all of the bodies. The canopy was so dense that I could only guess that it was already night by the time I buried them all. I gathered a few stones to mark their graves and left them behind. They didn't deserve to be left out for predators, no matter what they did.

By the time I arrived back to where our last camp was it was pitch black. I couldn't stop. I felt my strength leaving me slowly as my wounds kept bleeding under the make-shift bandages. The horses were all gone. Someone either stole them or set them free. I whistled, hoping that mine, Belac, was still around. I waited for a little, mostly because I needed to catch my breath and get rid of the heavy weight of the Gutagi head from my shoulder. I whistled again and to my relief I heard movement and soon laid eyes on the piebald horse. He came straight to me. I put the Gutagi head on his back and after a few tries I successfully got into his saddle too, beginning our journey away from this place.

I woke up to the feeling of falling, then I hit the ground hard. I yelled out as my wounds flared up in pain. Belac wasn't moving, he just stood there grazing the grass. My vision was pretty blurred from the impact but I could make out the border of Lendala in the distance. I was asleep throughout the whole journey? I remembered seeing a few things, but I must have blacked out more than once. It was a miracle that I was able to stay up in the saddle at all.

The Sun was starting to set.

My mouth felt dry. I stood up slowly, holding my side. I tried getting back on Belac but I simply couldn't. My pain was too unbearable to push myself up. I held his reins and we started our very slow walk towards the city.

By the time we reached the stable it was already dark again. I gave Belac to the boy, leaving the horribly smelling Gutagi head on his back. I had to pay an extra gold to make sure that it didn't get thrown out.

I started walking back towards the inn, holding onto the walls of the houses. People avoided me, no one offered their help. I don't think any of them even recognised me, but I didn't mind it. I just wanted to see my friends again.

Sam.

I wanted to see Sam.

I looked up as I arrived on the familiar street and I saw someone standing in the door of the inn, looking around. I tried to call out but my voice failed me - no more than a small grunt left my mouth. I fell to my knees, but I heard running footsteps and the voice of a woman before I blacked out again.

CHAPTER 10
BLACK ROSES
"SAM"

After I finished packing away everything, I sat down by the fireplace like I did every night.

I wanted to wait a little longer, I was hoping that the door would finally open and Killian would be standing there. It had been twenty days since he left. Tobias even started paying me - he claimed that I worked more than enough for just the price of the rooms. Neyra and Vendal were enjoying the sudden free time that fell on us while we waited for our last companion.

We had no news of his whereabouts or the group of people he'd gone off with. The man who'd hired them was just as surprised as we were. He said that the hunting usually took five or six days, ten in an extreme situation. I was worried, but mostly regretful; the day I left him at Leanne's house kept popping back in my mind. I couldn't help myself. I was rude. What if something horrible happened to him? What if he- no. That was impossible.

Vendal came down the stairs, he seemed full of energy and a huge grin was sitting on his face.

"Come on! Enough sitting around. You're barely sleeping lately."

He was right. I spent hours in the lounge in the evenings after my work was all done and was up very early in the morning to start over again. Even with the occasional help of Neyra, I didn't sleep enough. It showed on my face.

"Just a bit longer."

"Sam." He sat down in front of me and grabbed hold of my hand. The grin was gone from his face. "Killian is fine. Please believe me."

"How are you so sure?"

"Because I know him."

He winked, but it was the most horrible wink I'd ever seen. It made me chuckle.

"Good," he said. "Now, come on!" He stood up holding his hand out to me. I took it and allowed him to start leading me upstairs.

"Wait! I have to close the main door!" I exclaimed, quickly turning around. I opened it like I did every night. I felt Vendal's stare on my back but I had to check for my own peace of mind. There was nothing on the left side, but as I turned to the right, time stopped.

Killian was a few feet away from me, kneeling on the street.

"Vendal!" I yelled for the Druid and started running towards our friend.

"Oh, blessed Sagar!" I heard him say behind me.

Killian collapsed and I felt my heart beating at an incredible pace. It was dark out, but the light of the nearby houses gave enough to see that his clothes were slick with blood. Vendal lifted his friend up easily, but I took his other side to help him. Together we carried Killian back to the inn.

It took a lot of effort to get upstairs with him. We managed to get him on his bed and helped him get out of his shirt. Vendal wouldn't stop swearing under his breath. The three wounds looked bad - two on his arm and one on his side. They definitely weren't from an animal, that much I could tell. What happened out there? Vendal quickly got to healing them as best as he could, which resulted in Killian sucking in one deep breath instead of the rapid little ones. We watched as his chest calmed back down to a more balanced rhythm.

I ran to the small washroom and grabbed the water bucket from there. I dunked some cloth into the water and started cleaning the dried blood off of him.

"What the hell happened out there?" Vendal whispered. He was so nervous that he just kept walking up and down in the room, all while I cleaned his friend's body, trying to hide my tears from him.

"Something terrible," I replied, and stood up, dropping the rag back into the bucket. The water was tainted by his blood.

"I'll stay." Vendal said, but I put my hand on his chest, shaking my head.

"Go and sleep. I'll be here."

I pulled the chair next to Killian's bed. The Druid nodded and left briskly.

Killian was shivering so I tucked him in with the thick blanket. I grabbed his hand and just sat there until I eventually fell asleep.

The man ran into the water and lifted the beautiful woman out of it, taking her onto the shore. He was worried, looking around to see if he could call for any help. He started shaking the woman's shoulder but she didn't respond. Then, he pushed down on her chest over and over again until she coughed up the water that had filled up her lungs. I was standing there, watching, tears of joy running down my cheeks. She sat up with the help of the man and took a lot of short sharp breaths, trying to find the rhythm again.

And then their eyes found each other.

They did not speak.

They didn't need to.

They stood up and the man kissed the woman. I was happy to see them find their way to each other.

The feeling of skin on mine caused me to whip around.

The man was standing right in front of me, his face filled with sadness. He was yelling at me but no words left his mouth or at least I couldn't hear them. He started gesturing behind my back and as I turned around there it was: the woman's body floating on the surface of the water, face down.

I turned back to the man to beg for his forgiveness but his hands were quickly around my neck and anger was distorting his face. I tried to yell out but I couldn't. Black spots started to invade my view as I tried to breathe I couldn't breathe I couldn't-

A loud knock woke me up from the horrible dream and Killian was no longer on the bed.

I opened the door and Tobias looked back at me. He was fuming because I hadn't woken up in time. I apologised profusely, changed my clothes as quickly as possible and was down within minutes. I pulled down the chairs, wiped the tables and started helping with the cooking. My stomach was rumbling loudly as hunger slowly set in. The regulars started appearing one by one, sitting at their favourite tables. I didn't have time to ask Tobias if he'd seen Killian leave, but he must have because someone needed to let him out. When Vendal and Neyra heard that Killian had disappeared they left without eating.

To my great disgust, halfway through the breakfast the girl from the green-door house appeared. She didn't stay long as Tobias cursed her off after failing to show up to her first work day. I saw her noticing me and an envious look appeared on her face, but I just waved her goodbye, smiling politely.

By the time I finally got some food every wayfarer and vendor was out of the building. I took a seat next to one of the big windows so I would be able to see if someone was approaching the inn. Tobias was already hard at work on the lunch and I heard him cursing from time to time.

I was deep in thought when someone sat down in front of me. I looked up and almost dropped my last bit of bread. Killian sat down, looking like nothing ever happened to him, a wide grin on his face. Rage boiled over and I punched him repeatedly in the arm.

"You. Scared. Me. So. Much!" I said between my teeth, punctuating every word with a hit, but he just laughed and that was even more annoying than anything else.

"I'm sorry! I am- please stop hitting me, my lady," he said with a chuckle. I ceased my barrage. "Thank you for taking care of me."

"You would have done the same," I replied, not looking at him.

"I'm sorry I left early. I had to go and get my payment." He put a big pouch on the table that was heavy with gold. It clattered down in a satisfying heap.

"What happened to you?"

"Oh, you know. These hunting parties come together from mercenaries and low-lives. When we caught the beast, one of them tried to get me, which he partly succeeded in." There was a hint of regret in his voice. "It was... Alten Bar-"

"The King's Guard." Anxiety pulsed through my body. I remembered that Elf. He was the one who saw Killian save me in Yandana.

"Apparently, King Oberon and Queen Beatrice are quite upset with me for not showing up at their Royal Ball to choose one of their daughters as my bride. They say that I offended them deeply."

I nodded. He hadn't told me this before, but everyone in town knew that was the true purpose of the celebration.

"They want you dead?"

"Not...exactly. They want me back so I can fulfil their wish, which I will never do." He shrugged his shoulders and continued to smile.

"You find this funny, don't you?"

"I find it hilarious."

He winked. I shook my head in disapproval but didn't ask any further questions. After the relief that he was alright, I found I couldn't really look at him, so I returned to my food. I wanted to pick up my bread but he put his hand on mine. I didn't look at him.

"Sam." There was pleading in his voice.

"I spoke with Leanne..." I said, still looking down at my plate. He didn't let go of my hand. "We'll leave tomorrow, now that you're here. Vendal and Neyra went looking for you now, so they'll be pissed when they come back."

"Sam..."

"I can shapeshift, by the way, according to Rowland. He was quite amused by who I am, I guess. He seems to be just as weird as Felnard, so-"

"Sam, please. Look at me." I did. He was still smiling.

"What?" I asked, my voice shaking

"I know the stories you heard about me..." he started, and I was surprised that he wasn't talking about the hunting party. "...and what you've seen as well doesn't really paint me as anything other than someone who's after women all the time. But I want you to know that I left that life behind a long time ago."

"And why do you want me to know that?" I asked, my heart beating rapidly in my chest. I looked up at him, holding his gaze. It felt like a dare. He took a deep breath.

"Because you..." he hesitated and dropped his gaze to his hand that was still holding mine. "You're like a sister to me."

I nodded slowly. He still didn't look at me. I thought of the conversation I had with Neyra, my father, the events of the days behind us already and I let it all go, right in that moment.

"Well…" I pulled my hand away and said, "I better get back to work."

I stood up, grabbed my plate and took it back behind the counter.

I grabbed the broom, the clothes I used for cleaning, and I was on my way back upstairs. Killian, to my suggestion, went after Vendal and Neyra. I cleaned every room, the landing, the lounge and all the windows in the building and before I could notice, it was already dinner time. My three companions returned, laughing. They sat down and I took their dinners to them. Tobias told me to join them, but I refused.

After everyone was gone, I did the routine one last time, but when I closed the main door I didn't check the street. I headed upstairs. Killian was already asleep, so I tread very quietly, taking care of a few things before I also laid down on my bed. Sleep took me in its arms quickly.

The man was collecting stones into his pockets. When he had enough, he sat down on the shore and started building a triangle-shaped memoir to his love. He didn't look up at me, but I could hear his cries.

He was on the far side again. I carefully started walking towards him - I didn't want to startle him and I wasn't sure if he would react to me like last time. I automatically touched my neck and that's when I felt it:

My skin felt different. It was cold and rough under my fingers.

I looked at my hands and realised they weren't mine. Long fingers ending in strong, pointy nails, snow white skin.

They were a man's hands.

The clothing on me was different too: a long, flowy black dress. Soft, almost skin-like touch to it. I walked to the water's edge and looked down.

It wasn't me. I was in someone else's body.

A perfectly sculptured face was looking back at me, with full lips, straight, severe nose and red eyes. The ears were pointy and ended in big claw-like jewellery. My blonde hair was brushed back, sitting tightly on my head. Who was I? Suddenly my reflection smiled at me. I looked away in horror and found the other man was once again in front of me. He started doing the weird gestures with his hands, but strangely I finally understood what they meant.

'Why did you kill her?' he signalled. 'She was my love…'

'I didn't want to.' I pleaded, but instead I heard: 'She had to go.'

'Why?'

'I didn't want to!' I yelled, but once again something completely different left my

mouth:
> *'Because you don't deserve love.'*
> *I yelled out in frustration.*

I woke up once again to Killian shaking me, but I immediately jumped out of the bed. I didn't care about my nightgown or anything. He was looking at me, terrified. He was saying something, but I couldn't focus on him, the words just jumbled sounds in my ears. I pushed past him, making my way to the door and left, my breaths slowly steadying.

I headed straight down to the lounge and sat down next to the fireplace. A few embers remained so I dropped some wood on them, stoking the fire up once more. I was only sitting there for a few seconds when I felt Killian's hand on my shoulder again. I tried to pull away but he didn't budge. He sat down right next to me and when I looked at him, I realised that it wasn't him at all: it was Neyra. I hugged her tightly and she held me in kind.

We sat there for a long time, just staring into the fire. I wasn't sure what I'd done in my sleep, but it was clearly as frightening for them as the dream was for me. Eventually she helped me stand back up and we went back to our rooms.

When I opened the door, Killian stopped in his tracks. He'd been heavily pacing the length of our room before I arrived. He walked to me and there was so much worry in his eyes - I couldn't stand it. He hugged me and planted a kiss on the top of my head.

We stood there for a while in complete silence, but eventually parted ways and laid back down on our separate beds. He blew out the candle but I didn't dare to fall asleep again.

The next morning Tobias greeted us with a big bag of freshly baked goods. He thanked me for all my help and said that we are always welcome back, free of charge. I found myself surprised that I was going to miss him and the inn in a strange sort of way. We had found a peculiar kind of stability here, and out there...

But it was time to go. We thanked him, said our goodbyes and went to fetch our animals from the stables. We packed our things up on them and paid the stable boy for taking care of them.

Lendala disappeared behind us quickly, but I made an effort not to look back. We spent two days just travelling, eating and sleeping. On the third day, Vendal wanted to start teaching me again. I agreed. We found a clearing where we'd set up camp; Irkaban was still a very long way from us, so we decided to take our time. Neyra and Killian moved far away from us so they wouldn't bother us with their sword fight.

Magic's basis lies in connections. The easiest way to explain it properly was through silence, but it wasn't really silence at all. I understood it better when I closed my eyes for the hundredth time. As the world faded into darkness all around me, I felt like I was sitting in that quiet for ages, but soon a buzzing appeared. I searched for the source everywhere, trying to reach it with my mind and soul, and found it was the sound of worker bees on a tree. Then another sound appeared, this time much clearer than anything before. A loud, *whooshing* sound, big and strong. The river, somewhere deep in the forest, finding its way through heavy rocks and hefty logs.

As soon as I recognised what the sound belonged to, I was able to see it too, even though I hadn't moved. Heavy breathing found its way to me. Some kind of animal. A deer? Maybe something bigger? No... it was a hunting fox. For a second, I saw through his eyes. The world completely changed. I opened my eyes to see Vendal was smiling at me.

"How was it?"

"Incredible. I felt everything; it was much clearer than before."

"Well, it's a big improvement then, considering that you can barely produce any magic," he said, mocking me. "Also, I told you so!"

"What's the next step?" I asked, wanting to learn a lot more. Vendal raised one of his eyebrows.

"Well... the most important one, I guess. The awake vision. I came up with the name myself."

"I figured." I shook my head, smirking. "But what does it mean?"

"Well, you did the basic magic - you closed your eyes, connected and all that humbug. But, for a connection like this, you need deep concentration which you can't really do in the middle of a fight. So, everything you just experienced, you have to do with your eyes open this time."

"What?"

"Well... find something. For example." He looked around and found a small pebble on the ground. "This one." He opened his palm so I could see it too. "You won't be able to do it at first, unless... I guess, in your case, it comes from your bottled-up anger, but! You need to forget that, you hear me? I know the Unicorn's gift gives you protection from the Mark of Sagar, but I don't want you to practice magic that comes from spite." I wanted to say something witty but I couldn't, I knew he was right.

"Alright. I want you to break this pebble in half."

I rubbed my hands together, focused on the pebble, but nothing happened. I got a bit frustrated with it. I shook my head to clear it out. I tried and tried, but no matter what, I simply couldn't do it. The pebble didn't even move. Killian and Neyra appeared, I could hear their giggles. I tried to close their voices out, but it felt like they kept laughing louder. Vendal saw that I was getting fed up so he signalled me to take a deep breath. I did. Neyra snorted in laughter like a horse and the anger got the better of me. The pebble broke into half right in the middle.

"Sam!" Vendal yelled angrily.

"I'm sorry, okay? I just-"

He slapped me. It came so far out of nowhere and it even stopped our other two friends in their tracks. I didn't even have time to be angry about it.

"I don't want to hear any of your excuses again, you understand? True magic, REAL magic can only happen if you practice and work for it. Only the weak choose the easy way out. Anyone, and I mean anyone from the Druids, can do magic out of pure anger." He grabbed the sleeve of his robe and pulled it up. The Mark of Sagar was tainting his whole left arm; it was something that wasn't there before.

"That's it for today," he said finally, and stormed off.

Tension was high between us that night. Vendal didn't talk to anyone and I preferred to stay quiet too. Neyra and Killian got into some kind of conversation but I didn't pay any mind to them. I knew that Vendal was right in everything he'd said, but the weight of our mission had started to take its toll on me. I think what really pushed me on the edge was Rowland's tale of Amelaya.

She was a Paradion, like me, and she was able to shapeshift. Was that something that was expected from me, too? Ever since we started on the journey, the only times I was able to produce any kind of magic was when I felt angry or frustrated. The easy way out... the weak person's way out. I understood, even if I refused to admit to Vendal at that moment.

The next day a carriage appeared as we sat down around the campfire to eat our lunch. Killian had hunted some deer and there was still a loaf of bread left from the food Tobias had given us. A tall man and two young girls got off from the carriage and asked for a place by the campfire - their horses were tired from travelling. We said yes, understanding all too well how exhausted they all must have been. They told us they were vendors, travelling the Broken Grounds every Spring to Summer. The man was teaching his daughters how to run the family business. They had many good stories that they shared with us and they brought a much-needed ease with them. Once they ate, they thanked us for our help by giving us new very soft blankets and carried on their journey.

We continued practicing that afternoon. We didn't speak about the day before - Vendal was in a better mood but he kept pushing me towards my breaking point. We stopped when I collapsed on the ground, exhausted. The Druid, strangely, understood it.

Killian and Neyra didn't return until nightfall. They were in a much better mood than the both of us. The Elf, as soon as she saw her love, sat on his lap and gave him much-deserved kisses all over his face. They both giggled like teenagers who'd just found their first love. I went and laid down on my old blanket, but covered myself with a new soft one. It was magic, as ridiculous as that might sound. I hated falling asleep, even though I hadn't dreamt of the two men since that night in the inn, I was afraid of when they would return.

Especially the one whose skin I was in. He scared me more than anything else. That night I slept better than I had in a while.

The next morning, we broke down our camp and continued our journey through treacherous lands. As we were getting closer to Irkaban, it also meant that we were getting closer to the Dark Forest. We wouldn't have to travel through it, but legend said that even being near it made a lot of people go mad.

We were making our way through a pine tree forest as the sun was starting to set on another day when a strange sight appeared. Just in the distance, the outline of buildings. Vendal was frowning as he took out the map that Felnard gave him. A small little gasp soon escaped from his mouth. He didn't say anything, but we soon found out why.

We were heading straight for the Handor Empire.

As we got closer, we saw that some of the walls still stood basically intact, but most of them were in ruins, just like the houses. Nature had already taken back a big part of what belonged to it; thick greenery was surrounding most of the stone ruins. It was strangely beautiful. We got off of our horses and moved carefully towards what looked like the centre of the city. Vendal seemed nervous and kept looking over his shoulder. It made sense - last time we were close to ruins I got shot and we all almost died.

We arrived at a tall, still pretty intact-looking tower that appeared to be a part of a palace, or at least what was left of it. A thick rose bush had grown right at the base of it with blooming black roses. I looked to Neyra and Vendal, who both looked back at me, to each other. We knew exactly what that rose bush meant. Everything that Rowland told us was the truth. I noticed a writing on the tower wall.

"The last rose bloomed."

It was written in blood.

We all felt the tension in the air. This place felt haunted, and powerful, like old magic sleeping for a long time, or the potential for *something*. There was a silent agreement to be careful as we put down our packs near the bush and left the horses behind to look around and make sure that we were the only ones here.

I circled around, behind the tower. As I went, I noticed that a lot of furniture was still standing in its original place and even some valuables were still around some of the houses. I went into, what must have been at one point, the throne room. There were broken statues on both sides of the room. I read the writings on some of them, the ones that were legible anyway: they were all past emperors. I walked up the stairs that lead to the broken throne and I was surprised to see the skeleton of a Handor right in front of it. We didn't see any other skeletons anywhere; this was the only one. It was holding something in one of his hands. I crouched down and took it out, forcing the bony fingers out of the way. It was a piece of old parchment, caked in dust. I opened it up and the only thing I could make out was:

"Come back, Amelaya."

The Emperor, I thought. I felt sad seeing the downfall of a once rich and great culture all around us. All because of what? The spite of a Druid?

I stood up and before I could have done anything, I felt a sharp pain on my head and everything went dark.

I woke up in pain, radiating all over my body. I felt something binding my hands with a strong grip. I slowly opened my eyes but could barely see anything for a few seconds. The ringing from my ear faded and loud yelling and laughter took its place.

Men, all around me. As a shiver ran through my whole body I looked down and realised that I barely had anything on. My boots were gone, my trousers and shirt too, only my light undergarment was covering part of my body. I looked up in panic. My hands were tied either side of me, attached to two large wooden poles. I was back where the rose bush was. The tower behind it was in flames and the men were laughing maniacally, admiring what they had done to what must have been the last intact building of the Handor Empire. I saw another two poles not far from the bush.

Neyra and Vendal were both badly beaten up, and tied up the same way I was. Neyra's clothes were torn up and blood stained, Ven's robes were still on, but there were holes in them. Both of them were awake, but fear was written all over their faces as a few of the men were standing guard next to them. I was desperately searching for Killian but I couldn't see him anywhere. My sight fell on a house. A fire was lit inside it and to my horror young women were being raped by the men who captured us. I tried to pull on the rope that was holding me but I only succeeded in hurting my own wrists. An ugly laughter cut through the cacophony next to me. My stomach twisted as I turned to see him.

Cutter. He was admiring all the destruction he and his men created.

"Beautiful, isn't it?" He asked me, and I spat on the ground in answer. He laughed again.

"*Monster.*"

"Tell me something I don't know."

He held his hands up high and all the commotion stopped. I could only hear the desperate cries of the women in that house.

"Bring him out," he commanded and I immediately looked up. Two half naked men appeared holding a struggling Killian. He had a huge cut carved through his left cheek and it barely avoided his eye. Blood was dripping down on his neck from the wound. His shirt was in pieces, utterly blood stained, and so were his trousers. He stopped struggling so much when his eyes met mine

115

and I could see that he was terrified.

"You see, this honourable knight here is none other than the famous Killian Fin, Malion Arur, the bravest of men." Everyone started laughing. "He is wanted by the respected King and Queen of Yandana… His only luck in this situation is that the Leongrass do not respect anyone!"

The sound of even louder cheers broke out as they were all in agreement with their monster of a leader. I saw one of the men punch Vendal as he was trying to use his magic.

"Now. This brave man, not too long ago, was crying. What did he say, Marcus?"

Another man was standing on my left who I didn't notice before. He was smaller than Cutter, but just as ugly looking.

"'Please don't hurt Sam, kill me instead but leave her alone!'" He answered in a parodic tone. I suddenly felt Cutter's strong grip on my jaw. His face came uncomfortably close to mine.

"Is she your little love, boy? Hm? Do you want to fuck her brains out? Well, too bad." He forcefully turned my head to him and his disgusting lips were on mine. I tried to pull away but his grip was too strong.

"GET YOUR FUCKING HANDS OFF HER," Killian screamed and Cutter let go of me. I felt sick. The man started walking down towards Killian.

"You see, Malion. Arur… I have different plans with her." I couldn't see his face but I knew that the ugly smile was sitting on it. "She will be my obedient bitch by the time I am done with her."

They all started laughing again. I heard Neyra cry out and saw that Killian launched toward Cutter, but the men holding him were too strong.

"We shall start her training with some-"

"Lashes," finished Marcus and a burning pain struck my back. I screamed out and from then on everything slowed down around me.

CRACK!

The anger started rising inside me as Cutter turned back to face me. I saw from the corner of my eye that Vendal had regained consciousness.

CRACK!

Killian hit one of his guards in the stomach, the other in his crouch; they were both down for a few moments. A fiery snake rose up from the tower.

CRACK! CRACK! CRACK!

The wolf appeared out of nowhere and many followed. They took down the men Killian was fighting. Vendal's fire snake came down on the men in the building. Women were running out screaming.

CRACK! **CRACK!**

An enormous wolf jumped on Marcus which finally stopped the man from hitting me again. I could feel all of their strength flowing through my whole body, which I used to pull my hands free. Killian was fighting Cutter. Neyra and Vendal were both out of their bindings fighting the men around them. The wolves were tearing apart those who weren't fast enough. I suddenly felt something even stronger. I looked up and the griffon was flying down straight for me. Without thinking I took over its mind and changed its course. The animal's sharp claws cut into Cutter's flesh and raised him up easily from the ground. He was screaming in anguish. As I was trying to keep up the connection with the beast the pain came rushing back to my back. I fell on the ground with a big thud. I could see the wolves chasing away the rest of the men and Vendal's fire snake burning those fools who stayed behind. The world started spinning around me, the sounds died down and soon I was in peaceful darkness.

CHAPTER 11
THE LONG WAIT

"NEYRA"

The first two days dragged out for what felt like forever. Vendal healed Killian, Sam and I, then our two men went on to search for the women who'd ran into the forest. I stayed behind with all the wolves. They were sitting in a circle around our campfire, the biggest one was laying down next to Sam - they hadn't left her side since they'd come to our aid. We laid her on her stomach so the scars wouldn't get irritated by the rough blanket on the ground. It was hard to see her like that. Ven had no idea when she would eventually wake up, but he predicted a longer wait.

I washed her back every few hours with cold water to try and bring down the inflammation that had formed around the scars. The big black wolf watched my every move. There was an intelligence in his eyes, or maybe I thought I might have seen Sam through him. Ven was of the belief that the connection she had with the animals was the thing that was keeping her alive and she must be maintaining it somehow, even in the comatose state she was in. I checked her breathing so often that it had started to become embarrassing for me too.

When Killian and Vendal came back, they brought a small group of women with them - six of them to be exact. They were all kidnapped by the Leongrass from a small village nearby and they desperately wanted to get back. Killian agreed to take them the next morning even though he was dead set on not leaving Sam behind again, but Ven convinced him. I gave the girls blankets and they settled around the campfire, holding onto each other. I couldn't help but admire the strength they had, how closely they looked after each other. They said they were the lucky ones. Vendal's snake fire took away the men before they could turn their attention towards them. Those fucking bastards.

We only found two bodies; the others were all gone. Either the wolves took them into the forest or another predator came for them. We didn't know and we didn't care. As far as I was concerned, they got what they'd deserved for all the horrible things they'd done.

Vendal was weak from all the magic he used. He quickly fell asleep with his head in my lap while I caressed his face. The women were also out, although they were all a bit weary of the guarding wolves. It was only me and Killian, who was holding Sam's hand, looking down at her.

He loved her. I could tell. I had an eye for these things.

"Hey," I called over to him, "you can sleep. I'll take the first watch." He nodded only slightly.

He laid down right next to Sam. The wolf didn't even acknowledge him; it just lay on the other side of her. Killian didn't let go of Sam's hand as he fell asleep.

The next day, Ven and Killian helped the women on the horses that were left behind by the Leongrass men and the knight rode away with them, taking them back to where they belonged. Two wolves stood up and followed them. Vendal and I looked at each other, our shock mirrored in the other's face.

I went out in the forest to hunt, leaving Vendal watching vigil over Sam by the campfire. On the way, I once again found my way to the Handor ruins and arrived at where it all happened. The tower was no longer standing, but the flames hadn't done any damage to the rose bush. It was unbelievable to see. As I stared at the black roses, I thought back to the ones that were in the yard of my old house in Yandana.

My home there was the only thing I actually liked. As soon as I turned 50, I left my family house behind as most Elves did my age. The other Elves were just so hateful, so full of poison that I was praying every day to Silhoue to save me from them. My Ma wasn't always spiteful - it all turned for her when she met my Pa, who was just awful to everyone he met. It didn't matter if it was family, friends, other Nobles, or even royalty; other than our King no one could live up to his standards. Yep! Not even Ma, or me and my younger brother. I had to live through the years where my once sweet brother turned into the same as them. He held on for as long as he was able, but he got beaten by our Pa so regularly that he broke under the pressure. He became Pa's puppet, and with his help Pa was able to make his way into the royal palace. He made Gally marry into one of the main houses and soon he and Ma were invited to all the royal balls. They tried to force me into arranged marriage too, but I slipped out of their grasp as soon as I came into age. Boys had to marry younger than girls - that's how it's always been and that was the only thing that kept me alive. When I got my job in the royal archives it was also my way of keeping my eye on Gally.

I soon got a house from the court - everyone who worked there got one; it was our only payment - and made it into my home. It was the smallest house they provided, but it served me well. One large room and a separate washroom with a beautiful backyard overlooking the palace. I put all my drawings up on the white walls - my only real passion to do in my free time. The backyard had the most beautiful flowers that I planted myself. One of them was a rose bush. I never thought that I would miss those red roses one day like I did at that moment.

Gally visited me once in my small house. He didn't have a single good word to say to me. He was disgusted by my place and only came to tell me that my mother and father didn't wish to talk to me again. That was completely fine by me, but when my brother said the same, my heart broke a little. I honestly believed that he was just putting up an act for our parents, but clearly I was wrong. He got too used to the life he had, even though he was no more than a pushover in all of his relationships. I wasn't guilt free in that department either.

I eventually left the black rose bush behind and headed beyond to the trees. I was making my way into the forest, searching for any sign that either deer or boars were in the area when I heard a grunting noise. I followed the sound and it didn't take long to find what it belonged to. One of the Leongrass men lay on the ground, slumped up against a tree with a thick trunk. He was barely alive, his pallor incredibly pale giving him this slightly blue tinge to his skin, and he was not happy to see me.

I recognised him. He was the one who knocked down Ven when they caught us. An ugly, rotting wound was eating his left leg away so when I kneeled next to him he wasn't able to move too much. He looked up at me, elements of fear and disgust and hatred mixed into his expression. I smiled at him before whistling. I knew one of the wolves was following me. The man's eyes widened seeing the large animal slowly approaching him. I turned away and left, the last thing I heard was the wolf growl before attacking its prey.

I knew Vendal didn't agree with me, but especially after what happened with us, I couldn't help but think that Sam was heading towards danger for the bastards of the world, for the many who hurt her. Was it really something that we could ask her to do? How was she not bothered by it? When I first saw them in Allion, she was the only one who noticed me straight away, even though I was hiding in the shadows. She had a very good eye and was always on alert, and I admired that in her. At the end of the day, it was the thing that kept her alive for so long in Yandana.

I returned to the camp close to sunset, empty handed. There were no signs of any animals - other than the wolves - in the forest. It wasn't a problem, we still had supplies, I just needed to get away to be alone with my thoughts. Vendal was already cooking by the time I got back. He had our only small cauldron above the fire. He was making stew, the only thing he knew how to make.

"No luck?" He asked as I sat down next to Sam. She hadn't even moved an inch since I left. I just shook my head in answer.

"Hey," he called to me in a soft voice. I looked up at him, a kind smile sitting on his face. "She'll be fine. There are some wounds that take longer to recover from. That's all. Felnard was out for a whole week once after I healed him."

I nodded again as I didn't know what to say. Vendal knew exactly what was going on in my head.

"You're thinking about ending the quest."

"It's something we should consider, yes."

"You saw her power, right? Sorry, let me correct myself-" he gestured around us, there were now even more wolves sitting among the ruins, the big black one still lying next to Sam, guarding her. "You see her power."

"Ven-"

"Cutter and his men are horrible, yes. They hurt us, yes. But..." He stopped, he took his eyes off me and looked into the distance. "The Soulless will be a hundred times worse than them. And if he manages to free Radona, if we... if..."

He was just mumbling. He truly was terrified, I could see it in the way he held himself, his face, his every move. "Sam won't succeed."

"I understand," I said quietly.

"Do you? Do you really?" There was an edge to his voice that I didn't like at all. Ever since we'd gotten together, we'd avoided any fights successfully, but I felt it rising between us.

"What are you implying, Ven?"

"I love Sam too, just as much as you do, but she simply can't be more important than everyone else in the Broken Ground." He was almost yelling at me and I was taken aback by his sudden outburst. "Besides, we can't assume that she will die during this quest."

"What else could be waiting for her?" I snapped back.

He just shook his head. "You are impossible sometimes."

"Is everything okay?"

Killian's voice caused us both to jump. He returned with two horses both his and the other one was fully loaded with supplies for us. When neither of us responded, he gestured toward the second horse.

"They were really happy that I returned their daughters," he explained as we moved to take everything down. "Are you guys, okay?" He asked again but we both just nodded. He was already anxious; he didn't need our fight on top of everything that's been going on. He sat down next to Sam, and I watched as he fought with himself, trying to decide if it was okay for him to touch her. He didn't.

"Any change?"

"Nothing so far," I answered, but Vendal shook his head.

"Turn her over. The inflammation went down," he said and Killian did as he asked, but we all jumped back in terror. Sam's eyes were open, but they were completely white like snow. Vendal ran to her.

"I can't believe this," he exhaled.

"What's happening to her?" Killian asked with a panic rising in his voice.

"I only read about this, it's a…" he was trying to find the right word, "kind of a sleeping spell. It means that someone's controlling her dream."

"What? But who?" I asked and looked around. The wolves felt our fear and they were all on their feet; the large black one got closer to Sam, guarding her more closely.

"I have no idea. But it must be someone very powerful."

"Well can't you do something about it?"

Vendal glared at me a little. "Not right now, not while she's like this. If I tried, I'd just give her even more nightmares."

"So what do we do?" Killian asked, quietly.

Vendal closed Sam's eyes and laid and covered her with the warm blanket.

"We wait," he replied.

We   didn't   speak   anymore   that   night.

Four more days passed, but nothing changed. Vendal kept an eye on Sam. Killian was completely closed off, not talking to any of us. After exploring the entire area around the Handor ruins, he finally found a cave best suited to serve as a hiding place until Sam recovered. We packed everything up and followed him into the woods. We must have spent an entire day travelling among the dark trees.

It was a well-hidden cave - unless someone intentionally looked for it, it was impossible to discover. We settled down in it and it even provided enough space for our horses. The wolves refused to leave our side for even a moment so we didn't have too much to worry about in terms of protection.

I started going crazy next to the men. They refused to talk to me or to each other. I understood that everything that had happened was likely a lot for them, but anxiety and fear began to devour us all. On the fifth day, I finally gave up and got on a horse. I told them I was going hunting, but truthfully, I think I could have said anything because they didn't pay attention to me at all.

I didn't have to go too far. As soon as I got out of the woods I was greeted by a sign that pointed me to a small village named Enol. I imagined what it would be like to be among people again; to see laughter, happiness, hope. I missed all of those things. I wanted to drink, eat some fresh bread, talk, just live. Even if the whole thing couldn't last more than five minutes.

But it seemed the world didn't want to give me these simple things. I first noticed a chariot, broken into pieces on the side of the road, with four corpses around it. A family with two tiny kids. My stomach turned upside down at the sight and I was close to vomiting breakfast back up. The smell was unbearable and the flies polluted even the sky. Huge storm clouds started to gather, but I did not turn back. My gut told me that I needed to go further and investigate. Maybe there were others I could help. I made a promise to myself to bury that poor family on my way back.

By the time I reached the village it was already raining (at least it washed away the horrible smell of burning flesh). Houses all the way up and down the street were on fire, some only embers, some still raging infernos. Whatever happened only took place a few hours ago.

I rode into the village street, no more than fifteen houses around, but at least fifty poor people lying everywhere. Some of the bodies were missing one of their limbs or their heads. Blood was coursing along the dirt street like a small river; a dozen animals were burning in what must have been the stables, but the true horror only showed itself after I reached what must have been the small inn of the village.

The bodies of three young women, tied to poles. All of them had their throats cut wide open but there was not one drop of blood underneath them. What was going on around here? This couldn't have been the Leongrass. For all we knew, Cutter had been murdered by his own griffon and the morons that worked for him couldn't have regrouped already.

I heard a small cry and turned on my heels. A little girl, holding onto a ragdoll like her life depended on it, stood in the middle of the street. She had long ginger hair, big brown eyes and a wonderfully little blue dress that was a size bigger than her. How did she survive whatever had happened with the villagers?

"Hey, hey. Don't worry, little one. I'm not going to hurt you, okay?" I slowly kneeled down into the already muddy ground. The rain was hitting us harder than before. She pointed at a small shed that was untouched. We ran there quickly and burst open the door. Three more children were sat inside, all of them wrapped under a blanket.

"Oh my- what happened to you all?" My voice was smaller than I'd have liked.

"They put us in here," the ginger girl answered, her voice high and wavering. "They told us to only come out after they left."

"Who are you talking about my dear?" I looked around the shed. Nothing out of the ordinary about it, just tools. The only light was coming from three candles near the children.

"The soldiers."

I looked down on her. She was holding onto my skirt with her right hand so tightly. I came down to her level so she could look me in the eye.

"Humans like you?"

"No, it was all sorts of people," the little boy in the middle spoke up. He was the tiniest.

"They had a big monster with them," one of the blonde girls said. She and the other girl must have been twins; I couldn't tell them apart at all. They'd wrapped their hands around the small boy, protecting him.

"What kind of big monster?"

"A dragon," the ginger girl said. "A huge, dark green coloured dragon." A shiver ran through her whole body.

"Oh, dear Silhoue…"

Dragons barely came near the Kingdoms. No one really knew where they lived exactly as nobody ever dared to search for their nesting places. Whenever they did show up it was considered a sign of something terrible happening. In fact, the last sighting of a dragon was during the Great War.

"Neyra!"

I opened the shed's door. Killian had arrived, and was covering his mouth and nose while sitting on his horse.

"Neyra, what happened here?" He asked while looking around. I had no idea how he found me. The kids got up from their corner in the shed and came out of the shed. At the sight of them, he instantly got off of his horse.

"Oh, no…" I heard him whisper.

"We need to take them somewhere else." I helped the two identical girls on Killian's horse and the other two kids on mine. "Anywhere but here."

"What is going on?" he asked again, keeping his focus on me. We both climbed back up onto our horses and started making our way out of the burning town. I knew he couldn't make himself look around again. The bodies were more than disturbing.

"They said they were attacked by soldiers and a…" I looked at the kids as we were making our way out of the village. The girls held onto Killian as tight as they could. "Dragon."

"What? No, that's impossible."

"Well… How else do you explain the destruction?"

"I don't know." He scratched his chin, looking disturbed. I could tell there was something else in his mind.

"Why did you come after me?"

"Vendal sent me."

"And what is the thing you're not saying out loud?"

He sighed and looked back at the kids. They were numb, just staring straight ahead, not paying any attention to us. He turned back to me.

"Sam spoke. She didn't wake up before you ask," he said, killing my enthusiasm before it got out of control.

"What did she say?"

"We don't know. Ven thinks that it was the dead Handor language."

"What? How's that possible?"

Before the Sevens developed a shared language, every culture had their own, but they hadn't been spoken for centuries; there were barely any living beings who actually knew them, usually scholars or academics who studied them from old texts.

"It must be through the person who's controlling her dreams."

He shrugged, but it wasn't that easy 'I don't care' kind, it was more of the 'this bugs me so much but I can't do anything about it' shrug.

"That is worrying," I said.

"Yeah."

We rode for a long time until night fell on us. I wanted to stop, but Killian refused. He said that another village was close by and he wanted to get the kids to safety as quickly as possible.

I didn't know how much longer we were on our way, but we soon saw lights next to a small lake. It was a bigger village than the one we just left; simple wooden houses, farms and a lot of animals around. We approached the first house we came to. After we explained to the lady of the house what had happened, she was kind enough to take in the four children and promised to have them sent to an orphanage the next day. She told us the way to the inn as we didn't think that going back to the cave would have been a wise idea at this time of night.

The inn was so small that it only had two rooms, and one of them was occupied so we were stuck together. Killian let me sleep on the bed while he sat down on the chair by the window. Neither of us were talking, both of us deep in our thoughts. Eventually, however, he spoke.

"I can't lose her, Neyra."

I went to answer, but before I could do so I registered exactly what he said. It wasn't about what we just witnessed; he didn't talk about what the children said or who was behind the massacre - his thoughts were still with Sam. I sat up on the bed so I could see his face. He was looking out of the window, being very careful not to turn to me.

"You won't," I replied.

I started fidgeting with my fingers. Other than our combat practice I didn't talk much with Killian. I'd seen him countless times, as many had, way before our roads intertwined. Whenever he stepped foot into that palace, everyone flooded to him. I'd never seen Elves and Fairies treat a Human as kindly as they treated him.

I knew he'd done a lot for the King. When he and his men were sent out to hunt down the last remaining part of the Human resistance, he succeeded, lost everyone, almost his own life too, but he did exactly what was ordered of him. Elves admired bravery and obedience, and he had both of those things in him.

"Why did you... join the Elven army?"

"What?" My question pulled him out of his thoughts, disorientating him. Before he turned back to face me, he quickly wiped his face.

"I just realised I've never known your reason to-"

"Leave behind my own kind?" I nodded slowly.

"What was yours?

"I never belonged there."

"I never belonged among the Humans either." He took a deep breath before he continued.

"My father and mother… sold me to Elven slavers when I was ten." I felt my breath get sucked out of my lungs. I wasn't sure what I was expecting, but it wasn't that.

"That's not the worst part though," he continued, laughing humourlessly. "They sold my six-year-old brother too, separating us in Yandana. I was sold to an old couple - they were both near the end of their lives and needed help. The husband died first, and then the wife, on her deathbed, set me free. They left everything in my name… I turned eighteen, joined the army and did everything to find my brother." He laughed again, nervously. I realised that I'd forgotten how to breathe while he was talking. Every muscle in my body was tense.

"He'd died. The family he worked for, they… buried him. Treated him like their own son." A tear ran down his face. "The Elves I worked for treated me better than my own kind."

"Killian… I'm sorry, I shouldn't have asked."

"It's okay. Good to say it out loud, actually." He didn't bother with wiping his face again.

"I have a brother too." I said with a faint smile on my face. "Gally. I've never told him how much I loved him."

"You will, when we get back."

"Yeah." I didn't tell him that my brother probably didn't care about me anymore. "What was your brother's name?"

"Seán."

A huge smile spread across his face as he thought about him, and for the first time since our meeting I saw his humanity. Elves weren't as open about their emotions as other races were - we were taught to push them down as much as we could. Emotions were equal with weakness. Humans, however, when they loved, they truly loved. When they were happy, it lit up the whole world around them. I envied them for it.

"Hey," I said, regaining his attention. "Sam will be okay. She's strong."

"I know."

"But for Silhoue's sake, just tell her how you feel!" He wasn't surprised by my words, but there was regret in his deep black eyes. "What's holding you back?"

He told me everything, about the dreams, their quest to find Sam and his involvement in everything. I pondered it all quietly for a moment.

"So," I said finally, "you don't know if you love her for herself, or because of the dreams you had about her." He just nodded and I burst out laughing. He definitely didn't expect that because his eyes widened and an unreadable expression appeared on his face.

"Am I missing the joke?"

"No, sorry, I'm sorry." I took a deep breath to calm myself down, and then shifted on the bed so I could take his hand. "Killian. Even if your connection to her was first through dreams, we've been travelling together long enough that if you didn't like her for who she is, no dream could convince you otherwise." He looked a bit taken aback. I sighed, a little for show. "You men are so clueless sometimes."

"I said something stupid to her." He looked down at his knees, ashamed. "I told her that she was like a sister to me. But I just wanted to protect her-"

"From what? Are you really this much of an idiot?" I rolled my eyes.

"I might be." He folded his arms and leaned back on his seat. He was silent for a long second, before -

"I am an idiot."

"Yep."

I saw that sadness on his face again, the one that had been there so many times before.

"You need her just as much as she needs you. If it weren't for Vendal, I would have left already."

"Alright. I will talk to her, if-" he closed his eyes, collecting himself. "*When* she wakes up."

The next morning we paid the innkeeper and headed back to the cave. Vendal wasn't too happy with us once we arrived. After we told him what we'd witnessed, he went into a state of shock that lasted for a good few minutes. He had one question once he was back with us in reality:

"Did you say that there was no blood under the three women?" I nodded and all the colour flew out of his face. Killian and I were afraid that he was about to faint. "It can't be..."

"What is it my friend?"

"There were legends that..." he swallowed hard. "The Mark of Sagar could be reversed if the Druid drinks blood." He looked at us and I knew that Killian had the same thought as I did.

"So you're saying..." he shook his head and looked at Sam.

"The Soulless might have arrived already."

CHAPTER 12
AWAKENING

"SAM"

I was standing alone on the shore of the river; there was no one around me. I didn't dare to look down to see my reflection staring back at me. I took a deep breath and tried to wake myself up, but then I heard it.

A chuckle.

I opened my eyes. The man whose body I was in in my previous dream stood before me. He was a lot taller than me. I took a step back, attempting to get away, but he grabbed me by my waist, his grip far too strong. He leaned in closer and smelled my hair.

'Interesting,' he said slowly caressing my face with his other hand. 'I expected someone... different.'

'I don't know who you are, but please, just, let me go,' I begged, as I was unable to get away from him. He chuckled again and it made my blood run cold.

'But my dear, we are destined to meet very soon'

'You're not real. This is some awful dream, nothing else.' His red eyes were on me, drilling holes into my essence.

'Oh honey, I am as real as you are.'

He planted a kiss on my forehead and immediately screeched in pain. He stepped away touching his lips and laughed.

The Soulless

'The seal of the Unicorn, huh? Nice trick. Now... wake up!'

I sat up gasping for air. The Sun was shining brightly so I raised my hands in front of my eyes, trying to block out its rays.

I needed a good few minutes to realise where I was. When I let my arm down and looked around, I saw five huge wolves around me, guarding me. They looked like statues at first, but they were as real as I was. I looked around and realised that we were still in the Handor city, but I could not see my friends anywhere. The memories of what happened to us came rushing back to me and I found myself touching my shoulder blade reflexively, but there were no cuts on my back, and I didn't have any pain or anything. I just felt a bit lightheaded.

I slowly got up from the blanket and stretched my body as much as I could. It was like I hadn't moved in days. I stepped out of the ruins of the house and the wolves followed. I was wearing a dress that I didn't remember ever owning, but I was glad that I was no longer half-naked. I heard talking not too far from me so I made my way in the direction it was coming from. I turned left next to a lonely wall and saw the man and his daughters who we'd helped not too long ago. When they noticed me, they all immediately ran to me and helped me to the fire. They all acted like I was mortally wounded.

"What are you all doing here?" I asked, confused.

"Oh my lady, you and your friends saved my dear daughters from those awful men."

"Wait!" I cried. "You were their prisoners?"

"Yes!" One of the girls said, still shaken by the memories. "They caught us not long after we said our goodbyes to you and your friends."

"Did they hurt you?"

"They wanted to, but... you saved us all," the man answered, and I felt ashamed for not remembering their names.

"Where are my friends?" I asked.

"They should be back shortly. We promised them we'd take care of you while they were gone. They went hunting," the man explained as he took out a slice of bread from his bag. "This is all we have left." He held it out to me and I took it.

"Thank you. How long have I been out?" I asked, suspicious. Something felt... odd.

"For eight days," the younger girl answered. I almost dropped the bread.

"Eight days?"

"Yeah. After your Druid friend, Vendal, healed all your wounds we thought you were gonna wake up at once, but... you just kept sleeping. Your friends will be delighted to see that you are all right, my lady."

I nodded, but I was mortified by the information. The wolves were all sitting around me. The two girls seemed a bit scared of them. They slid closer to their father.

"No need to be afraid. They're friends." I smiled at the girls, trying to be encouraging. One of the wolves let out a low short growl in agreement. "And the-"

"Where is she?"

We heard the panicked voice a little ways off. I looked behind me and soon, from behind the wall that was blocking the view of the other ruined houses, Killian came running. He stopped in his tracks, panting slightly from the run when he saw me sitting there. Vendal and Neyra quickly appeared behind him and they seemed just as shocked as the knight. I stood up and turned to them, drinking them in, unexpectedly emotional about seeing them all alive. Killian came running towards me, and when he reached me he lifted me in the air and spun me around. He was hugging me so hard that I could barely breathe. I felt everything he felt in the warmth of that hug - the relief, the worry, the love. Another two bodies crashed into us from each side. Neyra was crying and, to my surprise, Vendal let out a sob himself. When we parted ways, they looked at me with such love that I felt my eyes tearing up.

"I am so sorry that we weren't here when you woke up," said Neyra, still crying her eyes out. "We were so worried about you Sammy."

Their faces were all healed; there was only a tiny scar on Killian's face where that big cut was before. I looked to Vendal, gesturing.

"You're starting to become a master healer."

"It sure looks like it."

Vendal kissed my forehead again, then grabbed hold of Neyra's hand and they both walked back to Martha, who had three dead ducks tied to her back. Killian kept staring at me, which made me uncomfortable and strangely calm at the same time. I touched the small scar on his face.

"I thought that…" he started, struggling to find his own words. "I thought that I- we were gonna lose you."

"I thought the same about you three," I replied, and I allowed a little edge to drip into my voice as I said, "but Cutter didn't know who he was dealing with."

"Yes, you should have seen his face when the wolves arrived." He took a deep breath. "I don't know what I would have done if you…" He lowered his head.

"Hey… I'm here. We all are. We're okay, Killian."

I closed him into a tight hug, and he held onto me like his life depended on it. We let go of each other when we heard our companions' footsteps. I kissed his cheek gently but as I pulled back, I yelled out in terror and hit the ground hard. Everything disappeared around me. The pale man was laughing at me, standing behind Killian, holding onto his shoulders.

"Him? Really?" He stepped in front of him and took a good look at the knight. He snapped his fingers and Killian disappeared too. "You could do so much better than him."

The Soulless

"Who the fuck are you?" I asked, swallowing down my boiling anger.

"Me?" He smiled, and it was evil. "I'm The Soulless."

I wanted to get away from him, but he was behind me in a split second, holding onto me, breathing heavily on my neck.

"Don't be afraid, Sam. I would prefer it if I wouldn't have to kill you, but our fight is inevitable in the long run." There was a hunger in his touch, one that intoxicated me, but I had one card against him.

"By the riverside," I managed to get out, "was that your brother?"

He stopped. He was holding onto me still and I could feel his cool breath on the small of my nape.

"Foolish girl."

Then I felt his hands, too tight on the sides of my face, attempt to snap my neck.

I woke up, but I wasn't sure if I really had. I looked around, but as I tried to sit up, crippling pain shot through my whole body.

I was awake. I was no longer in the dream. Was he telling the truth? Was he really the Soulless? I could still feel his touch all over my body; I hated myself for freezing in his presence. I forced myself onto my side, the pain unbearable. From there, I managed to force myself up into a sitting position. There was a fire crackling beside me, and beside that, a big black wolf looking at me, but no sign of the man and his daughters, or my friends. I tried to call out, but my throat was so dry that all that came out was a quiet rasp. I saw the horses, and to my relief, Martha. I was in a cave. When the realisation hit me, I was able to calm myself a bit more. I didn't want to wake up in the Handor city again.

It took great willpower to stand up from the ground. I slowly turned around and I finally saw two of my friends; Vendal was holding Neyra tightly, the two of them fast asleep and curled up by the fire, which meant that Killian was probably outside guarding the cave entrance. I took a shaky step and almost crumbled down back on the ground, but I was able to hold myself. Very slowly I made my way towards the cave's entrance where the moonlight shone through.

I was right.

Killian was sitting outside on a log. His leg in a nervous shake, fidgeting his fingers and an uneasiness in his posture. I didn't know if I should call out to him, or quietly approach, but in the end I didn't have to do anything. It was like he felt my presence. He turned around and his mouth fell open. I tried to gesture a small wave towards him but my strength was gone. Killian stood up slowly from the log, staring at me like he was seeing a ghost. He walked towards me and stopped only a few feet away. Tears were glittering in his eyes. I smiled at him and through a bit of struggle I was able to mutter:

"Hi."

My voice was shaky, barely audible. A sigh of relief left his mouth. He reached out a hand, allowing his cold fingers to touch my face. It felt like a test, like he couldn't believe that I was actually there. He took the last step closing the distance between us. I wiped his tears from his face.

And then he leaned down to me and kissed me on the lips.

I felt the immeasurable desire that was in him. His lips felt almost hot as he breathed more and more kisses onto mine. The hunger that was hidden in him appeared in that moment. My whole body trembled at his touch. But then he leaned away from me, ending that wonderful minute, or perhaps second, that I had longed for deep inside. He was searching my face to see if I was alright.

"I'm sorry," he whispered, but before he could pull his hand away from my face, I grabbed it. He pulled me against his chest, planting a long kiss on my forehead. "I am so glad you are here."

"Me too." I looked up at him; he was unbearably beautiful in the moonlight. "How long was I out?"

"Ten unbearable days."

I felt my legs tremble and he must have felt it too, because with one quick movement I was up in his arms. I rolled my eyes, playfully.

"I can walk, you know."

"At least give me a chance to play the role of a gentleman." He smiled and I did too.

"I kind of liked the man who decided to kiss me before asking first."

"Is that so?" He said, amused, as we began to step back into the cave, but I put my hand on his chest. He stopped.

"Can we stay outside for a bit longer?" I looked up at him longingly - I needed the air on my face. He just nodded.

We settled down under a large tree not too far from the cave. It was a warm night, with a dense humidity in the air around us. Everything seemed peaceful. Killian, on the other hand, was on edge. I could feel how his whole body had tensed up as he sat down next to me, his jaw clenched tight, his eyes darting every direction. I grabbed his hand and he jumped like he wasn't aware that I was right next to him. But when he looked at me, he calmed down and it made my heart sing to see his beautiful smile again. He gently touched my chin and pulled me closer to himself. He kissed me softly first, but when I didn't pull back, that hunger rose up in him again. His fingers were around my neck as he turned his full body towards me and his other hand found his way on my waist, pulling me closer. He was taking heavy breaths that became more rapid as his kisses grew more passionate. I placed my hand on his shoulder and he stopped. He pulled away a little, our foreheads still touched together.

"Forgive me, Sam. I've waited for this for a long time," he explained between two heaving breaths. I kissed the side of his mouth.

"Why did you?" I whispered back. He leaned back a little, his face again riddled with guilt. I watched him, curiously. "Why did you wait for this long, Killian?"

"Remember what I told you, with Vendal?"

"You mean the dreams?"

"Yes."

He slipped his hand down my left arm until our palms met. He closed his fingers on mine and told me everything.

"I just didn't want to hurt you, Sam. Knowing how I already did makes me sick to my stomach."

"So you… pushed away your feelings for me. To protect me or to protect yourself?" He tensed up again.

"A bit of both, I think." He looked at me again, resting his eyes on my lips first and then on my collarbones. "When you didn't wake up, I was mortified. Just the thought of losing you made me nearly lose my mind. All I could think about was how big of a fool I was for not telling you how I felt."

"Well, I think you've told me now." I smiled.

I wasn't angry with him at all; I understood what battle he was going through. It was the same kind I had to fight every single day. The self-doubt, the overthinking. I had to try really hard to follow what Felnard said before we said our goodbyes.

"It is not unrequited at all."

He pushed my hair behind my ear. "You don't know how much that means, Sam." I embraced him, resting my head on his chest.

"Your heart beats very fast."

"I wonder why." His laugh was so heartfelt I couldn't believe it was coming from the same Killian I knew.

"So you had naughty dreams about me?" I looked up at him, trying to tease. I knew I'd surprised him with my upfront question, but he leaned next to my ear and whispered, his warm breath tickling me:

"I will show you soon what kind of dreams I had."

I felt like my whole body got lit on fire. All I could do was laugh, but then he didn't pull back - he kissed my neck instead. I let out a small moan, that gave him even more courage. His lips were on my collarbones while his hands were discovering other parts of my body. I stopped him. It was definitely something I didn't want to happen in the woods plus my body was still aching all over in a way that was not pleasant. "I got carried away, I'm-"

I put my finger on his mouth. "Don't you dare say sorry again. Not for this. I just woke up, that's all. I need some time."

"Should we go back?"

His tone had changed in the blink of an eye. He was once again that worried, overcomplicating knight I knew all too well.

"A little warmth wouldn't hurt."

When we arrived back a panicking Neyra welcomed us. She came running out of the cave with Vendal at her heels. When they saw us, the Elf immediately started crying and ran straight to me, closing me in a tight embrace. She kissed my cheeks so many times that they became numb. We were all laughing.

The Druid was more professional. He shook my hand and then only after that he decided to hug the air out of my lungs. I was so happy to see them. Neyra gave me and Killian her usual "I know what's going on" look, which we promptly ignored, and we all headed back to the cave.

Inside, there were ten other wolves sitting on the rocks, and the black one was waiting patiently by the fire. The horses - and poor Martha - were nervously neighing. I walked up to the alpha. He placed his head under my open palm and I heard a voice in my head:

We'll always be here.

I looked into those big yellow eyes as I pulled my hand away. I gave him a small nod - my own little thank you. The wolf howled and as one, the pack ran out of the cave.

We sat around the fire as they told me everything that happened after I fell unconscious. When Vendal shared his worry about the Soulless, my heart was up in my throat as the images from my dreams flooded back to my mind. I had no other choice but to tell them everything.

"That's it." Vendal stood up abruptly once I was finished, causing a bit of a disturbance among the poor animals. He stepped in front of me. "Stand up!"

"What's... happening?" I asked and I saw the confusion on the others' faces as well, but I did as he said.

"I wanted to do this before, but when the person is unconscious..." He mumbled, shaking his head. He was talking mostly to himself as he positioned me in front of him, hands on each of my arms, holding me steady. He looked me dead in the eye as he said:

"Trust me, please."

I nodded my consent. He touched my forehead and it felt like lightning struck me. Everything went completely white for a second and when I was able to open my eyes again, I felt someone's hand on my face.

"She's okay," I heard Vendal say in a raised voice and as I looked behind Neyra I saw Killian standing merely inches away from him.

"Killian-" I said as Neyra helped me sit up. "I'm fine."

"Told you." Ven crossed his arms in front of his chest and shook his head in disapproval.

"What did you do to me?" I asked, still feeling a bit of pain in my forehead.

"It's protection magic. If I did it right, the Soulless won't be able to get into your dreams anymore." We all looked at him.

"If you did it right?" Killian raised one of his eyebrows.

"Well, I've never had to do it before." Vendal shrugged like it was no big deal. "But between the massacre that these two discovered and your dreams... Sam, our mission has become more urgent than it was before."

His words were grim and quickly changed the atmosphere in the cave around us. I watched as worry gripped all of them in different ways.

"Then we'll just have to get through this. And we will, I know we will."

My smile came easily, because for the first time, I believed in us full-heartedly. I knew that no matter what, we'd get through every obstacle like we did before. I was with my friends and that was all that mattered to me.

After a bit more small talk, the Druid decided to take the next watch while Neyra retreated to their place to sleep. I had my head against Killian's shoulder while we both just watched the fire dancing.

After a short while, he kissed my head and whispered, "I'll let you sleep."

As he was about to stand up I grabbed hold of his hand. He looked back at me and I didn't have to say a word in order for him to understand me. He laid on his back as I placed my head on his chest, wrapping my arms around him.

"Good night, Sam."

"Good night, Killian."

"CUTTER"

The Kingdom of the Giants, located West of Irkaban. Though lying in ruins, a few chunky-stone buildings stood the test of time. Although they had already been grown over by the plant life, the constructs perfectly showed the clean, modest conditions their owners once lived in. On the ground before the Kingdom several fallen skeletons lay, giving the place a terrifying aura. The ribs of the twenty-foot-tall titans rose ominously out of the grass. The jaw of one of the skulls was missing, but his eye sockets stared dangerously at those arriving.

Smarter people avoided the ruins. Legends had sprung up all over the land of the Broken Ground, that at night the restless souls of the Giants returned to walk the streets of their former city again. No more news came from the many people who still attempted to venture into their cursed land.

Menacing lights shone through the walls one night. I flew above on my griffon as three of my horsemen arrived, dragging thirty girls in snow-white clothes behind them. Their crying, anxious wailing filled the silence of the night. Passing through the old gate, following a few turns, they reached an empty stone square with a huge fire in the middle. Around it stood three dozen men, laughing, fighting, drinking. On the other side of the fire, a stone staircase rose, and on top of it stood a shattered grey stone throne. A figure shrouded in darkness occupied it. His body was covered in a long black dress, its barge spread out long on the stairs, reaching almost to the bottom. His alabaster hands ended in sharp black nails.

As soon as the three riders arrived, he ascended. Everyone immediately fell silent, turning as one to face him. Only the pounding of the horses' hooves still sounded.

The man stepped out into the light. His long, blond hair lay flat on his head; Elven ears ended in steel claws. The blood-red glow of his eyes mesmerized anyone who looked into them. There was an infinitely calm yet elegant smile on his face.

The riders stopped in front of the stairs. The chained women were organized into a group behind them, but they did not cry - they just hugged each other, desperately trying to hold some form of dignity as if we hadn't taken it already. I landed my griffon at the bottom of the stairs. I had bandages over my shoulders covering up the claw marks of the beast.

"My faithful subjects." He raised both hands high, turning his face to the sky. "We are approaching our goal day by day. To see how gracious Lord I am, I have brought you a present for the night." He lowered his hand slowly, turning his attention to the soldiers with a smile. The loud cheers of the men and the screams of the women mingled. The three men descended from their horses' backs and then, one by one, began to tear off the women's clothes.

"The charms of these women should give you renewed strength to fight."

The man walked down the stairs elegantly, stepping directly in front of the women. An otherworldly smile slid across his face as he caressed one of the women's uncovered breasts. They were all already watching him in fear. As he looked up, his eyes flashed.

"And you, ladies, the precious treasures of this Earth… will do everything, as these men desire. You will not resist, you will receive your masculine gift with pleasure, as if your own husbands, your love, embraced you."

The last crying voice was lost in the night. The chains were removed. The women mingled with the men enchanted, but as soon as body reached body, laughter and pleasure filled the space. The man waved his head at me and I followed him to the throne.

"Cutter." I fell on my knees.

"My lord…" I muttered.

"I see they didn't play around with you," he pointed at my wounded shoulders.

"You were right, my lord, that bitch was some kind of Druid…"

"Did all of them escape your captivity?" He asked as he sat back on his throne. I looked up at him in fear. I nodded moderately and he considered me carefully. "Why should I keep you alive?"

"I'm not making more mistakes, I promise, my lord."

"So you promise?" The man's blood-curdling voice rumbled. I shuddered. "This is not just a game. When I accepted you into my service, you said you and your team are the best. And now you're kneeling before me defeated, wounded…"

"My Lord, I'm so-"

"Quiet!" he yelled. Everyone stopped for a moment, staring back at him.

They didn't return to their time with each other until he let them with a simple nod. He knelt down, getting inches away from my face.

"You'll get another chance, but the next time you try to come back without the Destroyer, you better not come back at all." I got up from the ground and bowed gratefully to the man. He turned away from me as he said, "bring the women."

"Yes, my lord."

I tried to find my way among the clinging bodies, some gently embracing the women, others hard. The sounds of pleasure traversed the place, adorned with laughter. I joined a larger group where several people at once shared the pleasures of the body. I grabbed two girls by their hair, pulling them away from the soldiers. They screamed, but I didn't care, dragging them back to the stairs by their thick braids where I pushed them to the ground. I turned, caught a glimpse of one of the soldiers whose ornate black hair fluttered wildly down his back as he moved up and down in one of the women. I tore him out of the act and dragged the woman next to the other two.

I led them up the stairs, and they also fell to their knees before the great Lord. I walked over to the girl on the right side, cutting her throat in a single motion. The Lord threw himself at her, sucking the blood out of her and a healthy colour rose to his skin. I wanted to cut the neck of the next girl, but the Lord caught my hand. He wiped his mouth and stood up. The scar disappeared from his neck, his face as if rejuvenated.

"Bleed the remaining two."

He licked his fingers one by one. I nodded, led the two women away accompanied by my men, and led the victims to the poles that were set up on the left side of the square. My men hung them by their legs, pushed two cauldrons under them, then cut through their throats. They did not scream, for they could serve their Master with their blood. I hurried back to my lord.

"What else can I do?"

"Leave!" He screamed again, and I bowed deeply. "I have to get the Grabodan's message before the Destroyer, do you understand? Do whatever you need to bring it to me before they unravel the secret."

"I'll be on their trail, Master." The Elf leaned back contentedly, burying himself in the darkness.

Behind the throne, the huge head of the dark green dragon rose.

"Enjoy," my Master said, and the dragon grabbed the dead girl's ankle between his sharp teeth and then snuggled back into the darkness.

CHAPTER 13
THE WAY OF THE DRUIDS

"SAM"

We allowed ourselves a two-day rest in the cave before we got back on the road again. The mood amongst us had improved considerably in spite of all the crazy things we'd gone through. Vendal's old spirit returned and he told us story after story about how he and his uncle got into trouble by playing their childish games on the Masters. As it turned out, Felnard himself was a Master for a long time; he left the Academy after Ven did. According to the young Druid, his uncle was the most popular amongst the students because he always brought fun with him, which, naturally, made the more serious men in faculty quite mad from time to time. Apparently, the Heron family motto was that some people needed to learn how to have fun.

When Ven wasn't talking, Neyra usually broke out in song which meant that we never had a quiet moment on our journey to Irkaban. Even as we rode past the Dark Forest we didn't feel any of its infamous effects on ourselves.

Killian took the chance to be alone with me every time we stopped for the night, which made me even happier. We collected sticks together for the fire; he took me on hunting when our supplies ran short (or when Neyra was complaining that she wanted fresh meat), but sometimes he just simply took me away from our friends to steal a kiss. He was a changed man - the man who was always in there, buried deep under his worries, had risen to the surface to be with me.

It was our fifth day travelling when we arrived in Hilly. It was the bordertown of the Human land and the first sign that we were getting close to our destination. It was a far grimmer place than the ones we'd been in before; everything felt grey, most of the houses were in bad shape - almost all needing repairs on their wooden roofs or the whole brick structure itself. There were barely any people out on the muddy streets and those who we were gave us dirty looks. It was a gut punch to see the living conditions. We didn't dare to make a stop in the town's inn, which looked like it could crumble in itself.

Instead, we only stopped when we reached Lake Silhoue. It was named after the Goddess of Women, who was considered to be the creator and protector of every woman on The Broken Ground. As far as I knew every Kingdom was worshiping her. I'd never been involved with faith or belief so I knew very little about the Gods and Goddesses.

The mountains of Irkaban were another two days' travel from the lake so we set up camp on the edge of the forest, staying close to the water. Neyra and Killian took the chance to practice in the daylight and left pretty early on.

"What can break a twig?" asked Vendal as we settled on the ground.

"Well, if we step on it, if it's too old. If-"

"You pick it up and break it." Vendal picked up a twig and broke it in half. "How will YOU be able to break it using your mind?"

"Because," I thought a little, I didn't want to say anything nonsensical. "I understand it?"

"Can the trees be understood?" Vendal asked back, making me completely insecure. He stared back at my blank face for a long time before he finally smiled.

"Of course they can be, not the way I understand you when I listen to your story. A tree can't talk the way we do to each other, but if you pay close attention, you can see its whole story in it."

"Really?"

"Trees grow out of the ground. They experience great storms, animals live on them, around them - they are part of our history without ever saying a word. They are alive, just like us." Vendal put a twig in my hand. "Come on! Listen to its story."

I wanted to make an objection, but quickly remembered that it was better not to speak. I focused my attention on the twig. Suddenly I noticed that I could no longer hear Vendal's breathing or the sound of Neyra's mad carving in the distance. I could only see the twig in front of me, which whispered softly. It broke off his trunk under the weight of a large crow and landed on the ground where it was climbed by worms and beetles, picked up and thrown by humans. The pieces inside crackled as it whispered. Another voice seemed to say to me "I'm hungry, feed me!" Unexpectedly, a small flame burst through it. In horror, I threw the twig to the ground. I looked up at Vendal, behind whom Killian and Neyra stood, though I had no idea when they got there. They all seemed proud and satisfied.

"Nice work, you're starting to learn very quickly." The Druid said, nodding approvingly.

"I heard the fire," I replied, and Vendal laughed out loud. I wasn't sure if what I said was that funny.

"You may not even need me! I think you're starting to understand what magic is all about." I wasn't sure I was, but it was kind nonetheless.

"Nice work, Sam!" Neyra smiled, kindly.

"Now we don't have to be afraid of any bandits," Killian winked and I blushed. It became an instant reaction no matter what he did.

"Do you want to do more?" Vendal asked.

"Let's do it."

We practiced for a long time, and I tried to do everything as Vendal instructed. After a while, there was no problem with understanding, but rather with what to do with my newly discovered power. In the beginning I could only light everything on fire as the fire was constantly starving. Vendal reassured me that at first he had the same experience, as fire was the strongest element of the four great ones. This was then debated, as I argued with great conviction that the most important element was air and none of the others were as useful. Our long battle of words was stopped by dinner. Neyra made stew from fish and we ate in silence, only our Elf friend's humming filled the air from time to time. It warmed me to realise the quiet didn't feel awkward between us.

When we finished, Vendal stood up and held out his hand towards Neyra, she took it and they left, laughing like kids do when they are up to no good. Soon, their voices faded into the sounds of the forest.

I knew exactly why they left. We were stuck together all the time and they didn't exactly have a chance to enjoy each other's company on a more passionate level since we left behind Lendala. The realisation hit me as I felt Killian's gaze on me. My nerves got the better of me and I grabbed our small wooden plates, leaving without a word.

I didn't stop until I reached the lake. I started washing them without really paying attention to what I was doing. The pull I felt towards Killian had become different ever since he kissed me. I desperately wanted more, but at the same time I was terrified of the thought itself. I avoided a man's touch my whole life, not because I didn't long for it, but my only experience with it came from abuse - that wasn't successful, but the attempt was still there.

"Are you okay?"

I quickly glanced back to Killian. He just stood there all confused by my strange behaviour. I didn't even hear him approach.

"Yes, I just wanted to… clean these." I showed him the plates and he started laughing. He sat down beside me, I looked at his grin and I felt even more foolish than before.

"Hey… you know it's alright, Sam. Sure, I would love to enjoy your company on a different level too, but I can wait." He leaned a bit closer, taking one of the plates from my hands and washing it himself. "And if you decide you never want to, that's okay too. My feelings for you aren't bound up in whether or not that happens between us. Besides, just because they can't stop for a second doesn't mean that's the normal thing to do." I pushed him a little with my shoulder.

"I'm just scared, you know," I said aloud without thinking.

"That's normal. I was scared before my first time too." I looked at him mortified. Did Neyra tell him? I suddenly felt ashamed and incredibly angry at the same time.

"How did you know?"

"Just from watching you, I made a guess. I'm a good observer."

"You can shake hands with Neyra."

I buried my red face into my hands. It wasn't normal for women my age to be alone and not having been touched by someone. Fairies, for example - if they didn't have their first night before their 25th birthday, they were considered cursed and they were often outcast from their families.

"You have nothing to be ashamed of."

He kissed my shoulder and then wrapped his fingers around my wrists to pull them away from my face. "There she is," he whispered. His beautiful smile always had a strange effect on me.

"I'll wait for you. Okay?"

I nodded. He pulled me closer and closed me in an embrace. I kissed his neck gently, then his cheek and finally his lips. That fiery passion that always appeared in him was there in an instant. His right hand was deep in my hair, while his left slowly made its way down my side. He parted his lips slightly and his tongue soon intertwined with mine sending shivers down my spine. Our breaths grew heavier when my mind started screaming to stop. I gently pulled away and I could feel the desire in his hands resting on my back.

"Should we-" I couldn't stand his longing stare so I looked down on his lips, "go back?"

"If you want to. Or we could just sit here for a bit longer." His smile appeared again, I put my hand on his chest, feeling his heartbeat under my palm. I closed my eyes and suddenly I could hear his voice:

I want you to be mine.

"What did you just say?" I asked. Something... his voice didn't sound right.

"I said that we could just sit here for a bit longer."

"No, after that." He looked me in the eyes.

"I didn't say anything," he replied, surprised. I looked around us but there was clearly no sign of anybody else. "Are you okay?"

"Yes, yeah. Sorry. I think I'm just tired from practicing all day."

He nodded, but I couldn't shake the feeling that I heard his voice in my head. I quickly kissed the tip of his nose and his soft chuckle calmed me down too.

When we got back to the camp there was no sign that our friends had returned yet. I laid down on my blanket and stretched out as much as I could. I was tired so another dreamless sleep quickly took me away from reality.

The next day we were on the road again.

"I have a question."

"I'm listening," Vendal said. He was in a very cheerful mood. When they arrived back the previous night I woke up to their laughter.

"I can tame the animals, right? Can a person be controlled?" Vendal looked back at me a little disapprovingly.

"Why would you want to influence a person?"

"I mean," I knew it was stupid of me to even ask, but I couldn't get out of it, "if you don't want to pay a full amount for something, then-"

"Controlling people is the same dark magic as when you do something out of anger."

"And what about love?"

"What about it?"

"Well, can you get someone to love you with magic?" He looked back at me again, more and more suspiciously.

"Sam, love, hate and all the emotional connections we make during our life - these are all ancient things you can't influence, even if you really want to. Someone either loves you or not. It is that simple. Although we know of a case where someone managed to make someone fall in love with him, he soon realized that he had created an empty-headed being that followed him everywhere but felt nothing."

I nodded in agreement. "And nobody wants that."

"Certainly not." Vendal paused for a moment before speaking again. "But what you can do is read the minds of others." Even Killian and Neyra raised their heads, which made me realise they'd been listening the whole time.

"Really?" The memory from the previous night came crawling back to me. Could I have...?

"Yes, but Felnard says it's the hardest magic. The way an animal thinks is simpler than we do, therefore it's easier to get into its head. But a Human, an Elf, or any other kind of walking, talking race, is a far more complex being with a thousand thoughts." Vendal glanced back at Neyra. "And there are those who you don't have to try and read their minds, because what's in their heart is in their mouth too."

"As it should be," Neyra said proudly.

The conversation dropped after that. After a bit more than a day's worth of travelling, we laid eyes on the garrison that was the last stop before entering the mountain pass that led into Irkaban. The settlement had a wooden wall around it and watchtowers facing the main road with two Guards standing in front of the gate, big spears in their hands. As soon as we got closer, at least twenty archers rose up behind the walls, ready to fire.

"State your business," a strong voice called out to us. The recognition on Killian's face told us that we didn't have anything to worry about.

"Conor, is that you?" he called back. The huge gates opened just enough so a man could walk out of them. He wore completely black armour with a dark green cape. His helmet was under his right arm, long light brown hair was braided on both sides of his head, and a clean-shaven boyish face and big blue eyes which were squinting at Killian over the distance.

"Do I dare believe my eyes? Is that you Killian?"

He started walking towards us, as he was looking to see who arrived at his gates. As soon as he saw me a weird smile appeared on his face.

"It's good to see you old friend," said Killian as he got down from his horse. He shook Conor's hand, who annoyingly kept looking back at me. The archers on top of the walls lowered their weapons as soon as their leader signalled them. "We are on our way to Irakaban. Will you let us through?"

"Only if you stay for dinner and a night's rest; the mountain pass is not safe to travel through at night."

"It sure would be nice to sleep in an actual bed for once," said Vendal and we all nodded in agreement.

"Who are your friends?" Conor asked as we got off our horses and led them behind the garrison's wooden walls.

It was a much bigger area than I expected. Single large wooden barracks stood on both sides as we entered, with a bigger building in the middle that was much nicer than anything else in the enclosed area. It was built out of red stone and was the perfect copy of a Lord's mansion.

After the Elves and Fairies forbade the choosing of a new King for the Humans, different Houses took control over the new Kingdom. The Lords were the rulers of the three different regions in Irkaban: Malon gave home to the farmers at the bottom of the Mountain, ruled by Lord Gelart Molden. Haelion, where the richer people found a home, belonged to Lord Kell Arden. Elben, the home of the army, belonged to Lord General Olwen Han, who was the descendent of Grand Admiral Silen Han, the Human's hero during the Great War. The mansions of the Lords always stood in the middle of the major cities and were made from the most elegant red stone that the Mountain had to offer, built in a hexagonal shape with six towers looking down at the people they were guarding. The building that stood inside the garrison was the same shape without the towers.

A few soldiers came over to us and took away our horses so we were face to face with Conor, who was even more handsome up close and he clearly knew it.

"Conor, may I introduce Vendal Heron, Druid -"

Conor shook his hand and patted his shoulder, which clearly didn't impress our friend too much.

"- Neyra Lin -"

The second handshake didn't come as willingly, but Conor did what was expected of him, even though he couldn't hide his disgust at seeing an Elf.

"- and Samantha Tanan."

As he turned to me, that weird smile returned to his face. He grabbed my hand and planted a long kiss on top of it while looking straight into my eyes making me utterly uncomfortable. I saw the flash of jealousy run through

Killian's face during the awkward moment.

"My absolute pleasure," said Conor, still looking at me, before turning to everyone else, "to welcome you all. I am Conor Arden, son of Lord Kell Arden and the Commander of this outpost."

That explained the shape of the building.

As we stepped into his fancy house the difference was astonishing. Beautiful white walls, decorated with the paintings that showcased the whole Arden family. Five doors opened into different rooms from the main hall and all of them had a soldier standing guard in front of them. We followed Conor through the biggest door right in front of us. It led to the dining area where a circular table stood in the middle with ten chairs around it; all of them were crafted from willowtree, I could tell from the peculiar colour. Silver plates and cutlery were already set up for dinner. A servant appeared - a scrawny young boy, who couldn't have been older than fourteen.

"Set the table for four more people, boy." Conor didn't even look at him, the servant bowed deeply and left. "How long have you been travelling my friends?" He continued, gesturing towards the chairs, taking a seat in one that looked like a throne. Killian sat on his left, while Vendal took the right side and we sat with Neyra next to them.

"Months now. We're visiting friends and family." said Killian quickly, before Vendal could say anything. Neyra, Vendal and I caught each other's eye - the lie he came up with didn't make much sense and we didn't know why he did it. Did he not trust his friend?

"How nice," Conor smiled. "Who are you visiting here?" I saw the hesitation in Killian so I quickly joined in on the conversation.

"My friend, Polly Winigham. She is an excellent dressmaker."

"Oh, the widow of Baron Charles Winigham?" Baron? Polly never mentioned that they were a Noble family. I nodded. Conor kept his eyes on me. "She didn't announce any visitors."

"It's a surprise," I quickly added. "It's been a long time since we've seen each other."

"How kind."

There was an edge to his voice that made the hairs on my neck stand. I didn't like him at all and I definitely didn't like the way he was looking at me. I wasn't the only one.

"I will give you an escort to have safe passage to her house." More like he wanted to keep an eye on us. The servant boy came back, putting down the plates and cutlery in front of us. Conor took a sip of his wine before continuing.

"Killian and I used to serve in the Elven Army, you know. Though he clearly achieved more there than I did."

"Well, if you'd stayed I wouldn't have had a chance to reach the heights I did."

Killian's whole demeanour had changed. They no longer seemed like friends; they sounded like enemies. The real blow was struck with Killian's next question:

"How's Thana?"

Conor's face lost all its colour. Vendal's eyes widened and it looked like it was only myself and Neyra who didn't understand what was going on between the two men.

"She left. A few months ago." Conor cleared his throat. He couldn't keep Killian's eye anymore.

"Who's Thana?" Neyra asked the question that was in my mind too.

"She was Killian's bride-"

"And then yours."

Killian kept his eyes on Conor but under the table he squeezed my hand. I felt Neyra looking at me while Vendal was just fidgeting with his fingers, all the while I processed the reality of this situation: we weren't allowed in because of the respect these two men had for each other, but more because the guilt that was probably eating Conor up. They might have been friends once, but that was no longer the case.

"I'm sorry to hear that she left," Killian continued.

"It is what it is, old friend."

Conor snapped his fingers twice and five servants came out through the door that was behind his chair. They brought the most wonderful banquet out for us - roasted turkey, freshly baked bread, baked potatoes, salads and a big bowl of stew. They put everything down in the middle and bowed to Conor before leaving. Conor then stood up and carved the turkey, handing it out in such a way where the men got the better pieces just like in every Human household. As soon as he put down the last cut on Neyra's plate - the neck of the bird that barely had any meat on - both of the men swapped their plates with us. Conor didn't say a word, but his disapproval was clearly reflected on his face.

"Enjoy," he muttered, and so we did.

Neyra was a good cook, but eating stew or fish all the time had gotten a bit boring throughout the days we spent travelling. We were all very hungry, and the food was incredible.

As I was eating, suddenly I heard a voice.

I wonder what her screams sound like.

"What?" I looked up and everyone seemed confused. "Did one of you say something?"

"No one said a word, my dear."

I looked at Killian in disbelief - he'd never called me that before. As I saw Conor's expression change, I understood why he'd done it. I pulled my hand back from him; I didn't want to be a pawn in their stupid fight for dominance.

We all continued eating when I heard the creepy voice again:

I already took one woman from him; this one won't be a challenge either.

I looked straight to Conor who winked at me. I put down the knife and fork and stood up.

"I'm not hungry anymore."

"Billy," Conor snapped his fingers again and the young boy stepped up. "Take her to the guest quarters."

"Yes, ser."

I felt Killian's eyes on me, but I didn't care. I followed Billy and left the pretentious gathering behind.

He led me into a very spacious bedroom that had the same white walls as the hall, but light blue symbols were painted everywhere. Behind the big canopy bed was a small circular window looking out at one of the barracks. There was a small table and chair on the right-hand side with a candle on it. It felt quite empty, but the flowery smell that lingered in the room made it a bit better. Billy puffed up the pillows on the bed that were covered in the softest silk linen I'd ever touched.

"Anything else, my lady?" he asked, turning to me and I couldn't help but chuckle hearing the title he gave me. Even if I confused him with my behaviour, he didn't show it at all.

"Where's the washroom?"

"The house only has a bathtub, my lady. Would you like me to prepare a bath for you?"

Even though I was really tempted to say yes, I decided to stay in my room and manage a day without washing. Truthfully, I didn't feel safe enough here to put myself into such a vulnerable position.

He gave his leave and I laid down on the bed, closing my eyes. I couldn't get what Vendal said out of my head. Was it really possible that I was able to read minds? First with Killian and then Conor. I didn't think there was any other explanation to what I heard, unless of course I was slowly going crazy and had started imagining things. Wouldn't have been that big of a surprise after all of it, but I wasn't sure if I wanted to be able to read other people's minds. It definitely wasn't my business what they were thinking about. Maybe it was some kind of weird side effect of Vendal's magic that he'd put on me to provide dreamless nights. Either way, I didn't like it at all.

I must have fallen asleep because the next time I opened my eyes again it was already pitch-black outside. I sat up on the bed only to see Killian sitting by the table reading something by the candle light. As he heard me move around, he closed the book and came to the bed, sitting down on the other side.

"What happened at the table?" He asked without hesitation. I buried my face in my hands for a moment, wiping the sleep out of them.

"I don't know. I guess I was just tired."

"Don't lie to me Sam," he said, hurt creeping into the edges of his voice. I looked up from my hands to see him fully; he was drawing circles on the linen, concentrating on it like it was the hardest thing he had ever done.

"I think…" I tried to find the correct words, "that I might be hearing other people's thoughts." His finger froze in place and he slowly looked up at me. "I'm not sure, it's only happened three times so far."

"When we were at the lake, right?" he replied, and I nodded. "So what was I thinking?"

"Well, something along the lines that *you want me to be yours.*"

I put a little affectation on my voice as I repeated his words, and for the first time since I'd met him I saw Killian Fin blush. He laughed nervously.

"I might have thought that, yes." He cleared his throat. "So what did you hear at dinner?"

I really didn't want to say while we were still under Conor's roof, they already had problems, we definitely didn't need them to start fighting.

"Sam?"

"I think I heard Conor-" His face became stiff. Poor boy really had a hard time hiding his feelings. "And… it's better if I don't say."

"Was he… thinking something regarding you?" I nodded slowly. He almost jumped off of bed, but I was quicker and pulled him back down. Without even thinking I pushed him to his back and sat on his lap to keep him there.

"Please don't. I might be completely wrong. Maybe I just imagined things."

"So you fancy him?"

"No!" I yelled out a lot louder than I planned to and he started laughing.

"I'm just messing with you," he said through his chuckles. I crossed my arms.

"I don't want to read other people's minds."

"Then don't do it."

"Do you want to piss me off this badly?"

"Never, my dear."

There it was again. I froze. It sounded so weird coming from his mouth, but mostly because he was addressing me with it.

"He's not here, you don't have to call me that." I got off him but he grabbed my hand before I could get up.

"But I want to."

I felt a smile appearing in the corner of my mouth, but somehow I still felt incredibly uncomfortable. "Come." He opened his arms wide and I laid down next to him. "You should talk to Vendal about this."

"I will."

I was at the river again.

Panic took over me; I didn't want to see him again. I started running straight towards the water, but before I could reach it cold hands wrapped around my waist and started pulling me back, hard. The picturesque beauty of the river faded and I was in the dark. My breaths became heavy as the hands tightened around me. I fought as hard as I could, when I felt the kiss on my neck. I felt weak, my whole body trembled as the man slowly made his way up towards my face. I tried keeping my lips away from him but he forced me to face him.

It wasn't the Soulless. It was Killian.

I started laughing and turned to him, wrapping my hands around his neck. I let him kiss me but his lips slowly started to become cold. He was getting way too rough so I pushed him away only to have a silent scream leave my mouth. I fell backwards right into the river.

I was there again, in the cool water of the river. I saw the man walking towards me. He seemed even younger, wearing simple peasant clothes; his face had a brighter rosey colour and his eyes were blue. I looked down at myself - I was wearing the clothes of the woman whom I saw in my dreams previously.

"Give me your hand!" the man said, reaching out for me.

"No."

The words came out of my mouth but I wasn't the one actually talking. I tried to stand up, but the flow of the river was too strong. He was standing above me.

"Stop being stubborn!"

"Why did you kiss me? I chose your brother; it's time for you to accept that!"

"Oh, really?" An evil grin distorted his face. "Fine. I will send him after you."

His hands were around my neck in a second and he pushed me down under the water. I was trying to scratch him, punch him or kick him, but I couldn't fight him and the river at the same time.

"SAM!"

I was starting to feel dizzy.

"SAM!"

I felt multiple hands around my shoulders, shaking me. I opened my eyes and gasped for air as Killian, Neyra and Vendal looked back down at me.

"I'm awake. I'm awake…" I whispered.

"Was it him again?" asked Neyra, desperate but afraid to hear the answer. I shook my head as I sat up.

"It wasn't like before. I saw his memory again, I think."

"Or what he wants you to see." Vendal sighed, clearly disappointed in himself. I noticed that they were all dressed in their travelling clothes. Light had started to creep in the windows.

"I couldn't wake you up so I called them over," explained Killian as he saw my confused face. "Conor has his people ready so it is time for us to leave."

"Give me a few minutes to…" I looked down, the same clothes were on me, and I had nothing more with me. "I guess we can just go."

"Are you sure you're okay?" Neyra asked. Other than her worry, something was lurking in her expression.

"Yeah."

Conor kept his word and ten of his men escorted us through the mountain pass. The journey through the grey rocks wasn't anything spectacular, though it seemed even gloomier than it did when I left. Dark storm clouds were gathering above us as we got closer to Malon, a local farming settlement. It even started to rain which forced us to get off our mounts. We didn't go into Malon, though; instead, the soldiers took us up the rocky road that led to Haelion.

I used to live in Malon with my father so I didn't mind not seeing much of it. I did wonder if he was still alive or if the alcohol had finally killed him. Or someone else had.

By the time we reached the gates of Haelion the thunder had grown louder, and the horses were skittish. Thanks to the soldiers, the Guard didn't hold us up long.

As we entered the difference between the two regions was visible - every house was built into the rocks, they merged together where they were able to. It wasn't as glorious as the Elven or Fairy buildings, but it showed how smart Humans could be.

We didn't have to go far on the rocky road. The soldier who led us stopped at the second house on the left and knocked on the yellow wooden door. As it opened my heart skipped a beat.

Polly.

"Yes?" she asked suspiciously and I couldn't hold myself back.

"Polly!" I pushed through the men and as I arrived in front of her a wide smile appeared on her beautiful face.

"My dear girl.

CHAPTER 14
THE CELEBRATION OF LOVE

"KILLIAN"

Sam and Polly were inseparable. They had so much to talk about that we essentially never saw them.

After the soldiers were convinced we were telling the truth they retreated back to the garrison. Polly provided a room for everyone and welcomed us into her beautiful home as if we'd always known each other. A pleasant floral scent swung throughout the house; beautiful dresses were hung up everywhere - on the railing for the stairs, on the wall, even up on the ceiling. Polly had a really great sense when it came to clothes and interior design. Her house was full yet it felt empty. The dining room was so big that twenty people could easily fit in there to enjoy a gathering. The house had five bedrooms - she only used one of them, but kept all of them clean nonetheless. She didn't have any servants like other nobles, instead preferring to do everything herself. She cooked, cleaned, took care of the animals, and on top of all that she made the dresses too.

After two days of just resting and enjoying the delicious food Polly made, Vendal and I headed for the huge archive to ask for an old friend's help. Neyra – after wrapping a scarf around her ears, just to be safe – decided to have a look around in Haelion since she'd never seen it before. Sam stayed behind to help Polly some more; they had a lot more to talk about.

The Archive Building was home to all the relics, descriptions, and art from the Old Kingdoms. We were greeted by so many statues as we entered the huge marble hall that we could have easily gotten lost among them. The memories of great kings stood before us. It would have been a glorious moment, but the dusty smell that filled the place pulled us out of it quite quickly.

We made our way in and through, avoiding hundreds of piles of books that were lying around on the ground, eventually reaching the round table behind which sat a tiny little man.

Vendal couldn't believe his eyes when he realised he was looking at the sad face of an old Dwarf. As soon as the Dwarf saw me, however, his face lit up. He bounced off his chair, ran to me, and hugged my leg. Even though he looked ancient, he jumped up like a little buck. He giggled in his thin voice as I patted his back in welcome. I honestly didn't think he would recognise me - the last time we'd seen each other was when I was only just a boy.

"My dear friend, my dear friend!" He muttered, letting go of my leg. He glanced at Vendal. "And a Magic Bearer. An honour." He bowed respectfully.

In the old days, Dwarves respected Druids in the same way as if they were Kings. Every time the Druids visited them they held a feast that lasted for weeks.

"Dwarf, ser." Vendal bowed back. The man was stunned; to have a Magic Bearer bow his head in front of him? That had never happened before.

"Vendal Heron." He held out his hand and the Dwarf kissed it.

"Tidios Aldol, at your service," he stammered.

"We came for your help, old friend."

Tidios looked up at me from under his bushy eyebrows. He had grown his snow-white beard so large that it covered his mouth, meaning only his swollen cheeks and sparkling green eyes betrayed his smile. He'd aged so much since the last time I saw him. Before our parents sold us to the Elven slavers, Seán and I found safe haven beside Tidios. He looked after us, educated us and loved us like nobody else.

"Anything for you, Killian, you know that." He gestured toward the chairs, he himself getting back in his comfortable armchair. "Well?"

"We're heading up to the Grabodans' temple. We learned a lot from Leanne and from the Book of Sagar, but-"

Vendal hesitated. He looked around in the big hall afraid that someone might be listening even though it was only us in there.

"His book isn't finished."

"Well of course it is." Tidios chuckled. Vendal and I looked at each other, confused.

"What do you mean?"

"The pages are not empty. They were meant for the Destroyer."

I was even more confused by Tidios' words. How did he even know all this when – according to Vendal – the Druids themselves hadn't solved its mystery.

"How-?"

"It's written on the walls of his old house in Grabodan city."

"He had a house there?" Vendal had become incredulous. Nothing quite like a piece of new information to have you rethink everything you thought you knew.

"Of course. He spent his last few years with Crixus before he disappeared. He was the one who set up all the protection around the temple."

"Yes, about those-" Vendal said, clearly desperate to change the subject so he wouldn't feel like a fool anymore. I couldn't hide my smile. "Do you happen to know what tests await us up there?"

"I don't know about the tests," Tidios said, shaking his head but continued on. "It's just a legend, but if it is true then Crixus left behind a clue inside the temple that only the blood of the Destroyer would uncover."

My smile faded.

"Are you sure about that, Tidios?"

"It's just a legend my boy, but I wouldn't be surprised if it turned out to be true."

"Does the Destroyer have to sacrifice herself?" Vendal asked hesitantly, and as the Dwarf chuckled I knew my friend regretted his decision.

"Of course not. Well-" Tidios stopped, considering for a moment. "It wouldn't make much sense now, would it?"

"It just feels like a trap. I don't think that the Grabodans would ever come up with something like this. They were too noble to demand blood to reveal their secret." Vendal continued, thinking out loud, scratching at his scar.

"Don't forget, Magic Bearer; it was Sagar who set up the protection." Tidios' expression had changed; he was no longer smiling. "You are risking a dangerous journey by climbing the mountain," he warned us, voice intensely ominous.

"What are you talking about?" I asked. The Dwarf was a little insecure, looking at me and then Vendal not really knowing what to do. Vendal glared at me, so I stood up and crouched down in front of the old man so he could look me in the eye.

"Tidios," I started in a reassuring tone, "you know you can tell me anything, and Vendal will keep his mouth shut too."

Tidios sighed deeply. "They say there's a strange creature on the mountain," he swallowed hard, wiping his forehead in his nervousness. "Some kind of animal. No one has seen it yet. Old Gregoir was the only one to escape it but both of his cows were captured by the beast."

"Gregoir? The liar Gregoir?"

"Oh, you didn't see him, son. He was terrified. For days no one could pull a single word out of him, he just stared at the wall. When he finally spoke, all he said was 'death...'"

The air died in the room as silence took us. I sat back from Tidios, scratching at my chin, considering.

"Then we'll talk to this man," Vendal said, breaking the silence. He turned to look at me as he continued. "Whatever he says, we still have to go up the mountain."

It was agreed. We bade our thanks to Tidios and headed to the door. I shuddered a little as I found myself facing Neyra and Sam. They were both dressed up in what were clearly gifts from Polly; Neyra was wearing a golden yellow dress with orange coloured fire symbols on the skirt, while Sam had a beautiful black dress that was hugging her figure. I'd barely seen her in a dress - she always wore those too-big trousers and shirts.

She was gorgeous.

But clearly embarrassed by her own appearance, Sam started playing with the long sleeve of her dress. Neyra shot her a disapproving look. As she looked up at me, she blushed completely as I stared at her with my mouth open. When Vendal stepped out behind me he immediately started laughing.

"Sam, what's this ridiculous thing on you?" he asked. Neyra slapped his hand hard. "What now?"

"I think our Sam is very pretty," she replied disapprovingly, and the Druid glanced first at me and then at the increasingly embarrassed Sam.

"Well, I think she's much prettier when she's herself y'know? I mean, this dress doesn't even fit her- yikes!"

He raised his hands when the Elf tried to slap it again which resulted in Neyra hitting his side instead. I couldn't help but laugh at their absurd behaviour.

"Sorry for having an opinion!" yelled Vendal, fed up with how he was being treated by the woman he loved.

"You could be nicer sometimes, you dick!" Neyra snapped. "Sam do—" She stopped abruptly. "Where is she?" I looked back to where Sam was standing but she was no longer there.

"Great job you asshole!" I growled at Vendal and ran off the stairs, but I heard Neyra following me.

"Killian!" She yelled after me, but I didn't want to stop. There were ten different streets leading off the Archive's square and we had no idea which way Sam left. "Wait!"

"Neyra, we-" I turned to her and she slapped me so hard that I had to take a step back to keep my stability. Also, it hurt. "Why?"

"Why didn't you say something!? I am not the one who's allegedly in love with her and I have to protect her from my idiot lover?" She yelled so loud that people stopped to stare at us so I tried to gesture to her to keep her voice down.

"What has gotten into you?"

"She dressed up for you, you moron! Polly and I had to beg her to put on the dress because she was so insecure about how she would look." Neyra shook her head. "Why didn't you say something?"

I didn't answer. I wasn't sure why no words left my mouth. I looked back at Neyra, but she'd already turned her back on me and was on her way to Vendal, who stood at the bottom of the stairs still just rubbing his hand.

I ran towards the street that was closest to the Archive's stairs. The houses were differently built here; they resembled the narrow buildings of Allion, but definitely not the colours they used there. They had a washed-out brownish colour so in order to make them a bit prettier to look at, they were full of flowers. They hang from the windows, from the roofs, and they were planted in front of the doors in the street. The enormous flat ground that Haelion lay on gave them the ability to build up buildings. No wonder it belonged to the rich.

I arrived at a dead end so I turned back and tried the next street, then another, and another, until I decided to go where I was supposed to go and look for old Gregoir. I walked through the street from the Archive, feeling awful about the way I'd treated the situation with Sam. This new cobblestone street was much wider than the previous ones and it led to a smaller square that had a fountain in the middle.

And there she was.

I stopped. Sam was sitting on a bench by the fountain, throwing pebbles in the water. A few people walking behind her stared at her ears and gave her nasty looks, but she didn't care. I walked up to her.

"Fancy a stroll?"

She looked up at me and I realised why she looked different to me: Neyra put that red stuff on her lips as well. It was an Elvish obsession to look even more perfect than they already were, so they used different herbs and things to enhance their looks.

I gave her my best smile, bowing deeply.

"It would be my honour to walk with a beautiful lady like yourself."

She laughed and I took it as a win, but when I held my hand out to her she hesitated still. I made sure to look her in the eye when I spoke next:

"You look gorgeous."

"Did Neyra tell you to say that?" she asked in a quiet voice, trying to avoid my gaze.

"No," I replied, gesturing my hand to her again, and this time she accepted. "I'm just the idiot who couldn't say it when I saw you first."

She blushed, and smiled shyly - another win. That was my favourite smile of hers too; the way it lit up her face... Blessed Silhoue above, it was everything.

"Where are we strolling to, then?" She asked, her arm now hooked in mine.

"We're going to talk with old Gregoir. Just be prepared, he's famously crazy."

"What's another crazy thing on the list?" She finally looked at me with her ocean blue eyes that saw right into my soul.

"If you could know what I'm thinking right now."

"Probably something dirty."

"Excuse me, I think you're talking about yourself, or Neyra. I would nev-"

"You thought about ripping my dress off of me, which is flattering but Polly would probably kill you." She winked at me and I had a hard time keeping my composure.

"I hate that you can sometimes read my mind."

"I didn't," she smirked. "It was written all over your face." I couldn't help but laugh. "I guess I'm in a little trouble."

When we reached a crossroads, I stopped us. Shit.

"You don't remember which way to go next?"

"Not really, I'm not sure." I looked up at the sky, noting the sunset colours that had begun to paint across it. "It's not advisable to walk in this city in the dark."

"You have a sword and I have magic," she said, shrugging. I considered what she said, and she definitely wasn't wrong.

"Alright, then let's trust me to find the right direction on the first try."

Eventually we started to the right, walking down a narrow little street in complete silence, just listening to the sounds of the city surrounding us - the laughter from the inns and loud singing as a man confessed his love to his friend; the joyful cries of a child. But as we got further and further, the noise of the people subsided. When we reached the last houses on the street and found ourselves faced with a pinewood forest that grew over the side of the mountain, everything became silent around us. I spotted the small wooden house that lay near the trees - the only farming house in Haelion. Gregoir was given permission from Lord Arden to stay as his parents served King Herald.

We made our way over and knocked on his door. There was no answer for a while, but finally the door opened a crack and an old man looked out at us suspiciously. He was bald, extremely wrinkled and clearly half-blind.

"What do you want?" he asked in a hoarse voice.

"Ser Gregoir?" I wasn't sure that I was seeing Gregoir the Liar in front of me. He was famously good-looking back in the day, but that clearly changed.

"Yeah," the old man opened the door the rest of the way to take us in properly. "You come to hear about the monster?"

"Yes," we said at once, and Gregoir smiled humourlessly.

"I didn't tell anyone else anything about it - why should I say anything to you?" He measured us intently.

"Because we have to get up the mountain and it would be nice to know what we're up against."

Gregoir caught my shirt so unexpectedly that I didn't even have time to react. I reached for my sword, but when the old man started speaking he let go of me.

"There's only death waiting for you, boy. Death." His face distorted with fear, and his body started trembling.

"What is he talking about?" Sam whispered behind me.

"I saw... yes... I went after my cows... and... he just picked them up as if they were just feathers." He began to laugh and with that, backing back into the house and slammed the door.

"This was very scary," Sam said, not noticing that she was clinging to my arm. "You know how to show a girl a good time."

"It's a concern, that's for sure."

"Could we possibly find an easier way up to the Grabodan temple?" Sam asked as we headed back into the city. I didn't have a good answer; I only knew about the old path that every wayfarer seemed to use.

As we walked down the narrow street, she let go of my arm. We were once again surrounded by the noise of the city. When we reached the small square, we were in for quite a surprise. Garlands of flowers hung from each house and people in loose clothing that swung effortlessly, bounced around a fire that had been built in the middle of the square.

"What's going on?" I stopped a young man who hung a garland around my neck in response and hurried on.

The music, which at first we didn't even notice, suddenly accelerated and people began to scream at the top of their lungs. Sam was suddenly grabbed by two men and they dragged her away. I rushed right after them, but soon I was surrounded by a group of young women.

"Sam!" I shouted and saw the men lift her up high. I wanted to get away from the group that surrounded me, but suddenly they started throwing more flowers.

"Ladies-"

"It's a celebration of love! Let yourself go, soldier," one of them sang. I tried to keep an eye on Sam, who was put on the ground and they spread some strange cloak over her back.

"Come and dance with us!"

A woman with red hair pulled me quite close to the huge fire, which cut off my line of sight on Sam, but I saw unexpected familiar faces. Vendal lifted Neyra high, and she kissed him passionately while they laughed.

"Hey!" I yelled to them, and they both giggled as they hurried over. "Sam was taken away!"

"Who took her away?" Neyra asked, momentarily terrified.

"Some men dressed in masquerades." They both started laughing again, which pissed me off.

"It's a celebration of love, Killian," Neyra said, "and you both looked like mourners."

"Put me down!"

We turned around collectively to see Sam being lifted up by the men again. They put a flower crown on her head and then put her down right in front of us.

"What in Silhoue's name is going on here?"

"A celebration of love," Neyra pressed a kiss on her forehead. "We can relax a little." She grabbed Vendal's hand and they started dancing with the other people. Sam held a stern face, but I could see her warming to the sudden magic of it all. Still, she shuddered a little as she felt my hand on her waist.

"May we?" I asked, kissing her shoulder.

"I don't know how to dance."

"That makes two of us then," I said, pulling her closer and into the fray.

The music got even faster, permeating the whole space, and people adapted quickly. They danced more and more fiercely. Sam's laughter became heartfelt. I felt so good that I even forgot about the things that had happened to us and the ones that were probably still waiting for us. My gaze turned several times to other couples, who looked at each other with love, exchanged kisses and danced without care. Then I looked at Sam once more - she'd completely let herself go, which was a rarity for her.

Suddenly the people grabbed each other and the chain we formed was led through the small streets following the music until we reached the huge square in front of the Archive, where more people were waiting for us. The bonfire rose high, the buildings seemingly covered with more flowers than before. Musicians rushed to the top of the high stairs of the Archive and at least ten other people joined them. The music grew even louder. The bass of the drums, the flutes and the wonderful singing filled the place with the joy of life.

The city had literally come to life.

Neyra and Vendal soon escaped to one of the stairs from the dance to enjoy each other's company, and a few followed suit, yet the crowd seemed to only be getting bigger and bigger.

Men pulled their tops off thanks to the humid air. I had to do the same after a while and seeing Sam's eyes widen in surprise was already a good enough reason to do it. Drops of sweat rolled down my naked torso. My hair bounced up and down while I danced, and the more we danced the more it became wet. It bothered me at first but I quickly let it go.

I noticed Sam trying to run away, so I grabbed her waist and lifted her up in the air. I spun her around several times, but as I put her back down the music suddenly slowed down, a beautiful unearthly voice of a woman traversed the space. Vendal took Neyra in his arms and began to rock with her back and forth. I held onto Sam even tighter. The way she wrapped her hands around my neck made me incredibly happy.

I closed my eyes, letting the rhythm of the music guide our steps.

Finally, *finally*, bliss.

It was the sudden brightness that pulled me out of the moment. I let Sam pull away and looked up. Thousands of bright butterflies rose high above the crowd, but we weren't the only ones looking at the phenomenon in shock - everyone else was pointing at the sky. I glanced at Vendal, who winked at me with a smile.

"It's beautiful," I said. I felt her gaze while I watched the butterflies. "What miracles our little Druid knows."

"He must have done it for Neyra, she loves butterflies." I looked down to Sam as she lowered her head.

"Yes."

I tucked her hair behind her ears and she looked up at me again. The atmosphere, the lights - I found I wasn't afraid to say out loud how I felt.

"Sam, I-"

The butterflies suddenly stuttered. A shadow slid over us. The crowd became very loud as people began to guess what it might have been. They raised their heads to a loud scream, all eyes turned in the direction of the sound.

"RUN YOU FUCKING IDIOTS!" Gregoir rushed towards us waving his hand and yelling from the rupture of his throat. "DEATH HAS ARRIVED!"

And then it did.

The monster struck down out of nowhere. It took Gregoir in its claws and the man didn't even have time to scream for help. A dragon, dark green, its eyes glowing red, ripped Gregoir in two and threw him back to the ground. Panic struck as the people started running away in every direction causing chaos on the square.

Sam was the only one who ran straight to the giant.

"SAM!" I screamed after her as the dragon landed right in front of her. She reached out a hand but the beast roared up, causing Sam to crumble on the ground. Vendal sent a huge fireball towards the dragon but the animal flew up before the impact, flying back off into the night. I ran to Sam, picking her up from the ground. She opened her eyes, confused.

"Hey, you okay?"

"It was him. He was in the dragon's mind," she muttered.

"Who?" Neyra asked, still looking up at the sky nervously.

"The Soulless."

Then Sam lost consciousness.

We made our way back through the streets to Polly. It was amazingly strange that everyone disappeared in an instant, even though hundreds of people were dancing in the square a few minutes earlier. I could only think about how life had the worst sense of humour. The moment we allowed ourselves to let go a little, another horror hit us. But as I glanced at Sam in my arms, I knew that it didn't matter.

She woke up just before we reached Polly's house. When we stepped through the door she already knew about everything that had happened and worry sat on her face. She treated us like we were her children, bringing us tea and quickly started making hot soup to make sure that we had everything.

Vendal and Neyra went up to their room first, still shaken by the experience. We all agreed to not talk about it until the next day. Polly was next to leave, even though her worry for Sam was clear as day, but I told her that we were going to be fine.

The house became very quiet very quickly. Sam went upstairs while I stayed for a little while longer to check that all the doors and windows were closed.

When I made it upstairs, Sam was standing by the window. I walked over and took her hand gently, pulling it to my cheek and pressing a kiss on her palm.

"Good night," I whispered, looking deeply into her eyes, but before I could turn around, Sam kissed me. Our lips intertwined, handing over all the oppressed feeling that was lurking in them. I leaned away from her. I breathed a gentle kiss first on her forehead, cheek, and finally on her lips.

"Good night."

CHAPTER 15
THE GRABODAN TEMPLE

"SAM"

I woke up confused at first. I felt hands around me, but I didn't recognise the room. I looked to my side and as I saw Killian's peaceful face, I had to smile. He had his arms and legs wrapped around me, his warm breath tickled my shoulder. I closed my eyes, pinched myself and counted to three. When I opened them again, I found I was still in the room with Killian. I chuckled. The happiness I felt was something completely unknown.

I turned towards him as carefully as possible so as to not wake him up, but his smile appeared. He slowly opened his enchanting black eyes and looked at me.

"Good morning," he whispered, his voice dry from lack of use. I wanted to kiss his forehead, but he was quick, grabbed my face and pulled me into a passionate kiss.

"Thank you," he said.

"For what?" I asked, my eyes still closed, just enjoying the touch of his fingers on my skin.

"For choosing me." I opened my eyes to look at him, confused.

"I think I should be the one saying that." He shook his head.

"You still don't understand how special you are."

I wanted to answer him when we heard a loud knock on our door. I sighed, knowing our moment just ended. Killian sat up rubbing his eyes.

As soon as I sat up I became aware of my nightgown again. My shirt was laying right in front of the door, so with one swift move I pulled the blanket off of Killian and wrapped it around myself. I heard his soft chuckle as I tiptoed to the door. I opened it ajar just to find Vendal standing there.

"Tidios is here."

"Who?" I asked.

"We'll be down shortly, Ven." Killian yelled from behind me. As I was closing the door I saw that peculiar smile appear on the Druid's face. When I turned around Killian was already in his clothes.

"Are you gonna come down wrapped in a blanket?"

"No," I muttered. He smirked and as he strode by me he gave me a quick kiss.

"See you downstairs."

I didn't expect to see a Dwarf in Polly's dining room. The small man was sipping tea from one of the fancy cups Polly kept for the guests, while Neyra was helping my friend prepare breakfast and Vendal was deep in conversation with the Dwarf.

"Sam. This is Tidios Aldol, the local Archive's master." Killian came striding over, handing me a cup of tea. "Tidios, this is Sam Tanan."

"You're her, aren't you?" The Dwarf jumped down from the chair.

"I'm not su-"

"The Destroyer." I definitely wasn't ready for that. I took a quick glance at Polly who - thankfully - was deep in work. I forced a smile and nodded. "What an honour, Saviour."

"One title is more than enough."

I didn't want to be disrespectful, but I also couldn't get used to people calling me different names that sounded entirely foreign to my ear. What lay ahead was already too heavy to bear.

"Tidios," Vendal said, quickly inserting himself into the conversation, "is here because he found a way for us to get up to the temple without being eaten by a huge dragon."

"Really?" I was surprised how much the Dwarf knew about our quest, but didn't want to question anyone.

"It is through an old cave…" he got back on his chair, turning to the table where a map was laid out: a map of Irkaban. He pointed at the cave entrance which was only a few miles into the forest where Gregoir's farm was.

"This leads up to the Grabodan temple through the inside of the mountain."

"How are you so sure?" Killian asked. Tidios looked up at him and laughed.

"Because I already used it once."

"The things I find out about you, old friend." Killian smiled. The previous day's events had prevented us from talking about everything he and Vendal found out in the Archives, but his connection to Tidios was much more deeply rooted than I imagined.

"Did you think that I spent all my days in that old building?" Tidios had a huge grin on his face, and I felt I could feel his kindness shine through everything around him.

"It's perfectly carved out. There are flights of stairs leading up to a stone ledge halfway through where you can rest, and trust me you're gonna need it." He brushed through his long beard, gesturing with his other hand to another section of the map. "The exit of the cave is only a few miles away from the temple so you should have an easy way in there."

"This is a huge help, you beautiful Dwarf bastard." Vendal smacked Tidios' back hard and I saw a shy blush appear on the Dwarf's face.

"Tidios, would you like to stay for breakfast?" Polly and Neyra entered, putting down fresh bread, boiled eggs and bacon in front of us. The Dwarf nodded.

"You honour me, my lady."

And so we ate. Killian was in a better mood than he ever was before. I saw Neyra glancing at me with that "Know-It-All" smile sitting on her face, inquiring wordlessly. But I shook my head, making Neyra disappointed. I looked to Killian by my side, his smile never disappearing from his face as he talked and laughed with his old friend. I could barely take my eyes off of him. It made me immensely happy to see him in such a different light.

Was this what love felt like?

After breakfast we packed up our things, leaving the horses and Martha with Polly. My dear friend was smiling softly as she watched us put our bags on our backs, but I could see worry on her face too. Before we began to leave, I walked back to her and hugged her as tightly as I could. When I wanted to let go, she wouldn't let me, instead squeezing me tighter as she whispered in my ear so only I could hear her.

"You take care of yourself my dear, do you hear me?" There was an unmistakable sadness in her voice.

"We're going to be fine, Polly."

She tightened her hands around me one last time before letting me go. We pulled back to get a better look at each other, her eyes then darting behind me to where Killian was standing.

"I'm glad you've found someone who loves you." She looked back at me, tears glistening in her eyes.

"Me too."

I looked at my friends who were all ready to go and waiting for me.

"We'll be back soon Polly, I promise."

With one final squeeze on her arm, I turned and left, but I felt Polly's gaze on my back for a long time even after we left her house behind us.

We said our goodbyes to Tidios at the Archives and he made sure to remind us to take care of each other. From there, we headed for the mountain.

As we stood in front of the cave, we all felt a little clueless.

It all just *seemed* ominous, but we knew that if we'd have gone up the road carved into the mountain, danger awaited us. Eventually, Neyra took the lead and we followed her in, lighting our torches as we entered.

No one was expecting the sight.

The walls of the cave were covered with writing, deeply scratched into the stone - symbols of some kind of ancient language. We looked at Vendal, but the Druid looked as clueless as we were.

"I don't think this was done by smugglers…" Vendal said after a while.

"I don't think so either." Neyra nodded in agreement. However, unable to discern any meaning from the carvings, we agreed: nowhere to go but up. Killian closed our line.

The flight of stairs seemed endless as we walked. We got tired pretty quickly, the stuffiness of the air pushing down on us with full force was suffocating. It didn't help much that the heat of our torches was ten times stronger in the enclosed space. We were all starting to exclaim in between heavy breaths when we finally reached the end of the stairs. It led to a huge stone ledge that paved the way for another cave entrance. Vendal leaned wearily on the ledge and Neyra fell beside him. I leaned on my knees and took huge breaths to recover a little. Killian handled the climb relatively well. He wiped his forehead several times and gasped.

"I think we could rest here," Vendal announced.

"Couldn't we extinguish the torches? I am boiling in my own skin" Neyra fanned herself incessantly.

"Then we won't see anything, my love." The Druid turned to her.

"You don't even have to see me while I'm asleep." She turned to her side.

"Wait, I wanted to try something anyway."

I straightened up, closed my eyes, concentrated, and made the connection to the tiny creatures. One by one fireflies began to climb out of the crevices, covering the walls and their light and softly filling the ledge. Killian immediately grabbed the torches and extinguished them, though there wasn't much light left in them anyway.

"That's amazing!" Vendal exclaimed contentedly and immediately closed his eyes. I sat down on the edge of the ledge as the heat of the torches disappeared and we finally felt a slight small breeze coming from below. Neyra and Vendal fell asleep within seconds. Killian sat down next to me.

"Who do you think lived here?" he asked in a hushed voice.

"Do you think anyone lived here?"

"Of course, just look at the stairs or the writings on the wall."

I shrugged. "You may be right. Maybe it was the Grabodans' secret cave."

"Possibly. I think we all agree it wasn't built by smugglers, but why would they need another way up to the Grabodans?" He paused. "Maybe it was a secret lovers' cave?"

"'Love is a dark pit', isn't that what they say? Maybe that comes from here."

We laughed. Killian couldn't take his eyes off of me and I was very aware of that. He shuffled next to me, cleared his throat.

"How long have we been climbing these stairs?" I asked.

"It seemed long, but I don't think it would be getting dark outside just yet. Could be late afternoon?"

He leaned back, clasped his hands under his head, watching the thousands of glowing fireflies above us. "Beautiful."

"Yes…"

"When I was a soldier, I never had time for this. We always kept on the road, our only focus was the next fight... I started to think that I would never be able to see the beauty in this world again."

I couldn't help but look at him sadly, then. I understood why he had been shrouded in silence so often, just to enjoy the moment.

"I should sleep a little too. Or-"

"Go ahead, I'm fine."

He couldn't take his eyes off of the fireflies. I squeezed his shoulder as I got up and walked a little further in. I laid down not far from my friends and closed my eyes, leaving him there with the lights.

I didn't get much sleep. In fact, I woke up to someone holding my mouth shut.

I found myself facing Killian, who gestured to me to keep quiet. I sat up slowly and saw both Vendal and Neyra standing behind us with the Elf having pulled her sword out. I didn't know what was going on but I heard strange, strange sounds coming from the next cavern. Given what had happened between me and the dragon, I was a little scared to reach out into the darkness with my mind, but we had no other choice.

I closed my eyes and concentrated. Apart from the friction of the stones and a stream flowing deep in the mountain, I couldn't feel the presence of anything else and I found that extremely strange. I opened my eyes and shook my head, signalling to the others that we could probably move forward.

We set off pretty slowly towards the cave, almost reaching the entrance, when a strange shadow slipped in front of us. Neyra almost screamed, but Killian quickly closed his hand around her mouth. We heard the sounds again, but this time they came from behind us. We all turned around and were lucky that Killian's hand was still resting on the Elf's mouth.

Transparent figures appeared, made of some kind of strange golden light burning in them. We were only able to make out their shape.

"Ghosts," Vendal whispered. "Memories of the past."

"And should we worry about them?" Killian slowly let go of Neyra's mouth and she instantly clung to Vendal's arm.

"I don't think so," the Druid shook his head.

"Maybe if-" I held out one hand, but Killian pushed it back down.

"Don't. Let's just go."

We ventured into the cave. I made sure to keep bringing fireflies in so we weren't left without light. When we got through the short tunnel, we arrived at another spiral staircase. We started walking toward it when a huge ghost emerged from the floor causing Neyra to scream, her voice reverberating throughout the entire cavern.

The ghost held out his transparent hand, strange and formless, and pointed straight at me. I was scared, but also strangely calm at the same time. I glanced at my companions and began to move towards the ghost, drawn to it on some level - curiosity? Or something deeper? Killian grabbed my hand and looked at me begging. I caressed his cheek as if to say *it's alright*, as I slowly pulled my other hand out of his grip.

The creature shrunk down to become the same size as me. He - was it a he? Something told me so - touched my shoulder where I had the scar from the arrow Cutter's man had shot me with. Warmth overflowed my whole body and immeasurable happiness spread through me like wildfire, but it faded quickly as I started shivering from the unexpected pain. Suddenly frightened, I tried to take a step back but the ghost didn't let me. My pain became unbearable as he very slowly started to pull away his hand. A dark mass appeared from my shoulder, sharp and angry, like it was the shape of evil. I let out a scream as it left my body.

Then the ghost swallowed it whole. The golden glow inside him destroyed the dark matter in an instant, and I felt immeasurably lighter.

"But, this... how?" I asked in shock. "What is this?"

A deep sound resonated through the stone walls. "Nightmares," the ghost said, and with that he disappeared.

"He... cleansed you. He cleansed you from the darkness." Vendal was so excited he hugged me tightly. Neyra quickly did the same.

"This means that Cutter-"

"Worked for the Soulless." Killian finished my sentence and we all turned to him. I walked back over to him. "I am glad you are free from it." he whispered, holding onto my hands tightly.

"Let's get out of this awful cave, because, frankly, it scares me and, also, it sucks," Neyra said, intolerant of the entire situation and headed straight for the stairs.

The stairs led us a long way up; it felt like we climbed for days on end. Plus, the luxury of finding a stone ledge or rest area seemingly disappeared. Sometimes we sat down on the stairs themselves, but none of us dared to close our eyes. Finally, after climbing into what felt like infinity, Neyra suddenly exclaimed:

"Light! I see the sunlight!"

We all multiplied our footsteps, only wanting to get out of the cave as soon as we possibly could. We climbed out through the seemingly tiny hole and we were surprised to find that it wasn't the Sun shining, but the Moon.

"My deepest thanks to Silhoue," Killian said unexpectedly, and we all laughed.

"I don't care about anything but sleep," Vendal said, exhausted.

"Praise be to that!" Neyra was rubbing her legs trying to get them to move again.

"Come here, we can rest here tonight." I gestured towards the pine trees. The Elf sank down next to one of the thick trunks, the Druid joining her moments later, hugging her tightly.

"Considering how we almost died from the heat, I'm freezing now," Vendal said, grumpily.

"I'll make fire." Killian suggested, but I stopped him. I waved my hand and a fire ignited in the middle of the circle we formed. There it hovered between us, content to stay without a source to feed it.

"Thank you," Killian said, and he sat down leaning against another tree. I took my place next to him. He pulled out his cloak and spread it on us, smiling, then closed his eyes and tilted his head back against the trunk. I watched him for a while, then rested my head on his shoulder, allowing sleep to take me.

The Sun was high in the sky when we woke up. We soon gathered ourselves and were glad to find that we only had to walk straight up to the summit to reach the temple.

The huge edifice was like nothing we'd ever seen before, but it was just as Vendal described it for us after reading about it in the *Book of Sagar*; huge pillars, a golden dome with an enormous stone eagle sat at the top of it, watching us. Right in the middle of the temple stood a lake from which an empty altar rose. I saw the surprise on Vendal's face when we came across it - it mustn't have been mentioned in the book.

We stood in front of the open entrance in amazement - it didn't seem like it was protected at all. Ven took a careful step towards the two main pillars when the screaming rang out. Killian pulled him back sharply. The statue on the dome came to life trembling, throwing away its millennial stones. It rose high, then slammed hard on the ground and towered above us. The Eagle's feathers fluttered in gold; his head turned nobly as he looked at the four of us, spreading his monumental wings.

"Only those who answer my questions correctly can enter this gate," he proclaimed in a howling voice. We couldn't help but be taken aback.

"This must be what was missing from the Book of Sagar," whispered the Druid.

"Who will give the first answer?"

We looked at each other. Vendal stepped forward, confidently.

"I will be."

"I'm there for everyone, but if you don't cultivate me, I'll wither. I can be used for great good or menacing evil. What am I?"

"Um…" Vendal looked at us, questioningly. He had to think, but then he smiled. "Power."

The Eagle raised its wings and the Druid hurried under them. Killian took his place. The once-statue measured him well, only then did he speak.

"There are those who refuse me, there are those who lose me, but no one can erase me. You can live without me, but not in full. The lack of my presence makes you lonely. What am I?"

"Love," Killian answered with barely a thought. The Eagle nodded, content, and raised his other wing. Neyra stepped forward and the questioner spoke immediately.

"I'll give you warmth if you're cold, I'll embrace you in solitude. I'll wait for you with open arms, even if you're gone for years. What am I?"

Neyra stepped one more step forward and replied with great confidence.

"A house."

The Eagle began to scream, and we had to put our hands over our ears, it was as if the animal had laughed at the Elf.

"You cannot enter. The correct answer is home."

"What? But-" Neyra took another step but the Eagle slapped the Elf with its huge wing and the girl fell backwards. I tried to help, but she raised her hand to stop me.

"Damn it," she cursed. "Go, I'll wait for you out here."

"Neyra-"

"Just go!" She yelled at me, furious. I turned back to the Eagle. The noble gatekeeper bent down completely; he came so close that the huge beak almost touched my nose. His yellow eyes burned into my soul.

"I'm honoured to finally meet you, Destroyer." He straightened up. **"I am glad you made it here, but you have to answer my question also. Are you ready?"**

"Yes."

"I can be yours, but you don't own me. If I'm strong enough almost everything is possible, but when I am weak, I can slip out of your hands. What am I?"

I was confused. My first thought was love, but it was also Killian's answer. Maybe it was some kind of trick? I knew that if I didn't answer correctly, I wouldn't be able to get in the temple and then we wouldn't have what we came for. I took a deep breath.

"Hope?"

With shockingly little ceremony, the Eagle stood aside from the gate to let me in. When I entered, the entrance closed behind me again. My other two companions were already waiting for me.

"Where's Neyra?" Vendal asked.

"She didn't know the answer, so she had to stay outside. Relax!" I touched his shoulder gently. "Neyra can take care of herself."

Vendal took a deep breath, fighting whatever instinct he had to run back to her and somehow drag her in with us. "I know."

We headed for the lake, but when we got close, we saw hundreds upon hundreds of skeletons resting beneath the surface of the water. I glanced at the altar. It was surrounded by some strange aura that I could not see but I felt its presence. Vendal walked around the lake to see if anything had been written on the altar, but all sides were blank. He made to walk back, but almost immediately fell on his back. We found he'd stumbled on a piece of stone that was protruding from the ground.

I had a very strange feeling I couldn't shake looking at it. Something attracted me to the stone. I was a bit hesitant, but I touched it slowly.

Nothing happened.

"Sam?" Killian's voice felt like a pin being dropped in the quiet of the temple.

"This stone..." I whispered. "There's something-"

I tried to move it, but I couldn't. I stood back and tried to size it up. Meanwhile, Killian and Vendal tried to lift it but were unable to do so, as if someone had nailed it to the ground.

"Remember what Tidios said?" Vendal said, and Killian glared at him.

"What did he say?" I asked.

"That your blood is the key..."

"My blood?"

Killian hit Vendal in the back of his neck and he hissed from the sudden blow.

"What? She has to try!" The Druid said, a bit taken aback by his friend's aggression.

"No, you don't have to. What if it's a trap?" Killian was looking at me, pleading.

"Then what the fuck else are we supposed to-"

"Enough!"

I pulled out my small dagger and cut my palm, squeezing my spilled blood on the stone. At first nothing happened, but then the stone suddenly rose up high. It spun in the air a good few times, then slammed to the ground and broke in two, causing the group of us to jump back so as not to get hit. A roll of parchment fell out of it. I picked it up, opened it, and was instantly disappointed. Vendal took it from me.

"It's written in Grabodan. I can't read it." In his anger he almost threw it back on the ground.

"But maybe Tidios can?" Killian suggested.

"The Dwarf? How?" I figured he was smart, but did he really speak a dead language?

"He did a lot of research on the Grabodans, maybe he can help," Killian shrugged.

"Great, then we go back to the cave," sighed Vendal.

We were about to turn and leave when a huge roar shook the building. Killian picked up the parchment, put it in his bag, and rushed to the entrance. The Eagle was gone, so before we exited, we saw Neyra fighting a group of people attacking her. Killian drew his sword and roared into the battle. I wanted to follow, but Vendal grabbed my shoulder. He pointed to the sky. The Eagle was struggling with the huge dark green dragon. I glanced at the Druid.

Cutter appeared among the soldiers. I felt my stomach drop out from underneath me. Even though he was a ways away from me, I felt like I could smell his rotten breath on the wind. Vendal did not hesitate, just stepped forward. Cutter roared as the sword he held burned his hand and he was forced to drop it.

I panicked; there were too many soldiers arriving, and I felt fear flooding through every inch of my body. Although I saw what was happening, I didn't want to believe it. It was just too much, too fucking much.

Vendal concentrated. He swept a good few soldiers off the mountain with a huge gust of wind, while also setting the ground on fire under another couple. Neyra kept cutting down men, moving between them with ease, but no matter how many she killed, they kept on coming, running up towards us. Killian cut a man's head off in a single sweep, but I saw what he didn't: another soldier prepared to stab Killian in the back.

That snapped me out of my panic.

I screamed in anger, I didn't have to concentrate as I raised my hand, I felt the incredible power run through me. A huge lightning bolt struck the man who was trying to strike down Killian.

My anger grew further. I concentrated all my energy on the newly arriving soldiers. Giant roots broke through the ground, rising high up into the sky and blocking the arriving soldiers' way towards us. I turned towards Cutter, but I was too late. He pressed his sword to Neyra's neck, holding her. Killian immediately lowered his own weapon, backing away to Vendal and me. Only the sound of the battle of the Eagle and the Dragon above us filled the space while Cutter spoke.

"Give me what you've found in there," he snarled, pressing the sword into the Elf's neck, tears streaming down her face, not just in fear, but anger too. Vendal took a step forward, but I stopped him.

"We didn't find anything," I lied. Cutter laughed and a far more ominous voice intertwined with his. The Eagle slammed into the temple behind us, destroying it entirely. The holy site that had stood untarnished for centuries, gone in an instant. The Dragon, victorious, landed behind the remaining soldiers.

"We can do this easily. No one needs to get hurt."

"And I should just believe you when you say that you'll spare our lives if I give you what you want?"

My gaze bounced between the terrified and pissed off Neyra and the infinitely angry Cutter, but I finally settled on the dragon. I concentrated, but as I wanted to penetrate the consciousness of the living being, I was suddenly flooded with sharp pain. I fell to the ground, roaring with a scorching sensation.

"You can't control the dragon," Cutter yelled. Neyra screamed as Cutter pressed the sword further against her throat, blood now starting to trickle down her neck. "Give me what I want!"

"Here," Killian pulled out the parchment, holding it above his head. Cutter smiled.

"My dear boy, I knew you were the smartest of your friends. Come here!"

Killian swallowed hard then took careful steps towards the man, holding out the parchment.

The dark green Dragon rose up without warning, his claws were quickly around Cutter and Neyra, then with a swift move grabbed hold of Killian, who was fast enough in thought and threw the parchment right back to me. The soldiers started marching towards me and Vendal. I had no idea what I was doing, but my feet led me. I grabbed hold of the Druid's arm - who desperately tried to hit the Dragon with a fireball - and dragged him towards the edge.

We both jumped from the mountain peak.

Vendal's face was frozen in a silent scream, but I felt the change immediately. It was something I couldn't describe at all, but when it came down to it I knew I could do it.

I embraced the Druid as I felt my whole body changing.

First the scales pushed through my skin, followed by two huge wings that broke out of my back as I turned into a glorious white Dragon. I was still me, but I saw the world through dragon eyes. I raised myself back up, holding Vendal in my claws, but no matter which way I looked, I couldn't see the dark green Dragon anymore.

When we landed in front Gregoir's house I turned back into myself, barely able to stand on my feet, but Vendal caught me before I could fall. He wrapped his cloak around me as the clothes that I was wearing were gone.

"I lost them," I muttered as he lifted me up in his arms.

"We'll find them."

"KILLIAN"

The Dragon dropped us down on the stone ground and flew away. Before I could move, Cutter was already on his feet lifting up Neyra and then me. The Elf was terrified, I could see it in her eyes, but she held her face stern so as to not let Cutter see it. I grabbed hold of her hand and squeezed it.

We were in some kind of square, the Moon was already high in the sky, but it was the bonfire only a few feet away from us giving light to the place. A broken staircase stood before us, leading up to a huge throne. I knew where we were instantly as soon as I saw the monument:

The Soulless

The Giant's Kingdom.

I looked around again; there were skeletons everywhere to the left of me and on the right, three girls hanging from poles. Their blood was taken from them just like the ones we saw in that village.

My eyes darted back to the throne. There was someone sitting in it, hiding in the dark. The Dragon's head rose from behind it. Its huge scales had an almost silvery glow mixed with the dark green colour. It was the most terrifying beast I'd ever seen in my life. Neyra was quietly sobbing next to me, her facade cracked.

"Where is it?" A cold voice asked from the darkness.

"It's with this Elf loving Human." Cutter pushed me down on the ground and I started to laugh.

"Your pet failed its mission," I called out, voice raised. I looked up at the mysterious figure, raising both my hands up. "I no longer have what you are looking for."

"Wh-" Cutter fell on his knees behind me. I quickly stood up and dragged Neyra away from the man who was now coughing up blood.

"You..." The shadow figure stood up - "useless..." - it felt like he just floated down the stairs in his long black robe - "idiot!"

He clapped and Cutter's head blew into tiny little pieces. The man held out his hand and Neyra was gone from next to me in a blink of an eye.

"Leave her a-"

It was a small movement of the man's hand and suddenly I couldn't talk or move. He leaned close to the Elf, his red eyes full of hunger.

It happened way too fast. He raised those horrible boney hands and cut through Neyra's throat. His lips immediately closed on the wound and I watched as he sucked the life out of my friend, unable to do anything. When he was done, he dropped Neyra's lifeless body on the ground and slowly licked his fingertips.

"That was much needed."

A healthy peach colour rose on his skin, making him look a bit more alive. It seemed like all the muscles reappeared on his skeleton-like frame as he took a deep breath. He came to me with a strange smile covering his face.

"Ah, the lover," he whispered, leaning uncomfortably close to me. "What did you do with the parchment?" He gestured with his hand and I felt my voice return.

"Fuck you."

"You're not my type, pretty boy. Sam however-"

I tried to break free from the strange magic even though I knew I had no chance for it.

"I will kill you, you fucking monster."

"Now, now-" he appeared in front of me again. "Frankly, you're a bit boring. But..." he raised one of his long fingers, "I will make your life so.

Much. Easier."

"Torture me if you want, I won't tell you anything."

His laugh made my blood freeze. He came even closer and I couldn't stop staring in his eyes. He seemed oddly familiar.

"Oh, I ain't gonna torture you. I'll torture Sam."

He snapped his fingers and the world went dark.

CHAPTER 16
BETRAYAL

"VENDAL"

I couldn't believe that we let Killian and Neyra slip out of our fingers. What could we have done differently? We underestimated Cutter. We *constantly* underestimated Cutter. That was clear as day, and a mistake I refused to make again.

I carried Sam back to Polly's house where she rushed to our aid instantly. She asked so many questions, none of which we could answer. Sam was so tired that she was out on the chair where I put her down.

She wept all the way back to Polly's. I couldn't calm her down and after a while I didn't even try to. I was horrified by the thought of what would happen to Neyra. I was worried for my friend, sure, but in her I finally found someone who I could be free with. I felt like I belonged to her. I know Sam felt the same with Killian, I could see it in her.

Did we fail them?

We awoke the next morning to a loud banging at the front door. My whole body was aching - I had fallen asleep next to Sam on another chair, and clearly not well. We heard the door opening, but what came next was worse than any nightmare.

"Ma'am, we've been informed that a fugitive arrived at your home a few days ago. We're here to take her away." I looked at Sam in panic, but she was strangely calm.

"Go look for them, Ven."

"What?" I breathed out, baffled.

"We can't look for them with soldiers in our heels. Go. They're only here for me.”

“Sam-”

“I won’t risk Polly’s life or your life for mine. Don’t try to protect me.”

With that she stood up and she was out of the dining room before I could think to stop her. I heard the chains clanking around her wrists and the soldiers escorting her out of the house. Polly appeared a few moments later, sobbing.

“Why didn’t you stop her, my boy?”

“I don’t-”

I didn’t continue. It would have been too much to explain. I looked at the table, at the parchment was laying there. The wheels in my head spun.

“Who took her?”

“Elves.”

I nodded, put away the parchment and rose from my seat, a plan tying together nicely in my head.

“I will get her back, Polly. I will let you know when I do.”

“Thank you.”

I left the house behind hurriedly, taking the horses with me but leaving Martha behind with Polly. I made my way to the Archives where Tidios welcomed me with a big smile. It didn’t last long. By the time I told him everything that happened up on the mountain peak he was sobbing, fat tears were rolling down his face. It took a while to calm him down.

He was, however, excited to see the parchment with the Grabodan writing. As Killian suspected, Tidios was versed in the dead language. He needed a few books to translate it properly, but he was done within a few hours, eager to help in whatever way he could. I read his translation.

My resting place will be the hiding place for The Prophecy. I will leave my guard post and go to the grave at last. This message cannot go to anyone but the Destroyer, the only living being who can save us.
"I close my grave in eternal darkness."
- Crixus

“Do you know what it means, Magic Bearer?”

I shook my head in disappointment. I couldn’t believe how little the parchment revealed.

“It will have to wait,” I said, setting it on fire causing Tidios to give a sharp gasp.

“Why?”

“No one can find it.” I touched his forehead and within a second he started sobbing again. “Tidios. What did we talk about?” I asked.

“You… told me that they took everyone,” he said between two big breaths.

I nodded. It worked. I took away the memory of the parchment.

"And I will let you know when I've found them," I said, patting his shoulders. The second vow I made that day.

From there, I couldn't tell how much time got away from me. Everything blurred together, my thoughts were everywhere. If the Elves took Sam, she would be in Yandana before I could find Neyra and Killian. But who told the Elves that she was with us? And why now?

Next time my focus was really with me, I was back at the garrison and Conor wasn't happy to see me to say the least. He seemed nervous, almost hilariously fidgety, and couldn't bear to look into my eyes. His men kept their hands on their swords as I entered with the horses.

They didn't know I felt the air change around them. It was a hot day but around Conor it felt like deep winter. The air around him had a slight tremble to it that told me that he'd done something he might have regretted. My capacity to care about the consequences had long since run dry, so within seconds I had all of his men pinned against the wooden walls of the garrison by roots that ran underground. Conor tried to pull his sword out but I had my blade against his throat much quicker.

"Did you notify the Elves about Sam?" I asked, almost hissing. He was petrified. I didn't care if he wanted to send the whole army after me. Let them try.

"*Did you?*"

"Yes! Yes! For Silhoue's sake!"

"Why?" I pressed the blade against his throat even harder.

"I had a deal with their captain, okay?" He whimpered, "I was going to buy her from them, but that idiot Elf played me."

"Buy her? Like a fucking slave?"

"No!" He yelled. "Please don't kill me!"

It took every ounce of will not to drive the blade the rest of the way home. I pulled back, making sure to leave a small cut for him to question later as I took away his and all the soldiers' memories about what happened.

It took me days to find any trace of the dark green Dragon. Nature had all the evidence I needed to follow it. Said days blurred into each other as I made my way through the treacherous lands, only stopping if it was really necessary. I slept in the saddle of my horse most of the time.

It might have been the sixth or seventh day that I reached a farmhouse. It was separated from everything. The area around the house was populated by cows, lazily eating grass, and I saw a few goats too.

It seemed as if nobody was home, though the house looked to be in perfect shape. A strong animal scent filled my nose as I got closer to it; even if the Dragon flew by near it, it seemed like I'd lost its trace.

I got off my horse to knock but the door of the house opened instantly. A young maiden stepped out holding a bow aiming straight to my chest. I raised both my hands up.

"What do you want, Druid?" she asked. Her voice was incredibly high-pitched, almost child-like. She wore brown trousers and a white shirt, her black hair tightly braided. She didn't have an ounce of fear in her.

"I'm after a Dragon."

"The green one?" She lowered her weapon a bit, measuring me up carefully.

"Have you seen it? It took my friends away." She shook her head, her eyes suddenly full of tears.

"If it took your friends, they're dead," she said matter-of-factly, but I refused to accept that possibility. "It lives in the Giants Kingdom. It-" She quickly brushed her tears away, regaining her composure. "It took my father. I followed it, but I was too late."

"Is it far from here?"

"No. Half a day's journey, tops."

I quickly got back up on my horse's back. The girl put down her weapon, apparently satisfied I wasn't there to harm her.

"You'll only find death there."

"I have to try." I wanted to leave, but she stopped me with one sentence.

"A man came from there a couple of days ago. He was heading for Yandana."

"From the Giants Kingdom?" I turned back. Was it Killian? But if it was him, where was Neyra? None of it made any sense.

"Yes. He was tall, black hair and eyes. He seemed… lost, confused."

It must have been him. But if he was alone, that must have meant a terrible fate for my beloved. I had to take a deep breath.

"Was he alone?" I asked, and she nodded. I felt tears threatening to break. "Thank you for your time, and I am sorry for your loss."

I left before she could say anything else. I had to see it for myself. I needed to know if it was all true.

It was late at night by the time I reached the ruined gates that signalled the Giants Kingdom. The Moon had waned entirely, meaning the area was pitch-black and I didn't dare to light a fire. Smugglers and mercenaries often used the enormous stone buildings - what's left of them, anyway - to hide and ambush wayfarers. I left my companions' three horses outside and rode in alone.

It was dead silent. I felt the signs of destruction in the ground - blood had been spilled, many died in vain, but memories of pleasure also lingered there.

And a man.

I felt his every step resonating through the rocks. He'd left a dark mark on them, almost polluting everything that got in his way. I severed my connection to nature as I found myself in a large square where it seemed the main event had taken place - all the memories, the scents, the fights, struggles and the suffering. Dark magic surrounded every inch of the place.

I sent up an orb of fire and my stomach turned in disgust. The rotting body of a headless man lay only a few feet away from me, and it was only when I looked back again that I realised it was Cutter. Hundreds of flies buzzed and scattered with the introduction of the light; I had to swallow back my sickness. I raised a few roots to pull the man's body down into the ground, burying him and the smell. Then I saw it.

Next to the staircase was a neatly arranged pile of stones. I slowly approached it, my heart pounding in my chest. There were no other markings, but I knew that it was a grave. I crouched down next to it, barely able to hold myself. I was trembling so much. I touched the ground for only a second, but it was enough for Neyra's beautiful face to appear in front of me.

I fell backwards. A loud scream of anguish left my mouth, tears flowed down my face and I couldn't stop them. I didn't try - the ground was embracing the dead body of my love. The light slowly died around me as I lost my connection to the fire orb.

I sat there for what felt like hours, just sobbing, barely able to keep myself together. It felt like the pain was eating me from inside. I felt incredible anger for letting her go, for not trying harder to save her. Could I have done something differently? My chest hurt so badly that I wasn't able to breathe properly.

Maybe it was for the better. I didn't care if death chose my grave next to hers, I was happy to leave. But my consciousness eventually caught up with me. It took a lot of time to calm myself down, to slow down my breathing and to stop my tears.

I forced myself to stand up after a while, but that anger that was brewing inside me broke out without warning. I slammed my hand to the ground - I needed to see what happened.

Fear.

She was terrified.

Blood-red eyes in the dark.

His head is in pieces.

Killian.

Help me, please.

"This won't hurt at all. You are serving a greater purpose."

Yes, my Lord.

I pulled back. It was him, The Soulless. He drank her blood.

I couldn't take it anymore. I threw up the little food I was able to force down the previous day, instantly sobbing again. I didn't know how much more I could handle, but I needed to know what he did to Killian. I closed my eyes one last time.

The voices arrived with the wind.

"I will make your life much...easier."

"Torture me if you want, I won't tell you anything."
"Oh, I ain't gonna torture you. I will torture Sam."
Blinding Light.
Pain.
Emptiness.
Gods… this poor girl. Who is she?
Where am I?

His memories, all of them - gone. Resolve renewed in me as I knew I had to find him. I was weak from the powerful magic I'd summoned, but got back into the saddle. Collecting the other three horses at the gates, I left the cursed place - and my love - behind, and moved forward.

"SAM"

The carriage that served as my prison came to a stop. I looked through the barred windows only to see a fallen tree blocking the road. I sighed and sat back, leaning my back against the cold steel. I spent every day we'd traveled hoping to see Vendal, Neyra and Killian pop up, and each day it didn't happen I felt more and more lost.

We'd been on our way to Yandana for a little over ten days. The Elven soldiers only gave me stale bread and none of them would even talk to me at all, unless they had something rude to say. It was with glee that they told me Conor had betrayed us. The soldiers were originally after Killian, but his dear "friend" told them that he had a Halfling with him so they had a win on their hands either way. Of course, Conor was hoping to buy me from them, but the Captain of the Elves, named Gadev, refused to sell me to him. I felt disgusted remembering what Conor was thinking at the table. He was ready to take me from Killian in whatever way he could. Who knew that it meant calling the Elves on us?

One of the soldiers threw a slice of bread into the carriage. It already had mold growing on it so I didn't even touch it. That angered him - he called me disrespectful, but I didn't care. I only severed my connection to the animals around us when we stopped so they wouldn't notice that I was doing something strange. I'd made the Captain's horse drop him from his back more than once; it was my only entertainment to see the fury rising on his face.

Captain Gadev might have saved me from Conor, but that didn't make him a good man. I'd heard stories about him when I still lived in Yandana; he was famous for his methods of torture. When King Herald's family went into hiding, it was Gadev who forced the information about their hiding place out of the King. He also hunted Halflings for a sport when he wasn't assigned to lead a battle. It was only by luck I had been able to avoid him.

A dozen of the soldiers were working on getting the tree out of the way when a slim, red-headed private stepped up to Captain Gadev, who was sitting on the back of his horse waiting impatiently for his man to finish.

"Any news?" He asked, lazily. His long brown hair covered half his face as he leaned forward on the horse. He had an ugly scar running through his left cheek, making her lips uneven. His dark green eyes were fixated on me. I didn't look away.

"The hawk they sent back from Irkaban says that Killian is no longer there, Captain."

"Tell me something I don't know." He gestured the private away and led his horse next to my moving prison. He leaned down so he could look me in the eyes.

"I don't know how you bewitched one of my best men, but trust me, we will get him back."

I spat in his face. He didn't even budge. He wiped my spit down with one of his fingers, not breaking eye contact with me.

"You will learn your place soon enough, you disgusting little Halfling."

"THE ROAD IS CLEAR!" Yelled one of the soldiers. Gadev's ugly smile appeared and he rode away from me.

We were on the move again but I kept my eyes on the land behind us.

Hoping...

III
And Soon the the Darkness

CHAPTER 17
THE PALACE

"SAM"

The palace - if it was possible - was even more glorious from the inside than it was the outside. The floor was made from marble, golden and silver swirls embedded within it, making these seemingly impossible formations, and the walls in the main hall were painted a deep green - her majesty's favourite colour as I later found out. There were two staircases in front of us and an imposing red door right in the middle.

Captain Gadev pushed me so hard that I had the chance to observe the floor even closer. I barely had the energy to stand up. I'd spent twenty-one very long days in that carriage, eating only rotten bread and drinking stale water. They only let me out when I needed to relieve myself, once in the morning and the evening.

I couldn't sleep much; my nightmares woke me up most nights. I saw Killian die, then Neyra and Vendal too. I thought that they would free me before we reached Yandana, but after a while I gave up all hope and I accepted the punishment that was waiting for me. I did escape capture for many years after all, it was only a matter of time...

We entered through the red door once Captain Gadev announced himself to the Guard.

A long, royal blue carpet was laid out on the rough stone floor. It was a huge difference from the hall that welcomed whoever entered the castle; the floor might have been a disappointment, but the glorious pillars were definitely something spectacular. Each of them had Elves and Fairies carved into them in different positions. They surrounded the carpet that led to the throne, reaching their hands out and holding the torches that gave light to the enormous interior.

There weren't many people inside - a few royal families as far as I could tell from their clothes. All of them had a peacock's feather sewn into their sleeves

- the sign of royalty in Yandana. They were looking at me, haughty expressions clearly judging me, some even disgusted by my presence. As we reached the bottom of the small staircase that led to the throne, Gadev pushed me down to my knees.

King Oberon sat atop the dias. He and his Queen's throne were both carved out of the trunk of a Fairy tree. Both thrones were shaped to look like the antlers of a stag, but the King's was double the size of the Queen's. They were beautifully made, there was no question about it. On the King's right side a smaller throne stood, full of roses and lilies. The princess I'd seen on the day my life changed was sitting in it, keeping her purple eyes trained on me, expression unreadable.

Next to the Queen's throne was a similar one, but their son took that place. He was - just like his sister - completely flawless. His skin colour was the perfect mix of his father's dark brown and his mother's rosey skin. Big, dark purple eyes, small lips and long black hair that was braided in such an elaborate way that I couldn't tell where it started or ended. He had even smaller wings than her sister but they did have the same golden glow. He didn't even bother to look at me, he was too busy eye-fucking with one of the royal ladies.

Queen Beatrice was gorgeous. Her perfectly proportioned body was covered with a dress made out of white rose petals. Fairies had a way to preserve the flowers so that they wouldn't rot when sewn into a dress. She had sharp, close-set eyes, slightly red in colour, small lips and curly brown hair. Her wings were huge, beautiful, and iridescent. She was looking down at me, no more to her than the dirt on her shoes.

King Oberon, comparatively speaking, wasn't as perfect looking as his family. The right side of his head was shaved clean revealing a huge scar that ran through his cheek and ended on his collarbone. The rest of his long blond hair was in tiny braids. His blue eyes were fixated on me and the hatred I could feel coming off them was oppressive. Though he was wearing a long silver robe, one could easily tell he was a strong man.

Until he lifted his hand up there was small chatter from the guests all around us, then everything went silent.

"Captain Gadev." King Oberon had a very deep voice, one that seemed to echo across every corner of the hall. I was astonished by it. "Where's Malion Arur?"

The Captain struggled to hold his composure. "My King, we were unable to locate him, but she-"

"I don't care about this dirty Halfling!" snapped the King. I was ready to hear the judgement right then and there, but he continued:

"Where's the Human who was supposed to marry my eldest daughter?"

My head jerked up. I made immediate eye contact with the Princess, her face still stony and unreadable. So *this* was the woman Killian was supposed to wed. I wondered if he knew how pretty she was.

"My King, this girl was Killian Fin's travel companion," Captain Gadev said as fast as he could. Hushed voices rose up around us and I saw the surprise on the King and Queen's faces. Now the Prince's eyes were on me too.

"What?" asked the Queen, she swallowed back her chuckle. "Killian, with this ugly creature?" When she started laughing, the room followed her example.

Everyone except the Princess.

"We had intel about them from our inside person."

I felt like someone sucked all the air out of my lungs. Inside person?

"You mean the girl, the one who sent you on a false trail with her last report?"

Captain Gadev's whole body trembled, and I was near tears by the revelation. Neyra had been spying on us from the beginning. Then why did she send the soldiers to a fake location?

"We believe that to be a mi-"

"You can't be this much of an idiot, Captain Gadev," the Prince said, smirking at him.

"We have her brother in our prison, your Highness. I am sure it was a misunderstanding. Maybe her companions discovered her and forced her to-"

"Yes, we did."

I didn't know what got into me, but silence immediately fell on the throne room. Captain Gadev kicked my side but I gathered all my strength to stay on my knees.

"You're a brave little monster, aren't you?" The King asked. I looked up at him and stared him down the best I could. He didn't scare me at all, and I'd quickly decided that no matter what Neyra did, if they were keeping her brother captive, I had to help him.

"Why are you protecting the one who betrayed you?"

"I am not protecting her. The Druid who was travelling with us discovered her plans. We forced her to send false information about our whereabouts."

"Did you force Killian too?" The Queen asked, almost hissing at me. I nodded slowly. "I knew it, my love. You see? I told you." She grabbed hold of the King's hand, but he didn't seem convinced by my story.

"What should we do with her?" Captain Gadev asked. I held my breath as the King was ready to declare judgement on me, when the Princess coughed a little.

All eyes turned to her.

"Father. I would like her to be my servant."

"Aihyla!" The Queen snapped, but the King raised his hand to shush her.

"She's clearly up to no good, my darling. I don't think it would be wise to let her near you," King Oberon responded, his voice incredibly soothed. It became glaringly obvious that Princess Aihyla was the favourite child of the King.

"I think I will be able to change her, Father." She looked at me, but I was still unable to get a read on her. Pity, or cruelty? The King only pondered on his beloved daughter's request for a short while.

"If you insist." He turned his full attention towards Captain Gadev. "Take the Halfling to the Servant's quarters. There, order the head lady to give her a proper bath. This monster will be serving the Princess after all."

"Yes, my King." Captain Gadev bowed so deep that it was a miracle that he didn't fall on his face. He grabbed me by my arm and pulled me to my feet.

"And you, girl-" King Oberon pointed straight at me as Gadev began to drag me out of the room. "Make one move that my daughter doesn't like and I will personally cut off your head."

I held the King's gaze the rest of the way out of the throne room.

The Captain pushed me along what felt like a thousand-mile-long corridor, then down some very tight spiral stairs that led straight to the basement. It had a grimier look than the rest of the palace; there were ten doors on either side, but he led me straight to one that was facing the staircase.

He opened it without knocking. Inside, a plump woman was washing clothes in a laundry tub. Her massive breasts were almost out of her clearly smaller sized dress, and sweat was dripping down on her forehead, right on to her pig-like nose. She had her brown hair up in a tight bun on top of her head, not just for practicality, but a sense of pride that said this is a woman who has come to work. The biggest surprise, however, was that she was a Halfling just like me: half Human, half Elf.

"Anda, have this girl bathed, give her the royal servant clothes and tell her everything she needs to know. She'll be serving the Princess." Captain Gadev ordered and, without even waiting for a response, he turned around and left the room, slamming the door shut on his way out.

"The Princess must like ya, girl," she chuckled. Her voice was soft and kind. She stood up and pulled the curtains that were behind her apart. Behind them was a huge bathtub that was only available for the Royal Family. Anda's working place was full of the clothes that needed washing, it was quite messy, but around the bathtub everything was clean. Four other servants came in, all Halflings as well.

"Good, good my little birdies. This is-"

"Sam." I said quickly.

"The lovely Sam, she'll be serving Princess Aihyla." The four girls gasped. "Yes, yes. Moira, bring the royal servant's clothes in. Hannah, Jonna, please prepare the bathtub for her, put in the Princess' favourite herbs and white lilies. Katie, please fetch fresh food for this poor soul, she's barely able to stand."

"Yes ma'am!" the girl's choir sounded, and they split off to their tasks.

"Why are you so nice?"

The question came out before I could think about it. An all-encompassing smile appeared on Anda's face, making her small brown eyes almost disappear.

"Because no one else will be."

The two girls tasked with washing me pulled off my clothes without asking. I immediately covered myself (which was apparently very funny for them) as they guided me to the bathtub that was still filling up with water. They shook some yellow herbs in it that coloured the water, and dropped in the lilies which made the whole room smell wonderful. With their help, I got into the hot water and I felt my whole body ache with relief. They were very gentle as they washed my hands and poured water on my hair. Hannah, who was washing my hair, was tiny, like me, but she had this incredibly long white hair and big brown eyes. She was half Human and half Fairy - her wings had a dark, almost brownish colour to them, giving the impression of a moth. Jonna was also a Fairy Halfling - she had short blue hair, big green eyes and these purple wings. There was no way for her to be subtle, an explosion of colour like she was. I marveled at them as they made sure that every inch of my body was crystal clean. I had no idea what the different oils they put on me were, but some of them actually took away the pains I had.

I wasn't sure when I started quietly crying, I only felt Hannah's fingers wipe away my tears. I looked at her and she smiled at me encouragingly. Everything that happened had dawned on me all at once. I'd lost my friends, I'd lost Killian without even having the chance to tell him how I felt. Neyra betrayed us, even if she eventually changed her mind. The facts were there, but could I really blame her? They kept her brother - her brother, whom she didn't even mention - in captivity, forcing her to report our whereabouts.

Were they even still alive?

I felt the girls grabbing my hands and I stood up with their help. The sudden cold gave me goosebumps. Moira had come back with a pile of clothes. They dried me with the help of these enormous red velvet towels and immediately started to put all the undergarments, the underskirt, and finally the purple dress on me. It had black symbols sewn into the skirt area and was the tightest thing I'd ever had to wear. Jonna brushed out my hair and once they were finished they all left, leaving me with Anda.

"Sit down, dear." Anda gestured towards the chair next to herself, and I sat. "We were all taken from our families at a very young age. I've been serving the King and Queen for fifty years now."

I wasn't expecting the information to strike me as hard as it did, but as she said it I couldn't help but suck in a sharp breath. Anda continued.

"I know you must be sad now, but you lived free for years, so please, keep that in mind."

I didn't say anything; she was right after all. I'd enjoyed a freedom that they hadn't.

Katie, the fourth servant, returned with a big bowl of stew. I was so hungry that I ate it all within a few minutes. It didn't have much flavour but in that moment, it was the best meal I'd ever had. Once I finished Anda gave her work to Katie and guided me out.

The Soulless

As I found out, I wasn't going to live with them on the servant floor. I had a room ready right next to the Princess' so I could be there for her whenever she needed. Anda repeated everything at least three times to make sure that I understood her. The rules included:

- Only talk to the Princess if she asks you to.
- Always do what she asks you to.
- The Princess is always right.
- Only leave the palace if the Princess asks you to.
- Wherever the Princess goes, you must follow.
- Only go to sleep if the Princess orders you to.
- No talking back to the Princess under any circumstances.

Live at the mercy of the Princess, then, I gathered, as Anda led me through the parts of the palace that I needed to know about. The kitchen was enormous, full of hard-working men, and of course all of them were Halflings like every other servant. There was so much food everywhere that it was hard to comprehend; vegetables that I didn't even recognise, fresh meats and baked goods. The air was full of scents that I'd never known existed, and it was frankly a bit dizzying.

We went to the Royal dining room afterwards. It wasn't as big as the kitchen, but I soon found out that it was because they had the real dinners in another room three times the size of this one. This small one was only in use when it was just the Royal family around, which meant breakfasts and lunches usually. She did tell me that the Princess often chose to have her meals in her own quarters.

I noticed that they'd painted the walls of the main corridors in a deep red, while common areas usually were either white or brown. If it was for the public to see as well, they hung paintings of landscapes everywhere, but if it was just for the Royal Family then the walls themselves had Elves and Fairies painted on them. I didn't understand why they'd done it like this, but I didn't dare interrupt Anda while she was explaining everything.

Finally, she took me to the top floor where the quarters of the Princess and the Prince were located. There were only four doors as their rooms took up the majority of the space. Nearest to the staircase were the siblings' doors - one of them blue, the other green - and the furthest doors went to the two servants' room. As Anda led me into mine, I couldn't believe what was in front of me.

A vast canopy bed was next to the door, covered with red velvet sheets. Next to it was a cabinet that was far too big for me, made out of an oak tree with different symbols I didn't recognise carved into it. They looked like part

186

of the old Elven language but I couldn't be sure. The walls were all green to match the Princess' door and the floor was made out from a light brown wood. Despite all that, the enormous window was the thing that took my breath away. I stepped closer and almost started to cry - it opened to a clear view of the Noble Gardens. There were two other doors in the room - one leading into the Princess' room the other into the washroom. I opened the latter door and found a huge bathtub that greeted me.

"Are you sure this is my room?" I asked Anda. She nodded.

"Don't take this for granted, dear. The Princess famously gets bored of her servants quickly."

I wasn't even surprised. Anda made her way over to the door that led to the Princess' room and knocked three times. No answer came.

"She isn't here, good. Sam…" She turned back to me, suddenly incredibly serious. "Enjoy this quiet while you can. Welcome to the palace!" And with a smile that unsettled me more than comforted, she left.

The tears came right as the door closed behind her. All I could think about was Killian. I felt empty inside without him; I'd never known that people could get attached to each other this deeply. All I saw in my dreams was his cold, dead body. I still very faintly hoped that Vendal had found them and it was just taking time for them to reach me. But Neyra? I knew that it would break Ven to hear about her betrayal.

I wiped away my tears when I heard the footsteps approaching. I stood up from the bed just to come face to face with the Princess. She was two heads taller than me and even more beautiful up close.

She didn't say a word at first, instead taking a slow walk around me, taking me in. Uncomfortable was an understatement. She then sat on the bed and gestured to me to do the same. I approached slowly and did as she'd silently ordered. The speed with which she reached out and grasped my hand made me gasp.

"What's your name?" She asked, her voice soothing.

"Sam, your R-"

"No!" She snapped, but not from anger. It was more like desperation. "It's Aihyla. I don't want you to call me anything else when it's the two of us. Do you understand?"

I nodded quickly, and she smiled back in a reassuring way.

"Sam. I am going to be honest with you right now, more so than I've ever been with my own family. What I'm going to tell you can't leave this room under any circumstances."

I was so shocked by how her whole demeanor changed that I had a hard time forming words. "Alright."

"Neyra was reporting to me separately." My eyes widened. "She is my only friend in the world, the only one who actually understands me." She took a deep breath and I felt her hands tremble under mine. If this was a performance, it was a good one, but I was getting to the end of my rope when it came to people not being who they presented themselves as.

I had to fight to retain my focus on her as she continued.

"I do not wish to marry Killian, because-"

The words seemed to get stuck in her throat. She shook her head and stood up before I could say anything. It was practically brain-breaking to see someone so regal, so nervous. The way she held herself, how she suddenly seemed small and fragile was actually really... sad.

"What am I doing?" She whispered.

"Aihyla." I stood from the bed and she turned to face me. I felt a tipping point, and I decided to push. "I promise, I won't tell anyone what you want to say. I won't lie to you, I'm not sure who I would tell your secrets to."

She laughed a little at that, but not in a mean-spirited way, more like she wasn't expecting it. As I smiled back, I watched a little of the tension relieve itself from her frame. I crossed the distance between us and took her hands once more.

"I don't know what Neyra said about me, but you can trust me." Her smile appeared again, much brighter than before.

"You've already proved that she wasn't lying." She pulled her hands back, folding them in front of her chest and exhaling slowly before she spoke again. "I am in love with a woman."

The rule of royals: they were only allowed to marry the ones their family chose for them. There was no exception and definitely no chance for the heirs to marry their own gender.

"Aihyla, I am so-"

"I will help you escape, Sam, but only if you take me with you. I recognise our circumstances are vastly different, but I have just entrusted you with my biggest secret, so I hope you might be able to trust me with this."

I wasn't sure what I was expecting, but I didn't expect her to say that. I hesitated. So many thoughts were in my head I suddenly didn't know how to react properly. What else was there to do? I slowly nodded.

"Excellent. I think I have a plan for how we can do it."

"You think?" She laughed again and blushed a little.

"Yes, there are many things we have to consider. But for now, rest. We will start making our plans tomorrow. I made sure that we are left alone." She gave me a small nod and strode out of my room without saying another word.

Did that really just happen? I walked to the window and couldn't help but smile. The Sun was setting, bathing Yandana in a dazzling orange. The city seemed so peaceful. They had no idea what was going on all around them - too busy with how their clothes looked, who they would marry and who knows what else. I wanted so badly to go down to my willow tree but I knew I couldn't leave the castle without losing my head.

Instead, I walked back to the bed and laid down on the soft sheets. I closed my eyes thinking that everything might be alright.

"VENDAL"

I stopped a few feet away from my Uncle's house, quietly wondering how I could face him after the failure.

The house looked as it always did: lonely, old, rusty, and keeping a watchful eye over Yandana. I tied off the horses and walked up to the front door. I had to take several deep breaths before I raised my hands to knock, but before I could, the door opened.

Felnard, without hesitation, closed me in a hug so tight that it almost broke my spine, but I didn't care. It was what I'd longed for since I left the Giant's Kingdom behind, failing to locate Killian and making my walk of shame back to Yandana. He led me into the house, arm around my shoulder, and made me tea. The smell of the herbs were so strong that it made me feel a bit woozy. There was no fire burning in the fireplace. Summer had arrived, and it was hot day and night.

It took me a full cup of tea before I gathered myself properly and told everything to Felnard. He just sat there, listening to me closely, never interrupting to ask any questions. When I'd finished, he just stared at me. It was a bit scary, but I knew that he was thinking about what to say or, I guess... more like how to say it. He was never good at communication. I told a different and uplifting story about his time as a Master to my friends because I was a bit ashamed by his actions. In reality, when he was still a Master at the Academy, a lot of younglings had problems with the way he treated them. It didn't come from rudeness, he just simply looked at everyone equally so he often ended up treating young students like they were already adults who knew everything about magic, leading to a very short tolerance for failure.. He was soon placed on Library duty thanks to the multiple complaints.

That's when he started getting into Radona's story. That's how it all started.

"I have to tell you something too, my son," Felnard croaked out. I was surprised, I was expecting a scolding, but not the nervousness that was clearly in my uncle's voice. "Rowland... visited me."

"Rowland?" He nodded slowly.

Rowland knocked at dawn. Although surprised, I ushered the leader of the Order into my humble home. I offered him a place at my table and made fresh tea. There was a severe silence in the house until we sat in front of each other. Although the table was tiny, it looked huge, as if the two of us could not have been further away from each other, both in personality and in our ultimate goals.

Rowland cleared his throat before speaking. *"I hope life has treated you well, Master Felnard."*

"I guess you could say that…" I lifted my cup with a slightly trembling hand and sipped the rosehip tea. *"Why are you here, Rowland?"*

"It's about Vendal, and their mission." He stirred the tea again, though he had made the move several times before. *"It was foolishness to send them on such a perilous journey. Vendal doesn't know enough about magic to-"*

"I know my nephew very well, Rowland, thank you." Another sip. *"It's no coincidence that Killian is with them."*

"Malion Arur?" He almost laughed, but arranged his face with an elegant smile. *"Useless. Blinded by his own self-pity and his love for the girl. He doesn't think clearly."*

"If you're so worried, why didn't you go with them?" I put down my empty cup, poured myself another round.

"You know I can't leave."

"Then what are you doing here?" That genuinely seemed to amuse him.

"Felnard, I always forget that your foolish character hides a wise man." Rowland put down the spoon and took a loud sip from his tea. *"I entrusted one of the Masters with supervision while I am away."*

"But I guess you're not here because you're worried about a decision I made."

Rowland just watched me. His gaze was so penetrating that it would have embarrassed a young girl, or even a well-trained warrior, but not me.

"I am really quite worried about your Destroyer."

"Sam? But why?"

"She has huge power inside; I could feel it."

"And what's the problem with that, the Prophecy stated that-"

"I know what's in the Prophecy, Felnard, that's why I'm worried."

Rowland looked around. Seeing the small furniture, he began to grimace. *"Her soul may still shine bright and I am sure her heart is pure, but what will happen to her during the journey? They will face many dangers and the appearance of a dark Druid is the worst sign."* My hand trembled.

"What are you talking about?"

"Didn't you hear the news?" Rowland laughed, no longer trying to hide his emotions. *"People call him Bloodshed. He usually kidnaps virgins to drink their blood and he is headed straight to where your nephew and his friends are going. This is more than a coincidence, old friend."*

"It can't be," I shook my head, standing up so suddenly that Rowland shuddered a little. I scrambled around the room until I found the book that contained my notes. I sat back down, cracking it open and thumbing through the pages.

"I sent them so early because I knew that the path of the Destroyer and the Soulless could not intersect till the very end."

"Because if the path of good and evil intersects-"

"The Destiny of the Destroyer will be sealed." We finished the sentence together. I

190

continued to flip through the small book, finding the page. Tension began to overtake Rowland.

"It's here, too," I said, handing him my notes.

And then comes the time of the Soulless,
He will be followed by torment and death,
The bitter song of the people's cry.
He will be the only infection
Who can suck the soul of the Destroyer
And bring mayhem to the World's order.

"I know these lines well." Rowland rubbed his forehead. "If Sam is confronted with the So-" He swallowed hard. "The Soulless, before she is ready-"

"Let's not judge hastily, they have a long way to go."

"But will there be enough time for a person to change?" Rowland got up and went to the window. It was raining outside.

"I know only good intentions have guided you Felnard and to this day I regret that I didn't believe you sooner, but-"

"I wouldn't have believed you if you'd have stood in front of me with something like this." Rowland glared at me from over his shoulder. "It's hard to believe that what we thought was a fairy tale may be true."

"We have to do something to help them. We have to protect Sam." Rowland turned back to stare me down. The silence that followed was long.

"Sam is strong," I said eventually.

"And what if she isn't? If she's not strong enough and Radona gets loose-"

"Then He will show up for her." Rowland nodded slowly, but his eyes revealed fear and worry. I continued.

"You know that He understands true pain and reveals his secrets to those with broken hearts."

"I hope you're right Felnard, if not-"

"Let's hope for the best, my friend." I patted his shoulder. "More tea?"

I sat there, staring at my Uncle. He looked like a stranger to me.

There was another part of Elemris' Prophecy about the Destroyer, and he decided to completely withhold from us? There were so many things I would have done differently if I'd have known. I would have trained Sam more, I would even have trained myself to be better prepared. I couldn't even figure out how the Soulless got into her head until it was too late. I wouldn't have spent so much time with Ney...

I swallowed back my tears. I was full of anger and disappointment.

I couldn't look at Felnard.

"How could you not tell me about something so important?" I asked, trying to stay calm.

"There was a lot on your plate already, my son. I-" I raised my hand to cut him off as soon as I saw that he wanted to say more.

"I could have prepared myself more, maybe… just maybe… half of the things that happened to us would have been avoided. Don't you think so?"

I finally looked into his eyes. He was broken. I no longer saw my Uncle; I saw a man full of regret.

"I'm sorry, I simply wanted to make it as-"

I brought my fist down on the table hard, my anger breaking through my guard walls. Fire rose up in the fireplace, red as blood. Felnard didn't even flinch. He just lowered his head.

"I hope you can forgive me one day," he said quietly, before standing up from the table and leaving me alone in the Lonely House.

CHAPTER 18
UNEXPECTED NEWS

"SAM"

Keeping up the act of 'the good servant' in front of others was harder than I'd expected. Aihyla never failed to apologise for every order she had to give in order to keep up the illusion. We were only around the other members of her family during breakfast and lunch and - as Anda had told me - she usually asked for her dinner in her quarters. I had to withstand the ugly stares I got from the King and Queen while being in the dining room with them.

They were not happy at all with how well I acted. Queen Beatrice always tried to find something wrong with how I served the food or how my hair was done, but Princess Aihyla hushed her all the time. She wasn't popular with her parents after what she did to save me from probable death. Prince Bellion consistently glared at me but never said a word. He was kind of creepy, to say the least. The things they talked about were more boring than I'd ever imagined a conversation could be:

The Queen was in the middle of planning the Summer Ball, which gave a new chance to the Nobles and Royals to make engagement plans.

The King was on the hunt for more Halflings. In his eyes, there weren't enough servants in the palace, even though there were more of us than them.

Prince Bellion grabbed every chance to complain about a woman named Olenia Helron, who was his father's pick for him as a bride. He kept calling the woman ugly, boring, a pig and a series of other wonderful descriptors. I felt bad for her, not him. Aihyla rarely joined in the conversation and when she did, she kept her answers very short and usually managed to piss off her mother.

The Prince's servant - a boy named Milo - was the only one of us who was half Fairy and Elf. As I'd found out from him while we took our long walks to the kitchen, his family made him an outcast because he couldn't find a bride, but the Prince saved him from living on the streets. I was surprised to hear that a man like Bellion would do something like this for anyone. It felt like a half-truth coming from Milo. When I asked him why Bellion took him in as his servant he refused to answer my question.

Milo was as handsome as all of the other Noble Halflings. He had long blond hair, almost ashy grey eyes, defined cheekbones and jaw. He was really funny, kind and honest in a way that was so refreshing. I really felt bad for him whenever the Prince decided to punish him with harsh words.

On our fourth night of planning the escape I brought up the idea to take him with us, but Aihyla declined immediately. She said that it will be hard enough to get out even for the two of us, so we can't risk anything. I didn't have a good argument against it. It had proven to be a challenge to come up with an idea for our escape. The palace was heavily guarded with barely, if any, gaps between Guard changes. There was an underground escape route for emergencies but in order for us to go through it we would have had to go through the Guard's quarters, so that was out of the question.

"After long consideration…" Aihyla stormed into my room without knocking. I barely had time to grab my dress and pull it in front of myself. It was my sixth night in the palace but I couldn't get used to how she didn't have any normal boundaries in discussion, privacy or anything really.

"I think we only have one chance."

"I'm listening," I said, turning away from her and got into my dress so I wouldn't have to stand naked.

"The Summer Ball."

"What about it?" I asked and almost screamed as I turned around. There was barely any space between us; I didn't even hear her come up behind me. She put her hands on my waist and spun me back around without a word, setting to tightening the lace of my dress.

"That's gonna be the night when we will escape."

"Why is that any better than literally any other night?"

"Because the Guards only check the passengers of the carriages when they come *in*, not when they *leave* the palace," she smiled proudly. "That means that we just have to make sure to be in one of them."

"Alright… how will we do that?"

"Well, we will use the greatest weapon we have…" I felt like my heart was gonna jump out of my throat. I'd wondered for days if Neyra told her about my powers but it didn't seem like it at all. She grinned at me, head now around the side of my own so I could see her as she spoke, that small twinkle of mischief in her eye. Sometimes, it was very easy to remember she was part

Fairy.

"Seduction." She lowered her voice as she said it.

I started laughing, but when I turned around and saw the now-serious expression on her face I realised that she wasn't joking. I looked at myself.

"I don't think-" she put her finger on my mouth, shushing me entirely. My touch-starved skin reacted in revulsion and longing. I missed Killian.

"You can do it. You're gorgeous." She beamed at me and I couldn't help but smile back. Aihyla's energy was entirely infectious. She was about to continue when a knock came from the door.

"Yes!" She yelled as she turned towards it. Two Guards entered.

"King Oberon is waiting for you in the Throne Room," said the taller one.

"Oh, I almost forgot!" She grabbed my hand and said, "we have a guest." Before I could ask who it was, we were already on our way.

We couldn't talk much with the Guards behind our backs so my nerves started to get the better of me. I started sweating and felt shivers run down my spine at the same time. I didn't know what to expect. Aihyla subtly grasped my fingertips and squeezed them as if to say *it's okay*. I appreciated the gesture.

We entered the Throne Room and I had to take a deep breath as the King and the Queen came into view. Princess Aihyla took her place and I stood behind her chair. We didn't have to wait long before the door opened. As the figure of a man appeared my heart started beating uncontrollably, I was afraid that I might faint.

Vendal.

He looked different since I last saw him - thinner, and had these big bags under his eyes. He seemed not only tired, but weary. As he noticed me a slight smile appeared on his face.

"Druid. State your business." The King said already bored of a conversation that hadn't even started yet.

"King Oberon," he bowed. "Queen Beatrice, Prince Bellion, and Princess Aihyla." He straightened himself. "My name is Vendal Heron."

"No one cares!" Prince Bellion bursted out, I saw Milo finch behind him. "Just get to the point so we can leave."

"I am here to offer my services to the Princess." He looked straight at Aihyla. I coughed twice in an attempt to signal Aihyla, unsure if she was going to pick up on my meaning.

When a Princess turns twenty-five, she has the privilege of owning her own Druid, who makes sure that she is always in good health, her skin is flawless and - most importantly - that she is fertile.

"Well, Vendal, you honour me." Princess Aihyla stood up, turning to catch my eye for a second. I gave her the smallest nod I could manage. "If you may-"

"Hold!" The Queen raised her hand. "You just got yourself a new servant and now you want a Druid too?"

"Beatrice," King Oberon turned to his wife. "I already sent word to Rowland to get you a new Druid, please stop competing with your own daughter."

"But-"

"I said *stop it*," Oberon said, almost growling at her. The Queen stood up abruptly and stomped out without another word.

"One word from my daughter and you are out of here, Druid," he pointed at Vendal and left too.

The servants guided Vendal away to make sure that his appearance was up to the Royal standards. Aihyla and I went back upstairs, at which point I told Aihyla everything the moment the Guard left us. She was just as excited as I felt and definitely even more positive about our chances than before. We'd started making plans to leave even earlier when Anda arrived, leading Vendal in. He was wearing the palace's white Druid ropes, and they'd braided his thick hair even closer to his scalp so there wasn't a single strand out of place. As soon as Anda left I just ran straight into his arms and started sobbing.

"I've been so worried about you," I choked out into his torso. He squeezed me a little tighter as he replied.

"Me too, kiddo."

"Where's Killian?" I asked after I let go of him, but as soon as I saw his face I knew that something wasn't right. "Ven?" He looked at Princess Aihyla, who had kindly taken a backseat to our reunion. I found myself nodding uselessly.

"Oh, right, yes. Don't worry, you can trust her. We have a lot to tell, actually."

"Sam…" He took such a deep breath that I was afraid that he might never exhale all that air out. "Neyra is… she's… dead."

I wasn't sure what happened next. The world went quiet. I saw Vendal's lips moving and tears coming down on his face. I felt Princess Aihyla put her hand on my shoulder. I saw a bird flying outside. I wasn't sure how I ended up sitting on the floor with just the feeling of Vendal's hands on my face.

"I'm sorry I wasn't fast enough," I heard him say, and it brought me back to the room. I embraced him again, tears were streaming down my face but I didn't care. I felt his whole body shiver. "I'm sorry."

"It's not your fault," I whispered into his ear. His whole body started heaving with sobs in my grasp. I don't know how long we sat like that on the floor, but when we let go of each other I knew that what I was about to hear next was going to make me even more upset.

"Killian wasn't there," he said, wiping the tears from his face, "I believe that the Soulless…he took his memories of us."

"How is that possible?" Princess Aihyla asked. Vendal's brow furrowed for a moment, but he shook his head, apparently discarding the thought.

"With very dark magic," the Druid answered, eyes kept locked on me

"He doesn't know who I am?" I asked, my voice barely more than a whisper.

"Probably not."

"Oh…" Aihyla sighed behind me.

"Are you certain?"

Vendal nodded. "I tried to track him down. That's why it took me so long to get here, but my best guess is that he's gonna make his way back to Yandana anyway."

"If he comes back, my Father will probably punish him," Aihyla said.

"Why would he? Killian finished his service as a soldier; he was discharged by Oberon himself-"

"That's true, but he was supposed to marry me." Vendal's eyes widened.

I walked to the enormous window as Vendal got filled in, looking down at Yandana as it got taken over by the night. The street lanterns were all lit and young Elves and Fairies had begun roaming the streets.

"Since he received an Elven name, it is part of the tradition that he receives a Royal bride."

"But he's a *Human*," Vendal started to raise his voice.

"Yes, I know. I don't know why my father is this obsessed with him. The only thing I know is that he is dead set on making me marry him, even if I have no desire to do so," Aihyla finished breathlessly and had to take a deep breath to calm herself down. "I'm sorry. We are all a bit frustrated and-"

"Is it possible to bring back his memories?" I asked. Silence fell on the room. I turned back to look at them: Aihyla was visibly sad, while Vendal completely avoided my eye.

"Ven?"

"I don't know, Sam."

The pain came out of nowhere. I felt it shoot through my whole body, forcing me onto my knees. Both of them wanted to come to my aid, but as I lifted my hand to stop them, I pushed them to the wall with all the powerful force of the wind. I was dizzy, barely able to focus on anything. The pain concentrated in my chest. I pulled off the dress and screamed, not because of the pain, but because of a huge black mark that appeared right in the middle of my chest. I felt my head burn up before fainting.

"Sam."

"Samantha!"

"SAM!"

"Why are you shivering, Sam?"
"You fucking monster!"

"Killian, where are you?"

Red glowing eyes in the dark.

"You are alone, Sam… no one will love you"

"Get out of my head!"
"KILLIAN!"

"You invited me in and now you are sending me away?"

"Liar."
"Where are you?"
"LIAR?"
"Killian, I am so sorry."
"You're pathetic."
"Shut up!"
"Truth hurts little Sammy."
"I will kill you!"
"You will try."

"FUCK YOU!"
"Come and try it."

"KILLIAN!"

When I opened my eyes again, I was in my bed. Vendal and Aihyla were having a fight over something before the Princess slapped the Druid and left him alone with me in the room.

I sat up. The pain was gone, but I still felt dizzy. I looked down at my chest to see that the black marking had shrunk down to half the size. It looked like a deep cut that was burned into my skin. Ven sat down on the edge of the bed, his face full of concern.

"What in the hell is this?" I asked, referring to the mark on my chest, but as I looked up I saw my hair for a second. I had black strands now running through my red hair.

"I think it's some kind of old magic," Ven said, utterly despondent, "but I have no idea how it works."

"It felt like my heart broke in half." I wasn't sure if that was possible, but it was certainly the closest thing to how I could describe it.

"I'm sorry, Sam. I wish I could have come with better news."

"Don't even say that. I'm glad you're here," I touched his hand which made him smile a little. "I am so sorry for your loss."

"Is it true? What Aihyla said about her?" A jolt of irritation hit me; I couldn't believe that the Princess told Vendal about Neyra without me. I just nodded. "Oh for-"

"They had her brother captured." Ven was a bit taken aback by my words.

"Brother? But she never... Well, I guess that shouldn't be surprising."

"Ven-"

"No, it's okay. I'll be fine, I just. I can't believe how big of a fool I was."

"None of us knew, Vendal. She misled us all, but I think..."

I paused for a second, I did want to believe that Neyra wouldn't have done what she did if it wasn't for her brother's captivity, but truthfully I was still unsure. For Vendal, though, in this moment?

"I think the reason she started giving false information to the Elves was because of you."

"Me?"

"Come on, I know you felt it too. She loved you with all her heart." I smiled and I watched Ven's anger slowly dissolve from his face. It turned stony, into resolve.

"We have to help her brother."

"We will." It never failed to surprise me that I believed it.

"I heard your plan from Aihyla."

"Silhoue, how long was I out?" It seemed like they basically talked through everything without me. Vendal shrugged.

"An hour or more."

"I have to stop doing that." And for the first time since our reunion, we both laughed.

"KILLIAN"

The road back to Yandana felt longer than ever before. I met a few familiar faces along my way and they told me some concerning things. Some of them claimed that I had broken my oath to King Oberon and disappeared, while others told me that he was out for my head. I was full of questions; no matter how hard I tried I couldn't remember anything that had happened to me in the past few months. There were some faint memories of places, but nothing else.

What bothered me above all was the woman in my dreams.

Every night, a faceless woman would lead me through the streets of Yandana until we reached the Noble Gardens, at which point the scenery would shift in a haze and I would be holding her in my arms. I didn't know what it meant, but it felt strangely familiar. I kept turning it over and over in my head, questioning if it was someone I knew or just the weird coincidence of recurring dreams.

The Guards at the East Gate went into a full panic when I announced myself. I thought they would have me arrested, but instead they ordered a full escort to guide me to the palace. I was terrified by the thought of facing the Royal Family. If all the things I'd heard about myself were true, it meant the end of my life, and rightfully so.

The palace towered over us, casting a horrible shadow. I felt my heart pounding rapidly in my chest as the Guards led me through the main gate. People were whispering as we walked past them, not trying particularly hard to hide the fact they were whispering about me. The courtyard, on the other hand, was dead quiet as we walked through it. The soldiers around me didn't even look at me, which only spiked my anxiety further. It had taken me more than thirty days to reach Yandana and somehow, in that moment, I wished I wouldn't have.

The enormous red wooden doors of the palace slowly opened, but we came to a quick stop. My stomach sank as King Oberon, Queen Beatrice, Prince Bellion, and Princess Aihyla walked out with at least fifty people behind them. The Elven King seemed angrier than I'd ever seen him before. I fell to my knees, lowering my head to show my respect and, I guess, my guilt. The Guards stood to the side so it was only me and the whole Royal escort facing each other. It felt like the awkward silence lasted for hours, but it was broken by the sound of slow footsteps. I saw golden boots stop directly in front of me. I looked up at the King, who stared down at me and held out his hand. I swallowed down my fear and kissed the Royal ring on his finger.

"Stand, Malion Arur," he ordered.

I stood, but as I looked at the people behind him, I couldn't hide my surprise as I spotted my friend, Vendal, standing behind Princess Aihyla. Beside him was a Halfling servant girl with strange black strands in her red hair. She didn't look at me, her head kept down so I couldn't get a good look at her face. Another poor soul in the service of the Royal Family. But what was Vendal doing here?

"Your Royal Highness," I straightened myself even more, just like we learned in the army. "I owe you and your family an apology. I unfortunately can't provide a logical explanation for my disappearance as I do not have any memories of what happened."

"Bring her forward," the King said, completely ignoring me. Captain Gadev stepped up behind the servant girl with Princess Aihyla and grabbed her. She didn't resist, not even when the Captain pushed her down on the pebbles. She rose back on her knees with grace, strictly looking at the ground.

"Do you know this woman, Malion?" The Captain asked. Well, demanded really.

"I do not," I said, a bit taken aback. Captain Gadev pulled the woman up on her feet, grabbed her face and turned it towards me. Tears were glittering in her ocean blue eyes, she seemed broken and tired.

"Are you sure?" The King asked and I nodded.

"Am I supposed to know her?"

"She admitted her crime when she was captured. This Halfling monster and her companions kept you under a spell forcing you to lead them somewhere."

"Lead them...?" I looked at the woman and then to Vendal, who very slightly shook his head. "I am sure this is just a misunderstanding, my K-"

"We believe her Druid friend took your memories away so that they could avoid death," The King continued. I had no idea what was going on around me anymore. I looked at the woman once more as tears streamed down her face. Was it possible that she was behind my memory loss? She seemed innocent. She seemed...

"You really don't remember me, Killian?" She asked, her voice shaking from the crying. The way she said my name sent a shiver down my spine, the pleading and hurt in her voice was genuine. "Not-" Captain Gadev yanked her away.

"Shut your mouth, you stupid whore!" He pushed her back down on the ground with tremendous force and spat on her.

"That is enough!" The Princess yelled and was next to the servant in a few long steps, helping her stand up. "How dare you, Captain? Are you treating your wife the same?"

"Princess, I-"

"Shut your mouth or I'll have your head separated from your neck," the Princess hissed, angrily.

"You grow too attached to this criminal, my dear," the King said calmly. He waved his hand and two guards stepped out of line, taking the girl away from the Princess.

"Father! She is my servant, she did nothing wrong!"

"Not anymore. We can be grateful that Malion Arur is alive at all. Take her away!" The King gestured the Guards away; the woman showed no resistance. Suddenly, Princess Aihyla was in my face.

"Aren't you gonna do something?" She asked, that hissed ire now pointed in my direction. I was taken aback by her words. I couldn't go against the King's order. She turned away and hurried after the Guards with Vendal following close behind.

"Forgive her, Malion," King Oberon put his hand on my shoulder, patting it. "She's just excited about your engagement, which we will be announcing at the Summer Ball in three days time."

"Engagement?" My head was all over the place. "You aren't going to punish me?"

"For what? You were clearly at the mercy of these terrible people, my son," he laughed. "Come, we have much to discuss!"

It was late at night by the time I finished talks with the King and Queen, with all the Royal servants taking notes on the arrangements that they ordered. I had no desire to marry Princess Aihyla, but after everything, I couldn't deny their wishes. We parted ways in the Throne Room, and as the servant was leading me to my quarters, I once again had the chance to appreciate the glory of the palace from the inside. I liked the stillness and quiet of the corridors. The great big windows that faced out to Yandana showed the city in all its beauty. It never failed to amaze me.

We were heading straight for the stairs, but the servant stopped abruptly and bowed deeply. The Princess was arriving from downstairs with Vendal following her closely, whispering to her ear. When they noticed us they also came to a stop.

"Pr-"

"Oh good. Come with me. Katie, you may leave!" Princess Aihyla ordered the servant who left silently.

We didn't go up the stairs, but instead we took a left turn and walked in the direction of the War Room, a place that was far too familiar to me. The Princess sent the Guards away from the door and told them not to disturb us under any circumstances.

As we entered, the familiar smell of old parchment hit my nose. Some of the maps were older than the palace itself. The War Table was empty - there were no flags or figures on it. I hid my proud smile, as it was thanks to my unit. We were the ones who captured the last resisting forces of the Humans. The titanic black curtains were covered in dust as they hadn't been aired in some time. The cartographer's table in the corner had spiderwebs on it, giving an even more grim look to the whole interior. The shelves were fully loaded with maps and documents, logbooks and military records. It brought back so many memories.

Princess Aihyla closed the doors, forcing me to snap out of my daydreaming. I turned to them.

"Do you remember me?" Vendal asked, measuring me from head to toe.

"Of course, Ven! What kind of question is that?" They looked at each other.

"The Soulless did a more intricate job than I expected," he sighed as he stepped closer to me, which prompted me to take a step back. "Don't be afraid, old friend."

"It's hard not to be," I muttered as he put his hand on my forehead. "What are you doing, Vendal?"

"I'm going to try and restore your memory."

"But-"

It felt like a sharp blade cut through my whole body as brilliant light filled the room making me go blind for a second. When I opened my eyes again Ven was on the floor holding his head, Princess Aihyla crouching next to him, squeezing his shoulder.

"What in Silhoue's name was this?" I asked in agonising pain.

"Who is Sam? Do you remember?" The Princess asked.

"Who?"

"I felt the darkness; it forced me out of his head." said Vendal, slowly standing up, leaning against the wall. "Fuck. My magic is not enough for this."

"Can someone explain what's going on?"

"It's a very long story," Vendal said, trying to catch his breath.

"I have time."

And so he started talking. Told me everything about the servant girl, Sam, and our fight against an invisible enemy called The Soulless. He talked about dreams that led us to her, a long and treacherous journey, searching for answers and clues. Allion, Lendala, and Irkaban, and a Prophecy that needed to be found and destroyed at all costs. He told me about his love for our Elven companion Neyra, who'd lost her life to the Soulless, the menace who'd taken my memories of Sam away from me.

Sam.

Vendal said we were in love.

Was that the reason why she looked so hurt?

By the time the Druid finished the story we were all sitting around the War Table. My head was aching from all the information I'd gained. It filled all the gaps in my memory perfectly, but it didn't make any sense. Ven was a good friend, but the way he was talking about me and the things I'd done simply didn't sound like me at all. I would never have abandoned my King for a Halfling who's supposedly the saviour of our world. Falling in love with her on top of that was even more out of character - after what Thana had done to me,

I'd promised myself to never love again.

I stood up from the table and walked towards the door.

"Killian."

I didn't care about the pleading in Vendal's voice. I left the room without another word.

CHAPTER 19
THE SUMMER BALL

"VENDAL"

Killian avoided me.

If we happened to enter a room at the same time, he turned around and left. If he saw me at the other end of a corridor, he turned around and left. If he couldn't leave because I was required to follow the Princess around and they were forced to spend time together, he refused to talk to either of us. He clearly thought we were crazy, but I didn't give up. I kept bringing up stories of the time we shared on our journey even if he didn't answer me at all. And I made sure to continue and talk about his relationship with Sam. Every time, once we finished a walk around the Noble Garden or a dinner or lunch, he left without saying a word.

I knew him. I knew he was struggling to tell what was right and what was wrong. Getting under his skin wasn't a hard challenge since he didn't even attempt to talk about something else. He was forced to listen to us. The only time we heard him talk was during lunch, when the whole Royal Family was in attendance. He put on an act for the King and Queen, just like everyone else.

Sam, on the other hand, was a more worrying case. Every morning, early at dawn, I went down to her in the dungeons. She was kept in a small cell. Each morning I visited her, she stayed in the corner, her back turned to me. I kept her up to date on everything but she never responded. Her silence was more menacing than Killian's. Rats were cooped up around her - this giant black one kept its eye on me from her shoulder. I knew she was keeping up her connection to them even if it was draining all her power.

After I finished my visit, I would go down to the Noble Gardens with Aihyla, where my Uncle waited for us. We kept him up to date on everything. He said that no matter what was going on, we needed to keep Sam's spirit alive, which meant doing everything possible to bring back Killian's memories. Felnard contacted Rowland for help but heard nothing back from him. On the third morning however, the day of the Summer Ball, he greeted us with a big smile.

"I think I've found a way," he said cheerfully.

"Did Rowland write back?" Felnard gave me a look.

"Have a little faith in your uncle," he scolded me, which made Aihyla chuckle. I knew Felnard managed to charm her at their very first meeting. The man knew how to treat ladies.

"Fine. Tell me then."

"Tonight, you have to bring Killian along, no matter what happens."

"I don't think he will agree to come with us, Felnard," Aihyla said. She didn't say, but I could tell that she was starting to get stressed by the whole situation she found herself in.

"Make him drink this." Felnard pulled out a vial from his sleeve. It had a weird purplish liquid swirling in it. "Pour it in his drink. He will follow all of your orders, no matter what." Aihyla took it from him and put it in her small pouch. "And these," he pulled out two more vials, but the liquid in them was a dark green, "are for the Guards in the dungeon so you can get Sam and Gally out."

"Thanks, Uncle," I said as I put them away. "This is gonna be close."

"It sure will be, but I believe in both of you." Felnard stopped and just looked up at the trees. "It is good that this is happening tonight. The Soulless and his growing army destroyed another village."

"Shit," gasped Aihyla.

"He is getting bolder." Felnard brushed through his beard, his eyes darting back and forth as he ran through what might be ahead of us. "I'm afraid time might not be on our side."

"We'll be fine. We have to believe it," I said, which made both of them turn towards me. I wasn't in the best of moods ever since our first talk with Killian. "What? I can be positive."

"Good. We'll need it," Aihyla patted my shoulder. She was nothing like I'd expected her to be. She had nothing in common with her parents or brother. She was independent, brave, kind, caring-

She reminded me of Neyra.

We said our goodbyes to Felnard and headed back to the palace.

Every servant was in the Throne Room preparing for the celebration. As we walked in, long lines of tables had already been set up on both sides of the hall; Halflings were working hard to put down new carpet on every inch of the floor, covering everything in the colour of the Sun. The thrones were decorated by even more flowers and there were people up on ladders hanging up huge lanterns shaped like stars between the pillars.

When the news of the first destroyed village had arrived at the palace, King Oberon called "humbug" and dismissed it. When the second one was on fire, he shrugged. Since it was happening to Humans, he simply didn't care at all. Neyra's talk of how undeserving some people were kept creeping back into my mind. I was consistently disgusted by what I was seeing and couldn't wait to get out as soon as possible.

Killian was standing in the middle of the throne room in his classic black attire. He looked so different from the man I knew, and it didn't help that he acted different as well. Aihyla and I walked up to him.

"It's a bit much," he said, strictly looking up at the room. Aihyla did her usual stealth move, and I know I saw Killian jump a little when he realised how close she was to him. I had no idea how she was able to manage that with literally everyone.

"My mother likes it like this," she answered, disappointment in her voice. I had to hide my smile seeing the way her expression changed.

"I am guessing you do not." He looked at Aihyla and I noticed that familiar stare he used around ladies. The Princess noticed too.

"What's with the face?" She asked, confused by the change in Killian's behaviour.

"Well, today is our engagement after all," he shrugged. "We might as-"

Aihyla slapped him so hard that it echoed through the Throne room, causing everyone to stop at what they were doing.

"You are not yourself, Malion Arur." The Princess had lowered her voice, but she was angrier than ever. "But that will change."

We left him behind. We didn't stop until we reached the staircase that led down to the dungeons. Aihyla started pacing up and down to calm herself down. I understood her frustration.

"Tell me about her," I asked.

She smiled, and told me about her beautiful love down by the sea.

After the Sevens were broken, the Palace of Peace and everything around it was changed into a new city called the Shells. Inhabited by Elves and Fairies, under the rule of King Oberon and Queen Beatrice's first born - Steward of Shells, Abelyon. Aihyla's chosen one, Marion, was a Halfling girl - half Human and half Elf. She was a servant, Aihyla's servant. The Princess liked her from the moment she started working for her. She didn't care about the rules the Royal family created; Marion took every chance to talk back to her, to ignore some of her orders while also giving the worst attitude one could have imagined for a servant who's life always hung in the balance. She was steadfast in herself, and Princess Aihyla loved the challenge she set up for her, the excitement of something new. Talking back turned into flirtation, fliration turned into stolen kisses in the dark, and soon they'd realised they'd fallen in love with each other. This, however, only gave them reason to fear that someone might discover their relationship.

Prince Abelyon, older brother to the Princess, was - according to Aihyla - a lot like her, so when she asked him to take Marion in until she could get away, her brother agreed. The Princess was supposed to leave on the day Killian rescued Sam from the Guards. When he didn't show up in the palace, King Oberon doubled the Guard presence around the whole city, which meant that Aihyla couldn't get away.

We were the reason she couldn't reunite with her true love. How cruel and strange the world could be sometimes. In order for us to have had the fortune to get Sam, Aihyla had to suffer. The domino effect we have on others lives weighed on me, along with the guilt of holding up Aihyla's happiness.

Aihyla stopped pacing as she finished her story. She turned to me a lot more composed than before.

"I'm fine."

"I can tell," I smiled. She shook her head, apparently not convinced. "We can do this. Okay?"

"Yes. I know." She nervously brushed her hair away. "Go to Anda. She has a dress ready for Sam and attire for Gally. Once the Guards are out-"

"I will make them change into Ilyons and put masks on them - I know Aihyla, we made the plan together, remember?"

"I'm sorry. I am just nervous, Vendal." She took a deep breath and said, "I will take care of our friend Killian."

"Good. See you soon."

I collected the Ilyons from Anda, who was a bit suspicious and asked me about the Princess' strange request. I told her I couldn't share any information which stopped her asking further questions.

I hid the clothes behind the statue of a Guard (how creative) near the dungeons (Aihyla chose the spot because literally no one walked through those corridors). When I was sure no one would stumble across them, I made my way to the kitchen.

The cooks were running around like crazy to prepare everything the Queen wanted. There were more than fifty of them in the huge area, running with cakes I'd never seen before, making meals only Nobles and Royals knew about and they paid me no mind at all, which made my next job a lot easier. I snatched the food that was prepared for the dungeon Guards and left with it.

Just before I reached the Guards, ensuring I was out of eyeshot, I poured the potions Felnard had made into their drinks. They were playing cards.

"Dinner? Already?" asked the one with the broken nose. He told me his name, but I didn't care.

"Because of the Summer Ball, all of us have to eat earlier. I grabbed yours because one of the servants wanted to take it for himself."

"Fucking Halfling monsters," growled the other, who had an ugly scar on his cheek.

"I know, right? They have no respect." They started laughing and took their trays. "Enjoy!"

I left them, going straight back to the statue to gather the clothes. I didn't have to wait long before I heard them crumble to the ground. I ran down, took the keys from Broken Nose, opened the cell that was furthest from the stairs and dragged them in there, locking them in.

Feeling pretty confident the plan was going well, I first went to Gally. He was very skinny and looked sick. I opened the door and as he looked up at me I couldn't believe how much he resembled Neyra. He had the same face shape, exquisite deep-set grey eyes, small lips and long black hair.

"Gally, my name is Vendal. I'm Neyra's-" I had to think about what to say next - "friend. I am here to help you."

"Where is she?" His speech was slow and his voice was hoarse. It occurred to me that he probably hadn't talked to anyone since they closed him in the cells.

"I will tell you everything once we are out. Put these on, we need to blend in." I handed him the Ilyon. He looked a bit confused, but didn't ask questions.

As he started to change, I stopped him.

"Before I forget," I said, bringing a quick wave of water through the stone walls, showering his dirty body, and then used warm, thick air to dry him. He stood frozen for a moment, jarred by the sudden experience. I shrugged at him. "We have to be convincing."

When I went to Sam's cell I almost screamed. She was already standing by the door when I went to open it. The rats had all left except for the black one that still sat on her shoulder.

She didn't look like herself at all. It seemed like there were more black strands in her hair, her eyes were red from all the crying, and the strange scar on her chest had grown bigger. It had small, black, vein-like lines coming out of it.

"Sam. Do-"

The rat ran down from her shoulder and landed on the floor with a thud before disappearing in the dark. I opened the cell door and gave her the crystal blue dress Aihyla picked out for her. She went back and I left her there so she could change in peace. I heard the water running again and I smiled. She'd been listening all along.

With the help of my magic I made the deep bags disappear under Gally's eyes before putting his mask on. Sam emerged from the cell in the beautiful dress and the butterfly-shaped mask already on her face. She didn't want to let me at first, but I changed her hair to make it thicker in order to cover her ears, and was able to take the redness from her eyes.

We went back upstairs, passing the Guards who were still passed out in the cell. When we neared the Throne Room, the sound of the crowd was already audible. Gally seemed nervous but Sam was... devoid. It was scary to see her like that. She didn't react to anything, not emotionally anyway; she was just staring ahead of herself, focused on ahead. We made our way to the doors into the Throne Room. People were flooding in from the main gate, and everyone was wearing masks - nothing better to make a jailbreak than a masquerade ball. The only unfortunate thing was that we had to keep up the act until the announcement of Killian and Aihyla's engagement. I told my companions to stay close to me at all costs. They just nodded.

As we entered, it was overwhelming to see the amount of people already inside. Many were dancing to the live band, some of them were drinking and just talking, but most of them were already flirting with each other. The scenery and the mood of the room was completely transformed. On top of it all, everything smelled like flowers. We stood as far away from everyone as was possible.

A few Elves did come around to talk with Sam, but Gally, incredibly, played his part perfectly. I told him on our way up to pretend that Sam was his lover and he did an honourable job, charming folks who tried to strike up conversation and debuffing further inquiry.

Sam looked stunning in the body-tight Ilyon that the Princess had chosen for her. I don't think she ever realised how beautiful she really was. The only thing that was casting a shadow on it was the immense sadness that sat on her shoulders. I squeezed her hand and she looked up at me with blank eyes. She was fading away.

The band brought the music to a satisfying close and ceremonial trumpets sounded. The chatter ceased and the crowd shifted to open the way to the throne.

First came King Oberon and the Queen, both of them in the same golden-coloured Ilyon. Behind them arrived Prince Bellion in a bronze one, holding the hand of a slightly plump Elven woman. She was quite beautiful, but he didn't seem very satisfied. The crowd started murmuring the second that Princess Aihyla entered with Killian by her side. I heard people gasping around us, some of them surprised to see Malion Arur back in the palace, others claiming they knew he would appear again. Aihyla was wearing a long silver Ilyon, with black symbols sewn into the skirt. I instantly recognised Polly's work. I looked at Sam, but she was back to staring at the ground. It broke my heart to see her suffer. The instinct to scoop her up and escape right then and there was overwhelming, but I settled for grabbing her hand and squeezing it. She didn't react.

After the crowd quieted down the music started up again and people began to mingle. Fairies flew up with their partners and started dancing around the lanterns, while Elves seemed to prefer eating the various delights provided by the staff I knew were working their asses off below us. Princess Aihyla made her way towards us, Killian following behind her.

"Sam," she smiled and I saw that she had a hard time holding herself back from hugging the girl.

"Your Highness," Sam bowed as she spoke for the first time. She didn't look up at all.

"My mother wants to announce the engagement right after the ceremonial dance." I almost hushed her, but a peculiar smile appeared on her face.

"Look at this," she whispered as she turned to Killian, who was just looking around. "Killian." His eyes immediately darted to her. "I order you to dance with Sam." Princess Aihyla pointed at her and before either of us could protest against it, Killian held his hand out towards Sam.

"Why are you doing this to me?" Sam asked, her voice broken.

"Please, it might help," the Princess pleaded. "I will dance with Gally." She took his hand and quickly disappeared with the man.

"My lady," Killian said, still holding out his hand toward Sam.

"Go," I whispered. She nodded, if a bit resentful. She took Killian's hand and he led her into the crowd to dance.

I watched them closely. Sam kept her head turned away to the side, barely looking back at him. But Killian's gaze rested on her face during the whole dance. I knew he was under Felnard's enchantment, but felt I could see him remembering something. Maybe the night they danced together on the square in Haelion? Whatever it was, it disappeared quickly when Sam couldn't handle it anymore and left him behind, coming back straight to me. She just stood next to me taking big breaths, while holding her hand on her chest. I put my hand on her shoulder and squeezed it a bit.

The night went on for what seemed like hours. Princess Aihyla ordered Killian to pretend to be in love with her in front of everyone so they could sell the act to her parents. Gally and Sam stayed close to me, not daring to speak a word. Finally, the trumpets sounded again as King Oberon slowly rose from his throne.

"My dear subjects," he started projecting out to the crowd. "We are here tonight to celebrate Silhoue's favourite season!" Everybody started cheering. The Fairies were dropping flower petals down on us from above. "But!" He raised both of his hands which prompted everyone to fall silent again. "It is also a celebration for our family." Queen Beatrice stood up, joining the King by his side.

"We are honoured to announce the engagement of our daughter Princess Aihyla to Killian Fin, Malion Arur!"

The crowd burst out in loud laughter and applause as they stepped forward, holding hands. Time slowed down around me. Sam ran from my side before I could react at all. I bolted after her, pulling Gally with me. There was an outcry as we all pushed through the crowd. I saw Sam falling on the ground as one of the Elves pushed her over. We picked her up and it was at that point I realised why she'd run off: scales had started to appear on her hand, just like that night at the Grabodan Temple.

"Sam!" I whispered in her ear. "You need to control it!"

"I can't!" She shouted at me, which stopped the celebration. All eyes were on us. I saw Aihyla's concerned face in the midst of them.

"Of course you can!" I said between my teeth.

"What is happening to her?" Gally had huddled in.

"I don't-" Sam pushed us away as she fell forward on the ground. Several people backed away, leaving Sam spotlighted by the lack of people surrounding her.

"Sam!"

She screamed out in pain as blinding white light burst out of her chest, washing over the whole Throne Room. I heard the panic that took over the crowd all around us while I desperately tried to find my way back to her. The light suddenly dissipated and in Sam's place stood an enormous white Dragon, but her chest was still tainted by the black scar. Many of the people were on the floor crying in fear while others were fleeing towards the doors.

Sam's blue eyes stared back at me from the Dragon, but instead of sadness there was something else reflecting in them. She didn't care about me. She launched her long neck forward without warning, bringing her eye to eye with the Royal Family, which was followed by more screams. Aihyla was petrified, but as Sam slightly gestured with her head, the Princess pulled Killian away across the dancefloor, straight towards myself and Gally.

"King Oberon," Sam growled, her voice completely changed. "Know that you locked in your dungeon the only Halfling who could have prevented Radona from taking over this world. You have brought destruction to your people."

For the first time in his life, King Oberon was speechless. He was just staring at the Dragon, unable to understand how a *woman* could use such powerful magic. Fear was etched into his face, but not just of the Dragon: the fear of the unknown. Queen Beatrice was crying, her wings desperately folded around herself in a protective shield, completely shaken by the sudden events. The funniest sight amongst the chaos was definitely Prince Bellion who was hiding behind his partner, trying to cover himself with her skirt.

The Dragon let down her huge wing and I quickly ushered everyone to climb up onto her back. Once we were all settled, Sam turned around and ran through the door, destroying it. She leaped out on the courtyard, her wings spread open wide and we were high up in the sky with the blink of an eye. I screamed at her as loud as I could even though the wind made it impossible to hear anything unless it was right by someone's ear.

"WE NEED TO GET FELNARD!"

I wasn't sure if she heard me until she suddenly turned her wings vertically and stopped in the middle of the air.

Yandana looked unrealistic from above. The city formed a perfect hexagon with the Fairy trees creating a perfect circle around the palace inside the city walls. I saw the others look down at it with the same amazement I felt. The moment passed quickly as Sam turned around and flew towards the forest behind my Uncle's house. We landed by the lake, scaring away a herd of stags. I got down from her back quickly.

"You three stay here! I will grab my uncle!" I yelled.

I ran through the forest as fast as I could. My feet felt heavier with every step, but I didn't care. Getting to Felnard was all that mattered. I was hoping he would have a good explanation as to what happened to Sam. She just… turned, completely spontaneously. Maybe something triggered it, perhaps to do with the scar on her chest, but I wasn't and couldn't be sure about it. All I knew was that now King Oberon and everyone else in that room knew the truth about her. What was waiting for us? Were they gonna send armies after us? We'd taken the Princess, also. Seeing as much as I had of the King and Queen's behaviour, I wasn't sure what to expect from them. They didn't even care about the destroyed villages. Would a woman who can turn into a Dragon change their view on things? Sam said Radona's name out loud too. Was there a chance that people still remembered the legend?

I broke through the last trees and pushed at a faster pace to reach the house. Felnard was already out putting supplies on the three horses' backs. He had a bag around his shoulder with herbs sticking out of it.

"We're in big trouble!" I yelled even before reaching him.

"I know, dear boy!" He yelled back as he rushed to the house, closing the door and raised both of his hands up in the air.

"Stand back!" I grabbed the reins of the horses and pulled them away.

Massive roots broke through the ground and encased the Lonely House. Within a few seconds, huge, scary looking, black flowers bloomed out at different points, giving the building a grim and unwelcoming look. He lowered his arms, pulling the roots tighter around the structure until the windows shattered and a few wooden planks cracked and crumpled too.

"There. Just as we found it when we came here," he said, practically barking with laughter. I think he enjoyed destroying the house a little too much.

We made our way back through the forest on horseback. As we reached the clearing, an unwanted scene greeted us. Gally and Aihyla stood in front of Sam holding up their hands, shouting at Killian who had his sword out. I got off my horse and ran to them.

"Killian, stop it!" I yelled at him. Uncle's potion had worn off. Killian looked flustered and confused, but ready to fight. Ever the soldier. "Put your sword down!"

"Why the hell are you protecting a *Dragon*?" He demanded, his eyes darting from us to Sam.

"Because it isn't a Dragon." He turned around quickly as he heard Felnard's voice.

"Felnard…" he whispered.

"Sam, if you may, please?" My Uncle gestured with his hand. The Dragon turned around and walked straight into the lake.

"Sam?" Killian looked back at the creature just as that same light from the palace shot up to the sky, leaving Sam in the lake. "What kind of witchcraft is this?"

"The most ancient kind, my boy." Felnard put his hand on Killian's shoulder. "Now sleep."

He collapsed right there and then.

"What are you doing with him?" I asked. My uncle just laughed.

"I am going to bring back his memories, dear boy. Come, we'll need Sam," he said as he crouched down next to Killian and started taking out herbs from his bag.

I turned towards the lake as Aihyla was already wrapping a cloak over Sam's shoulders. Her hair had turned almost completely black; one single red strand was left peeking out of it. Aihyla held Sam close to her as she walked her back over, desperately trying to give her some physical comfort, but Sam's eyes were dead. Felnard had started chanting something in a language I'd never heard him speak before. Gally was sitting in the grass, his arms wrapped around his legs. I still hadn't had the chance to really explain what was going on to him.

Blessed Sagar, everything was fucked.

"Sam!" My uncle stood up and said, "I'm going wake him and I'm going need you to kiss him."

Sam didn't respond, still staring blankly ahead.

"Why?" I asked in her stead.

"That's the only way the magic will work. Well, according to Rowland at least."

"Sam? Are you okay with this?" Aihyla asked, but she didn't answer. "Sam."

"Yes." Her voice cracked as she spoke. She was staring at the sleeping Killian, expression… Well.

I stepped closer to Felnard and whispered in his ear.

"This has to work or we will lose her."

"I know, son," he nodded. He snapped his fingers. Killian sat up, dazed and confused, looking at us like we were all strangers to him. He stood up slowly holding up his hands.

"Go, Sam."

She stepped forward. For the longest time, they just stared at each other. Eventually, Killian slowly lowered his arms, and Sam put her fingers on his cheek and kissed him. It lasted less than a second. When she took a step back, we watched Killian with anticipation. He opened his eyes.

"Ven? Felnard?" He asked as his eyes met ours. Then he looked around, finally resting his eyes on Sam. "Who are these people and what are we doing here?"

Felnard sighed. I saw tears running down Aihyla's face as she tried to take Sam's hand into hers, but the Halfling turned away from us and walked back into the water.

"I'm sorry, son." Felnard said.

"We just have to find another way."

"I will take you all to Shells." We heard Sam's deep tremble as the white Dragon walked out of the water. "And we will part ways there."

"Sam-"

"Don't even start, Vendal," she growled as she let down her wing so we could climb on her back again.

No one said another word. It took a bit of convincing to get Killian up on the Dragon's back, but he did as he was asked eventually. I wasn't gonna let him go - I had to have faith in reversing the Soulless' magic back even if Sam didn't. The horses weren't thrilled as the Dragon grabbed them and lifted them from the ground.

We flew above the clouds the rest of the night and throughout the next day. We made it to Shells late into the next night, just as a storm arrived at the shore.

The city was built on a peak that rose above the ocean. The houses were all built around the Palace of Peace, which served as the home for the Steward of Shells. It was nowhere near as glorious as it used to be; I had seen drawings of the building in its heyday in books. Back during the days of the Sevens, it was built to reflect all of the different nations: The glory of the Elves, the modesty of the Giants, the intricate designs of the Dwarves, the unique shapes of the Handors, the colours of the Fairies, the accuracy of the Humans, and the nobility of the Grabodans. However, during the war, it had been heavily damaged and the Elves decided not to fix it in order to keep the palace as a reminder of what was. Each of the seven towers, except for one, were in ruins. The dome-like roof of the main building was covered in holes, and the eagle that was sitting on top of it was missing one of its wings. There was nothing glorious about it anymore. The walls were covered in greenery and they'd planted trees all around it to make it look a bit nicer.

Sam put down the horses first, then landed a few feet away from them. We all got off her back and before I could say a word to her, she took off from the ground and rose high above the clouds.

"What now?" I asked, voice low. "We completely failed her."

"She'll be back," Felnard replied, annoyingly confident. "Have a-"

"Oh, dear Silhoue!" Aihyla cried out. We both turned to her as she and Gally grabbed hold of Killian, who was near to fainting. They buckled under his weight, the three of them collapsing to the ground. We ran to them, my uncle taking Killian's face between his hands and inspecting him.

"What's happening to him, Felnard?" Aihyla asked.

"His memories are coming back." My Uncle smiled. I immediately looked up at the sky - clear and empty.

"Is this supposed to happen?" asked Gally, voice appropriately panicked as they sat Killian upright in the grass, my Uncle not letting go of his face. "Felnard!"

"Patience, my child, patience!" he hushed them. Black tears started streaming down Killian's face as he began silently screaming from the pain. He started coughing uncontrollably, hacking up black ooze so hard I thought he might bring up a lung in the process.

"Uncle-"

"Come on boy, that's the way. All of it out..."

Killian bent forward violently, shaking us all off. Finally, he spat out the last bit on the grass and it burnt everything around it instantly. He fell on his back, taking rapid breaths.

"Killian?" Felnard said, trying to pull his focus back to earth. His eyes stopped spinning in their sockets. We helped him up. Aihyla tore a piece from her Ilyon and gave it to him, which he gladly accepted and started wiping down his face.

"Are you okay?" she asked.

"Where's Sam?" Killian asked, spitting once more. "Where is she?"

"She left." I answered. "How much do you remember?"

"Everything. I remember everything. I was screaming inside, hoping that she would hear me," he sobbed. "Ven, I am so sorry I couldn't save Neyra-"

"What?" We all looked at Gally, now white as a sheet. "What is he talking about? Where's my sister?"

"I'm sorry Gally," I replied, "she's gone." He shook his head in disbelief.

"No, don't say that. Please, don't say that." We watched as he started to crumple in on himself with grief. "What happened?"

"The Soulless took her life like he took my memories of Sam," answered Killian, almost growling in anger. "But trust me, we're gonna kill that cunt."

CHAPTER 20
THE SORROW OF SOULS

"KILLIAN"

Ten days had passed since Sam disappeared. We were welcomed by Princess Aihyla's brother, Prince Abelyon, the Steward of Shells. He and his sister were the black sheeps of the Royal family; both of them clearly despised the ways of their parents. The palace from the outside wasn't too appealing, but they'd done numerous renovations on the inside. The rooms we got were all in the west wing. There was no ceiling, but they'd put up dome shaped tents, enchanted by the court's Druid to repel water. The walls were painted with gold with thick greenery growing through the holes, contrasting the ostentatiousness of money with nature in a way I'd never seen before. The bed frames were made out of thick oak, covered in the softest linen. The floor, interestingly enough, was pure white sand throughout the whole palace. We were required to take off our boots at the entrance. Prince Abelyon said that it was the wish of the late great rulers to keep the palace pure, hence why they used sand instead of wood or stone. It was weird at first, but we got used to it pretty quickly.

Gally followed me everywhere. He didn't talk much; he seemed to be scared of everything. His resemblance to Neyra destroyed me whenever I looked at him for too long. Younger than her, less mature, less sure of himself. When we asked him about his life before, he fell silent. After a while we stopped trying and let him be.

We barely saw the Princess. Finally reunited with Marion, they spent every minute they could together. The reunion was filled with tears and embraces, the both of them holding each other so tight as if they let go they might disappear again. Whenever I saw them, walking near the shore, or at the dinner table holding hands, my heart ached.

Sam left in the belief that I didn't remember her. While I was trapped in my own head, I'd tried to scream as loud as I could, hoping there might be some chance she might hear me, but the Soulless' magic was too powerful. Seeing the pain on her face after she kissed me the night she left haunted my dreams. I just… the only thing I wanted was to hold her in my arms again. I tried going after her, but Vendal and Felnard stopped me each time - no matter which way I went, they were right behind me. Felnard believed that Sam would find her way back to us, but I was doubtful.

Every morning, I left the palace and walked down on the shore to see the sunrise. It calmed my thoughts after the horrible nightmares I would have. Neyra's death replayed over and over again; Sam's broken heart; and Him. The Soulless was always there, lurking in the shadows.

When I arrived back at the palace, I usually got the news on new attacks throughout the Broken Ground. The Soulless had reached the Elven Kingdom with his army, growing stronger and stronger with every town hit. It always started the same: young boys and girls disappeared from the villages before an attack that left the places in fire and smoke. On our ninth evening, a message arrived from King Oberon to the Prince. He voiced his concerns, asked about his daughter and called a meeting in preparation for war. He wanted every high-ranking soldier in the Palace of Peace the next day and there was no way Prince Abelyon could say no to him.

o

The Royal carriage arrived at midday, followed by an overwhelming ring of Guards. King Oberon was so concerned about his own safety that he brought at least half of his army with him on the journey. Vendal, Felnard and I stayed close to the War Room, situated in a closed off area next door. Prince Abelyon sent Aihyla and Marion away, to make sure that their father couldn't pull something underhanded.

We watched from the window as they marched toward the Palace. Vendal wasn't too happy that we'd stayed - he was very clear that he thought we should follow Aihyla and Marion - but we had to hear what they were planning.

"Oh, great Sagar!" Felnard gasped as the carriage door opened. Rowland stepped out after the King. "What on Earth is he doing here?"

"This is very odd indeed," Vendal nodded in agreement.

Rowland and the King walked towards the stairs and disappeared from our view. Felnard seemed concerned as he started pacing back and forth, mumbling to himself.

"This is not a good sign Killian," Vendal said, his voice full of concern. "My people took an oath not to interfere with events unless it was inevitable. If the Head of the Druids is here in person…" He paused; I'd never seen Vendal so afraid before. "It means that the threat is too big to stay silent."

Before I could respond we heard the doors of the War Room opening. The Guards entered, taking their places along with the high-ranking authorities. We stepped even closer to the thin wall. Felnard stopped pacing and sat down on the chair that was placed there for him.

For a few seconds everything was awfully quiet. No one spoke, we only heard the servant unpacking the little figurines onto the war table. Once they left the room and the door closed, the King took a deep breath.

"War is upon us," he said, his voice broken. "This so-called 'Soulless' and his army are marching right toward Yandana." I heard as he pushed one of the figurines on the table. "The last report came from Gandon, the Guard City near the border of the Human Kingdom-"

"I am sorry, my King," a high-pitched voice sounded somewhere further from our wall. I didn't recognise it. "Did you really say The Soulless?"

"Yes, General Eldam."

"The Soulless. From that very old fairy tale?" he asked, doubtfully.

"You can laugh, General," Rowland spoke instead of the King, "but it is true. He has arrived."

"A *fairy tale* can't be true, Master Rowland," the General said, voice dripping with condescension. The room erupted into chatter, creating chaos, but it was all quickly silenced by a clap. King Oberon did always like to be dramatic.

"Bring her in!"

My body tensed, the three of us looking at each other. Was it possible that they caught Sam? We heard the doors open again; the three of us waited quietly. I was ready to burst through the door when King Oberon spoke again.

"This is Lilian." I let out the breath I was holding in. I was relieved and sad at the same time that it wasn't Sam. "My child. Tell us what happened."

Silence fell on the room again. I heard hushed voices and then the squeaky voice of the little girl.

"They came at dawn," she started, and it was clear that she was afraid. "Men in dark armour. My mama hid me in our shed and..." she stopped. I heard another woman's voice, but it was too quiet to make out. "I heard them demanding for 'the virgins'...? to be given to them."

Felnard gasped at the same time as the people in the room. I watched as he shook his head, tears glittering in his eyes. Vendal just stood next to the wall, his ear pushed against it, he didn't even dare to take even one breath at that moment.

"How did you survive, Lilian?" General Eldam asked in a raised voice.

"Once they took the virgins, they left. My mother-" she started sobbing silently, taking big deep breaths to try and calm herself down. "She sent me away with the other kids."

"Their carriage was found by hunters in the forest, far from their village." The woman spoke up. "When they went back to check on the people, they found only destruction."

"And whose orders were they following?" General Eldam asked, impatiently.

"The Soulless."

From that revelation onward a lot of arguing began. General Eldam was unshakeable; he simply refused to believe that the tale of the Prophecy was true. We listened as they discussed strategies, but our interest in the matter started to deflate. The turning point, however, was the second they mentioned Sam. It was Rowland who brought her up.

"We're going to need to get her back," he said. There was no kindness in his voice.

"After how we treated her I doubt she'll say yes." Vendal arched his eyebrow at me.

"It doesn't matter. It's her des-"

"The girl is far away from here." We both swung around to see the empty chair. Felnard had snuck out behind us and was already raising his voice against the men in the war room.

"Felnard, what a surprise," Rowland said, his voice feigning sweetness. "Do you know where she is?"

"I do not."

"Then we shall send out search parties. If she is still in the body of that Dragon-"

General Eldam once again cut off the King. "The body of a Dragon? Do you all think we are complete fools?"

"General, with all due respect, your stubbornness in this matter will cost lives." Felnard said.

"According to you. The Soulless? The Prophecy? The Destroyer? Do you really want us to believe all this without any proof?" He was practically laughing, his voice slowly gaining octaves the less he believed.

I couldn't take anymore of their arguing. Vendal tried to stand in my way but I shoved him aside. I marched through the small corridor that led from our room to the War Room and burst through the door.

I took in the room, noticing familiar faces as I walked up next to Felnard. Everyone was sitting around the enormous round table - the King's best Generals, Admirals and, slightly unexpectedly, a number of refugees from the Human Kingdom. Rowland wasn't the only Druid either; there were at least another five Masters in the room. Vendal quickly came running in after me and stood next to his uncle and I.

"Malion Arur," the King rose up from his seat. "I should have your head."

"Not so fast my King." I said between my teeth, desperately trying to suppress the anger I felt taking over me. "I am your only chance if you want to find Sam."

"The girl?" I ignored the King and moved closer to the table.

"She is our only hope in this war against the Soulless," I said as confidently as I could, the eyes on me made me nervous. "Vendal, Felnard and I spent five years trying to find her and help her on the journey that lay ahead. In return for her bravery she didn't receive anything but hate…" I looked around, taking in all the emotionless faces that stared back at me. My gaze found its way back to the King, who'd become visibly shaken by my accusation.

"The Soulless himself took my memories away in order to cause her more pain. No matter what you decide, we - I - am going to keep fighting to help her. I love this woman."

Everyone started talking at once. In the noise of the chatter, I found a calm in my proclamation. The King and I stared each other down until Felnard snapped his fingers and darkness fell over the room, silencing it.

"Master Rowland and I think that she will find help wherever she is," Felnard said, moving next to me. "Reginald the Great always comes to the aid of those who need it the most."

"I had enough of this!" General Eldam exclaimed as he stood up. "You add more and more tales into this madness with no proof behind it all. I am leaving!" He stomped toward the door, before looking around waiting for others to join him. No one else stood up.

"Do you all seriously believe them?"

"We saw the girl turn into a Dragon, General Eldam," Admiral Xelion said. He was the leader of the Fairies - fearless, battle-hardened. He rarely spoke, but when he did, his words carried weight. General Eldam turned pale as he looked around. He slowly sat back on his chair, shamed.

"Who is this Reginald you are talking about, Druid?" The King turned to Felnard as General Eldam was defeated.

"Reginald the Great is the Guardian of the Sorrow of Souls, your majesty." Felnard clapped his hands twice and the darkness evaporated. Brilliant light shone through the windows leaving everyone blinded for a moment.

"He appeared around the same time as Sagar did. Many believe that he was created by Sagar himself."

"He appears to those whose souls had been tainted by darkness which - we believe - has happened to our Destroyer," Rowland had stepped up to the War Table as well. He raised his left hand, creating a small circle of light that shone on the Needle-Shaped Rocks on the map.

"The very few who encountered him described this place as his home."

"However, a month ago, the Needle-Shaped Rocks became tainted by darkness." Rowland pinched his fingers together sharply and the light burned, leaving the map blackened where it had been. "So, he's either still there or he moved somewhere else, in which case he could be anywhere-"

"Or he's dead," General Eldam said, still sounding unconvinced.

"Actually, to the best of our knowledge, General, Reginald is immortal," Rowland replied, unbothered by the soldier's words. "I would start the search there, your majesty. But-" he raised one of his crooked fingers, "Sam must meet with him. You cannot interfere with that at all."

"Why is that so important?" Admiral Xelion asked.

"Because if the Destroyer's Soul stays dark, she won't be able to help us at all."

I felt fear gripping hard onto my heart as Felnard said those words. I felt responsible for what happened with Sam, even if I knew that I was just a puppet in the Soulless' plan.

"Do we know where the Prophecy is?"

The King's voice pulled me back into reality. With everything that had been going on, I'd forgotten about the Grabodan's message. Vendal caught my eye and shook his head slightly. *Later*, he seemed to say. I nodded.

"My nephew and I are working on that problem," Felnard said, trying to sound as reassuring as possible.

"Rowland, provide all the help they need," King Oberon said, not even looking at the man as he said it. Rowland bowed as deep as his aching back would let him.

"Killian, you will be the leader of the search."

"Yes, your majesty." I bowed too.

"Excellent. Generals, Admirals, I expect reports every day. This summit is dismissed for now."

He left without another word, his servants and Guard following close behind. Prince Aberyon wasn't too thrilled with how the events had unfolded, but he did as he was asked to. After all the other officials left, Rowland guided Vendal and Felnard away, leaving me alone in the War Room.

I took deep breaths to calm my racing heart. I couldn't believe my own boldness. Admitting my feelings towards Sam right in front of the King was probably the dumbest thing I'd ever done in my life. I saw the look on everyone's face as I said those things out loud. They were judging me.

Well,   fuck   them.

○

The army movement in Shells doubled as soldiers came flooding into the city. Within five days I was able to find the twelve best men and women to join me on the search for Sam. Vendal and Felnard gathered three other Druids to their side to help them decode Crixus' message about where his resting place could be found. Princess Aihyla stood by her brother's side in every matter. She helped organise the new barracks that were built outside of the city, while her lover, Marion, gathered together the women to help take care of the children.

The threat of the Soulless grew bigger with every passing day. The reports were disturbing. It looked like he avoided Lendala and the villages that surrounded it. The thought was he was afraid of the Druids and the possibility of them stopping his march forward. No one could figure out what he was planning as his attacks on towns were seemingly random.

Rumours started spreading very quickly. Many believed that he used the virgin girls who were abducted to provide an heir for him. Others thought that the virgin boys were turned into monsters, as the sighting of strange flying creatures came in from everywhere. But I knew what he was doing with them: the more dark magic he used, the more pure blood he needed to clean off the Mark of Sagar. In reality those poor women and men were all guided to their deaths.

The report of the white Dragon came in on the fifth day of preparation. I was in the courtyard of the Palace when Vendal came running, waving a piece of parchment.

"They saw her!" He yelled as loud as he could. I ran to meet him, practically snatching the parchment from his hand.

"Xillion. That's only a day away from here." I said, feeling more hopeful than before.

"Yep. I already told your soldiers." Vendal smiled, very proud of himself.

"You are the best."

"Tell me something I don't know," he said as he winked at me.

We made our way back into the palace, purpose now in our steps. It felt like the number of people in the area had doubled in a blink. We navigated our way towards the main gates where my team was waiting. Just as we were about to reach them, Gally stepped in front of us, stopping us in our tracks.

"I want to go with you," he said, voice uneven. He had had a hard time getting over his sister's death these past few weeks; it wasn't hard to see how it pained him every day. I went to say no, but he immediately cut me off.

"I want to go. This is what Neyra would want from me."

"Gally-"

"Killian," he said, more confident than before. "I want to go."

I took him in, then, properly, measuring him fully. His posture had shifted, and the look in his eye spoke of a new resolve.

"Alright," I nodded. "Grab your things and-"

He patted the bag already on his back and grinned.

"Perfect. Follow me then."

I'd never seen anyone so happy before.

We walked to my team who were eager to get going. Vendal started to address my team, providing a little last minute tactical advice before we headed out. I gathered my things, and changed into the black armour I'd gotten from Prince Abelyon with my favourite bird - an owl - carved into the shoulder pad.

We left the Palace of Peace behind on horseback and, for the first time in weeks, I was hopeful.

o

"VENDAL"

Felnard was all over the place, to say the least. Ever since I'd told him word for word what Crixus' message said, he hadn't stopped searching. The three Druids who'd been assigned to help us were useless; they didn't know anything about the Grabodans, or the Prophecy for that matter. Felnard put them on research duty - they had to read through all the books Rowland provided and let us know if they found something that could be connected to the message. After so many failures they didn't dare to step forward with their ideas anymore. Felnard was... unkind, to put it lightly.

With Killian leaving the Palace behind to search for Sam, Felnard had become even worse. He kept repeating the last line, even in his sleep:

"I close my grave in eternal darkness."

On the third night - when I couldn't handle it anymore - I simply walked out of our room and didn't stop until I reached the courtyard. There was a stone bench right next to the stairs, so I put my blanket there and laid down. He was driving me mad. I couldn't eat properly, I couldn't sleep, or just simply exist. Plus, on top of his annoying behaviour, I kept thinking about Neyra.

If I managed to get a bit of sleep, I saw her every time - calling out to me, searching for me. Memories kept coming back to me of the days we'd spent together, her sweet touch on my face. But then I'd remember how she misled us all along. Was she really feeling something for me, or was it all just part of the act? Getting close to the stupid Druid...

o

I was in the study that Abelyon let us use when Felnard marched in with a bunch of books in his hand, followed sheepishly by the poor Druids carrying even more behind him. They dropped everything on the table and my Uncle said something I'd never thought I would hear from him:

"I give up."

"What? What happened?"

"I can't figure out what he means. I just can't. I've looked into tales, legends, history... the only other place where eternal darkness appears is Radona and Elemris' legend and- what now?" He snapped angrily at the poor Elven Druid boy, who couldn't have been older than fifty.

"Well, Master, I think, um," he started, his voice small, "I think we were looking at it the wrong way."

"What do you mean?" I asked him before my uncle could say something horrible to the poor kid.

"Well, you said it yourself, Master, this is a translation. But... what if we look at the Grabodan language itself?" The room froze for a moment, digesting the idea.

"Uncle, what's eternal darkness in their language?" I asked, trying to stop myself from getting too excited too quickly.

Felnard started laughing uncontrollably. It took him a good couple of minutes before he was able to answer.

"*Harea nóu Ase*, which is the other name of The Unknown Land that's beyond the Enormous Sea!"

The three other Druids let out deep sighs of relief as they started patting the Elven boy's shoulder, huge grins on their faces. I felt so stupid for burning the parchment; we might have solved the mystery much sooner if I hadn't.

"Now," my uncle turned to the three boys, "we need to wipe this from your memories."

"Uncle!" I exclaimed in surprise. The boys were just as mortified as I was. "You ca-"

"Yes, I can. I have to. Trust me, I don't want to either. But if they will ever get captured by the Soulless, our headstart will be gone."

"They helped us," I said, even though I knew that Felnard was right in the matter. The Elven Boy stepped up, took a deep breath and nodded.

"It's okay, Master." He'd said it to my uncle, but he looked at me.

I left the room, unable to watch. They deserved better after all the help they gave us.

o

Killian and his team had been gone ten days when the first message came in. Sam was no longer in, near, or around Xillion. They had started making their way towards the Needle-Shaped Rocks as their two trackers were certain that Sam was heading there.

Felnard sent the boys back to Lendala with ten Guards to take care of them during the journey. I didn't talk much with him after what happened and he wasn't interested in talking either.

I spent my days helping Prince Abelyon in the preparations for the possible war - wrote messages, helped organise the troops, guards, and whatever else he needed me to do. There was not one calm moment in the palace as the days were passing by; the news that was arriving was no longer as bad, thanks to the troops who were sent out more and more victories occurred. It turned out that the Soulless himself wasn't present when his men attacked the villages; many people had seen his Dragon flying high above, but that was all. One of the captured men from the Soulless' army had gone through hell by the time the

Druids were able to clear his mind from the dark magic. As Master Rowland described it, the process was very similar to what Killian had to go through. The man had no memory of the past five months so he couldn't even tell us where the Soulless was hiding while he was sending his mindless troops to tear villages down.

Nights were the hardest. Not because of Felnard, but because my mind was able to roam free. I felt like a failure. I'd failed Neyra, Killian, and Sam. No matter how hard I was working to make it right, I kept thinking about what Felnard said when he told me that I needed to be the one who travels with them:

No one else can protect Sam but you.

I didn't pay much attention to her at the beginning. She kept telling those stories about her life and I couldn't bear hearing them. I was selfish. My good mood and fun was more important than her, or anyone else's, well-being. I knew how Killian felt about her ever since the dreams had intensified but I kept stopping them with my stupid stories. I wondered how many times I hurt Sam. I saw how she looked at Killian and still I…

I was horrible.

I barely slept. If I did manage to close my eyes, my nightmares woke me up. Neyra was dying in each of them, no matter what I did. She kept begging me to help her, she kept screaming my name. The Soulless was there, a wide smile on his face that cripled me with fear. I usually woke up bathed in my own sweat and crying. My Uncle had to help me calm down each and every time.

But I didn't tell him what had been going on. I couldn't talk about it - it was too painful to even think back on it. The first and probably only woman I loved was gone and I had to live with the knowledge that I couldn't save her.

"GALLY"

When we finished talking with everyone who'd seen the white Dragon, Killian lost it for a second. I wasn't sure if the others had noticed it too, but I saw it: he was angry with himself. It only appeared on his face for one quick second, but I knew that expression all too well. I felt it every day, ever since I'd betrayed my own sister - the only person who had ever stood up for me, who ever really cared for me. I carried that weight.

We left Xillion behind, following the trail the two trackers - Jalak and Gelion - had found. We talked with ten separate people and they all remembered different directions the Dragon went in, so we had to spend an additional two days around the town trying to pick up the right trail. When Jalak found the scales of the dragon north from the town Killian made us move immediately.

He didn't talk much; by the fifth day he'd gone basically silent. I knew he was suffering, like how I was suffering.

I tried to tell him more than once about what happened between my sister and I because I was sure Neyra had never talked about it. If they'd have known how awful I was to her, they wouldn't have saved me, I was certain of that. However, each time I tried to talk with him, my courage left me. He had enough on his plate - he didn't need to hear my sad story on top of all that. Instead we'd just end up talking about something completely unrelated to Sam or Neyra, if at all.

The other soldiers in the team were a lot of fun. They had many crazy stories, not just about themselves and their experiences, but about Killian as well. Our leader was not too thrilled, but always interjected with how he remembered them. He was a legend among us Elves - the Human who'd declined to follow the path of his own kind. Was it weird for him? Of course, the Elves were nothing but accepting of him from the beginning, but I always wondered if he felt like an outsider.

I definitely did.

Following the strict rules, marrying into a family I hated, with a woman I had to share my bed with was nothing but a nightmare for me. I honestly never had any desire to touch any man or woman in my life. The way Elves and Fairies were so open and free when it came to their sexuality and sex itself always scared me. The idea of me doing things like that? My skin would crawl in revulsion. I didn't belong.

I had to ruin the only good relationship I had in my life in order to protect my sister. Our mother and father had awful plans for her, and I knew I had to hurt her in order to protect her.

I'd often see her face in my dreams - that look of disappointment and sadness when I told her I do not wish to see her again.

Killian sat by the fire when I woke up from my nightmare. I wasn't surprised that he was awake. He usually took the first watch, but if he woke up - which he did, every night - he switched with the person who was on the lookout.

I sat down next to him on the wide log. He didn't look at me, just stared ahead into the night. He was holding a small piece of fabric that I'd seen in his hand before. I didn't dare to ask what it was or where he got it from; I knew the answer.

"My sister died thinking that I hate her."

I said it out loud, more to myself than to him, but it definitely got his attention. He put the fabric in his pocket and turned to me.

"I am sure that's not tr-"

"It is true." The weight on my chest started to ease up a bit. "I knew she never mentioned me to you all the minute I met Vendal."

"What happened?" he asked, his voice was full of empathy. No wonder so many people liked him.

"Our parents were horrible people. They forced me into marriage so they could get into the Palace. Neyra was the only person who stood by my side during those years. She listened when no one else did."

"Yeah, she was pretty great." Killian smiled.

"She left our home before our parents could force her into marriage too, but she-" I took a deep breath, Killian gave a hard squeeze to my shoulder, reassuringly. The pressure helped calm the rage that bubbled when I thought about them. "She didn't know, but our parents were planning to sell her into slavery."

"What?"

"Elven children usually get cast out from families if they can't find a partner, but in some rare cases they get sold on the black market so they can be of use to the family. Of course, it's not legal, but it happens."

I didn't dare to look at him. This was a well-kept secret among noble families - not many people knew about it.

"If I'd have told her what they were planning, she would have tried to rescue me from their claws. I knew if she tried we'd both end up dead, so instead, I told her that our parents didn't want to see her anymore. And that I didn't either."

I felt the tears burning my eyes as I tried to hold them back. Killian patted my shoulder.

"You did what you had to, kid."

"I'm... married to Captain Gadev's sister." I said, barrelling on before he could respond. "They knew that my sister could be forced to go after you if they threatened her with killing me."

"Why did they send Neyra instead of a soldier?"

"Because they knew that you would recognise an Elven soldier. Neyra had access to archives, she was quick and she was always great at pretending." I saw the sting of that last sentence flicker across Killian's face. "She only did it to protect me. I know her betrayal hurt you all."

He stared at the fire for a long time, processing. It was like he was breathing through each emotion that came through him before he finally spoke again.

"I don't think she was pretending to be our friend. She loved us, loved Vendal. I don't think you can fake that."

I let out a laugh that was all relief, like I'd been holding my breath the entire conversation and hearing him say she found someone... Air filled my lungs once more.

"Thank you for listening, Killian."

"I am glad you finally decided to open up." He smiled again, although he was definitely more sad than beforehand.

"We will find Sam." He nodded, heart not in it. "You know, she talked about you a lot, when we were in the dungeon."

"Really?"

"Yeah, when I finally met you all, it felt like I knew you better than myself."

"I can't imagine what kind of crazy things you must have heard."

And he laughed. He laughed a lot. It was infectious; I couldn't help but laugh too.

"Only the best ones," I said, and I turned to look at him properly. "Neyra was lucky to have you."

He looked back at me.

"And now you have us too."

o

It took us another ten days to reach the Needle-Shaped Rocks. They were named pretty aptly - certainly needle-shaped, but in addition they were a light-stealing shade of black, tainted with darkness just as the Druids said. Killian sent out the trackers to look for clues while we set up camp near the formation. He kept searching for a way in but the spaces were way too tight for anyone to fit through them. It was pretty clear he was getting close to losing his temper. No one dared to say anything.

The trackers came back at nightfall, big grins on their faces; they'd found the Dragon's white scales by the lake that was close by, which calmed Killian exponentially. He ordered the patrols to go through the forest nearby and set a group of Guards next to the Needle-Shaped Rocks. He was certain that Sam was already there; he walked around it so many times that I lost count.

After three days of nothing, Killian decided to send some of the men away to keep on searching. He was starting to get anxious over the situation - there was no way to get between the rocks, no sound came out of them and there was no sign of life in there at all. Surely, it must have been under the spell of Reginald - or whatever the Druids called him - but the quiet was starting to get to all of us.

The six soldiers who were sent away were visibly relieved to leave the place behind. Those who stayed were starting to lose their sense of time; the days seemed incredibly long, unrealistically so, but the nights passed by like they were nothing. Strange dreams started to wreck all of us. Dreams about lost loved ones, missed opportunities, hopes and fears. One of the trackers, Sheela, was so shaken by one of her dreams that she spent a whole day crying. None of us could calm her down, and eventually Killian decided to send her back to Shells. She didn't want to go, but our leader insisted.

Only seven of us remained.

As time passed - incredibly slowly - the dreams intensified and some of us started to see apparitions when we were awake.

I saw Neyra. More than once. She wouldn't say a word, just laughed as she walked by. I often saw her sitting on one of the branches of the large oak tree that provided us with some shelter.

Killian kept returning to one of the rocks. It was a peculiar one as it was the only rock that didn't stand up straight like the others. Instead, it was slightly leaning forward and there was a tiny white spot on its peak. Killian stared at it every day. He would just stand there, motionless.

Not long after Sheela's departure, another two of the men had to be sent away - they would scream constantly, every night. Their eyes would be wide open but they didn't react to anything, no matter how hard we tried to wake them up. As soon as the sun started rising on the horizon they stopped screaming.

I didn't know how many days passed in the end, but eventually only Killian and I were left. And Neyra. She wasn't talking, but she came closer every day, sat by my side, holding my hand and just smiling. I knew it wasn't real, but it gave me peace.

I was sitting by the fire as night was falling one evening. A cold breeze brushed through, carrying with it the scent of flowers. I took a long deep breath and tried to figure out why it seemed so familiar when I heard the quiet sobs from Killian nearby. I got up and went over to him to find him sleeping under one of the tents. He woke up easily, but he seemed disorientated. His eyes kept flickering to a spot behind me, so I turned around.

A tall man was standing in front of the rocks. Killian was quickly on his feet and walking towards him. I followed, a little ways behind.

As we reached him, words failed us. He was a Halfling - half Elf and, to our surprise, half Handor. A huge grin sat on his wrinkled face; his Elven ears wiggled a little.

"I am always amazed by the power of love," he giggled like a child, causing his long grey hair to bounce up and down on his chest. A long black robe covered his body, but scales were visible on his hands, neck and forehead.

"Who are you?" I asked, finally finding my voice.

"How silly of me," he said as he bowed. "My name is Reginald Ludius Mayheart. Nice to meet you Gally Lin, Killian Fin." I didn't have time to let shock take over me as Killian spoke immediately.

"Is she in there? Is she alright?" Reginald nodded, his grin never leaving his face.

"She is on a road she needs to take alone, my dear boy." He put his unnaturally long hand on Killian's shoulder. "They need you back in Shells. Leave Gally here; he'll be able to guide Sam back when the time comes."

Killian was sullen. "I don't want to go."

"I know." Reginald said, still smiling. "But she'll be fine. I promise, you will be able to hold her in your arms again soon."

"It's okay, Killian. I will bring her back," I said, trying my best to convey my conviction. He slowly nodded.

"Excellent." Reginald turned to me. "I am afraid you have to stay outside."

"That's fine." I looked back to the fire where Neyra was sitting. "I'll be fine."

CHAPTER 21
THE NEEDLE-SHAPED ROCKS

"SAM"

It was dark by the time I ascended from the clouds. I landed next to a lake and turned back into myself, shedding my Dragon skin. The clothes I stole were a bit too big, but I didn't care. I put them on, all the while taking a long look at the growing black mark on my chest.

Fifteen nights had passed since I left them all near Shells. I spent most of my time in Dragon form just flying over the Broken Ground. I didn't have any desire to walk among others or talk to anyone. I felt nothing. Neyra was dead. Killian no longer knew me. I was nothing but a filthy Halfling in the eyes of those I was supposed to save from certain damnation.

My nights became dreamless. I didn't step into someone else's memories or face my enemies. Every morning I got up from the cold ground and the mark grew a little bigger. My hair had turned completely black, the red gone. I washed myself in the lake and was ready to leave when I noticed the strange rock formations in the distance. I was aimless anyway, so I decided to check them out.

I stood in front of the Needle-Shaped Rocks. It wasn't hard to recognise them, but they looked much more ominous than the way people spoke about them. It was as if the place didn't even belong to the Broken Ground, surrounded by a scary, frosty atmosphere. The rocks were all truly needle-pointed, staring at the sky like trees, their menacing exterior keeping everyone away from setting out to explore the maze behind them.

I looked at those horrible black rocks and I had a feeling that I was being called. I started toward the gap that opened between two sloping rocks, but before I entered I paused for a moment. Breathing deeply, I closed my eyes tight and knew that all my strength would be needed to embark on the journey, which seemed even more threatening than I'd first thought. But what did I have to lose?

I didn't move quickly through the narrow corridors, so it took hours of walking before I finally reached a wide-open meadow with a tree planted in the middle. The incredible hanging branches of the willow tree comforted me more than I could express. It looked so similar to the one that was in Yandana, it made me feel like I was back in the Noble Gardens. I'd only taken a step when the rain – without any warning at all – started pouring down.

I ran.

Although I didn't have to go a long distance, I still got a little drenched. When I made it under the thick canopy of the tree, lightning struck above me. I hugged the tree trunk tight, screaming and crouching down, but my fear was soon replaced by the feeling that I was not alone. I looked up to see a great snake crawling out of the canopy. It made its way to the floor, curling up in front of me and proceeding to just stare. Its head was almost the size of mine and it seemed extremely scary at first glance, but some strange peace and tranquillity emanated from it at the same time.

"Greetings." I screamed in horror as the snake spoke, otherwise quite politely. "Oh, I'm sorry," he laughed in amusement.

The sudden bright light blinded me for a moment, but when I could see again, an old Handor man was sitting next to me with a wide smile on his face. I couldn't believe it. All of the Handor people became savages after the curse of the black roses. He was old, and as I looked him up and down, I realised how it was possible: he was a Halfling, a mixture of Elf and Handor. His scales did not cover his whole body; they were covering his forehead in a V shape, his neck and arms.

"Better, isn't it?"

"Who are you?"

"How rude of me. Reginald Ludius Mayheart, dear Sam."

He knew my name. The last one who surprised me like this was Ki… him. I swallowed it.

"Ludius?"

"My mother named me after Amelaya's sweetheart." He reached under his dark blue cloak and took out two apples. He threw one for me and from the other he bit a big chunk.

"You know the story, if I am not mistaken."

"Y-yes," I stammered.

"My mother loved that story even if it didn't end well," he laughed, though it sounded more like a cough than a laugh.

"But… the Handor had all gone-" I didn't know how to put it without offending him.

"Oh yes… Mother too. Feel free to say it. They became savages. What a strange word, isn't it? Interesting…" Ludius stopped for a second, just staring into the abyss… then he continued like nothing happened.

"They are back to their roots. My mother also suffered the fate of her people. Dad died shortly after she left." He wiped his face. "I haven't had a visitor in a long time."

"How could you turn into a snake?" Rowland had made it clear that only Paradions like me could do it, so how…?

"My father taught me. He was one of the most famous Copiers."

"Copier?" I had to be careful, my gut told me; the old man didn't seem like he was fully sane.

"Maybe you don't know. Sagar could copy the shape of any animal. He spent most of his time as a Unicorn." He leaned closer, which forced me to lay flat against the trunk of the tree. "They say he didn't die, but lives among us as a Unicorn still. But because he spent so much time in the animal's body, he can no longer change back." He laughed so hard at his own story, it was as if he'd just told the greatest joke in the world.

"Hold on a second - that would mean he's immortal."

"Well… yes." He scratched his head.

"What?"

"I think he's the father of Radona and Elemris and he came among us to give us power in case his daughter came back to destroy our world." He finished his apple, even going so far as to devour the apple seeds. He left nothing for the mice.

"You've had a lot of time to think about this, haven't you?" I tried distancing myself from him without any success.

"I mean, someone has to, right?" He laughed again, coughing.

"And how did you know my name?"

"I felt it." His long gray hair fell on his shoulders as he rose. He was only two feet tall, lean, and although his body was old, he himself was not at all.

"Before you, that stupid one stopped by here… The one who drinks the blood of the unfortunate victims."

"The Soulless?"

"That fool… he has poisoned my beautiful rocks with his wickedness." He pointed around us.

"You mean these rocks aren't really black?"

"Oh, no, they're white. Life permeated them, large tendrils wrapped around them. This place was beautiful before he came along - full of flowers, trees, animals. These paths were walked by creatures you will have never heard of or did not know existed." He pointed to where I came from. "My friend Henry - he was a raccoon with his little family - lived there. And in the other direction," he pointed behind himself, "that's where the Centaurs lived."

"Centaurs? They are just creatures from-"

"Fairy tales, right? That's what you wanted to say."

"Yes," I said, getting more and more convinced that Ludius was mad.

"They were real. I knew all of them by name," he said. As strange as I thought the old man was, I felt sorry for him then. His body caught up with his age unexpectedly; he even squatted a little as the deep pain pervaded him.

"They were my friends, my second family."

He wiped his face and I noticed that I was also crying. I didn't realise that Ludius' grief had such an effect on me, but I knew how it felt to lose someone you love.

"We played a lot, we laughed," he continued. "We understood each other. This place has been our garden of paradise for many years." He crouched down, looking at me with sad eyes.

"I'm really sorry."

"It was the only place that was never tainted by blood. And as soon as it happened," he looked around again. He sighed so deeply that for a moment he seemed to take his last breath. "They all died of sadness. All that was left was this tree."

He stroked the willow's trunk. The rain began to pour even harder, as if the sky felt Ludius' pain.

"Why didn't you leave?"

"I tried, but I couldn't leave my last friend here. As long as he lives, I will stay with him."

He tapped the trunk again and then with a snap of a finger his expression changed. The sadness vanished and utter joy took over.

"Let's stop being sad now! It's bad for our health!"

"Um… sure…"

"No, no. We talked enough about bitter things. Life… is not always fair. If we accept this, every step will be a bit easier along the way. To be bitter about what had happened is just a waste of another precious minute, in my opinion."

He let out another barking laugh. I didn't understand how he was doing it, to change so quickly from one emotion to another.

Then he suddenly started jumping and dancing.

At first I just stared at his strange behaviour, but - unexpectedly - I started to feel a smile appear on my face as I watched his clownish steps. Warmth ran through my whole body, something I had only felt amongst my friends before. I didn't even notice for a moment that we'd both started laughing. The old man reached into the canopy, lifted out a lute and started playing as he kept dancing. I jumped up and started dancing, not even caring that I wasn't good at it at all.

And we laughed.

We just laughed; all our worries were gone.

"Yes! This is it!"

"I don't understand what's wrong with me!" I exclaimed, still screeching with laughter as I spun around and around in the rain.

"What would be wrong?" The melody got even faster; I didn't even know I was able to dance at the same pace. "Are you happy?"

"Yes! I am happy!" I yelled back.

Ludius started to sing:

If a song comes through your heart and soul
Your life will be happier so
Sing with me brother and sister, my friend
Jump up and dance dear ones I pray
Our song will fly higher
Into a world much bright
So sing with me sister you gorgeous soul
Bring out your smile my brother for more
Ay-la-la-la La-la-la-la
Ay-la-la-la La-la-la-la

I sat down on the ground. As I laughed, my eyes filled up with tears. I leaned against the chunky trunk of the tree, closed my eyes, and let the dream captivate me.

The garden was filled with so many different colours that it was nothing like I'd ever seen before. All the colours were so vibrant, the flowers adorned the trees and bushes, the grass was thousands of different shades of green, and the unique scents of the flowers came to me in harmony. It felt like I was in a fairytale.

I walked along a small path lined with variegated bushes and reached a meadow. I was so impressed by the sight that I could not move for a moment. Huge willow trees framed the meadow, on which thousands of tiny flowers had opened. A river cut the landscape in half; its water was as crystal clear as the one I once bathed in with the others. I started walking towards it, the soft grass stroking my legs, but instead of getting closer to the river I felt it moving further and further away from me. I stopped, looked around, and realised I was barely making any progress. Dejected, I sat down on the grass, wondering what I could have done wrong, why I couldn't reach the water.

"There are things unattainable in life."

I looked up, recognising the woman stood before me immediately. Her skin was dark as night, features soft, with a beautiful round face, full golden lips, and white eyes all framed with long - literally floating - curly blonde hair. Her dress was made out of flowers and branches, like she was a manifestation of nature itself.

"Elemris," I muttered to myself.

She looked down at me and, as she smiled, rain started to fall. It didn't bother me at all, though - it was the most beautiful smile I'd ever seen. This miraculous phenomenon sat down next to me on the ground and a hundred more flowers opened around us.

"What do you think of this place?"

"Too good to be true."

"Not many people have had the opportunity to enter here." Elemris drew a circle with her finger in the air and a wreath full of purple and pink lilies and bright green leaves fell to the ground. She grabbed it and put it on my head.

"This is my home."

"Isn't this just a dream?"

"It's just a dream for you, but it's my reality," she smiled. "Sometimes we have a hard time believing what's in front of our eyes."

I felt the familiar touch on my shoulders. As I turned around, Killian looked at me and caressed my face, putting my hair behind my ear. His gaze was so penetrating that it made me blush. He spoke, but no words came out.

"What is he saying? I can't hear him," I said, turning back to Elemris, who was staring at the sky.

"Then close your eyes and listen."

I closed my eyes. I felt Killian's breath on my ear, then heard it. Very quietly, but he was there.

I love you.

I opened my eyes, but Killian was nowhere to be seen. Elemris stood and started toward the river. I followed, marvelling at the way she walked so gracefully, it was as if she was gliding.

"I don't understand this. I knew Killian loved me before-"

"Knowing and believing in something are two completely separate things."

We reached the river together; I had to acknowledge in shock that we'd reached it with just twenty steps. Elemris crouched down, picking up a pebble by the riverside.

"If I throw in this pebble, what will happen to it?"

"What? Well, it will sink."

"How do you know?"

"Because I've thrown pebbles in rivers before."

It started raining again. Elemris threw the pebble, which sank nicely into the depths of the river.

"Can I find the pebble I just threw in?" She straightened up, still looking out beyond the river. I looked at her in disbelief.

"There are thousands of pebbles in the depths of the river."

"Then I ask my question like this: Do you believe I can find the pebble?"

"No."

Elemris laughed and a huge lightning bolt struck one of the trees on the other side, but instead of destroying it, suddenly hundreds more flowers bloomed on it.

"Here's the problem-"

She took my hand, and I was inundated with endless calm and peace.

"What are you trying to tell me?"

"You know things, and you take them for granted, but when it comes to believing in something, you shy away."

Elemris let go of my hand, and I was flooded again with the bitterness and sadness of the last few weeks.

"But it wasn't always like that…"

I went to respond when I heard the laughter behind me. I turned, but I was no longer in the meadow, but on one of Yandana's rooftops. I looked at the roof tile under my feet - it was the same roof I was on in the morning when my whole life changed.

As I turned to look around, there I was next to the chimney looking down at the people before jumping down to head for the market.

"Sammy!" I turned, and it felt like someone took my legs out from under me - Polly was walking towards me.

"Polly! I was going to surprise you!"

My voice sounded very cheerful. I looked myself up and down and found I was now much younger. It was a memory I didn't recall at all.

"I brought you something!" Polly reached into her small purse, pulled out a blue little flower and put it in my red hair.

"This is gorgeous, thank you Polly."

"I saw it and it reminded me of you. I had to bring it for you." She planted a soft kiss on my forehead like she always did.

"I will always be here for you; I hope you know."

"I know." My younger self chuckled and suddenly the location changed. My eyes filled with tears almost immediately.

Neyra sat by the fire.

"Your turn!" I said while playing with the Mood Flower.

"Hm… ravens."

"What?" I laughed sincerely. "Are you afraid of ravens?"

"I can't help it; they're so damn scary. One attacked me when I was little, nasty flying beasts they are, nothing else," Neyra grimaced as she recalled the memory.

"I'm surprised you're not afraid of Vendal then."

"Hey!" Neyra tossed her shoes at me, but grinned. "That was very rude."

"I'm sorry, I had to! Sometimes he sits by the fire just staring in front of himself with his hair all messed up."

"I saw you blush today when Killian looked at you." The Elf changed the subject quickly.

"I didn't."

"Oh, really?" she smirked

"Yeah. Really!" I stuck out my tongue.

"You little fool…" she laughed, sticking her tongue back out at me, which made me laugh in turn. "Well, if you're going to stay alone forever because you're afraid to speak to any man, you can live with me and Vendal. We will build you a small cottage next to our own."

"You see *that* I can believe!"

I sank down on the grass as Neyra disappeared from view and I was back in the meadow. I was weeping already, suddenly feeling immeasurably alone. I tried to force myself to stop, but as my tears were racing down on my face, I felt something dark and heavy leaving my body - something I should have let out a long time ago.

The dark mark on my chest visibly pulled back as I crouched in the grass and let myself mourn everything I'd lost.

I felt Elemris lift me up and pull my head onto her chest. She started humming softly until I was overwhelmed by the light that brought calm with itself.

The next time I opened my eyes, it seemed like days had gone by. I felt my skin tense where my tears had run so I wiped my face with the sleeve of my shirt.

I sat up; Elemris was sitting a few feet away from me, quietly watching. It had turned dark during the however long I was out. When Elemris caught my eye, she pointed up at the sky, so I turned and my breath caught in my chest.

I had never seen anything more beautiful.

All the stars were out, shining as brightly as the Sun itself. I didn't even remember ever seeing the sky as clear before. The millions of stars up there filled the hearts of all those who looked up to them with some kind of peace that couldn't be experienced otherwise; the feeling of it all sitting on top of you, weightless and heavy at the same time. I reached out, wishing I could take a star out the sky and lock it in my heart forever. I wanted to speak, but as I turned to Elemris again, I almost fell back in fright.

Neyra sat across from me. She was beautiful, but completely changed, not the same rebellious Elf that I'd known. This woman was different - calm, like someone who had seen a lot, lived a lot, loving and wise. I knew I would have been unable to utter anything meaningful, so I left the speech to my friend.

"Hi Sammy," she smiled at me kindly.

"I'm so sorry, Neyra." I said instantly. She looked surprised.

"Why?"

"I wasn't there to protect you," I lowered my head in remorse, but Neyra just kept smiling.

"Oh, Sam. I can see that you are suffering; truly I think anyone could. Dissatisfied with yourself and the way things are going, but… we all knew from the beginning that this was not going to be an easy task. I knew when I joined you." Neyra took a deep breath and looked up at the sky. "Even if at first I did it for the wrong reasons."

I knew what she was talking about but I didn't care. She had her reasons, valid ones. She just wanted to protect her brother.

"Did you regret joining me?"

"No," she laughed. It was like music. "Otherwise, I wouldn't have known you, my dear Vendal, or Killian."

"I miss you."

"I know." Neyra stood up, sniffing the fresh, cold air. "I was weak, Sam. It's hard to admit, but it's the truth. I wasn't happy with myself, my life. My brother hates me, you know. But when they-" She stopped for a second, searching for the right words that didn't seem to find their way to her.

"I have plunged you into trouble that I will never be able to forgive myself for. But... I think you're stronger than any of us."

"Me? Then why am I here? I left everyone behind because-" I looked down at my chest. She stepped closer and as her fingers slowly traced the black mark it shrunk a little more. I gasped. I locked eyes with her and just spoke.

"I didn't know how to proceed because... something broke inside me and I couldn't get it back."

"Doubts... always just doubts," Neyra said quietly, her lips curled in a teasing smile. I stood up too and we started walking towards the trees.

"Wouldn't you doubt yourself?"

"Of course I would!" She spun suddenly and grabbed my shoulder. "But I never had any doubt in you. Vendal told me when you found out what your fate was, it didn't take long for you to accept it and set off."

"I think he was being kind-"

"When I met you, I was terribly jealous of you."

"Me?"

"Of course! I saw the strength in you even if you didn't. Whatever comes, it won't be able to beat you."

"Well, sorry to disappoint."

"You should believe in yourself a bit more."

"Yeah, I've heard that before." I stroked the willow branches as we passed under it. Each leaf laughed, aware of the gentle touch.

"I *know* you're missing me and you're blaming yourself for my death." I went to speak, but she put a finger over my lips to shush me. I was reminded of Aihyla - I could see how they were such good friends.

"I *know* that you think the Soulless was able to take away Killian's memories of you because his love for you wasn't strong enough, but I believe that you are strong enough to return nonetheless."

"Why do you believe in me so much?"

"Because I know you."

She said it so simply, and for the first time I felt I believed her. What a strange, mortifying thing to be known, and how badly I wished it would stay, but some part of me - deep in my gut - knew what was about to happen, even if I wasn't quite ready to look at it yet.

Neyra stopped at the willow trunk. She touched it gently, her palm resting flat against the bark.

"I'm... going now."

"Where?" I felt the panic rising up in my stomach.

"To Rest."

And there it was. Neyra came over and hugged me tightly, whispering in my ear before letting go.

"I will always be your friend."

"I forgive you."

Neyra turned to dust in my arms, which then carried away in the wind. I had no more tears left to cry, and found that I was smiling. The weight of grief still sat in my chest, but with it came a sense of reassurance.

Out of the corner of my eye I spotted something red.

"You're on the right track." Elemris stepped out of the trunk of the tree as I examined the colour that had returned to my hair.

"I think so too."

"Come. You still have to meet someone."

We walked in the shade of the willow trees. The leaves of each tree adorned different colours - purple, blue and yellow shone around us. When we reached the last tree, Elemris paused for a moment, as if looking for something. Stepping out of the cover of the last willow tree, a huge desert unfolded before our eyes. I no longer asked what or how - instead, I surrendered myself to it all. I glanced at Elemris, who gestured to me to leave.

And so I did.

I walked all night, cold bit and crawled under every inch of my body. I rubbed my arms, blew on my fingers to keep them from freezing; it was as if the coldest winter had greeted me.

But as the Sun began to rise, it began to warm.

It hadn't even reached the highest point in the sky when I found I could barely breathe in the great heat. Sweat covered my whole body, but there was no breeze to give me relief. The Sun burned my skin without mercy. I tore off a larger piece from my skirt and twisted it over my head. Even my short hair bothered me; I didn't even dare to think about what it would have been like if I hadn't kept it short.

I wanted to let myself collapse, but something took me further. I knew that I had to move forward, no matter what happened. One step. Two step.

I lasted until the evening - that's when all my strength left me for good and I collapsed. I didn't care about the cold setting in or the now strong wind, I just wanted to lie in the sand and let redemption come.

Then it hit me; the other consciousness struck mine like a bolt of lightning. I raised my head from the sand, my mouth filled with tiny grains but I didn't care. A beautiful male lion stood in front of me; the wind caught his huge mane, providing a very majestic sight in the blank of the desert. His consciousness was stronger than I had ever experienced before; it felt less like an animal, and more like a human trapped in the body of a huge wildcat.

I had a hard time getting up, but when I managed it I found the lion was much bigger than I'd expected. I reached out my hand in front of the animal's chest, the moment frightening and exhilarating at the same time. The lion gently took my right hand in her mouth and we set off. As we progressed, the cold didn't seem so awful anymore, and after a while I forgot about it completely.

We crossed dunes that looked like monsters. I felt like we'd been going for hours, but the darkness didn't want to go away; the moon and the stars were our only light.

Our long journey led to an oasis - a small lake, huge trees and… a boy. A little blond boy was sitting on the beach.

The lion released my hand. I hesitated a little, but walked over to the child. I sat down next to him.

"The fish are beautiful," he declared. I nodded and it wasn't until I spoke that I realised what happened: I was a child again.

"But they're not as beautiful as owls."

"Do the owls eat fish?"

"I don't know," I shrugged. My long red hair was clad in two braids. "Why are you sitting here alone?"

"I don't want to go home." There was too much sadness in his voice for a boy so young.

"Why not?" The boy didn't answer, just threw a pebble into the lake. The fish swam away from it.

"Now they're scared."

"Sure." I waited a little to see if he would start talking again. "Why don't-"

"Because I tore my clothes." He stretched out his legs, and indeed, above both knees, his beautiful trousers had two big holes in them. "Mom worked on it a lot, and I don't want her to cry again."

"What happened?" I was a bit concerned.

"Thomas pushed me. He is a very mean child."

"Did you say something nasty to him?"

"No!" The little boy was indignant. I nodded.

"I believe you."

"But I'll get back at him. I've already figured out how." He smiled, and with it his eyes darkened.

"How?" I asked, a bit scared to hear his answer.

"I'll grab his ugly dog and beat him to death."

The little boy was no longer a boy - it was my father. The pair of green eyes almost shone as he stared at me. I also changed. I was his skinny, clumsy daughter again.

"You can't do that."

"I can do whatever I want." He stood up, I followed suit and grabbed his hand to stop him. "Leave me!" he yelled.

"Why are you doing this? Why are you so evil?"

"Because the world is evil too! Or maybe you don't see it?"

"Then fucking stop it," I burst out and stared at my father who stared back, taken aback by my fierceness. "Hurt people will hurt people. I reckon if we take a closer look at those who have ever hurt someone… they were just the same as those they chose to pick on. Maybe that's how they try to feel better about themselves. I think you're doing exactly the same thing."

"Stop it." My father shook his head.

"I think you're just a person who has had to suffer too much and now you think that's the only way you can achieve anything... by hurting me. Why did you do it?"

"You talk too much, as always. You don't understand anything, you're just a stupid kid." He spat on the ground.

"I'm *your* stupid kid!" And I slapped him.

I suddenly felt stronger than ever, but the black mark started to spread again. I didn't care. The moment had come to give back the many evils I had to endure for years. I raised my hand again, but as I looked at my father, I saw his terrified expression. He was the little boy who got pushed around by others; a man stood before me who was broken by life. I raised my hand again, but as my father hunched over in fear, I was unable to follow through. I felt my lips tremble as tears were threatening to come out again.

"Why did you do it?" I asked again.

"Because you deserved it," he snarled. I grabbed his shoulder and shook him hard.

"Liar! Answer me honestly!"

He gritted his teeth, holding it in. I grasped his face and made him look at me.

"TELL ME."

"You! She left because of you!" He blurted out, tears flooded his face.

"What?"

"Iliandre, your mother… left me because of you," he sobbed. "She left me after you were born. I had no idea what to do with you, and every time I looked at you, I saw her."

"Why was I the reason she left?" I asked, letting him go, still unable to process that after thirty-one years I'd finally found out my mother's name.

"She always had big plans. She wanted to be more than she actually was and raising a child didn't fit into that." My father slapped the ground. "I told her that when you were born, we would give you to others who want you, but I think you were just a good reason for her to walk away…"

He began to cry again, buried his face in his hands so I could not see. I waited for the pain of truth to hit me, but, surprisingly, I felt nothing but relief.

"You never loved me? Not even a little?"

"I only ever loved her." He looked up.

I started laughing uncontrollably.

"I feel sorry for you," I said, once I calmed down.

"Why?"

"Honestly? Unrequited love is perhaps the cruellest of all. You had me to take care of without even wanting to care - the girl you couldn't see the opportunity in. You could have loved me and I would have loved you back."

"Samantha-"

"And I'm sorry you've made your whole life dependent on one person."

"She was everything to me," he said as he collapsed on the sand.

"I believe you."

"Can you forgive me?"

"No. But I'm tired of the constant hatred and being angry with you. I'm not going to forgive you, but I think I'm ready to let go of what was."

I closed my eyes. I could feel the grains of sand sweeping through my face, crashing against my clothes and hair. It felt like a huge stone had rolled off my heart.

It started raining again. When I opened my eyes the oasis was gone, and the lion sat opposite me. It seemed unbothered by the rain; he was just watching, listening, and I laughed because I realised what I was actually looking at.

The lion suddenly turned into a billowing blue cloud and crashed straight into my chest. I fell backwards and just laughed, opened my mouth wide, and let the rain fill it. I jumped up, and found myself stood once again among the Needle-Pointed Rocks. Ludius grinned at me. I looked down at my chest and found it bare - the black mark was gone.

I ran to Ludius, the two of us throwing our arms around each other and started to dance. Ludius quickly cast something and music kicked up around us. The music was uplifting - it was as if huge waves crashed as the melody flew around us. The flutes evoked the sounds of thousands of beautiful birds, the harps roared majestically like the most amazing singing voices, and I felt like nothing could stand in my way anymore.

The next morning, the Sun shone so bright that I had to cover my eyes. I heard laughter from all directions, got up and realised why it all seemed brighter: the rocks were snow-white again. Everything was overgrown with vines, flowers and dozens of animals running up and down. Old Ludius hugged three raccoons to his chest.

Sudden pain pierced my chest. I backed up against the willow tree. I clung to my torso, but, unable to hold myself, I slipped on the ground. My heart pounded so hard that I screamed out in pain.

I felt Ludius' rough hand on my face. He didn't look worried; there was a wide smile on his face. He said something but I couldn't hear it, so I concentrated on his mouth and read his words from his lips:

You're ready now.

In one fell swoop I found myself outside, in front of the opening where I had entered the day before, or perhaps several days earlier. The rocks closed, their colour remaining the same white and shining in their old light again.

I spun around, feeling something massive arriving. A white Dragon landed a few feet away from me, but as she lowered her enormous scaled head only a few inches separated us. I felt her consciousness and it was strangely familiar.

"I will protect you, Sam," I heard her whisper. I took a step back in surprise.

"SAM!" I turned in the direction of the voice.

"Gally?"

He dropped the wood that was in his hands and started running towards me. I didn't hesitate either; as soon as we reached each other he closed me in a tight hug. I felt like crying from happiness.

"I am so happy to see you," he said, face buried into my shoulder.

"How did you know I was here?"

"We were following your tracks and it led us here. The others went back to Shells, I stayed behind to take you back." I wasn't sure if I was ready to go back, but I knew what I had to do. Gally grabbed my hands. "We need you, Sam. The Soulless is destroying villages and towns, kidnapping innocents-"

"It's okay," I said, reassuring him. "I'm coming with you."

We started walking back towards the dragon when I noticed the brown leaves in the grass. I stopped in my tracks.

"Gally... How long was I gone?"

"A bit over two months. Autumn arrived." I let that sit with me for a moment.

"I left everyone behind."

"You needed to find yourself." He smiled. "Let's get back; there are people who are eager to see you again."

CHAPTER 22
THE CALM BEFORE THE STORM

I named the dragon Neyra.

Gally loved it. He told me everything on our way back; it sure sounded like Ludius was taking care of us both. Gally had become a lot more talkative, fun and he definitely reminded me of his sister more. He was finally himself: free.

I - on the other hand - was deeply stuck in my head. I wasn't ready to face my friends. The journey I'd gone through had helped me a lot to see my past mistakes - how judgemental I was towards others, how I was often unaware of other people's feelings or what they were going through. I could see, now, how self-absorbed I was and I knew that if I wanted to do better, I needed to change. I needed to make the effort to change.

It took us two days to reach Shells on Neyra's back.

As we arrived at the border of the city, Gally pointed out the people who were celebrating on the streets. I first thought it was some kind of festival, but I soon realised that they were all pointing at us.

I asked Neyra to land in the Palace's courtyard. As we were getting closer to the ground, I saw Vendal and Felnard making their way towards us. Princess Aihyla was hand in hand with her love, Marion, but no matter where I looked I couldn't see Killian anywhere. Neyra put her enormous head on the ground and we both slid off her neck.

The people around us were all either singing or celebrating, hundreds of them. I heard them yell things like:

The Soulless

"Our saviour is here!"
"Silhoue has blessed us!"
"Long live the Destroyer!"

A lot has changed since I left.

Before the sudden celebration could overwhelm me I found myself in Vendal's arms. He held me so tightly that I was afraid that he was going to break all my bones. Then Felnard joined, followed quickly by Princess Aihyla and Gally too. I couldn't help but laugh. When they all let go of me, I felt Vendal grabbing my face.

"Your hair is red again!" He sort of... yelled at me. He was clearly emotional.

"I know!" I yelled back, everything had become so loud around us that I could barely hear myself.

The crowd parted ways as Prince Abelyon and his Guards made their way towards us. I felt fear creeping over me, unsure of what to expect. My friends stepped away.

Prince Abelyon looked a lot like Aihyla, though his skin was much lighter than his siblings'. Many rumours had been spread for years that he was actually a bastard. He was taller than all of us, his hair longer than mine used to be, but a deep, rich black. His features were just as striking as the rest of his family's.

"I am honoured to welcome you, Sam Tanan, to the Shells," he said ceremoniously, his voice was very, very deep. The crowd started cheering again as he said my name. He shook my hand. "I heard a lot about you, Sam," he continued, his voice lowered so only I could hear him. He winked at me, giving me a smirk.

I went to reply when Neyra roared up behind us, silencing everyone. The Dragon looked at me with her huge green eyes.

"*Listen.*"

I heard her voice inside my head. I turned to see the smirk Prince Abelyon had given me had shifted into something more.

"SAM!"

The voice was very familiar, but I knew that it was impossible that it was him. Vendal stepped beside me and put his hand on my shoulder.

"*SAM!*"

"Is that-"

I couldn't finish. Killian broke through the crowd, stopping abruptly next to the Prince. He'd changed - his hair was longer and he had a beard, which infuriated me with how good he looked. He looked at me, eyes disbelieving. I didn't know what to do until I heard Gally's chuckle next to me.

"I couldn't reveal the biggest surprise," he said, gesturing with his head.

I turned back to Killian who was only a few steps away from me, breathing heavily. I reached out one of my hands to feel his skin. He grabbed it gently and planted a kiss on it, looking deep into my eyes. I couldn't hold myself back. I closed the distance between us and kissed him. I heard the cheers around us again, but I didn't care.

I was so afraid that I was dreaming.

But it was him, I knew it from the way he was kissing me. He held me so close to himself it made me feel like he was just as afraid as I was. When he let me go I caressed his face, just one more time, to make sure it was real. A tear ran down his cheek, but he was smiling brighter than ever before.

"I am so sorry," he whispered.

"It wasn't your fault," I replied, unable to let go of his face. I pulled him into a tight embrace, just wanting to be in his arms, feeling his heartbeat, his familiar scent.

"I love you."

He said it desperately, like it had been building up inside him and he couldn't contain it anymore. I leaned away from him.

"I do, with all my heart."

"I love you too," I replied, and it came as naturally as breathing. He kissed me again. I felt my heart beating faster than before.

o

We spent the whole day in the War Room. As happy as I was previously, my mood quickly degraded as they told me everything that had happened. No matter how many troops they sent out, it seemed like the Soulless couldn't be stopped, only slowed down. Refugees from Irkaban escaped to Lendala and beyond, the only place where they were safe. The Soulless didn't dare to step foot into the Druid Capitol or the smaller towns around it, though. The Humans took the first blow of the attacks. Irkaban was in flames. Reports had also come in that he'd destroyed the Grabodan city and everything that was left from their civilisation.

I just sat there, listening. Killian held my hand the whole time. When the three Generals who were in the room finished talking, all eyes were on me.

"So, do we have a plan about where we should confront him?" I asked, but all I got back was puzzled looks.

"You won't fight him," Felnard said, standing up from the table. "You will need to go after the Prophecy."

"What? But he's gonna-"

"Go after you." Felnard brushed through his long beard with his fingers. I looked at Killian, then Vendal. They both nodded. "This is the only way."

I sat with this for a moment. I couldn't help but think about how this felt like the opposite of what my instincts were telling me. But I had to trust my friends.

"Fine."

"I'm coming with you." Gally ran through the door.

"Of course you are," Killian smiled, standing up from the table. "Vendal and I will come too."

"Just like old times," I nodded, even though we knew it wasn't. But it was close.

"You'll have to leave in secret. We will wait a few days before starting to spread the news that you left." Prince Abelyon nodded towards the door. "Felnard will tell you everything."

We all left the War Room. Felnard and Vendal guided us into their room, where another table was already set up with a map laid out on it. To my surprise, the map only showed the Enormous Sea and the shores of the Broken Ground. I looked at them suspiciously. Vendal closed the door behind us and we all gathered around the table.

"Crixus' message gave us a bit of a headache," Felnard started saying as he put a tiny piece of parchment on the map. "But now we know where you'll have to go to find the Prophecy."

"*Harea nóu Ase*," Gally read the three words out loud. "I feel like I've heard this somewhere."

"Well, if you ever read history books, then you might have," Felnard winked. "It is the other name of the Unknown Land beyond the Enormous Sea."

"Hold on!" I said, taken aback by their revelation. "You want us to go to a place that no one has ever returned from?"

"Yes." He nodded, entirely nonchalant. "Easy peasy."

Sometimes I felt like Felnard wasn't really living in our reality. I threw my hands up in the universal sign of 'fuck it'.

"Sure. We don't know how long it will take to get there. We don't know what's in the sea below us - we don't know anything, but let's do it." I said, still a bit shocked by how much he didn't really seem to be bothered by my points.

"I am sure you will have great stories to tell when you come back."

"If we come back," I said under my breath. I sighed. "Alright."

"Excellent! Now, Vendal, my boy. It's time to erase this from my memory." Felnard turned to his nephew. Vendal didn't seem too thrilled. "You know that this must be done. No one can know where you all go."

"I know," he said. The piece of parchment caught on fire, burning a hole into the map as well, then he put his finger on Felnard's forehead and nothing happened. Or so we thought.

"I feel a bit lost," Felnard said after a few seconds, blinking rapidly, trying to find his train of thought. "What are we doing here?"

"Nothing, Uncle. We were just celebrating Sam's return."

"I must have drank too much beer," Felnard laughed, quickly brushing away his confusion. "Should-"

"I think we should leave Killian and Sam alone for a little," Vendal suggested.

I blushed instantly. Felnard looked at me and that made it worse. He didn't say a word as he left with the other two men.

The room felt bigger than before. I wasn't sure why my nerves had gotten the better of me until I felt his gentle touch on my back. It made me jump a little, like I wasn't aware that he was standing right next to me. I turned to him, but instead of kissing me he closed me into his arms, breathing heavily into my shoulder. I wasn't sure what was happening until I felt the warm tear fall on my bare skin.

I leaned away from him. He didn't look into my eyes, but I could tell he was ashamed of himself. I wiped away his tears with my sleeve and he sat down on the bed closest to us. I wasn't sure what to do, but eventually took my place next to him.

For what seemed like forever, we were in silence. I heard footsteps passing by the door; the laughter of children from outside. A fly was buzzing in the far right corner of the room, irritating me greatly. I was ready to jump up and hush him away when Killian spoke:

"I saw you by the Needle-Shaped Rocks."

"You were there?" He nodded. He started to drift back into his thoughts but snapped out of it as I put my arm around his shoulder.

"Killian, talk to me."

"It gave us these visions, hallucinations, and some of my men had horrible nightmares. Gally was the only one who handled it well." He looked at me. "I saw you as-" He stopped himself, his left leg shaking. "The Soulless killed you. Each time in a different way, and I couldn't move. My legs were like rocks, my whole body frozen. I screamed inside just like I did when I arrived in Yandana."

"Wait. In Yandana?"

"Yes, I was... locked inside my own mind." He finally looked up at me. "I thought if I scream loud enough you'd be able to read my mind, but the Soulless' magic was too strong."

I reached up and played with the hair at the top of his neck. "I'm so sorry you had to go through all that. But I am alive Killian, your memories are back. I think we are on the right track."

He smiled, genuine, warm and charming just as ever before, but I still saw how broken he was inside.

"I will always be here for you Sam. I promise." I kissed him quickly as I couldn't stand his gaze.

"I believe you." I leaned away but he pulled me back without a second thought.

His kiss was soft and gentle, it was the feel of his skin under my fingertips that made my hunger grow for him. The familiar feel of his frame leaning on mine made me dizzy for a moment. I felt his arms wrapped around me, holding me tight; I parted my lips and felt him washing over like the heat of the summer air.

My heart was beating so rapidly in my chest I was afraid it might burst as he slowly laid me down on the bed, claiming my mouth over and over again. As my fingers slid under his shirt, I felt his strong muscles tighten under my touch. It was like the whole world stopped existing around us. He was full of passion and hunger that wasn't unwelcomed. I missed his gentle touch, the way he made me feel like I was the only woman in the world.

He deepened his kisses as he slid his hands under my shirt. I became very aware of what we were doing so I gently pushed him away. I felt his heart beating fast under my palm. He looked at me a bit confused, his hair tickling my face.

"Are you okay?" He asked, his voice full of worry.

"Yes, it's just-" I couldn't stand his gaze, so I looked down at his lips, "No one has ever touched me like you have." He kissed my forehead, slowly sliding his hand up on my face. He tilted my head up gently.

"We can wait if you are not ready," he whispered, his voice mixed with understanding and a bit of disappointment. I shook my head.

"I'm ready," I said, with no doubt in my mind. I was more than ready. I wanted him, all of him. I wanted to kiss him again when a knock came from the door.

Killian got up, very annoyed by the interruption. He walked to the door and opened it. I didn't hear or see who he was talking to, but it got heated very fast. He left without a word, slamming the door.

I just sat on the bed for a moment, my heart slowing down a bit. I was disappointed that our perfect moment got ruined with just one knock at the door, but I still felt his touch lingering on my skin. It made me smile a little.

After a few seconds I finally stood up, fixed my shirt and walked to the door. As I wanted to open it I had to take a step back; Killian came back, his expression unreadable.

"Is everything okay?" I asked as he closed the door with a key and turned back to me. "If you need to-"

But I couldn't finish. He took me, kissing me passionately without warning, his warm hands wrapped on my face. He let out a low moan as he devoured my lips, passion rising up in his every breath. Before I could think about what I was doing I was already untucking his shirt. He leaned away for just one second to pull it over his head, but his lips were quickly glued on mine again, the warmth his body was giving off making me feel hot.

We backed up onto the bed, sitting me down as he slowed down a little, sweat dripping down his quickly rising chest. His fingers skimmed my face gently. He untied my shirt, waiting for me to move and so I did; I dropped the white clothing on the floor revealing my femininity like I'd never done before. His eyes were on fire as he looked at me, making me blush with his intense stare.

His hands slid around my head pulling me back to his mouth. We laid down on the uncomfortably hard bed as our hands were exploring each other's curves in quick motion. He left my mouth behind just to plant kisses all over my body, making my toes curl up in the process. I dug my fingers into his hair as soft moans left my mouth, sounding utterly unfamiliar to my ears. As he rose above me again his scent was in my nose making me hypnotised. His lips crashed into mine once more.

"You're beautiful," he said, half moaning half growling the words, so it was hard to decide what made my heart skip a beat. As he deepened his kisses, his tongue demanding mine, I felt his hands on my pants. He pulled them down easily. I had no idea when he got out of his trousers but as our bare skin touched together I felt a shiver run down my spine. I let the raw sensation take control of me. My legs wrapped around his hip as I tightened my grip on his back letting him know what I wanted, how much I desired him to be fully mine.

I didn't have to beg for long as he pulled me even closer to himself. The pain was unexpected, I felt all my muscles tense up for a moment to which he answered with kisses all around my neck. Our breathing became heavy as our hips started to move together in an unwritten harmony.

I was clasping into his shoulders as his rhythm changed. It was easy to get lost in him the same way he got lost in me. Our connection was stronger than I'd ever felt before. I felt his body shiver the same way mine did as we stepped into a new universe through our unity. Our breathing, movement and feelings were in a perfect sync and I never wanted it to end, but all good things must come to an end.

He rolled on his back, taking me into his arms, basking in the afterglow. I didn't dare to look at him as I felt my shy self come forward again. I heard his heart thumping in his chest, felt the little goosebumps on his arm, heard the soft chuckle as he planted a kiss on top of my head. I was very aware of the fact that I was naked and so was he. My legs intertwined with his, he was playing with my hair with one hand while caressing my arm with the other.

"Are you okay?" he asked, his voice no more than a soft whisper. I felt his warm breath on me. I looked up at him and as I saw his face again, his black hair all messy, his eyes glittering with joy as he looked at me, all my doubts flew away.

"Never been better," I replied, a huge smile on my face. He laughed, pulling me closer and kissed me again - gentle but passionate.

"I'm the luckiest man." He said it with his eyes still closed.

"And I'm the luckiest woman." He looked at me, his thumb brushed through my lower lip. I snuggled in closer. "So, was this like how you dreamed it before?"

"No," I leaned away as he laughed. I was ready to say something nasty but he put his finger on my mouth. "It was better."

"Good. You were very close to being struck by lightning for a moment." I tried to put an angry face on but the way he was smiling at me, all while eating me up again with his eyes, stopped me.

"Stop looking at me like that." I wanted to get up but he pulled me back on his chest.

"Don't go anywhere, please. Let's enjoy this moment," he whispered.

And so I stayed.

o

Killian fell asleep quite quickly but I couldn't.

I dressed and left the room as quietly as it was possible so as not to wake him up. It was late in the afternoon. The palace was quieter than before. Other than a few guards, I didn't meet many people on my way out to the courtyard.

Neyra was sleeping peacefully among the bushes, a few of them had been destroyed in the process. I figured that no one really dared to make her move away from the spot. I petted her nose gently; the scales were warm from all the sunlight they'd absorbed.

I walked around the garden and, although it wasn't as glorious as the Noble Gardens in Yandana, it offered the much-needed peace I was looking for. I eventually found a spot from where I could look down at the beach. There were a few people lingering down there - lovers, friends, families. For a moment it made me feel like there was nothing else going on in the world; it was all so peaceful. I leaned against the trunk of the oak and closed my eyes.

"So here you are."

The familiar voice made me open one of my eyes. Princess Aihyla sat down next to me, sneaking up on me the way she used to in the palace. She was in a flowy green dress, her hair up in a bun. This place looked good on her.

"What's that smile on your face?"

"I'm happy," I said and as she looked me dead in the eyes, I felt like I was looking at Neyra and her knowing stare. It made me chuckle as Aihyla gasped, putting things together.

"You and Killian?"

"Maybe," I replied, blushing like crazy. Her laugh was like the sound of bells ringing.

"You naughty woman, you." I playfully pushed her a bit which made her laugh even more. "Tell me, how was it?"

"Aihyla!"

"What? It's a completely normal thing to talk about, don't be prude!"

"Fine, fine! Hold your horses." I couldn't really look at her, she resembled Neyra in so many ways that it made my heart ache a little bit.

I missed my friend.

"It was perfect," I told her. "He was very gentle and caring and..." I swallowed hard. "Very passionate."

"I bet he was. With all the mess you two went through he must have been dying to be with you in bed as well." Aihyla laughed softly, putting her hand on mine. "I'm happy for you Sam. You deserve this."

"Thank you. How are things with Marion?"

"Just perfect. She means everything to me, that is why I..." She stopped herself, pulling her hand back and started fidgeting with her fingers. "I want her to go with you Sam."

"What? Aihyla-"

"My Father and Mother found out about her." She pulled out a letter, handing it to me with shaking hands. "All that is waiting for her here is death."

"Aihyla, I can't promise you I'll be able to keep her safe. We don't even know what's waiting for us yet."

"I know, but at least she'll have a chance. If she stays here," she looked at me, eyes brimming with tears. "I can't lose her again, Sam. I won't."

"Alright," I nodded, squeezing her hand a little. "Alright."

"Thank you. She can't find out about why she had to go with you, okay? She would want to stay then. She's an excellent archer. The best on the Broken Ground."

"I will come up with the best excuse."

Aihyla smiled and planted a quick kiss on my cheek in gratitude.

"Do you want to come back for dinner?"

"I'd like to watch the Sunset, if that's okay," I said, and she nodded as she got up. She took a deep breath, taking in all the smells the wind brought with it, and walked away.

The letter lay beside me. The way she'd left, I knew she'd left it on purpose, so I opened it up and read through it.

King Oberon had written the most awful things to her. He threatened her with the execution of Marion multiple times. The words on the page betrayed a deeply twisted and cruel man, the kind who thought children were property; only worth love if they did as they were told. I lit the letter on fire to make the harsh words disappear.

The sky took up the deep orange of the Sun as it set down beyond the horizon. The sea was gorgeous but terrifying to comprehend. Was there even anything beyond it? No one had ever returned from the other side. Was it possible that they all died on their ships, never reaching another land?

The sound of footsteps made me turn. I wasn't even surprised to see Killian, who quickly made his way to me, sitting down by my side taking me into his arms.

"It's not nice to leave me behind like that," he said, staring straight ahead with a forced angry look on his face.

"Were you scared without me?" I teased. He didn't say a word, just slightly turned his head away from me. "You were snoring like a bear."

"No I wasn't!" he exclaimed, horrified by my accusation. His shocked face made me laugh. "You are so mean."

"You brought out my wild side."

"Hmm, sure looks like it." He kissed me softly, taking my face into his hand. "I'm not complaining."

"I hope not."

o

The woman was sitting on the log again. My heart skipped a beat as I found myself on the shore of the river I knew from my dreams. I looked around, searching for the Soulless to no end. It was like she knew what I was thinking about she said:

"Don't worry, he isn't here."

I looked back at her. She changed. Her hair was still black, but her eyes were blue like mine and her face resembled mine a little.

"Who are you?" I was a bit hesitant to walk closer to her.

"A memory, a future, a past or maybe a present."

"I don't think I understand."

"You will." She stood up from the log very gracefully. She was much taller than me, but as she closed the distance between us it felt like her figure downsized. "You have to be careful."

"Yes, Sammy." I turned in the blink of an eye only to find myself in the arms of the Soulless. His red eyes were on mine, hungry, terrifying. "Be careful," he said, smelling my hair.

"Get the fuck off me," I said between my teeth. His laugh was cold. He grabbed my chin, turning my head up. He was merely an inch away from me.

"You feel strong now, because you broke my magic over your lover but your confidence won't last long." His long black nails were pushing against my skin hard. I had to swallow back my pain. "He will turn from you. There will be someone better along the way for him. Someone who-"

"Your venomous words mean nothing." I looked him dead in the eyes. I saw surprise flicker in his eyes, but his smile didn't disappear for a second.

"We'll see about that, Destroyer." His lips crashed onto mine. I struggled to push him away from me. He bit my bottom lip before leaning away.

"Tasty."

I screamed into the darkness as he disappeared from view.

CHAPTER 23
A BEAUTIFUL LIE

"KILLIAN"

Vendal was pacing back and forth in front of the door; I'd never seen a man less able to stay still when he was stressed.

Felnard had asked for privacy with Sam. When she woke up in tears it scared me to death; she wouldn't let me touch her and she kept asking for Felnard, utterly hysterical. The old Druid had arrived and made us leave the room what seemed like forever ago, which was doing nothing for my nerves. I couldn't stop thinking about how the Ghost in that cave cleansed her. Unless the Soulless had poisoned her somehow without us noticing, I didn't understand how the dreams could have come back. The worst part was knowing something was wrong, again, and again, I couldn't do anything to help her.

"Would you please stop pacing?" I asked, louder than I expected to. Vendal looked at me, nodded, and kept moving. "*Ven.*"

"I'm sorry, I just- Did we miss something?" He finally stopped pacing and took a step closer to me. "First there was the Ghost, then Reginald h-"

"I know. That's what I was thinking about too."

We both looked up as Aihyla came running towards us, Marion by her side.

"What happened?" She asked, out of breath. I guessed the two of them ran here. "We came as soon as the servant said that there was something wrong with Sam."

The door opened as I went to respond. Felnard stepped out and invited us all in wordlessly. We filed into the room; Sam was sitting on the bed, her eyes were red from crying and it seemed like her face had lost all its colour. I wanted to run to her, but Vendal grabbed my arm, stopping me. I heard the two women gasp as they saw her too. Felnard locked the door behind us and grabbed my hand, pulling me to where Sam was. The others followed, but stopped as the Druid raised his hand.

"Did you two seal your love for each other?" He asked, I looked at Sam. She was just staring at the floor.

"I'm not sure that's your-"

"Answer the damn question, boy."

Sam looked up enough just to catch my eye and nod as if to say it's okay. I crossed my arms.

"Yes, we did," I said, curt.

"Sit down." He pointed at the space next to Sam. I did as I was told, but when I went to touch her hand he yelled:

"NO! Do not touch her!"

"Felnard, what's going on?" Vendal stepped closer but his uncle shot the dirtiest look towards him, forcing Vendal to stop in his tracks.

"Close your eyes Killian." I did as he asked.

I felt his cold finger on my forehead and it sent a heatwave through my whole body. I tried my best to stay calm, but I couldn't get Sam's terrified face out of my head. Just as I felt panic riding farther than I wanted it to, I felt a sharp pain rip through my palm. I screamed in agony and opened my eyes; a small blade was buried deep in my left palm.

I looked up at Felnard; he was holding a small black mass in his hand, amorphous and awful, it hurt my brain to even comprehend it, like the fact it existed to be observed was wrong on a fundamental level. Thankfully it didn't last long, as Felnard tossed it up in the air and it lit on fire, the flames burning a bright blue, consuming it entirely.

He turned back to Sam, who had a similar blade stabbed into her right hand. The Druid got down right in front of her, indicating to her to focus on his eyes. She was taking sharp breaths between her tears.

Felnard started to draw a circle with his hand in front of Sam. He did it once, twice and the third time his hand stopped at Sam's chest. With a blink-and-you-miss-it motion, his hand shot forward, cut through Sam's skin like butter and pulled out that same black mass that was previously in his hand. I heard Aihyla let out a small yelp. Felnard pulled out the blades from our palms at the exact same time and dropped them on the floor. He grabbed our bleeding hand and pushed them together.

"Hold it!" He yelled. Sam was mortified so I had to stay strong for her.

Felnard started murmuring something in a different language, eyes closed. A cold breeze washed through the room even though all the windows were closed. Our hands started glowing; black gooey drops began dropping to the floor, burning a hole in the wood.

"DO NOT LET GO!" Felnard yelled again.

A burning sensation ran through my whole body; next to me, Sam was suffering as well. Vendal and Aihyla came up behind us, holding us down by our shoulders. Felnard kept canting and the glow grew brighter and brighter, blinding us all.

"LET GO NOW!"

I fell backwards as a huge black wall formed from the black ooze flying out of our palms. It started morphing, twisting awfully into the form of a man. The face remained featureless, but I recognised him nonetheless:

The Soulless.

"Well done, Druid, well done indeed," the faceless figure said, but it sounded like there was more than one person talking all at once. Felnard didn't even flinch, but I saw Marion and the others take a step back.

"You impressed me with how you broke the memory block on that fool, and now this-"

"You are smart, but not smart enough," Felnard cut in, sounding proud.

"What did you do to us?" I was unable to stop myself.

"I let you carry a piece of me with you." He laughed. The features of his face started to form slowly; I saw the outline of his ugly smile. "To see what you see, hear what you hear and taste -" he turned to Sam "- what you taste."

I locked eyes with her, but instead of shock in her eyes, there was something else. She stood up slowly, with purpose.

"Sam," I whispered, but she didn't even look at me. She reached out a hand to the now smoke-like apparition of the Soulless. She barely moved her fingers, but the figure erupted into flames, leaving the man screaming.

"I hope you feel this wherever you are, you son of bitch," Sam said, angrier than ever as the Soulless' screams filled the room all around us until it disappeared completely.

Sam took a deep breath and looked at her palm - the wound had healed by itself, no sign of a scar from the blade. Felnard stepped to me and took my hand in his; it only lasted a brief second and my wound disappeared as well. I stood up with his help, our friends stood around us in silent shock.

"What the actual fuck happened?" Marion asked the question that was in all of us. Felnard looked at her, letting out a small, dishonest chuckle. He walked to the bed and sat down. He seemed much older out of nowhere.

"Very old magic, the kind we can only read about in books," he said, sounding out of breath. "It is as he said it. He left a piece of him in you when he hid all your memories of Sam away."

"He was *in* me this whole time?" I asked. My body felt wrong at the thought of it.

"Just a tiny bit of him." Felnard started coughing, his breathing haggard, exhausted. The room felt bigger than it was. "When you and Sam made love, a piece of him was able to poison her mind with the dream again."

The reality of it mortified me. I looked at Sam, but her face was emotionless - she was just staring at the wall. Our moment of passion and love was tainted by evil. Emotion whipped me in different directions, all of it too big.

"Would it happen again?" she asked, not looking at any of us. I heard the pain in her voice.

"No. I got it all ou-"

He started coughing again, even worse than before. Vendal grabbed his shoulder and helped him lay down on the bed.

"He needs rest," Ven said, sounding very worried.

We took our leave. Gally, Prince Abelyon, and his Guards were all waiting for us. I walked ahead to say something, but was distracted by Sam, who'd walked away entirely. I excused myself and asked Aihyla to explain what happened.

Sam had disappeared from the corridor so quickly that I had to just follow my instincts. I reached the courtyard just as she was climbing up on her Dragon's back. I ran towards her but backed down as a low growl bellowed from the creature, its green eyes on me, staring me down. I raised both of my hands in the air to show that I meant no harm.

"Let him," Sam said.

The Dragon laid its huge head on the ground; I climbed behind Sam's back and we were quickly up in the cold air. The Sun had already started to rise, the mixture of yellows and oranges reflected on the sea. It was beautiful, but I couldn't concentrate on it.

The Dragon dived down and landed on the sandy shore. Sam quickly got down and I followed suit. The wind was very strong and incredibly cold; it didn't help that we both wore the lightest clothing. She just stared at me, as expressionless as before.

"Sam," I took a step towards her but she took a step back. "Hey."

"Was it you?"

My head reeled, confused. "What?"

"Were you the one who made love with me or was it him?"

"Sam! How can you even ask that?"

I tried to get closer but the Dragon's enormous head was quickly in my way. It was growling, its huge teeth showing. I swallowed my fear.

"Sam, please."

"Neyra."

It made my heart jump to hear her say our friend's name. The Dragon raised its head and with a swift movement flew up into the sky, blinding us for a moment as the Sun's light reflected back from its white scales. Sam just looked at me.

"I don't know what to believe anymore, Killian."

"Sam, you *know* me." I took a step closer to her and was relieved when she didn't pull away. I took both of her hands in mine. "It was me. I promise you."

"How do you know?" She asked, defeated.

"I know. I just know." I pulled her hand toward me and put it on my chest.

"In here, I know."

I was just as terrified as her, but I couldn't show it. I couldn't lose her again, not because of the Soulless, not because of me.

"He kissed me, in my dream," she said, making me sick to my stomach. "It felt like I was kissing you."

"Everything he's doing is designed to shake your faith - in yourself, in me-"

I took her face in between my hands and kissed her very gently. Her soft lips closed on mine, trembling a little. She tasted like the sweetest apple. I leaned away, but didn't let go of her face.

"This is real. What we had, what we did together, was real." Lightly, I bumped my forehead to hers, closing my eyes. "We have to trust each other."

"I don't want to lose you again," she whispered, her voice breaking a little as she swallowed back her tears.

"You won't."

I closed her in my arms, her small figure leaning against mine, making me feel all sorts of ways. I wanted to protect her, love her, adore her, but I was also scared - scared that we would never get free from the Soulless. He was able to poison Sam three times already, turning her dreams into nightmares. She needed me more than ever before, I knew it, I felt it in my bones and I wasn't going to fail her again.

I brushed my hand through her soft hair and rested it on the small of her back. She took a long deep breath as she held onto me tighter. I felt her shiver a little.

"We should go back," I said and almost jumped out of my skin when the Dragon landed next to us. I didn't even hear her arrive. Sam laughed.

"Already ahead of you." She let me go, but I stopped her.

"Hey, there's something different about you." She seemed surprised. "I can't quite… but it's good. It looks good on you."

"I think it's all Reginald's doing. I learned a lot while I was there." She got up easily on Neyra's back. I followed her, taking my place behind her wrapping my arms around her waist and planting a soft kiss on her neck.

"I can't let the Soulless corrupt my mind."

"I know that won't happen."

"How?"

"'Cause he's already failed three times."

o

The days after the incident flew by uneventfully.

We started preparation for the journey and agreed to travel on Sam's Dragon after she reassured us that it's able to take on very long journeys. She didn't entirely explain how she knew that, but I trusted her, and everyone else trusted her, so on the Dragon it was. Vendal kept an eye on Felnard, who seemed to have aged ten years since he cleansed us from the Soulless. He usually wandered in the palace talking to the Druids who'd stayed behind to help protect Shells in case the Soulless' army would ever reach it.

Reports kept coming in about attacks, but it seemed like the numbers had gone down. This was either thanks to the Elven and Fairy forces or the Druids who sent out their Masters and best students into every town and village to provide extra protection. The cleansing magic they used had saved a lot of young men from the Soulless' grip.

After a while, it wasn't the men who were the issue - it was the Dragon. It showed up at random and burnt down entire villages. A scouting party was set up to follow its movement but as soon as the creature flew above the clouds it was impossible to track it down quick enough to prevent a future attack.

While we prepared for the journey, Sam asked Marion to join us which came as a surprise to all of us, but after the Halfling woman showed us her archery skills it seemed like a completely reasonable choice. Princess Aihyla didn't seem too bothered by the invitation; I wondered if there was some kind of agreement we weren't privy to.

I spent a lot of time training Marion and Gally in close combat while Vendal was back to teaching Sam again. Their lessons seemed much more successful than before, which was probably thanks to Sam who'd become much better at controlling her emotions. I, on the other hand, had a much harder time with my two new students. Marion might have been a master of archery but her skills with the sword were non-existent. Gally got scared each time I raised the wooden practice sticks so I had to find something else for him. He was really quick, there was no doubt about that. The short blades seemed like a good fit.

He was a natural; he could easily dodge all attacks I rained down on him and by his third try could disarm me in just five steps. We had a lot of fun and that was definitely needed for all of us.

I spent less time with Sam than I wanted to. It was either that she finished her practice late and I was asleep or the other way around. She was right next to me each time, though. Prince Abelyon was kind enough to provide our own quarters so we had all the privacy we needed. Each morning she left before I was awake and her absence was starting to get on my nerves. It seemed like everything was fine since our talk on the shore, but she felt distant from me. I knew she needed time to process everything that happened, but I'd hoped it would be a much quicker progress. I missed her soft touch on my face, her kisses, her soul. It felt like we could never get a moment to be on the same page, like a life spent swimming in different currents. She loved me, and I loved her, but the idea that might not be enough ate at me from the inside, as if it was all just a beautiful lie we told ourselves to pretend that here on out we'd be okay, no matter what happened. I found myself wondering if too much had happened already.

On the tenth day - as we were getting closer to our eventual departure - a message from King Oberon arrived. He'd announced his arrival within the next few days and requested the appearance of the Destroyer. Sam wasn't thrilled as Prince Abelyon told her the news.

"He put me in a dungeon," she said, her voice calm and even, like she was just simply stating facts.

"I know, Sam." The Prince nodded. "My father isn't an easy person to get along with."

I watched Sam gear up to say something else, so I cut in. "Is it a good idea to have them both in the same room?"

"Well, probably not. Especially since you declared your love for her in front of him."

"You did what?" Sam's eyes widened in shock. There were many things we didn't talk about since she returned.

"It might have slipped out."

"*Slipped out?*" Her voice hit a high-pitch I wasn't even aware she was capable of. It didn't even seem like she was the one talking. She seemed pissed to say the least.

"It's not ideal." Abelyon said, cutting me off from answering. "You received an Elven name; that binds you to the Royal family. My father is very keen on tradition, but-"

"Is he in danger?" Sam asked, now impatient and fuming.

"No. I will revoke his Elven name."

"Wha-"

"Do it," I said, without hesitation. Sam looked at me in disbelief, but I just took her hand in mine. "It's just a name, you mean way more to me than a title."

"But-"

"I don't care about it. I care about you." I planted a kiss on her forehead before looking back at Abelyon. "You would honour me, your highness."

He smiled. "You will be the first Human who received an Elven name and also lost it."

"Good," I said, and I meant it. He nodded.

"We'll do it when my father is here; that will free you from your duties towards the throne."

"I appreciate it."

We left the War Room and headed to the courtyard. Vendal, Gally and Marion were already waiting for us. Before I could stop Sam to pull her aside and talk to her, she'd already left with our Druid friend. Gally came up next to me and patted my back.

"You okay? We can skip practice today if you want to."

"No, I-"

"Hey, she'll be fine," Marion said.

Marion's voice was really deep and a bit rusty. She'd definitely inherited much from her Elven father, with her tall figure and lean body, but she was toned too. In all the ways Princess Aihyla was soft and elegant, Marion was sharp, a real rough-and-tumble type. Her brown hair was short and messy, framing her square face perfectly, and she had these piercing brown eyes, light as sand.

"Give her time. I may not know you all that well, but I recognise when a woman needs to spend time with herself."

"I just wish she would talk to me. I miss her."

"I know you do, and she will talk to you when she's ready to." Her charming half-smile appeared as she winked at me. "Now, can we please practice some more? I could teach you guys archery."

"That actually sounds like a great idea," Gally agreed almost instantly. I looked towards the way Vendal and Sam left before joining the two of them.

The rest of the day went by quickly. We laughed a lot, mostly at me, as I turned out to be really bad at archery. No matter how hard I concentrated or tried, my aim was off all the time. Marion tried to explain it all in many different ways with no success. She showed me different techniques that made it even worse. And she was merciless in her mockery of me, which I appreciated. I left the field defeated, but refreshed. Spending time with the two of them made me feel like I was back with my soldiers. We used to have a lot of fun together; they were all good men.

We reached the gates the same time as Vendal did, but Sam wasn't with him. When I asked where she was he didn't know; he said that she didn't want to practice after a while so they just called it a day. My nerves almost took over but I thought about what Marion said before: Sam probably needed some time on her own. We all went our separate ways as we stepped foot in the palace. I couldn't wait to get down to the bath area.

When they'd built the Palace of Peace, the Dwarves dug deep into the ground, gifting everyone who ever stepped foot in there with their famous baths. It was like stepping into a different world - three big bath holes all full of warm spring water. There was nothing else down there but these little paradises. I loved spending time there; I was usually alone with my thoughts while the warm water washed away the worries of the day.

I went for the one furthest from the stairs, took off my clothes and sat in. I'd barely closed my eyes, just enjoying the warmth, when I heard footsteps. I was a bit annoyed, but as I turned around I couldn't help but smile.

"I knew you were going to be here," said Sam as she walked toward me. She was a sight for sore eyes for sure.

"Am I that predictable?" I asked, trying to pull my most charming smile. I knew it worked on her, because every time I did it a small blush appeared on her cheeks.

"Turn around," she gestured.

"I've already seen you naked, you know."

"I'm still allowed to be shy, idiot."

I laughed, but did as she asked. I heard as she got out of her clothes, desperately wanting to look back at her, but I didn't. She stepped in and sat down next to me.

"You know that this water is completely clear, right?" She sighed and pulled up her knees to her chest. "You are unbelievable."

"It is what it is," she said, looking at me. I couldn't resist her. I leaned closer to her and kissed her beautiful lips.

"Killian-" She pushed me away lightly. The way she said my name, I knew immediately that something was wrong again. "Are you sure you want to throw everything you have away only for me?"

"Are you seriously asking me that?" She turned away from me, avoiding my eyes. I shuffled closer to her in the water. "Sam. I don't know how else I can prove how much you mean to me. I told you, I showed you. If I have to, I will tell you a million times more. I love you."

"But why?" She looked at me, her eyes full of doubt. Not in me, in herself.

"Well, there are the obvious things: you're kind, caring, loving, absolutely beautiful... sometimes a bit dramatic and loud, but I love those things as well. But, mostly..." I gently pulled her hands away from her knees and she slowly let her legs down, revealing herself to me. "I think you're incredibly brave. You've gone through a lot since we turned up and asked you to come with us, and a lot before that still, and yet no matter how many times the world has thrown something at you, you've adjusted. That is a rare strength, Sam, and it not only makes you resilient, it makes you admirable."

"You think really highly of me and I don't know if I deserve it."

"Of course you do. I hope you can one day stop doubting yourself so much." I kissed her shoulder.

"I love you too, Killian. I never thought I would ever feel this way about someone. You, Felnard, Ven and Neyra gave me so much to live and fight for."

As she leaned closer her scent made me feel weak. She carried the scent of roses mixed with sweet vanilla; it drove me wild whenever she came close to me. Her lips closed on mine softly. She put her right hand against my chest as she turned to me, butterflies dancing in my stomach, I was so happy to hold her so close again, to feel her soft skin press against mine. I always flinched a little as I put my hands on her back, feeling the scars under my fingertips. I'd dreamt about that night a few times; it made me sick whenever I did.

We only separated when we heard the laughter from the top of the stairs. Within a few seconds Gally, Aihyla, Marion and Vendal arrived, ready to jump into the warm water. Sam pulled a bit away, but I kept my hands around her waist.

The others soon joined us in the water, making Sam incredibly uncomfortable. She kept so close to me, trying to hide her own body with mine that it made me chuckle a bit. Our friends didn't care at all though - not about us or about each other. As we talked more and more Sam started to loosen up a little bit. She didn't let go of my hand, but was a bit more open and chattier. Aihyla had an all-knowing smile sitting on her face each time I looked at her. She sat there looking like a proud mother hen, caressing Marion softly, keeping her eyes on her chicks. Vendal seemed a lot more relaxed than before - Felnard was feeling a lot better than before and it made the young Druid calmer. Gally had changed the most. He loved hearing his own voice and the more he talked, the more he resembled his sister. I knew Vendal noticed it too, but I wasn't sure if it made him sad or happy.

We could have talked for hours just sitting down there, but life had other plans for us. The warning bells sounded up out of nowhere. First we weren't even sure if we heard it right or just imagined it, but they grew louder and louder. We were out of the bath quicker than lightning and ran up.

It was chaos.

Guards and Soldiers were marching through the palace, making their way towards the main gates. We all ran outside after fighting our way through a battalion of people. The sight was unreal. What seemed like a million torches were lit, signalling the Soulless' army down at the bottom of Shells. They were forming a semi-circle around the stone walls, just standing there, motionless.

"How did he get so many people?" Aihyla asked, still out of breath from running. Prince Abelyon arrived, standing next to us. A hawk was sitting on his shoulder - one of the messenger birds.

"Those are not people," he said, we all turned to him. "It's the Handors."

The dark green Dragon roared up behind the army, sending a wave of fire up through the air, giving light to the thousand upon thousand wild Handors. Felnard came running up the stairs; Vendal grabbed his hand to help him.

"You all need to leave now. He is here for you, Sam." He said so fast that at first I wasn't even sure if I'd heard him right.

"No," Sam said confidently.

Neyra landed on the stairs, making some of the soldiers jump into the bushes on the side. Before I could grab her hand she was already gone, sprinting down to the dragon, easily climbing up on her back. They took off before any of us could say anything.

CHAPTER 24
AND SOON THE DARKNESS…

"SAM"

I wasn't sure what I was thinking, but I knew that I couldn't just run away leaving all the people of Shells behind to die. Neyra took me high above the clouds for the briefest of moments before diving down to where the Soulless was. She landed seamlessly. The dark green Dragon let out a low growl as it laid his enormous head on the ground so his master could get down. Neyra did the same, not taking her eyes off the other beast. As soon as both our feet touched the ground the two Dragons flew up, getting into their own fight high above.

He was much stronger than how I saw him in my dreams. His long dark black robes looked more like clouds than clothing. That ugly, evil smirk sat on his face unbothered by my presence. I started walking towards him, ignoring the hungry yellow eyes of the Handors looking at us.

I stopped two feet away from him. He was so much taller than me, but it didn't scare me at all - not anymore. I was keenly aware of my own breathing in the silence that surrounded everything. He slowly leaned forward, his long blonde hair looking white in the moonlight.

"So, we finally met. Did you miss me?" He winked and as I looked into his deep red eyes a strange kind of familiar feeling overwhelmed me.

"Fuck you," I said, shaking it off. He laughed and it started a chain event as the Handors made some kind of noise that barely resembled laughter at all. My blood froze in my veins as he raised his bony hand elegantly silencing his minions.

"Maybe a bit later darling," he said, keeping his eyes on me. "You have something I need."

"I have many things you would need, a soul being one of them." The smirk disappeared from his face; I knew I touched on a sensitive point.

"We're playing dirty I see."

The liana struck up from the ground, sending dust cascading all around us, but I was prepared and sent a whip of fire towards him that cut through his black smoke of a robe, making it disappear. His bare chest was covered in scars, just like his hand - scars that looked like they were caused by whips. The Mark of Sagar was on his left hand, but only on his wrist. I knew if I could make him use magic enough times the Mark would take care of my problem for me, crushing his black heart. He launched forward making even more lianas appear from the soft ground below our feet. I was able to defeat most of them with counter attacks, but the last one cut through my side, making me scream out in pain. The Handors were screaming from the top of their lungs as the Soulless suddenly pointed towards the city.

I didn't hesitate to attack him again. He wasn't prepared for the huge brown bear whom I'd made a connection with way before Neyra and I landed. He fell to the ground, screaming in pain as the giant animal tore into his flesh, but what I would never have done was easily taken care of by the Soulless himself. The bear roared to its side as the Soulless crushed its spine with the power of mere thought. His dark action was not without a trace, the scar crawling nearer to his shoulder.

"You sneaky little bitch," he exhaled. His flesh was hanging on his shoulder blade, black blood pouring out of it. "I wi-"

The sudden sound of battle horns stopped him. The gates of Shells opened and riders started streaming out in full force, their swords at the ready. The archers on the wall were already sending down flaming arrows on the Handors who were disorganised in their attack, but thanks to their thick skin endured more than any other soldier could have. The Fairy soldiers flew out above the riders, easily shooting out Handors with their arrows.

The Soulless screamed out in annoyance.

"You fools," he said, followed by a maniacal laugh. At least a thousand more soldiers appeared from the edge of the forest, running straight into the unfolding battle.

"Sam!"

I heard and turned towards the source of the voice. When Vendal appeared, he easily cut through the Handors with whips of fire. He stopped a few feet away from us, taking a very deep breath and I knew what he was about to do. I jumped away just in time as he blew out all the air in his lungs, creating a strong wind that sent at least a dozen arriving soldiers flying high into the sky. The Soulless was smarter than his men were and managed to dodge away like I had. Another three Druids arrived behind Vendal and with his leadership they all marched towards the newly arriving soldiers.

"I've enough of this game!" The Soulless exclaimed, he raised both of his hands high and as he brought down multiple lightning strikes from the sky, destroying not just his enemies but his own men as well. He didn't care about them.

I ran towards him, sending waves of strong winds at him just to try and make him stop. I was horrified by the thought that Killian, Aihyla, Gally and Marion were also on the field, not to mention Felnard.

The chaos grew.

The clashing of the metals grew so deafeningly loud that it was hard to bear. Cut limbs and heads laid on the ground all around us. The battle tainted the previously green landscape with blood. It was near dawn, but the battle of the swords had not abated. Wounded soldiers, recovering from the Soulless' magic, rumbled for mercy from those who attacked them; Elves and Fairies tried to help their injured comrades flee the battlefield, only for them to get cut down. As the cries of the people filled the air, so did the smell of burning flesh and blood.

I caught a glimpse of Aihyla at one point, covered in blood and fighting mercilessly with a short sword in each hand. She'd picked up a heavy breastplate and tied her hair back, spinning the blades with such finesse and power that her combatants were falling one after the other in the blink of an eye. She was a great warrior, but it was definitely something I didn't expect from her.

No matter how hard I tried to force the Soulless to use his magic, he kept grabbing a soldier to drink their blood. Even if it was a few drops, the Mark of Sagar pulled back enough that he didn't have to worry. If I got closer to him, he found a way to put space between us again. Making a connection with anything became more and more tiring, but not just for me - The Soulless was visibly struggling. His attacks missed more than they hit, or he struggled to call anything to himself.

What stopped our struggle was the dark green Dragon. He crashed into the ground, killing the many unfortunate souls on impact. It tried to get out from the hole it created, but Neyra arrived, pushing her enemy back down and biting through its neck, vanquishing it. The Soulless screamed out in pain, his hand shooting up to his neck. It was my chance to strike him down but before I could, a wave of fire shot merely inches away from my left side, catching my shoulder.

Tired, panting, bathed in blood, we faced each other. The Mark of Sagar was at his collarbone. I attempted to strike him but failed, I had no more strength left. Unable to connect with anything to help, I bent down for a sword that was lying inches away from my foot. As I rose, I was surprised to see that the Soulless had finally fallen to his knees. I knew the time had come, that I had to finish him. I stumbled over, holding onto every bit of strength I had left and stopped in front of him. I raised the sword high, but I was unable to strike down. I looked down at the man, who seemed weak and broken. I shook it off, prepared again, but something hit my ear that I'd never thought I would hear.

The Soulless was crying.

Stunned, I lowered my sword entirely.

"That's enough, please... don't force me," he sniffed, looking up at me. I saw the unimaginable. His features changed - his red eyes turned blue, his skin had a slight rose colour to it, but the biggest difference were his ears. They were not Elven, in fact-

"You're a Human," I muttered to myself.

"Seán?"

I turned around. Killian was coming towards us out of the battle, his sword lowered to his side.

"Who?" I asked, but the answer came from the Soulless.

"Brother!" The world started spinning with me. Killian had a brother? "I couldn't help it brother, you have to believe me. She forced me." He sniffed again, huge tears falling down his face. His sobs were heart-breaking. I turned back to Killian and watched as his face distorted in horror. I felt the Soulless' cold fingers close around my neck, his blade at my chest.

"Let her go!" Killian screamed. Marion and Aihyla arrived behind him, giving support to a visibly hurt Gally.

"Where's the Prophecy?" He hissed still panting. "Tell me or I will kill her."

"Don't say anything to him!" Vendal appeared. His robe was tainted with blood but he had no visible wounds.

"That would be foolish of you, but then again you aren't too bright," he laughed, his cold breath was caressing my face.

"Let me go, you monster," I said between my teeth. He whispered in my ear so only I could hear him.

"I'm a better lover than him, you know."

"You sick bastard." My skin tingled in revulsion under his touch.

"That's no way to talk to your future brother-in-law now, is it?" Killian was fuming as he locked eyes with the man he'd called Seán. I saw the same disbelief on the other's faces that I felt. "So what will it be?"

"I think... death."

Neyra roared up. I used the opportunity to burn the Soulless' blade-holding hand. He screamed in agony as he leapt away from me, pushing me on the ground. Neyra's neck bent backwards as she prepared to release her fire on the man who was struggling to find his footing. The fire came crashing down on him, the heat unbearable. Killian helped me up to get me further away from it all.

The few Handors that left were gone in a blink of an eye as the magic that kept them prisoner broke. The soldiers seemed clueless about what they were doing in the middle of a battlefield as they dropped their swords. The fire died down but there was no body, just ashes flying in the air.

The pain was beyond imagination. It pushed me to the ground. As I screamed out loud the ground shook. I saw Vendal running straight toward me from one direction, and from the other Gally, Aihyla and Marion. Killian was holding my head as the world went dark.

"VENDAL"

"Sam! Sam! What's happening?" Killian asked, sobbing as he hugged her. Her hair slowly turned black and her whole body trembled.

"She's lost part of her being," I said in shock. They all turned towards me.

"What? He was not part of-"

I cut Killian off. "But of course he was. Just think about it." I couldn't believe we never realised what's been going on. "The heart of the Soulless is dark, the soul of the Destroyer is pure. They are the perfect representatives of good and evil, but if one is lost…"

Sam coughed, suddenly jumping out of Killian's arms, barely able to stand on her own two feet but staggered forward. She grabbed her hair, panicked, her breathing accelerated, she was on the threshold of hysteria.

"It won't ever be truly lost. The question is, which will be her dominant side?" I asked, desperately waiting for her to turn to us.

And so she did.

Next to her jet-black hair, one of her eyes became darker and her skin even paler than before. She surveyed the people watching her, then spoke in an almost unearthly voice.

"And soon the darkness," she said, and with that she collapsed. Killian ran to her and took her in his arms again. Aihyla came to me, grabbing my shoulder.

"I'm sorry about your uncle, Ven. We tried to save him, but-"

"It's okay. I know you did everything you could."

It took a lot out of me to hold back my tears. Felnard had been on the battlefield, backing up Aihyla with protection spells and some offensive work, but he hadn't done a good enough job protecting his flank. A Handor had snuck up behind him and stabbed him through. Aihyla took the soldier out quickly, but it was too late for him. I was too far away from them to help.

Killian put Sam up on the Dragon's back, where the scales had also changed colour; they were a dark, onyx black. We helped Gally up and Aihyla too as they were both hurt as well.

The Dragon landed on the courtyard at its usual place, dropping us all down from its back. A group of Guards ran out of the palace straight to Aihyla.

"Your highness," one of them stepped forward holding out a silver cloak. "Prince Abelyon fell in the battle."

"Is he-?" Aihyla asked, but the Guard just shook his head.

"I'm sorry, your highness."

Aihyla gasped; Marion was next to her in the blink of an eye. "Oh, my dear brother."

"Ven," I turned to Killian who was holding Sam in his arms. "Can you help?"

He nodded towards Gally who was sitting on the ground. I went over to him. He had an ugly wound on his side.

"This will only take a second," I said as I put my hand on it. I felt the energy flow from me to him and as I let go it was only a faint scar.

"Thank you Vendal," he said, taking a deep breath, relieved from the pain. I helped him stand up and moved over to the princess.

Aihyla had the silver cloak over her shoulder as tears were streaming down her face. She steeled herself as she spoke to us.

"Vendal, please help the wounded. Killian, take Sam to the royal quarters - she will be much more comfortable there."

We all did as she said, but all that had happened lingered in our minds no matter how hard we tried not to concentrate on it.

o

It was midday by the time I finally made my way to the royal quarters. As I opened the door I saw what I expected to see: among all the glory - the golden walls, the huge bed and fancy furniture - was a man holding onto his love's hand.

I silently walked over to him, took a chair and sat by his side. Sam looked peaceful; all the blood and dirt had been cleaned off of her, and she'd been dressed in an emerald green dress. I was sure that it was Killian who took care of her.

"Any change?" I asked, but he just shook his head, kissing Sam's hand. "So-"

"I don't know how it's possible, Ven." He looked at me, his eyes full of guilt. "I thought that Seán was dead."

"I know, but maybe he-" I stopped, not wanting to make it worse for him. "Maybe he modified the Elven family's memories of him and they thought he died. He was a very powerful Druid, Killian."

"He never showed any sign of magic while we were little, Ven. He was the sweetest little guy I'd ever known. How could he-" Killian's voice broke. He couldn't keep his tears at bay anymore.

"I don't know. I really don't," I said, patting his back. "I'm not sure if we will ever get the answers we are looking for."

Sam started coughing. Killian was up on his feet in a split second and helped her sit up. But she didn't open her eyes, and as the coughing stopped Killian laid her back on the bed. It was horrible to see his suffering.

"When will she wake up?"

"I'm not sure, my friend." I stood up and put my hand on Sam's forehead. Closed my eyes and searched for her in the dark. "She'll wake up. I'm certain."

"Hey."

Gally came in, followed by Marion. They both sat down on the other side of the bed. They had fresh clothes on, and other than a few bruises on their faces they were fine. "How's she?"

"Resting." I answered instead of Killian. "She'll be fine."

"Aihyla wants us to leave by tonight." Marion said, a bit hesitant.

"Why?" I asked in surprise.

"She doesn't want us to be here when her father arrives. He'll be furious when he finds out that his son is dead."

She was right. I looked at Sam, then at Killian who just nodded.

"Grab your things then, let's go as soon as possible."

They both got up and left. I squeezed Killian's shoulder one more time before leaving.

By the time I got back out to the Dragon, they were already there waiting for me. Killian was already sitting on the back of the animal with Sam in his arms; Gally was strapping the saddle the blacksmith had fabricated for the Dragon's back so we could all travel in comfort on its back. I passed my bag to Marion, who placed it among the others.

"Aihyla will be here soon," she said, sadness washing through her words.

We didn't have to wait for long. Killian placed Sam on the saddle, tucking her in with a warm blanket before getting down. Princess Aihyla wore a long black dress. She was ravishing, as ever, but this was mourning garb, and this was not the time. I knew what she was going through. As I thought about Felnard again, my heart ached.

"So, this is it," she said.

Four Guards stepped forward, holding out different weapons for us: a beautiful wooden bow and arrows, for Marion; silver longsword for Killian; two daggers for Gally and a little vial for me. I looked up at her because I didn't really understand it. A strange, white liquid was swirling in it.

"Felnard left it for you."

I couldn't keep my act up. My tears broke out mercilessly, blinding me for a second. I felt Killian's arms wrapped around me.

"He was a great man, Vendal. We're gonna honour him, I promise."

"Thank you," I mumbled. I'd lost everybody who was dear to me - Neyra. Felnard. They were both gone forever.

"The journey ahead of you is unimaginable to all of us, but if anyone can succeed it's you all," she said, looking at us one by one "May Silhoue follow you on your way."

"May Sagar watch over you all," I answered, bowing down and the others followed my example.

Aihyla stood next to Marion, and that was our queue to get on the Dragon's back. We watched as they said goodbye to each other in tears, giving one last kiss before parting ways. They held each other's hands until the last possible second. Gally helped Marion up on the saddle and embraced her as she sobbed into his shoulder. The Dragon didn't need any order from any of us; it swiftly departed from the ground and Shells soon became nothing more than memory as we flew over the Enormous Sea.

o

"HE"

The ashes were falling on my face like snowflakes. My whole body ached as I forced myself to sit up. I looked around in the dark - there were wolves eating from the dead flesh of people making awful noises. My head was spinning as I saw the bodies all around me. I got up, shivering in the evening cold. I had no clothes on, just black ash sticking to my skin. My wounds were gone, all of them, and as I inspected myself my hair came to view. To my surprise it was no longer the same colour: it was black.

A sharp pain forced me back on my knees. I screamed silently as I shut my eyes, at which point I felt the cold fingers on my face, lifting me back up. I opened my eyes.

"Mother of all Darkness," I whispered. Radona smiled, her razor-sharp teeth showing for a moment.

"My favourite little pet."

"I failed you, Mother." She laughed cheerfully.

"Oh no, my child. Everything went exactly as I planned it." She planted a long kiss on my forehead. "Time for the real work to begin."

END OF BOOK ONE

Quotes from Beta Reader Reviews

"Ultimately, an excellent outing for a first-time author. A well-painted world, a strong cast of characters, a hero's journey to save the world, and a journey of metamorphosis, literal and figurative for the unlikely heroine at the heart of the story."

- Jeffrey Pierce

"I can't wait to see how Killian, Vendal, Gally and Marion (who I think has the potential to become a real fan favourite) grow into their own people outside of Sam's quest, which I think is the most exciting thing about any fantasy novel, outside of the compelling world that has been created."

- Katie Volker

"Much like The Lord of the Rings or Harry Potter, the story does not solely depend on its main character. While Sam is a wonderful character on one hell of a journey, the story told in The Soulless is an ensemble piece."

- Kevin Clawson

"I was so invested in the relationships between the characters that were explored throughout, especially the relationship between Killian and Sam. Being a romantic myself, I always root for two individuals that have developed a clear, obvious connection, and I really appreciated how Lily managed to show this development."

- Olivia Diaz

"From the first two chapters I just wanted to know more. Every little detail caught my attention, whether it was events that took place or just small moments between characters."

- Yasmin Gibson

"The ending of the book left me at the edge of my seat, and I'm very much excited for anything that the future holds for this book. I did not expect so many twists in the end, my heart was racing all the time."

- Dani Adam Octavian

"I experienced all the highs and the lows with the characters we follow. I am left now eagerly hoping for a book two so I can find out where this adventure is heading next!"

-    Nadine Martin

"The novel itself reminded me of an epic. In a similar vein to Tolkien's The Lord of The Rings, Lily has captured visceral depth in each of her characters. Some of her passages were descriptive and covered the five senses, to the point where I felt I was enduring the adventure with the protagonists."

-    Jonna Robertsen

"While the fantasy genre is usually not my go-to genre, this book turned out to be entertaining and captivating nonetheless. Due to the carefully placed and unconvoluted world building that takes place, it does not hinder the flow of the plot and serves to elevate the atmosphere of the specific scene."

-    Jasper James Thieme

"For perhaps a more jovial reason, the Druid Felnard became my favourite minor character. There's something chaotic and lovable about a brilliant hermit with a heart of gold that propelled my attachment to his cause: defeating the Soulless with the help of Sam, the Destroyer."

-    Armineh Davis

ABOUT THE AUTHOR

Lily K is a 'renaissance woman', as her good friend Rick Worthy calls her. Her interest towards the creative fields showed very early on: school plays, theatre plays, her own acting company, an interest in drawing (although she developed a true passion for it much later on), as well as directing, acting, becoming the Sean Bean of Extras and of course: writing. She, like many of her generation, started with fanfiction, and although she wouldn't like to admit it, MANY of her pages were filled with stories where she inserted herself into her favourite movies and TV shows. While Lily tried to build her own worlds, many failed halfway through which put a stop to her writing. She didn't create anything until a short story competition caught her attention. *Poe Pao and Carl Junior, Junior's Incredible Friendship* won a place in the book among many talented authors and it gave a boost to Lily to keep pursuing writing.

The Soulless has been sitting in her drafts for a long time.

Going back and finishing it proved to be one of the greatest journeys she ever ventured forward on and Lily can't wait to start writing Book 2.

Printed in Great Britain
by Amazon

68995507R00163